Prologue

They Call Her Eiya

Footsteps echoed around the corridor of Skyfall Penitentiary as prison officer Mortim Parkhurst paced slowly towards the solitary confinement unit. He eyed the plastic food tray he was carrying with distaste. Mashed potato, tinned carrots, a bit of ham, even some kind of gloopy mullsquash dressing. If it were up to him he'd be serving his prisoner gruel, if anything at all, never mind this luxury stuff.

Ever since the former president of Endrin, Kan Darklight, had been sentenced to life imprisonment for the kidnap and torture of Danney Plum and the murder of twenty people amongst other crimes, Parkhurst had been assigned to keeping a watch on him, much to his displeasure. Most prisoners were monitored in batches, but not Darklight. No, Darklight had received special treatment, there was no doubt about it. The fact that he had been placed in solitary confinement just confirmed this. Usually, prisoners were sent there for being a danger to other inmates, but with Darklight, it was the opposite. After being targeted during the first couple of weeks by other inmates, he had been put there *for his own protection.*

Should have let him get ripped apart, Parkhurst thought.

Before he reached the cell, Parkhurst just about resisted the temptation to spit into the potato.

"Dinner," he said. "Stay on your bunk where I can see you."

The only satisfaction Parkhurst got out of visiting Darklight was seeing his physical appearance. It was a far cry from the sharp businessman image he had maintained as

Endrin's CEO. In fact, you'd be forgiven for not recognising the man. Darklight's slicked-back, greasy black hair had been shaved off, his one-eyed face was now marred by two scars from knife attacks by other prisoners, his cheeks were noticeably gaunt, and the jumpsuit he had to wear was a world away from the thousand-note suits he used to don during his television appearances.

Despite this, Darklight seemed quite content with his current situation, never getting angry or raising his voice, a constant smirk always apparent on his smug face.

Parkhurst unlocked the hatch on the cell door and slid the tray in.

"Officer," Darklight said, and even the sound of his voice made Parkhurst's skin crawl.

"Yes?" Parkhurst said impatiently.

"Do you have any children?"

Bile rose up Parkhurst's throat. *Just walk away*, he told himself. *Don't let him start a conversation.* He slid the hatch shut in silence, but after a few moments of letting his blood boil, he said, "I have a son, not that it's any concern of yours."

"How old?" Darklight pressed.

Parkhurst took a deep breath to control his anger.

"The same age that poor boy Danney Plum was when you abducted him for your sick experiments, you Gedin forsaken piece of crip."

Darklight chuckled lightly.

"I find it fascinating that nobody appreciates the scientific breakthrough that Project Suffer really was. I made myself a killing machine; a beast that I could control at will. Is that not worth a small bit of praise?"

"Praise? *Praise?*" Parkhurst spat. "You think you should be praised for cutting open a child, sticking electronic devices inside him, and then electrocuting him from the inside?"

Darklight closed his eyes, grinning.

"I have to say I did enjoy that part of it. Sometimes I knew that I was taking it too far; that I was just electrocuting him for my own pleasure. One time I just kept going, just pressing that button over and over again until his frail, little arms looked like they were going to snap in half from the spasms."

Parkhurst turned to walk away. He was going to scream at the top of his lungs if he didn't.

But as he turned, he jumped back in shock.

Standing in front of him was a burly man dressed in a ripped overcoat.

Parkhurst fumbled for his pistol, but as he did so, the intruder whipped the gun out of his grip with some kind of flesh-coloured tentacle that had shot out of the sleeve.

Horrified, Parkhurst made to run towards the nearest alarm, but the man reached out and grabbed him with inhuman force, wrapping a gag around his mouth, stealing a pair of handcuffs from his belt, and handcuffing him to the bars of Darklight's cell. Parkhurst flailed about, but there was nothing he could do except scream through the gag and hope that someone would be able to hear his muffled cries.

Parkhurst couldn't believe what was happening. How had someone infiltrated the prison? There hadn't been a break in for two decades. And where were the rest of the officers?

Darklight hadn't made a sound during the whole thing. Instead, he had backed up silently against the furthest wall of the cell, his eyes wide with fear, an expression Parkhurst had never seen on his face before.

As the intruder used Parkhurst's keys to enter the cell, Parkhurst's cries for help slowly dimmed, silenced by the appearance of the monstrosity before him.

This was no normal human being. The tentacle that had seized his gun was just the beginning. The creature he was staring at was a freak of nature, a half man, half . . . sea creature, whose face was writhing, pulsating, as if there were worms wriggling underneath his skin.

Darklight was now scrambling around as if he were trying to find a way out through the bricks.

"Who on earthia are you?" Darklight said. "What do you want?"

"Kan, I'm insulted," the creature said slowly. "Don't you recognise your old friend?"

Darklight's movements slowed and he stared at the creature's face with horrified realisation.

"K . . . *Kevan?*"

"I guess you didn't hear I'd returned from the dead. I'm glad. I like this expression on your face."

Parkhurst recognised the name Kevan. Was this Kevan Kayne? The Endrin employee and long-time friend of Darklight who had mysteriously disappeared sometime last year?

"Kevan? . . . I . . . shot you . . ." Darklight stammered. "I buried your lifeless body at the Endrin headquarters."

"Yes, I know," Kevan Kayne said bluntly. "I was there."

"How are you . . . how . . . are . . .?"

"You buried me in the wrong place."

Darklight was silent for a moment.

"I buried you with the diseased worms in the Cultivation Unit. Those worms should have ravaged your body and eaten your remains. They were swallowing up all the modified helitonium that my Divinita Machine was spewing out. That's why I buried you there, so they would destroy any traces of you along with the toxic waste."

"Well, unfortunately for you, Kan, those worms are the reason I am here today," Kayne mused ponderingly. "It was the worms that brought me back to life."

Kayne cricked his neck and a bubble of pus just above his shoulder popped, dribbling thick, green liquid down onto the collar of his coat.

"Of course, I didn't know what was happening at first. One minute I was staring at your gun, the next I was waking up to darkness, suffocating. I scrambled around until I found oxygen, which didn't take long. You really should have buried me deeper. It took me a moment to realise where I was, but when I did, I made a run for it. I escaped through the sewers and hid in the shadows of the city for the first night, and first thing in the morning, I left. I boarded a train to Arivel; a place where nobody knew me. A place where you wouldn't be able to find me."

Kayne winced in pain as a small, thin, fresh tentacle burst

out of the back of his head, wriggling around like an eel through his unkempt, long, brown hair before slithering back into his skull.

"I had no idea how I was alive," Kayne continued. "I knew you had shot me, not because I remembered it, but because I still had the bullet wound. This big, gaping hole."

Kayne shrugged his overcoat off, letting it drop to the floor, revealing a mutated torso that was bubbling and pulsating even more than his face. But the most incredible thing about it was the bullet-sized tunnel cutting straight through the left of his chest, directly through the heart.

"I had no pulse," Kayne continued, "but somehow I was still here in the world of the living. It was only when I started to feel ill and I threw up that I found out what had really happened. There were dead worms floating in my vomit. I figured they had to have crawled into my mouth while I was buried, and found their way to my stomach. Whatever demonic form of helitonium those worms had been devouring had altered the reality around them. They had given me some form of second life."

Parkhurst was no longer trying to escape the handcuffs that were restraining him. He just stood, watching, mesmerised by what was unfolding.

"I had to do what I had to do to survive," said Kayne. "I found myself a small place to rent in Arivel, but I soon began to realise my existence wasn't permanent. My skin was beginning to decay, my consciousness was coming and going, one of my little fingers . . . dropped off, and these tentacles started popping out of me. I needed more worms to keep me going. I couldn't come back to the city in case you spotted me, and I was too weak, but I could send somebody else in. So I found the records of one of your village evacuees; a young boy named Seckry Sevenstars. He was the perfect candidate; small enough in stature to have an easy time sneaking in through the sewers, and most likely harbouring a resentment for Endrin due to the Extraction Project. I was correct. A few days later, the worms arrived on a train. I couldn't believe he managed it so effortlessly. I paid him generously for his troubles, of course."

"It was *you* that sent that brat into the headquarters?" said Darklight. "That boy ruined everything for me!"

"Yes, Kan, it was me. I have to say it is somewhat satisfying knowing that I inadvertently caused the collapse of your presidency and your ultimate imprisonment."

"So what have you come here to do?" Darklight said. "Kill me?"

"Of course," said Kayne.

"This isn't going to change anything, Kevan," said Darklight, chuckling nervously. "You can kill me and get your revenge, but you'll never get what you really want. You'll never get Elenya back. Your wife is dead. I murdered her. And killing me in return isn't going to change that. You will always have to live with the memory of me blowing her brains out, and it spattering over the wall beside you in tiny . . . little . . . *bits*."

Kayne gripped Darklight's jumpsuit with his large fingers and slammed him against the wall of the cell. Two thick tentacles slid out of slits in his forearm and wrapped around Darklight's neck like twin snakes, squeezing until his face was blue and his eyes were bulging.

"I've got a secret to tell you . . ." Kayne said softly, leaning in close to Darklight's ear. "*Elenya's also still alive*."

Darklight wriggled violently, grabbing the tentacles and trying the wrench them away, but he had no strength against this mutant.

"You buried her just a few yards away from me," Kayne continued. "Of course the worms gave her life. They gave her even more of a second life than me. You see, helitonium is chaotic, unstable, and . . . unpredictable. You should know that more than anyone, Kan. It didn't just reanimate her existing body, it gave her soul a new body entirely, one modelled on Elenya as a teenager."

Darklight's mouth began foaming from suffocation.

"Yes," said Kayne, as the final morsel of life was squeezed out of Darklight, and his arms dropped to his sides. "Ropart tells me they call her *Eiya*."

Chapter One

The Birthday

It was the twelfth of September in Skyfall City, a date that was important to one particular boy who lay sleeping in the smallest bedroom of flat seventeen, block four, Kerik Square. That boy was Seckry Sevenstars, and today was his sixteenth birthday.

Unlike last year, school term time didn't begin until two days later into the year, so Seckry was enjoying what was to be one of his last lie-ins for some time.

Seckry's eyes slowly flickered open and focused on Eiya's bed, which was empty and neatly made. He shook a few strands of sandy hair away from his face and sat up. As he did so, a note that had been lying on top of his quilt fluttered down towards his legs. In Eiya's cute bubble writing, it read:

Back in a bit X

Seckry's feelings for Eiya had grown so strong since the day he had found her that even the sight of her empty bed had given him slight palpitations of concern about her safety. But Seckry had no need to worry; above the distant rumble of the monorails, he could hear the faintest sound of her humming out in the kitchen area. Seckry smiled silently as he realised it was The Broken Motion's latest song, and lay back down, sinking into the comfort of his warm sheets.

Seckry Sevenstars had been an ordinary boy leading an ordinary life in the quiet village of Marne until just over a year ago, when the Endrin Corporation had come crashing into his life, taking away his home, obliterating everything he knew, and changing his life forever. After being forced to move to Skyfall City, Seckry had been homesick, but over the course of the year, Seckry had bonded with the city in a way that he never had with Marne. Even though Skyfall was a mess of decaying buildings, scaffolding, and rat-infested back alleys, this was where Seckry now truly felt at home.

It was amazing to think back at the memories he had of his first year in Skyfall; meeting what were to become his best friends, playing Friction for the very first time, competing in the Mega Meltdown and actually winning, thwarting the plans of the Endrin Corporation, discovering that he had spawned an entire religion, and finding, or indeed creating, the most important person in his life, Eiya.

Back in Marne, if someone had told him what his future had held, he would never have believed them in a million years, but Seckry had the strangest feeling that the crazy events of last year were just the beginning of his adventures.

One event that Seckry was certain was going to be explosive this year was the Friction Mega Meltdown. After the Eastern Eidolons' dramatic win last time, they were going to have to train extra hard if they wanted to keep their trophy from the revenge-driven clutches of the vicious Mobbins and the Northern Nightmare, not to mention the Western Warriors and the Southern Slayers, who had struggled to keep up for the last few years but were always a viable threat.

The thought of Friction and the next Mega Meltdown sent butterflies fluttering through Seckry's stomach. He couldn't wait to get into the stadium again and compete. The trepidation and excitement he had felt as they prepared to enter their pods amidst the heaving crowds of spectators and the rush he had experienced when they were cheered by thousands of fans were second to none.

The fact that Seckry now considered Friction to be one of the most important things in his life was more surprising to Seckry himself than anyone else. When he had arrived in Skyfall, he had never even heard of the game, never mind played it. But it wasn't long before he found out that he was a natural; a few games in and it had felt to Seckry like he had been playing all his life, and the Eidolons had been happy to accept him.

Without realising it, Seckry sunk into a hazy half sleep filled with fleeting avatars and flying arrows. Then, around an hour later, he woke with a start as Eiya jumped onto his bed, dropping a heavy hamper which bounced on the mattress.

"Happy Birthday, Seck," she said sweetly, smiling that smile that gave Seckry goosebumps every time she did it. "I thought I'd let you sleep in while I got to work."

"Got to work?" said Seckry. "What have you been up to?"

Eiya slapped her hand on the hamper.

"Go ahead," she said, "look inside."

Seckry lifted the lid and the most wonderful smell of freshly baked bread filled the room. Inside was a mouth-watering array of cheeses, biscuits, and slices of exotic meats alongside warm, crusty bread, a bowl of potato salad with junerbush berries mixed in, and chunks of fresh, bright green meltmelon.

"Your mum's been giving me some cookery lessons over the last couple of weeks. If she hadn't have helped me, that loaf of bread would probably be more like a breeze block right now, in all honesty."

"Eiya, this looks delicious," said Seckry, his mouth watering.

"They reckon this is the last batch of good weather before the cold starts creeping in, so I thought I'd take you to Featherduck Park and we could have a picnic."

A picnic in the park with Eiya? Seckry couldn't think of a better way to spend his birthday.

After opening presents from his mum and his sister, who had both gone to work and left Seckry asleep, he and Eiya caught the monorail to the park, lugging their hamper and resisting the urge not to nibble on the way.

Skyfall was a busy, dirty city, so escaping to one of its rare grassy areas was a much needed treat, especially in the warm, humid, late summer weather. When they arrived, they had fun throwing a FrisDisc around and trying to climb a couple of trees before tiring themselves out and taking shelter from the sun underneath the park's largest tree (which was humming with sleepy glowflies) and delving into their picnic.

"Do you know what Tenk is up to?" Seckry asked Eiya, leaning back against one of the tree's giant roots as he licked crumbs from his sticky fingers. "I haven't heard from him all day."

"I think he's . . . um, with his new girlfriend."

"I haven't heard from Tippian either, or Loca, or Kimmy."

Eiya averted her gaze uncomfortably.

"I, um . . . have no idea to be honest."

"Oh," said Seckry. Had he done something to offend them? It wasn't like he wanted them to spend the entire day with him, but he hadn't even had a text from any of them to wish him a happy birthday.

When Seckry suggested they start heading back home, Eiya asked him to stay in the park a little longer, and kept glancing at her watch off and on until around 6 p.m.

"I feel like something weird is going on," said Seckry, and the fact that Eiya didn't respond just confirmed his suspicions.

When they arrived back at Kerik Square and began making their way up the external, steel, grated stairway to the third floor of Seckry's block, Eiya picked something up off the floor that looked strangely like a party popper and shoved it into her pocket quickly.

"Litterbugs, eh?" she said. "Kids have got no respect around here."

As Seckry fumbled to find his keys, he noticed a pair of bespectacled eyes peering at him from behind one of the curtains on the other side of the window.

"Oh my Gedin, *Tippian?*" said Seckry, startled. "Eiya . . . why is Tippian in the flat, hiding behind a curtain?"

"*He can see you! Get down here!*" somebody hissed, a hiss that sounded suspiciously like Loca's. A female hand suddenly reached up, gripped Tippian by his t-shirt, and yanked him out of sight.

Seckry opened the door carefully, and around thirty people popped out from behind sofas, curtains, and tables, with someone even emerging from underneath the kitchen sink.

"Surprise!" everyone yelled, except Tenk, who was trying but had a mouth full of food.

Seckry did his best to look genuinely shocked.

"This is where they've been," Eiya said affectionately. "They didn't forget about you."

The flat was heaving with familiar faces, and it took Seckry a few minutes to register exactly who was there. Aside from his mum, his sister, Tenk, Tippian, Loca and Kimmy, the first bunch of people he noticed were Tenk's mum, dad, and brother Longo. Then there were a few of the neighbours from his floor, and even Henrei, the arcade vendor, and his wife, Marberry, who raised a glass of wine each to him from a distance. Seckry smiled and raised his keys back at them.

After thanking his mum for going to all the effort of creating the surprise party and saying hello to everybody, Loca handed him a paper plate and said, "Happy birthday, Seck. You can be the first to try the food. We've been holding out until - Tenk, did you eat a sausage roll?"

"No . . ." Tenk said meekly, licking a flake of pastry from the side of his mouth.

"You were supposed to wait!" cried Loca. "It's Seckry's party!"

"Well you got me hiding under the food table!" said Tenk, looking genuinely upset. "I could smell the things."

Seckry laughed and told them it really didn't matter.

Tenk slapped his hand on Seckry's shoulder.

"You see, Loca, this is why me and Seckry are friends. We understand each other."

"Where's Richelle?" Seckry asked him.

"Oh, she had to . . . um, visit some relatives," said Tenk. "She sends her birthday wishes though."

At the beginning of the summer, the group had bumped into the mystery girl Tenk fancied who had been, until then, known as the Chip and Milk Girl. After spending the entire Friction match chatting to each other in the corner of the stadium, they had arranged to meet up again, and were now officially boyfriend and girlfriend. Seckry was elated for Tenk, since Tenk had been dreaming of finding her for ages, but Tippian wasn't so pleased because he was now the only one left in the group without a partner.

Seckry filled his plate so as not to be rude, but in all honesty he was still feeling fairly full from Eiya's homemade hamper, so he stuck to drinking pop most of the night, much to the delight of Tenk, who said, 'more food for me!'

Tenk's stomach was somewhat of a mystery to the rest of them, because there was rarely a day when Tenk wouldn't eat an entire meal at lunchtime and then continue to scavenge the group's leftovers.

"Gedin, Tenk," said Loca as Tenk shoved his seventh cheesebread into his mouth. "How on earthia do you do it? You scoff your face every day and you're still as lanky as a rake."

"It's getting eaten up by his metabolism," said Tippian, who decided to respond on Tenk's behalf because Tenk's mouth was still full. "In a couple of years, his metabolism's gonna drop and a massive stomach's gonna pop out of nowhere."

Tenk swallowed and glared at them worriedly. "Why's my metabolism gonna drop?"

"It just does," said Tippian. "Everyone's does as they get older."

"But . . . I'll still be able to eat two roast dinners on a Sunday, right?"

After a brief moment of silence, Tenk continued.

"What about my chocolate ice cream that I always have before bed?"

"You have ice cream before bed every single night?" said Loca, aghast.

Tenk said nothing in response and wandered off, lost in contemplation.

After a few people had said 'happy birthday' to Seckry for the second time, Tenk's dad, who seemed to have had a few drinks already, shuffled up to him and slurred, "Word of advice. Never get married. The mother-in-law will make your life a living nightmare."

He obviously knew nothing about Eiya's creation.

"That bad, eh?" Seckry said.

"All I ask is to be able to watch an hour of sport on a Sunday, and do you think the old cow will let me?"

"Tenk's nan is living with you?" Seckry asked. As far as he knew, Tenk's grandparents on his mum's side lived in a quieter suburb of the east partition somewhere.

"The bag's been with us for a week now," Tenk's dad said. "Though it seems like a lifetime to me."

As he walked away, Seckry got the attention of Tenk, who was now trying to blow into a balloon as much as he could before it popped.

"Your dad really isn't happy," said Seckry. "How come your nan is living with you?"

"Granddad's gone into hospital for a while," said Tenk, who was looking a little spaced out from oxygen depletion. "She's staying with us for the time being."

"Oh, I hope your granddad's okay," said Seckry.

"Don't worry about him," said Tenk. "He says it's like a vacation, not having to put up with my nan."

Seckry had often wondered what it would be like to have grandparents. His mum's parents had both passed away when he was just a baby, and his dad . . . well, he had believed his dad's parents to have died before he was born, but if what Vance had told him was true, then his dad had no parents to begin with, just the scientists that had created him in a laboratory, Adelbert Endoman and Rikard Ringold.

A few moments later, Coralle dimmed the lights and Leena wheeled out a gigantic cake as everyone began singing 'Happy Birthday.' It was only as he neared it, ready to blow out the candles, that Seckry realised his mum had made an intricate icing illustration of his avatar, Anikam on top of the cake, along with the official Friction logo. Seckry was blown away. He couldn't believe his mum had gone to so much trouble.

"I'm calling dibs on the Friction logo!" shouted Tenk.

Once the cake had been sliced and distributed amongst

everyone, Seckry was finally feeling like he could no longer physically fit any more food into his stomach, and sat down at the kitchen table, keeping an eye out for a clear pathway to the bathroom in case he had to run to it to be sick.

After a while, Tenk joined him, fuming with anger because Longo had fired a party popper directly into one of his ears.

"Mate, I still can't believe you're the Messiah," Tenk said.

"*Tenk!*" Seckry whispered furiously.

"Oh, sorry," said Tenk. "Not the Messiah, the Son of Gedin. I thought the Messiah was the same thing though."

"*No, I mean, stop talking about it! People are gonna hear!*"

Shortly after everything that had happened with him being sucked into Darklight's time portal at the beginning of the summer, Seckry had decided to keep those moments to himself, his family and his closest friends. If everybody knew about it he wouldn't be able to walk down the street without somebody making a comment. And besides that, who was to say anyone else would believe him? He might be branded as insane, or even worse, as a blasphemer, and then get attacked by religious fanatics or something.

Tenk put his hands up and made a silent zipping motion across his mouth.

They watched Loca and Kimmy dance for a while, and Seckry noticed that Tippian was sat alone at the other end of the living area, seemingly talking to himself.

"You see him too, right?" said Tenk, and Seckry nodded.

"Loca, come here!" Tenk called. "I want to ask you a question!"

Loca joined them and sighed.

"Tenk, for the seventh time, I'm not gonna start calling you The Tenkmeister, it sounds ridiculous."

"What? No, not that," said Tenk. "I want to know if you think Tippian has been acting strangely recently."

"Yes!" said Loca, exasperatedly, slapping her palm on the table. "Thank Gedin someone else has noticed it too."

"I'm seriously getting concerned about his mental health," said Tenk. "There! Look at him!"

Seckry craned his neck and watched Tippian close his eyes

and start making strange, silent gestures with his mouth, as though he was chewing some invisible marshmallow that was making him go through the entire spectrum of emotions in a matter of seconds.

"He's been sat there muttering gibberish to himself for the last hour," said Tenk. "I think there's something seriously wrong with him."

After their stomachs had settled a little, they decided to approach Tippian to make sure he was okay.

"Yellow," Tippian said to himself as they got closer. "Yeeeellllooowww."

"*I swear to Gedin, the guy's lost the plot,*" whispered Tenk.

Even Seckry was getting a little concerned now. Tippian was starting to sound like Mr Gobbledee during one of his Chlorocalm outbursts. But when they tried to talk to him, Tippian just hushed them, got up, and walked away, muttering other random words under his breath. Even Marberry, Henrei's wife, seemed to be noticing it.

"Dear Gedin, Hen," Seckry overheard her nattering. "I know they say kids should be pushed to their limits in school these days with the XL-Ent curriculum and all that, but seriously, I think they're pushing them a bit *too* far."

After around half an hour, Tippian shouted, "Yes!" from a corner of the kitchen, and the group approached him cautiously.

"I got it!" he shouted, spinning around and thrusting a palm-sized object into their faces. It looked like some kind of primitive mobile phone or radio receiver.

"Guys," said Tippian. I proudly present to you . . . the Voicemaster."

Loca spoke for everyone when she said, "What?"

Tippian reached into his pocket and pulled out a scruffy flyer before handing it to Loca.

"The Andersun Wellworth Young Inventor Award," Loca read out loud, narrowing her eyes. "Submit your unique invention now for a . . . Tipp, there's a ball of used chewing gum covering the rest."

"Oh, sorry," said Tippian, pulling it off and throwing it

into his mouth. "It says submit your unique invention now for a chance to win the prestigious award in its twenty-fifth incarnation."

"Who's Andersun Wellworth," asked Seckry.

"He's famous for providing the metal used in really expensive trophies - a pure form of the strongest metal in the world, utainium. They use Wellworth utainium in all the major trophies. If you get a Wellworth one you've made it. They're worth a fortune. Any award that uses his utainium has his name before it. Like the Andersun Wellworth Fine Art award, and the Andersun Wellworth Young Composer Award. I think he provides the metal for free in exchange for having his name attached to it. So he's a sponsor."

"And this is your invention?" said Tenk. "The Voicemaster? What does it do? Make your voice deeper or more high pitched or something to make you sound weird?"

"Oh, my good friend Tenk," said Tippian, "it does a lot more than that. How would you like to speak into the device and have your voice come out exactly like your favourite actor?"

"Umm . . . Tipps, I love Serra Simmony but I'm not sure I'd want to sound like her."

"That sounds awesome, Tipp," said Seckry, who was aware that Tippian was getting slightly insulted.

"Only thing is," said Tippian, "for the software to be able to fully emulate someone's voice, it has to record them saying a set number of certain words before it can work."

"What kind of words?" said Tenk.

"This is what I've been trying to figure out. It has to be a selection of words that express every combination of intonations and expressions in the Unilan language."

"Every intonation?" said Loca. "Wait, so that's what you've been doing, muttering all these words under your breath and making weird faces and noises?"

"'Course," said Tippian. "What did you think? That I'd gone mad?"

"Deranged is probably a better word," said Tenk.

"But, every intonation?" said Loca. "That'd be loads,

wouldn't it?"

"Surprisingly, no," said Tippian, who was now in his element. "I've had most of them figured out for ages, but I was stuck on one word, one magic word that would allow the thing to run smoothly and pretty much never glitch or sound false."

"What word was it?" asked Seckry.

"Junikrapogswash," said Tippian.

"Excuse me?" said Loca.

"Yep, junikrapogswash," said Tippian again. "It must be the Arivelian accent that makes it the magic word. Don't ask me why or how, even I have no idea to be honest, I'm just relieved that the thing finally works, in its primitive form at least."

"Tipps, what on earthia is a junikrapogswash?"

"It's an insult of Arivelian descent. It's considered quite rude in Arivelia so I wouldn't go shouting it around. I think it roughly translates as 'son of a decrepit mule.'"

"Hmm, this thing does sound pretty cool actually," said Tenk. "Think of the possibilities. You could capture my voice, then ring my mum, and she would never know the difference!"

"Um . . . yeah," said Tippian. "Wasn't what I had in mind, but definitely doable. Although I'd probably rather not get a telling off about leaving my dirty washing all over my bedroom."

"Can we test it now?" said Loca.

"Not yet, I've still got a ton of work to do before I want to show it, and I'm gonna need to make it a lot smaller than this to be portable and discreet. The award isn't until winter, so I'll be working on it for months yet."

After shoving the Voicemaster back into his pocket, Tippian finally began to enjoy the party like the rest of them, and even joined everyone in a dance when Coralle turned the music up.

By this point, most of the adults were on at least their third glass of wine, and Seckry and the others were all buzzing from some fizzy drink that Tenk had brought over called Mental, which was made with some kind of new sweetener that was, according to the can, twice as sweet as real sugar, and gave you six times the amount of sugar rush. Tenk, manic from the energy, decided to gather up all of the non-helium balloons that were floating around and take a running dive on them, popping them and making Henrei and his wife duck for cover. Then, as he was about to take a second run at the remaining balloons, there was a vicious rap on the door.

Coralle answered it to an old man with slits for eyeballs who was holding his fist up as if he was going to take a shot at someone.

"Mr Mulk, I'm so sorry," Coralle apologised, before the man even had a chance to speak. "I'll turn the music down. It's my son's birth-"

"I don't care what the occasion is, Ms Sevenstars," the man interrupted. "It sounds like a bleedin' world war is going on in here. I want absolute silence from now on!"

"Mr Mulk, we'll keep the noise down," Coralle continued. "You won't hear any more balloons popping."

"Did you not hear what I just said?" Mr Mulk thundered. "I said *silence!* This party is over. Now!"

He grabbed the door and slammed it on himself. Everyone was motionless as Coralle turned around slowly, and they heard his footsteps disappearing down the corridor.

Chapter Two

Carved Coordinates

"*What a rude pig!*" whispered Loca.

"Who on earthia was that guy?" asked Seckry. In the entire year they had been living there, he had never seen the man before.

"He lives in number fifty-nine up on the top floor," said Coralle. "He doesn't get out much."

"The *top* floor?" said Tenk. "How can he hear the noise all the way up there?"

"I don't know, love, but it *is* getting pretty late. I think it's time to call it a night."

Everyone helped clear up the flat before leaving, and on the whole managed not to make too much noise, except for when Tenk accidentally stumbled backwards onto a couple of the balloons, popping them in succession like a machine gun let loose. They all stared at the door for a few moments, expecting Mr Mulk to start rapping on it for a second time, but luckily they were left to clean up the rest of the mess in peace.

After the last of the guests had said their goodbyes and left, Coralle yawned.

"I am absolutely shattered, you guys," she said. "I hope you had a good birthday Seck, 'cause a lot of work went into that."

"It's been the best day ever," Seckry said with a smile. "Thanks for everything."

"No problem darling," said Coralle. "Now if you don't mind, I'm gonna love you and leave you both. I'm asleep on my feet."

When Coralle had gone to bed, Seckry and Eiya decided to get some fresh air, since the flat was still boiling and sweaty from all the guests. Being a flat without any form of garden, it was hard to relax out in the open, but they did what they could with what they had, and made their way out onto the grated staircase, leaning over the railings and looking out at the square.

At some point during the party someone had to have wandered outside to get some fresh air too because they had tied a helium balloon to the railings.

"I wonder who left this -"

Seckry cut himself off as he turned the balloon around. A cute animal had been drawn onto the surface in colourful felt pen, and the words *Happy Birthday Seck, from Eiya*, were written underneath.

"I did it while you were in the bathroom earlier," she said, with that half guilty, half innocent blush that made Seckry's heart melt. She began untying the balloon to give it to Seckry, but as she loosened the knot, the string slipped through her fingers and the balloon began floating upwards.

"Oh no!" she said desperately. She clutched at the air, jumping as high as she could, but there was no way she could reach it.

Seckry launched himself after it too, but he had no chance.

"Don't worry," he said. "I'm not letting it get away."

His flat was on the third floor, and there were five floors above him. If he could sprint up the stairs, maybe he could make it.

Before Eiya could tell him not to worry, Seckry had darted upwards, skipping three steps at a time.

When he reached the eighth floor he thought he had caught up to it, but as he reached out, the string just evaded his grasp. He glanced around wildly looking for another way up, but this was the end of the stairs.

Then he spotted some kind of maintenance ladder leading up to the roof. He jumped onto it and climbed frantically until he mounted the roof and jumped one last time.

"Yes!" he said triumphantly, as he gripped the string tightly and pulled it down towards him. "I got it!" he called down to Eiya.

"Seck, be careful!"

"Who's that making a racket now?" came a raspy voice that sounded like Mr Mulk's.

Seckry whispered, '*sorry!*' and took a deep breath. He hadn't done this much exercise since the Mega Meltdown last winter.

When he regained his composure, he realised how high he was. He looked out over the moonlit horizon in awe. It was like seeing Skyfall City for the very first time.

"*Eiya, come and have a look at the view!*" he whispered excitedly.

She made her way up, being careful not to clank too loudly on the metal ruts.

"It's beautiful," Eiya mouthed softly, as she joined him on the rooftop.

"Look, there's the Friction Emporium!" said Seckry, as the words 'Brace Yourselves for Battle' scrolled across the building's huge LED-lit exterior.

"Oh, look, Seck, you can see Endrin too," said Eiya, pointing.

Seckry looked over at the huge, illuminated letter E that was slowly rotating atop the Endrin headquarters. The sight of that building had used to make Seckry's stomach churn, but now that Jenniver Layne had taken over as CEO, it actually made him feel a little hopeful.

What had once been a daunting and unfamiliar skyline was now a skyline that made Seckry feel instantly at home, the only unfamiliar thing about it being a gigantic new chocolate factory that had opened at some point during the summer. Massive, chunky, lowercase chocolate-coloured letters adorned its rooftop, spelling the word 'chococorp.'

"Tenk tells me we have to try their extra thick chocochomp bar," said Eiya. "He says it's delicious."

Seckry made a note to try one, even though taking food recommendations from Tenk was usually pointless, since

Tenk had once eaten goobergrubs and found those delicious too.

Far in the distance, to the left of the main cluster of the city's buildings, Seckry could see a collection of warehouses lining the bank of the river.

"Oh, Gedin, Seck," said Eiya, following his line of sight. "Do you think one of those warehouses is the one that Darklight used? I can't even look at them."

Seckry and Eiya had found out over the summer that Darklight had been using an abandoned warehouse on the riverfront to keep the captured innoya locked up before he had transported them to the Endrin headquarters to meet their death. They had heard from Sanfarrow that Darklight had been keeping them chained to the walls, and had left them practically to starve, while Darklight set up the Divinita Project.

"It could be," said Seckry, solemnly.

"I just can't imagine such a horrific last few months of living," said Eiya. "It must have been pretty much torture."

"I can't understand how nobody would have heard the screams," said Seckry.

"Maybe they couldn't scream," said Eiya, and Seckry felt sick, thinking of the innoya being gagged for all that time.

As Seckry turned his head away from the warehouses, he caught a glimpse of something carved into the concrete of the wall close to his right hand. He examined it more closely to find that it was two different Ancient Klaxion numerals. Each were three digits long. Seckry wondered what they meant, but concluded that they had to be something the builders of the structure had put there during the construction for some reason.

They stood for a while, gazing out at the colourful nightscape and listening to the distant sound of traffic, enjoying the warm breeze. Seckry realised then that there was something missing from the atmosphere of Kerik Square that had been a constant at one point; Mrs Plum's lullaby. Since they had rescued Danney Plum from the clutches of Darklight, he had been kept in secure care, and Mrs Plum had been allowed to visit him now and again until he had been brought back to normal health. As soon as Danney had been released, Mrs Plum had taken him out of the city, and as far as Seckry knew, they had settled in a small fishing village somewhere far away.

As they watched the moon slowly drift across the starry sky, Seckry's thoughts turned to his previous birthday.

"He didn't come this time," he said.

After a moment of silence, Eiya said, "I'm sorry, Seck."

Seckry smiled feebly.

"I know it's silly. I knew he wouldn't risk coming here for a second year. I guess I just . . . always had a little bit of hope that I would catch a glimpse of him."

On his fifteenth birthday, Seckry had received a birthday card with no signature on it. At least that was what he had thought, until at the beginning of the summer when he had caught an indentation in the blank space which faintly read, 'Love, dad.'

"Can you believe he was here?" Seckry said ponderingly. "My dad was actually standing outside the front door of the flat at some point, and I was asleep inside."

"When you told me about the blank birthday card, I didn't even think to question it," said Eiya.

"I didn't really question it myself," said Seckry. "I just assumed one of the neighbours had shoved it through or something without bothering to write on it."

"You've been watching the letterbox all night, haven't you?" said Eiya. "I saw you glance at it a few times during the party."

Seckry smiled guiltily.

"I should have known better. I mean, if everything Vance said is true, then my dad vanished because he's protecting us from Lux. He must have really gone against his intentions to post the card last year. He would never take that risk again. It just doesn't make any sense that he came here at all, you know? Why take that risk in the first place?"

"Maybe he just wanted you to know he was still out there somewhere, still thinking about you. Maybe he just wanted you to know that he's alive."

Seckry nodded. If that's what his father had wanted to tell him, then Seckry was grateful. He had been wracked with fear last year that his father was dead. At least now he knew he was still out there. Somewhere.

At that moment, Eiya put her small hand on top of his and interlaced her fingers with his gently.

Seckry swallowed. Every time Eiya touched him, it was like a wave of euphoria spread through his body, and he just wanted to take her in his arms and kiss her, tasting her beautiful lips and smelling her soft skin. But the truth was, Seckry hadn't kissed her since that first time in the abandoned reactor.

It wasn't that Seckry hadn't had the opportunity. He wasn't even sure what was stopping him. He just couldn't pluck up the courage to kiss her again, even though his entire body longed for it. Ever since that night, he had sometimes wondered if Eiya had even wanted to kiss him again. He had never kissed anyone before, so for all he knew, he had been terrible at it, or he had had bad breath. So a mix of nervousness, embarrassment, and fear of rejection had made Seckry wait, and hope that Eiya would make the first move once again. Except she hadn't.

"Seckry, what on earthia is that smell?"

Seckry jolted out of his trance, realising that he had been staring at Eiya, completely glazed over.

"Smell?" he said. Seckry couldn't smell anything, but he wouldn't have been surprised if the eggy sewerage vapours that sometimes emanated from Mr Bobsworth's, of number twenty, were making their way up to the roof now as well.

"That guy needs to get his place fumigated, it's getting beyond a joke now," said Seckry.

"No," said Eiya, "It's from this direction. It certainly isn't coming from Bobsworth's."

Seckry followed Eiya around some maintenance pipes to the other side of the roof, and the most wonderful, sweet, sticky, sugary aroma wafted into his nostrils. It was so strong that he was sure he was getting a sugar rush just from the particles entering his body.

"Is that candy?" Seckry suggested.

"It's . . . not as artificial as that," said Eiya, "and it's got so many . . . layers to it. There's freshly made bread in there somewhere too, you can feel the warmth of it. And what's that flowery smell? It's beautiful."

Seckry sniffed again. Eiya was right, there was a fragrance in there that seemed to be a fresh flower. A very particular flower.

"It's teraflower," said Seckry. "It's this rare flower that we used to have a few of in Marne."

Seckry leaned over the edge of the western facing edge of the roof, and spotted a single, warm, orange light that was spilling out of a large window and illuminating the backstreets. The sign above the window read:

Softspoon's Bakery
The freshest bread, now back in business.

"There's our culprit," said Eiya. "Gedin, Seck, we've got to get something to eat there sometime, my mouth is watering."

"Why are their lights on at this time of night?" said Seckry.

"Maybe they're baking stuff for the morning," suggested Eiya.

As Eiya closed her eyes and took in the delicious scent, Seckry looked to his left and his eyes widened.

Attached to the railing just a few yards away was some kind of brass, antique telescope, intricately patterned with ornate engravings.

Seckry approached it and brushed his hand over the old metal. It was cool, but covered in a fine layer of dirt. Evidently, it hadn't been used in quite some time.

"Wow, I wonder who that belongs to," said Eiya, joining him.

"Look at the old patterns," said Seckry. "This must have been sitting here for years. I bet nobody even knows it's up here."

"Can I be first to look through it?" said Eiya sweetly, and

Seckry smiled as she placed her eye on the eyepiece.

"I don't think it's working," she said. "It's just black."

Seckry tried peering through as well, but Eiya was right, the lens was being blocked. He leaned over the railing to see if there was a cap at the front, but there didn't seem to be anything covering it.

"What are these?" said Eiya, who had flicked open a small latch at the base of the telescope to reveal two circular dials with Klaxion numerals engraved onto them. She turned one slowly, making a gentle clicking noise, and after a few moments, a whirring rattle came from within the scope itself and began spinning clunkily to its left before stopping abruptly.

"It's like, some kind of clockwork machine," said Eiya.

But Seckry was lost in his own thoughts. The Klaxion numerals he had seen engraved into the wall on the other side of the roof. Were they coordinates for the telescope? He jogged back to them and made a note of the numbers, before returning and turning the dials until they showed identical symbols to the ones that had been carved.

The telescope jittered into action and tilted to its right, then downwards slightly before coming to a stop.

"This is so cool," said Eiya, placing her eye on the eyepiece once more. "I just wish we could see through it. It's still black."

Seckry pressed his face up against the side of the machine, trying to get an idea of what the coordinates had pointed the telescope towards, but to him it just looked like the corners of a couple of old buildings.

There had to be a way of getting it to work. Seckry examined the telescope from all angles, to see if there was some kind of switch to activate it. He couldn't see anything obvious, but as he backed away, he noticed a thin cable coming out of the bottom of the scope and disappearing into a small hole in the concrete.

"Eiya, look," he said.

"That must be how we turn it on," said Eiya. "Where does it lead?"

They glanced around them but couldn't see any obvious cables of the same thickness reappearing out of the structure of the building. It was only after a bit of snooping around that Eiya shouted, "I got it!" before hastily covering her mouth with her hand from the noise she had made.

"It's right here by the ladder," she said. "We came right past it earlier."

Seckry leaned over and followed the cable until it disappeared into the wall of the top floor.

"It's going straight into somebody's flat," said Seckry. "I wonder if they know about the telescope."

"Well it doesn't look like anybody's touched it for decades," said Eiya. "I bet whoever made it died a long time ago. Maybe they lived in that flat at one point, and now there's someone living there who has no idea what that cable is for."

"We should totally tell them about it," said Seckry. "They've probably been wondering what that cable is connected to since the day they moved in. I bet they've never bothered venturing up here."

"Yeah, we totally should!" said Eiya, with infectious excitement. "They might even be able to tell us who lived in the flat before them. We could find out who made it and why they put it there."

"Come on," said Seckry, climbing down the maintenance ladder. "Let's find out what number flat it is."

Eiya followed him down carefully and they glared at the flat door number.

It was flat fifty-nine.

"Seck . . ." said Eiya. "Is it me or does the number fifty-nine ring a bell?"

Seckry groaned internally. The flat they were staring at was none other than Mr Mulk's.

Chapter Three

The Sheltering of a Criminal

Seckry and Eiya had gone to bed feeling slightly deflated that night. If the flat had belonged to anyone else, they imagined the residents would have been thrilled to find out that there was a secret cable running up to a telescope on the roof, but somehow, they imagined Mr Mulk wasn't going to be that enthusiastic about it.

When morning arrived, Eiya got up early to have some breakfast, and Seckry slept in again, savouring his last lie-in before the beginning of school the next day. His lie-in was cut short, however, when he heard Eiya gasp from the living area.

"Oh my Gedin, Seck!" she cried. "Come here!"

Seckry threw off his sheets and darted out of his bedroom, worried that Eiya was in danger. The fragility of her existence made him constantly worried for her safety. But Eiya was perfectly fine, her eyes locked on the TV and her mouth slightly open.

It was the morning news, and Darklight's face was all over it.

"Former CEO of Endrin, Kan Darklight, was murdered last night in his cell by an intruder. Prison guards describe the intruder as having severe physical deformities. Guards attempted to restrain the man, but they were unable to, and he gained access to Darklight's cell. The Patrol are appealing to anyone with information."

"He's . . . dead," Eiya said vacantly.

"Murdered . . ." said Seckry.

"Do you think it was one of the innoya?" said Eiya.

"Someone taking revenge?"

Seckry shook his head slowly. He had no idea.

"Severe physical deformities?" he said, screwing his face up.

Seckry's phone started buzzing in his pocket.

It was Ropart Sanfarrow.

"Mr Sanfarrow," Seckry said.

"It's okay Seckry, you don't have to keep calling me that, please, call me Ropart. Seckry, are you watching the news?"

"Yeah," Seckry said. "Who on earthia . . . ?"

"Seckry, I need to talk to you. And Eiya. Both of you together. Can you come to my new office today?"

"Uh . . . yeah, I think so," said Seckry.

"Good," said Sanfarrow, and his voice sounded pained. "It's at the new construction site in the west partition on Chronoway Crossing."

"We'll be there as soon as we can," said Seckry, and ended the call.

"He must know who did it," said Eiya, as they boarded the monorail to the Chronoway district in the west partition.

Neither Seckry nor Eiya had seen much of Ropart Sanfarrow over the summer. After everything that had happened with Darklight being arrested and Jenniver taking over as CEO of Endrin, he and Jenniver had quietly got married at a ceremony which just close family and friends were invited to, and then he had begun work on an ambitious, new project; the renovation of the longest monorail track in Skyfall, one which had collapsed decades ago, and had never been rebuilt.

It had seemed strange to Seckry at first, that a scientist would be in charge of a construction project. But it was soon revealed that Sanfarrow wasn't just rebuilding the track, he was designing a new way of travelling; a new track, with new vehicles that would use magnetic technology to hover, effectively travelling at super-fast speeds.

As they exited the carriage at Chronoway Crossing, they caught sight of Sanfarrow's new office. It was a bright white structure in true Endrin fashion, and was the size of a three-bedroomed house. It sat on the platform, right in place of where the collapsed track used to begin.

"It's good to see you again Seckry, and Eiya," said Sanfarrow, greeting them at the entrance with a genuine smile, but still looking as shaky and on edge as when they had first met him last year. "Please, come in."

The first thing Seckry noticed as they entered was the stunning view of the city through the office's glass-panelled back wall. Part of the collapsed track was still visible, jutting out across the cityscape before cutting off in mid-air, where several cranes and a load of scaffolding were congregated. Seckry could just about see the tiny silhouettes of workers constructing away.

"Forty-two years ago was the last time a train travelled this track from Chronoway to Mechaner's Clifftop," said Sanfarrow. "It was one of the most useful tracks for commuters. It cuts out four different stops if you need to get to the other side of the city."

"Why do you think no one has ever tried to rebuild it until now?" asked Eiya.

Sanfarrow sighed.

"I guess it still has that notoriety. People have largely been scared of rebuilding it in case it collapses again. It wasn't an easy 'yes' from the government, let me tell you that. The thing is, it's been forty two years. The technology we have today is way beyond what they had back then. The accident was simply a sign of the times."

"What actually happened, anyway?" asked Seckry. "Why did it collapse?"

"One of the fixtures came loose and altered the track. It was a Sunday afternoon, so it wasn't very busy, but there was one carriage carrying seven passengers. When it hit the misplaced fixture, it derailed and all seven passengers were killed. Luckily it derailed above the Plaqua industrial estate and nobody was in work, being a Sunday, so there were no other deaths, just financial losses for the companies whose buildings were destroyed. The force and the weight of the carriage pulled the track apart though, and it spread like a kind of domino effect, causing the entire thing to crumble. Luckily, only thirty-seven people were injured from that, and there were no other casualties."

Sanfarrow organised a few papers on his desk and shuffled them into piles.

"Anyway," he said. "I imagine you've guessed why I asked you both to come here today."

"Darklight?" said Eiya.

Sanfarrow nodded.

"Do you know who killed him?" asked Seckry.

Sanfarrow swallowed hard.

"Yes . . . yes I do."

"Really?" said Eiya. "Who was it?"

"A man who was desperately seeking revenge," said Sanfarrow.

"Do you know where he is now?" said Seckry.

Sanfarrow slowly tilted his head to the left.

"Yes," he said. "He's right behind that door."

Seckry and Eiya said nothing. They were too shocked. Whoever it was had broken into Skyfall Penitentiary and murdered their most high profile inmate. The Patrol were searching high and low for him right now.

"Seckry . . . Eiya . . . I'd like you to meet . . . Kevan Kayne."

"Kevan Kayne?" said Eiya softly. "But he's dea-"

Eiya cut herself off as a figure opened the door. Seckry reeled back at the sight of the man. He had dank, dark hair that was dripping down his grey face, and was wearing a brown overcoat that was littered with holes, sprouting what could only be described as flesh tentacles, writhing around.

The most unnerving thing, however, wasn't his physical appearance, it was that his eyes had been locked on Eiya's face since the moment he had entered the room, and they still hadn't moved.

"As you can see," said Sanfarrow. "Kevan is still very much with us. Although not in a form of existence that I've ever encountered before."

"It's good to finally meet you in person, Seckry," said Kayne, his eyes still staring at Eiya. "Thank you for the worms. They . . . are the reason I am here right now."

"What?" said Seckry, quietly, glancing back and forth between Kayne and Sanfarrow. "Wait . . ." He scanned Kayne's strange body. "You're the one I sent the worms to on the train? You're the one who blackmailed me into breaking into Endrin?"

"I apologise I had to put you in that position," said Kayne, though Seckry didn't get the sense that the man was genuinely sorry at all. "I was a desperate man, and if you hadn't retrieved those worms for me, I wouldn't be standing here today."

Sanfarrow was now sweating.

"Dear Gedin, Seckry, I have a lot to explain. Please take a seat, both of you. Would you like a drink?"

Seckry and Eiya shook their heads, unable to take their eyes off the pulsating flesh of the undead scientist before them.

"You . . . killed Darklight . . ." said Eiya.

"Ropart tried his best to dissuade me. But this world needed to be rid of the man who conducted those experiments, and who shot me and my wife."

Seckry didn't feel any contempt towards Kayne for the murder, just fear at being so close to someone who was capable of it.

"How . . . how are you here? Didn't Darklight kill you?"

Seckry spent the next half hour listening to the story of how Kayne had been reanimated by the toxic helitonium inside the worms and how he had fled to Arivel to regain his strength.

"So the worms are . . . keeping you alive?" said Seckry.

"Alive may not be the correct word," said Kayne. "But yes, they are keeping me in this world for now. During my time in Arivel I managed to successfully breed the worms that you collected for me, giving me a constant supply of them. Luckily, the helitonium inside them carried seemed to carry through to their offspring."

Kayne suddenly winced in pain and something around the area of his left bicep popped, spilling blood all over the floor of the office.

"We need to patch that up," said Sanfarrow, quickly.

"It's quite alright," said Kayne, grimacing and clutching the wound with his right hand. "I'll see to it myself. And then I need to lie down." He gazed up at Eiya and said, "I look forward to speaking with you again sometime," and disappeared into the adjacent room.

"Mr Sanfarrow," said Eiya as soon as the door closed. "You're sheltering a murderer. That's a serious crime! Aren't you scared the Patrol will catch you?"

"I've spoken to the Patrol," Sanfarrow said.

"What do you mean?"

"The . . . Patrol is very aware of Kevan's whereabouts. I had a very long talk this morning with the head of operations. He's a personal friend of mine, and we came to an . . . agreement."

"Oh my Gedin," said Eiya, softly.

"Let's just say that the riddance of Darklight from the face of the earthia was unwelcomed by very few people," said Sanfarrow. "And with the right amount of influence and money, the Patrol have been persuaded to stay away."

Seckry felt more than a little uncomfortable. Bribing the Skyfall Patrol, although for entirely different purposes, was the kind of thing Seckry thought only Darklight would do.

"Believe me, I'm the last person who would have thought I would ever consider bribing the Patrol," Sanfarrow said, looking away in shame. "But . . . Kevan is the exception. I have owed him my life for the last forty years, and only now am I close to repaying him."

"Why do you owe him your life?" asked Seckry.

Sanfarrow took a deep breath.

"When we were seven years old, I fell into the river, not far from the Endrin headquarters, strangely enough. We had been trying to catch some fish with our bare hands by leaning over and reaching down. Well, you can imagine how easily it would have been to slip in. Before I knew it, there I was, plunged into the cold, dirty water, terrified and unable to swim. Kevan, without hesitation, jumped in to save me, even though his swimming was just as bad as mine. He almost drowned himself. He just about managed to keep me afloat long enough for a maintenance worker to throw us a rope and drag us up the bank."

Sanfarrow wiped his sweating forehead with a tissue.

"The worst thing of all, is that when the tables were turned, and it was his life that was in danger, I didn't help him in return. I ran. He needed me . . . and I *ran*."

"When?" asked Seckry.

"The night he and his wife were shot. We knew Darklight had turned against us. He had already begun wiping our existence from Endrin. When Jenniver told me that Darklight was planning on killing us, and that I should escape, I knew that Kevan and Elenya were in the building. I knew they were there but I chose to escape on my own. I chose to run without telling them because I was afraid Darklight would find me. I fled the place and just hoped that Jenniver would be able to help them out too. I only found out that he had been killed when you two brought me the message from Jenniver when I was hiding in that underground lair. Before that, I still held on to the hope that he and his wife had escaped.

"That letter that you had the scan of, telling Kayne my whereabouts - I thought he had received it all those years ago when we were in university. We were friends with Darklight at the time, but we knew if we made it to the top of Endrin with him, there was a possibility he could turn on us. That disused reactor was always a favourite hideaway for me and Kevan when we were young, and it was one place that neither of us had ever mentioned to Darklight. When I escaped, it was the first place I thought of hiding. If Kayne had escaped too, it would have been the first place he would have come looking for me. I placed all of my hope in the fact that he had seen that letter years ago and he would remember my instructions."

Sanfarrow whimpered, his lip quivering.

"After finding out that he was dead . . . I can barely believe that he's back. He revealed himself to me in a café by giving me the combination code for the locked cube he had given me previously. Inside, it had simply said, 'It's me.' When we were growing up, we were always playing spies, and we would come up with these elaborate ways to identify each other if we were undercover. He explained, recently, that he had originally made that cube as a light-hearted reference to those times, but had never anticipated the circumstances in which he would ultimately have me open it."

"We can barely believe that he's back, either," said Seckry.

"You can understand why I'm sheltering him, can't you? Even this doesn't feel like enough. I fear I will never be able to repay him for how he saved me and how . . . how I betrayed him in return."

Seckry and Eiya could see that Sanfarrow was getting emotional, so they politely told him that they were about to start heading off.

"Of course," said Sanfarrow. "Of course. I've kept you for long enough. Seckry . . . before you go . . . I would like to talk to you in private, if that's alright . . . without Eiya."

Seckry glanced back and forth between Sanfarrow and Eiya. "Why can't she hear?" he asked.

"Please," said Sanfarrow. "Just a few moments."

"It's no problem, Seck," said Eiya, "I'll see you outside."

She exited the office, leaving Seckry alone with the unstable scientist.

"Seckry . . . the . . . the reason I asked both you and Eiya to come here today wasn't simply to meet Kevan Kayne."

Seckry listened motionlessly.

Sanfarrow started to speak a few times before cutting himself off, trying to find the right words.

"Seckry, Kevan Kayne believes that . . . that his wife, Elenya, has come back to life."

"You mean . . . the same way he has?"

"No, not quite . . . me and Jenniver checked the soil and the body was still there. We've since provided a proper burial. No . . . Kevan thinks that Elenya has returned to this world in a new body, a kind of . . . reincarnation. And . . . he believes this reincarnation to be *Eiya*."

It took Seckry a moment for what Sanfarrow was saying to sink in.

"Eiya? I don't understand."

"During those first few days after revealing himself to me, I told Kevan everything that had happened with Darklight and the Divinita Project, and of course, Eiya came into the conversation. It was only when I finished talking that I realised something had changed in his eyes. He kept asking me questions about her afterwards, becoming obsessed. By the end of it, he was utterly convinced that Elenya had been reincarnated."

Seckry sat down, taking this in.

"Did you tell him he was wrong?" said Seckry. "That Eiya was created out of my subconscious?"

"Yes, of course," said Sanfarrow. "This doesn't mean he believes me. I mean, my theory of Eiya's creation coming from your subconscious is still just a theory, and Kevan knows this."

Seckry stared at the ground.

"There isn't . . . a possibility that he's right, is there?" he said.

Sanfarrow ran his fingers through his grey hair and closed his eyes in frustration. "You have to understand, something like Eiya has never happened before. The multitude of unknowns surrounding her creation are infinite, despite my best guesses. Look, Seckry, everything that I've concluded suggests that my original prediction was right, and Eiya was somehow created from your brain."

"I mean," said Seckry, "if Eiya was a reincarnation of Elenya, why doesn't she remember who she is?"

"Exactly," said Sanfarrow, "it makes much less sense than my original theory, and I will be trying my hardest to convince Kayne that Eiya is not his dead wife. I daresay he has much time left with us anyhow."

"What do you mean?" asked Seckry.

"Well, he is still technically dead," said Sanfarrow. "He has no heartbeat, no pulse, and alongside all these strange mutations, he is slowly decaying. I estimate that he has around six to seven months to exist in some form before his consciousness slips away for the second time and he is gone for good. The thing I'm worried about is what state he will be in physically before that time comes. He is already growing these strange tentacles, and, well, you've seen the state that his body is in. One can only imagine what will happen to him over time."

"Dear Gedin," Seckry said, disturbed. "So is he going to stay here in your office for the entire time he has left?"

"I hope so," said Sanfarrow. "If his body doesn't begin to expand beyond the walls."

Seckry shuddered at the thought of the undead man growing like some hideous inflation.

"Don't worry, Seckry, I'll do my best to bring Kayne to his senses. It's amazing how grief can warp the mind. In the meantime, it would probably be best to keep this information from Eiya. I doubt the idea of being someone's dead wife is a pleasant one."

Seckry nodded and said his goodbyes, re-joining Eiya out on the platform.

"What on earthia was that all about, Seck?" said Eiya, who was sat on the edge of some kind of modern art sculpture.

Seckry had zero intention of keeping what Sanfarrow had told him a secret. He kept nothing from Eiya. He had to tell her.

"His wife?" Eiya spat, stopping in her tracks.

"That's what Sanfarrow said."

"But . . . wait a minute. How old was this wife of his? If that guy thinks I'm in my forties I'm gonna be really offended."

"He thinks you're a reincarnation of her soul in a new body," said Seckry.

For the entire journey back, Eiya said very little, lost in her own thoughts.

That evening, to take their mind off the grotesque image

of the undead Kevan Kayne, Seckry and Eiya decided to knock at Mr Mulk's and enquire about the telescope. They doubted the grumpy man would even be interested in hearing about it, but as long as they could get him to activate the thing, they'd be able to look through and see what the coordinates were pointing to.

"Of all the people to have taken over that flat and gain control of that button," said Eiya, as they made their way up the staircase.

"Wait, what are we gonna say to him?" said Seckry. "If we just ask him about the telescope straight away he's gonna tell us to leave him alone. We'll have to butter him up by being nice to him first."

Eiya nodded and knocked the door gently. They heard a few groans and some muffled swearing before the door opened.

Mr Mulk glared at them.

"Yes?" he said impatiently.

"Hi Mr Mulk, I'm Seckry and this is Eiya. It was my party last night and -" Seckry trailed off as he realised that the man was wearing only a shirt and a pair of Y-fronts.

"Your . . . um . . . that's a . . . um, lovely shirt you have on today, Mr Mulk," said Eiya.

Mr Mulk looked down at his own torso.

"It hasn't been washed for two weeks, it's got several holes in it, and it's patterned with a hideous floral design; the shirt is revolting. Now what do you want?"

"We wanted to . . . um . . . apologise for the noise last night," said Eiya. "We weren't thinking about the other residents in the building, were we, Seck?"

But Seckry's attention had left Mr Mulk and was scanning the flat behind him, probing for any cables coming from the ceiling. He caught sight of one in the far left corner of the room, which snaked down the wall until it reached a little white button, like a doorbell.

Mr Mulk threw his head over his own shoulder to see what Seckry was glaring at before turning back to him with a piercing stare.

"Cut the nonsense," he said. "What do you want with that button?"

Seckry gulped.

"We'd like to press it, sir," he said.

Mr Mulk lowered his head towards them like a teacher boring down on pupils and said quietly, "You think I am *that* stupid?"

"Excuse me?" Seckry replied, backing away.

"I know what we can do as a joke!" Mr Mulk said mockingly. "We can tell old, senile Mr Mulk that all we want to do is press a little button on his wall, we'll get inside his flat, and then we'll steal his cash and his passport and his rare collection of vintage bottle caps!"

"No Mr Mulk, that's not it at all," said Seckry. "We honestly just want to press it, we're not trying to steal anyth-"

"Well I can save you the trouble," said Mr Mulk. "I've pressed it one thousand and one times, and the bleedin' thing does nothing!"

Seckry and Eiya glanced at each other.

"Mr Mulk, sir, I think we know what the button does. There's a teles-"

"Look," Mr Mulk interrupted, "I don't need some teenagers telling me what that Gedin forsaken button does, okay? I've lived here for sixty years and I'm telling you, the thing does *nothing!*"

"But, sir, can you just press it one more -"

"But, sir, nothing!" said Mr Mulk. "You're not making me press that useless, ugly building fault one more time, and you are certainly not stepping one foot inside my flat."

"Can you at least tell us who lived in the flat before you?" asked Seckry.

Mr Mulk grabbed the door handle.

"Go back to your own floor!" he said viciously. "You're stinking the place out with your filthy hormones." With that, he slammed the door shut.

Seckry lay awake for quite some time that night. He wasn't sure what was playing on his mind more; Darklight's murder,

Kayne's return, or the simple frustration of not knowing what the telescope on the roof was pointing at.

As he concentrated, he realised that Darklight's demise had absolutely no effect on his emotions. Whether the man was rotting in prison, or gone completely, as long as he was no longer able to carry out any more horrific experiments, Seckry was happy. Kayne's return, however, was something that made his stomach churn. Not least because of his delusional idea about Eiya being the reincarnation of his wife. The only thing that helped ease his mind was the decision that he would stay away from Kayne as much as possible and, more importantly, keep Eiya away from him. From what Sanfarrow had told them, the mutating man only had a limited time in this reanimated state before he completely vanished into the netherworld, so Seckry would just let the man enjoy his brief second life at a reasonable distance.

The telescope, as trivial as it seemed, was probably the biggest cause of Seckry's insomnia. He hated being so close to uncovering something secret and having somebody as rude as Mr Mulk standing in their way. The task of pressing that button was going to be a bit harder than they had expected, and if they were going to get the telescope working, it was going to have to be without Mr Mulk's cooperation.

After tossing and turning for what seemed like hours, Seckry stuck his earphones in and played his unique version of The Broken Motion's Looking for Tomorrow.

Chapter Four

Fringe Science

No, Seckry thought. *Not again. This can't be happening.*

He was in the Divinita Chamber, and Darklight was standing right in front of him, pointing a gun at his head.

"You're dead," Seckry said desperately. "Kayne killed you."

"I have no idea what you're talking about," said Darklight. "All that helitonium messed with your mind when you broke into my building. You're hallucinating. I'm not dead. I'm right here in front of you. Now if you'll excuse me, there's somewhere I have to be."

Darklight, still pointing the gun at Seckry's head, made his way up to the Divinita Machine and pressed a button.

"Extraction initiated," said an electronic voice.

I have to save Eiya, Seckry thought. *Where is she? I have to save her. I have to stop the Divinita Machine before it kills all the innoya, and Eiya dissipates.*

Seckry looked down at his hands. Gripped tightly in his left was the vial of gimmypug blood they needed. But what was he supposed to do with it? The innoya were floating in water tanks. How would he get inside them and get the blood into their bodies?

He held the test tube firmly, trying not to drop it, but the thin glass started to crack between his fingers. He tried to hold his shaking hand steady but the more he concentrated on it, the more he crushed the thing. Before he knew it, the glass was in bits, falling to the ground, and his hand was soaked with blood.

"Seckry," said the sweetest voice he had ever heard. Seckry looked up to see Eiya kneeling in front of him, so close she only had to whisper.

"Eiya," he said longingly, showing her his soaking hand. "The blood . . ."

"Seck . . . it's no use," she said softly. "This day has already happened, and you can't change it. The innoya died, and so did I."

"No," Seckry said desperately. "No, you're still alive, you're here, you're here with me right now."

"Am I?" Eiya replied. "Or are you just imagining me?"

"I . . . don't know." Seckry tried to concentrate, but his mind was filled with anxious fuzziness.

Without Seckry realising it, Darklight had crept up behind Eiya. He grabbed a hold of her collar and ripped her backwards, sticking the gun to her temple.

Seckry tried to get up, to run to her, but he couldn't because both of his hands were now locked tightly to the wall behind him by some kind of rusty clasps. He squirmed violently until they began cutting into his wrists.

"Eiya!" he screamed. "Eiya, I've got to save you. I can't let you die."

He tried to find a way of squeezing his hands through the clasps, but the more he struggled, the more they seemed to tighten.

"Seck," Eiya said softly, and even though she was far away, her voice felt as though it were being whispered into his ears. "Don't struggle. There's nothing you can do to change what happened. The innoya are going to die and I am going to die, and there's nothing you can do about it. This is just a memory; a memory you can't change."

"No," Seckry said. "The innoya died but . . . you lived . . . I'm sure of it." Seckry tried hard to concentrate, but his mind was clouded with fear and desperation.

"Seckry, you couldn't save me that night," Eiya said, and her eyes filled up with tears.

Seckry opened his mouth to speak but nothing came out. He blinked and Eiya was gone.

"*Eiya*," he said with agony, tears streaming down his face.

Eiya's voice then whispered softly in his ear, "I died that

night Seckry. I'm gone. Don't you remember?"

"No!" Seckry screamed.

There was a loud bang and Seckry was suddenly sitting upright in bed, gripping the mattress tightly and drenched in sweat.

"Who is it Seck?" shouted Leena. "I'll get 'em!"

His sister was standing in the doorway of his bedroom, swinging what seemed to be a giant marble in a pair of knickers.

Eiya was sat up in bed too, shocked at the sudden outburst of noise.

"Don't tell me you were just having a nightmare," said Leena, accusingly. "Are you serious? It sounded like you were being tortured in here!"

Once Leena had calmed down and returned to her own bedroom, Seckry propped up his pillows and leaned back on them, his heart still racing.

"What time is it?" he asked.

"Three a.m." Eiya said gently. "What were you dreaming about?"

Seckry swallowed hard.

"Just Darklight, that's all," he said. "I dreamt he had come back."

Eiya nodded in understanding, but she had no idea that the true cause of pain was Seckry's fear of her dying, and of him not being able to prevent it.

Seckry lay awake for a long time after that, thinking about the day they had stormed the Divinita Chamber. It was only by luck that Eiya was still alive. For all he had known, the innoya in the chamber had been the only innoya left alive, and if they had died then so would have Eiya. The fact of the matter was that as hard as Seckry had tried to save Eiya, he had failed, and it was only by a miracle that there were more innoya hiding in the city to keep her alive. It was a fact that tormented him, but one he couldn't change.

Eventually, he managed to push his anguish aside by telling himself that no matter what, Eiya *had* survived that night, and she was still here right now, sleeping in the other bed, and that was all that mattered.

When Seckry's alarm woke him for school, he felt groggy and exhausted, partly because of the restless night, and partly because he had become used to sleeping in until around ten o'clock over the holidays.

After a large breakfast of toast and cereal, Seckry was starting to feel a little more alert, and, even though he wasn't the biggest fan of tea, his mum practically forced him to drink a cup to wake him up.

Before Seckry had time to think about it, they were getting off the monorail at the entrance to Estergate, joined by Tenk, who looked even more tired than Seckry, and shortly afterwards, Tippian, who had been driven to school by his mum.

The courtyard was swarming with pupils, all brightly clad in freshly washed uniforms; green blazers over white shirts emblazoned with the Estergate badge (a circular logo with a cityscape encased inside), and smart trousers for the boys, and chequered pleated skirts for the girls.

As they entered the building, Seckry realised he had forgotten how unique Estergate smelled. It was a strange mix; the pleasant, plastic hum of the corridors was the main one, but it was combined with the occasional spurt of acidic disinfectant, the unpredictable and sometimes downright offensive odours that wafted from the osmology rooms, and if you sniffed hard enough, the faint odour of blood from the pathology labs.

"Sounds like Butterkins is getting mauled by the yapyaps again," said Tippian, as a distant wail emanated from the direction of the labs. "She's only got eight toes left 'cos of those things, she claims."

As they queued up to get their new timetables for the year, Seckry eyed the crowds around them nervously. He was happy to see most of his classmates again, but there was one person in particular that he was not looking forward to being reacquainted with; Snibble Knotting.

The last time Seckry had seen him, he had smacked the

bully in the face with his fist and left him bloodied on the side of the road. Seckry had actually been amazed that the Patrol hadn't come looking for him afterwards to charge him with assault. The only explanation Seckry could come up with is that Snibble was too afraid to talk to the Patrol because of all the things he had done himself over the years.

"Don't worry, Seck, I haven't seen him yet," said Tenk, understanding why he was looking so sheepish.

"I still can't believe what I did," said Seckry. "I punched him. I actually punched him. I've never punched anyone!"

"Yeah, well the guy deserved it, there's no doubt about that. I just wish I had been there to see that ugly mug get smashed in."

"But, what's he gonna do to me when he sees me? I am dead meat."

"Don't worry, we've got your back, Seck," said Tippian, throwing a few weak punches into thin air before straightening his glasses.

"Thanks, Tipps," said Seckry.

When the receptionist handed the group their new timetables, Seckry scanned over it and noticed that their first lesson of the day was something completely new.

"Fringe science?" said Tenk. "What in Gedin's name is fringe science?"

Seckry shrugged his shoulders. Neither Tippian nor Eiya had an idea of what it was, either. They made their way to the classroom indicated, trying to guess which teacher they would be getting. Seckry imagined it would either be Mr Spundle, who had taught them once last year as a replacement for Mr Kobold while he had been off sick for a few weeks, or Mrs Verymill, who was an electronics teacher alongside Cutson, but who had never taught Seckry's class. But when they reached the second floor and Seckry saw the classroom door, his face lit up.

It was Vance's.

Adding to Seckry's delight was the fact that, even though Snibble was supposed to be in the same class, he was nowhere to be seen, and Seckry was sure he overheard one of the other pupils saying that Snibble was skiving off school already.

Once everyone was seated, Mr Vance entered the room carrying a briefcase. He clicked it open and pulled out a holographic projector box before plonking it on a stand at the front of the class and flicking a switch.

"Did everyone have a nice summer?" he said brightly.

There were a few replies of, 'yes, sir' and, 'wicked, sir' and then the class began chatting amongst themselves about their vacations and escapades over the holiday whilst Vance configured the machine. After a few minutes, Vance tightened his tie and cleared his throat to indicate he was ready to start, but a few of the girls had a hard time stifling their giggles after Seckry overheard them discussing who was going to flirt with Vance the most this year, and referring to him as Handsome Vancesome.

With his chiselled jaw, stubble, and kind, world-weary eyes, Vance was often the subject of swooning stares from teenage girls, and even the occasional fellow teacher. Seckry was sure Mrs Furrowfog had a dreamy twinkle in her eye every time she was in the same room as the man. Seckry wasn't sure of Vance's exact age, but he guessed that he was somewhere in his late thirties.

"Fringe science," Vance said, putting a stop to the chatter, "covers subjects like time travel, invisibility, force fields and parallel universes, amongst others. Subjects that are on the outside of the main body of science, but that are vital to our technological growth and advancement on Earthia. We won't have time to study all of these in one academic year, so I have decided to focus on just one, for now. Teleportation."

"*Teleportation?*" someone blurted. The class erupted into excited murmurs.

"Indeed, teleportation," Vance said, wiping his whiteboard clean. "The transportation of matter from one location to another, without traversing the distance between them physically. It's something that humans have dreamed of creating for centuries, but has never been realised."

He pressed a button on a remote control, and the

projector fired into action, morphing a 3D model of a man at the front of the class, who placed his hand upon a palm-sized cube and then vanished, reappearing just a few yards away, his hand now pressed to an identical cube.

"Now, who can tell me some popular theoretical uses for teleportation?" said Vance, pacing the front of the classroom, being careful not to walk through the hologram.

A few hands shot up.

"Miss Dunkork, is it?" said Vance, unsure if he knew the girl's name, since he hadn't taught any of them directly before.

"Yes, sir," said Arelia Dunkork, "I think teleportation could be used for going on holiday whenever you wanted to."

"Yes, that is, no doubt one of humanity's biggest desires in terms of teleportation; to be able to travel instantly at will, without having to pay for expensive flights, or endure the longevity of them. Anybody else? Corby Harbourson."

"You could teleport food," said the boy named Corby, who was sat towards the back. "To, like, countries with poverty and that."

"Excellent," said Vance. "A very ethical use of the technology. Yes, teleportation could be used to feed those in need in an instant, and also provide immediate emergency services to places where a natural disaster has occurred. One thing we would have to consider, though, is that a teleportation device would actually be a set of two devices, and one would need to be close to the place of the disaster to begin with."

"Two devices?" someone queried.

"Yes, it is a popular misconception that a teleportation device would be a single object," said Vance. "People often assume that they would just be able to conjure up an image of a certain place in their minds and then they would magically be transported there, or they would type the name of the place into the machine and it would grant them their wish. In reality, if a device were ever to exist, you would need two of them. A sender and a receiver, so the matter could teleport from one to the other. Now, can anyone tell me the environmental benefits of teleportation over transportation?"

"Less pollution," offered Tenk.

"Exactly. Well done, Mr Binko."

Tenk looked elated. He wasn't usually one to offer answers during lessons.

"Now, before we get ahead of ourselves, let's think of the practicalities of using a simple teleportation device ourselves. What would you guys, as pupils of Estergate, like to use a teleporter for? The boy with the earlobe tunnels over there. Sorry, I don't know your name."

"Benn Karter, sir," said the boy. "I'd use it to teleport myself to school in the morning so I could cut out the journey and get an extra hour of sleep."

Vance chuckled.

"A popular use amongst you all, I would imagine."

"Do you think teleportation actually could be invented, though?" said a girl named Perra Flomonger. "Isn't it impossible?"

"That's a very good question, Perra," said Vance. "And one that, until now, I have been very unsure about. But there has been a small scientific discovery here in Skyfall city that changes the possibility greatly, which leads me on to my proposition to you all."

Vance switched the projector off and scanned the room as though sizing everyone up.

"How would you lot . . . like to help me invent a working teleportation device by the end of the year?"

"Oh my Gedin!" someone yelled. "Are you serious, sir?"

"We have the basics," said Vance, "and I'm sure, with the help of an intelligent class like yours, we can work together and achieve the impossible."

The class erupted into cheers and claps and Seckry couldn't help but join in, a huge grin across his face.

The rest of the lesson was spent brainstorming ideas for size, structure, and practicality of the devices, and before Seckry knew it, the hour was almost over. When the bell rang, it was the first time Seckry had ever heard an entire classroom sigh.

In fact, the only one who hadn't been completely enthralled by the class was a girl named Anjilla Wotsmoor, who had been disappointed from the start that fringe science hadn't been about how to maintain the perfect side swept fringe in various weather conditions.

Their second lesson of the day was ethnobotany, closely followed by a double helping of computer programming before lunch. Finally they were treated to a period of graphic design, but all of them now seemed pale in comparison to fringe science.

When the bell rang, Eiya wanted to go to straight to the library to do some research on Elenya Kayne, so Seckry took the opportunity to catch Vance on his own. Seckry hadn't seen him over the duration of the summer holidays, and there hadn't been any time to speak to him one-on-one during their first lesson, but Seckry was anxious to share the mysterious birthday card from his father, which he had brought to school in a tightly clipped plastic container so that the edges wouldn't get scuffed in his backpack.

Vance caught Seckry's eye through the window of his classroom and winked as he was saying goodbye to a few straggling pupils from his last lesson.

"How did I do this morning?" said Vance, kindly, as the final pupil filtered out. "The subject is new to me too."

"Oh, it was awesome, you can rest assured," said Seckry. "I think you're gonna have a hard time getting the class to leave at the end of the lessons though."

Vance powered down his holographic projector and the spinning DNA strand it had been projecting disintegrated into a mess of pixels before vanishing completely. "It's good to see you again Seckry," Vance said with a smile. "How was your summer?"

"Great, thanks," Seckry responded.

"No trouble from religious extremists?"

"I've been lucky so far."

"How is your sister coping?" said Vance.

"Umm . . ." Seckry had to think about this one. "She hasn't burst into tears and started trashing the flat for at least two months . . . so I think she's starting to accept things."

Leena had definitely taken the revelations about their father badly when Seckry had first mentioned them to her last year. She had spent weeks crying off and on, and went through a dramatic cycle of straight up denial, anger, and finally acceptance.

"Sir, about my dad . . ." Seckry said. "There's something I want to show you."

Seckry pulled the plastic container out of his backpack and popped it open.

"It was posted by hand on my birthday just over a year ago. For all this time I thought it was blank. It was a mystery. But feel it with your finger."

Vance opened the birthday card very carefully and smoothed his fingertips over the barely visible, indented text.

"Unbelievable . . ." he mouthed, holding it up to the light.

After a few moments, Seckry asked, "Do you really think this was from him?"

"It's hard to imagine why anyone would try to fool you," said Vance. "I mean . . . the only person I could think of would be . . . Lux. But if Lux was the one who posted this then that means he already knows where you live and . . . well . . . if his intention is to kill you then why not kill you there and then?"

Seckry's heart started pounding away in his chest at the thought of Lux outside his flat.

"But, on the other hand," said Vance, "it just . . . doesn't make any sense that your father would put your anonymity at risk for the sake of saying 'happy birthday', the anonymity he erased himself from your lives for. This is very strange indeed."

Vance turned the card over and over again, examining it from every angle and under every type of artificial light in the room. Eventually he flattened it out gently on his desk.

"I have no idea where the card was bought," said Seckry. "There's no company logo or trademark or anything on it."

Vance pulled his phone out of his pocket and snapped a shot of the barcode.

"The number's not recognised by the scanner . . . Seckry, this card may not have even been shop-bought. Your father may very well have made it himself. This fake barcode was probably printed on there to make it look authentic. Bear with me one moment." He disappeared into the storage cupboard behind his classroom and started pulling out an array of strange looking equipment.

"There must be something more to it," he called to Seckry. "I've got a prober here that will scour the surface of the card for any other indentations or abnormalities, in case your father has left you anything else, like a another message or a numb-" Vance suddenly cut himself off and said, "Seckry, how many digits does that barcode number have?"

Seckry counted. "Thirteen."

"And what are the first five numbers?"

"Zero, two, five, four, sev-" Seckry stopped talking and turned his gaze upwards at Vance, who was slowly placing down the equipment he had found.

"The Skyfall area code . . ." said Seckry.

"I can't believe I didn't notice it earlier," said Vance. "Seckry . . . that's a *telephone number*."

Chapter Five

The Chequered Shirt

Seckry thought he was going to be sick; his stomach was in knots from a mixture of excitement and anticipation.

"Here, call from my phone," said Vance. "We don't know for certain that it was your father who posted this, and if it wasn't, it's probably best not to hand your mobile phone number to the imposter on a plate."

"But what about them tracing the call to you?" said Seckry.

"I hacked my own mobile a long time ago so that it's untraceable," Vance said simply. "You can never be too cautious in Skyfall City."

Seckry's heart was pounding. In mere moments, he might be talking to his father; the man he had waited over nine years to speak to again.

Seckry dialled the number and waited.

It rang once, twice, three times.

Seckry closed his eyes and swallowed hard.

It rang for a fourth, then a fifth, then a sixth time.

The ringing stopped.

There was a beep.

A recorded message.

There were a few moments of silence before a single word was spoken.

"*Seckry*," said the voice on the message softly, and Seckry's eyes darted open.

Waves of emotion flooded Seckry's body and vivid images of Marne and fields and laughter and summer evenings flashed through his consciousness.

Vance's eyes were wide open too, scanning Seckry's

fervently for any indication of what was happening on the other end of the line. Seckry simply nodded.

"Seckry," said his father's voice once again, and Seckry heard the pain and the longing in its tone this time. "Gedin, I don't even know if you're going to call this number, but it was the only thing I could think of that wouldn't raise any suspicion if it was intercepted. I paid a young boy here in the Draindug district to deliver it by hand. I didn't want it going through the Skyfall postal system. Seckry, I know it's a formidable area to venture into, but I want you to meet me at The Axe and Cleaver Inn, Carnaj Street, Draindug district, south partition on the twenty-second of September at one p.m. if you're able. Say the name Pawl Sevenstars to a man named Grolt and he'll let you upstairs."

There was another moment of silence, as if Pawl wanted to say something more but was stopping himself from doing so, then the message clicked off and there was silence.

Seckry slowly removed the phone from his ear and wiped away the tears that were streaming from his eyes.

He passed the phone to Vance, who listened to the message whilst Seckry composed himself.

"It was him," Seckry said incredulously. "It was actually my dad's voice. But he wanted me to meet him . . . oh Gedin, that was September last year . . . he would have been waiting there for me and I didn't turn up -"

Vance put a firm hand on Seckry's shoulder. "He may very well still be there," he said, and looked at his watch. "I can pick you and Eiya up from your flat at around seven o'clock tonight. It'll take just twenty minutes to get to Draindug."

Seckry nodded gratefully. This morning had been just an ordinary day back at school, but it was about to become one of the most important days of his life.

"What's he doing in Draindug?" said Seckry.

Seckry knew very little about the Draindug district. In fact, the only things he could remember about it was that it was in the south partition and a person shouldn't venture there if they valued their life, especially at night.

"Draindug is the roughest district in Skyfall," said Vance.

"I've never been there. To be honest, I would say most people haven't been there, unless they're already residents. It's not exactly a tourist hotspot, that's for sure. How on earthia your father managed to settle there without being severely ostracised or even attacked by the locals is beyond me. But if you think about it, it makes perfect sense. He's basically using the same tactics that the innoya used last year to hide from Darklight, when they hid in the Blacklear. He's hiding from Lux in a place that people are too scared to venture. Simple but effective."

When Seckry got home and told Eiya what had happened, he sat down on the edge of his bed and began rocking back and forth uncontrollably, while Eiya quizzed him about the message.

When Vance pulled up outside the flat at seven o'clock, they both sped down the grating, relieved they didn't have to wait a moment longer.

"Your mum knows we're heading there, right?" said Vance, as they clambered in.

Seckry gulped and gave Vance a guilty look.

"I don't think I'm gonna be getting an ellonberry pie this year, am I?" said Vance, after a while.

Seckry hadn't mentioned a word about it to his mum because he just didn't know how she would react. As far as she was aware, he and Eiya were calling at Tenk's house to play some video games. Even though Coralle had eventually accepted Vance's explanation for his dad's disappearance, Seckry knew her well enough to guess that she would probably try to stop him from entering the Draindug district to find him on the grounds of how dangerous it would be. Seckry didn't want any barriers. He had found his dad, and he was going to meet him, no matter what.

As Vance drove off, the hum of the car's smooth engine and the potent smells of coffee, aftershave and faux leather brought back memories of the time Vance had first introduced himself after saving Seckry from getting beaten up by Snibble.

The district of Draindug wasn't far, and as they entered, Seckry could see the change in the streets, the buildings, and the atmosphere. The roads were wet, narrow, and littered with broken glass, empty beer cans, and masses of take away paper and packaging. Seckry was sure he could even see the odd speck of fresh blood amidst the debris. Blocks of emaciated flats rose high on either side of them, making the rusty framework of Kerik Square look like a royal palace in comparison. Clotheslines full of tattered washing were webbed above them, attached from window to window.

Before they had found Carnaj Street, a gang of burly, heavily tattooed men, mostly dressed in vests or bare chested, formed a line in the road, preventing the car from going any further. A couple of them were swinging what seemed to be wooden bats wrapped in barbed wire.

Vance gradually pressed his foot on the brake until they stopped just a few metres away from the blockade.

The most athletically built of the lot strolled towards the car, cocking his head to see them through the front windscreen.

Vance opened the window.

The guy eyed Vance up and down.

"You've taken a wrong turn. Ain't no offices in Draindug Mr Businessman."

"We're actually looking for The Axe and Cleaver Inn on Carnaj Street. Could you give us directions?"

The guy laughed and called to the rest of the gang, "Another one after Grolt! The guy's famous!" He turned back to Vance. "Listen, Grolt provides services for Draindug and Draindug only. You ain't from the 'Dug and you ain't getting anything from Grolt, you hear me?"

Seckry exchanged looks with Eiya. Services? Who on earthia was this Grolt?

"Look, we just want to speak with -"

The guy shot his hand into the car, gripped Vance's collar and stuck a pocket knife to his throat with his other hand.

"I don't think you know who you're dealing with," he said.

Vance cleared his throat.

"I don't think you know who you're dealing with, either," he said, and grabbed the guy's right arm, yanking it down and snapping it on the car door. Then he shoved his left arm out of the way and threw a right hook at his face, knocking the brute out and sending him sprawling on the concrete, his penknife clattering into the gutter.

Seckry and Eiya could only watch, wide eyed, as Vance said, "Time to let us through, boys," and stamped his foot on the accelerator.

The car screeched forward and the gang readied their weapons before panic hit and they dived out of the way in all directions, letting them speed through.

It came as a surprise when Vance pulled the car up because Seckry and Eiya had both been so distracted by glaring out of the rear window to see if any of the thugs had followed them that they hadn't been concentrating on the directions.

They stepped out cautiously to find themselves at the entrance of a seedy looking pub. As they entered, the low hum of gruff chatter ground to a halt and the background music cut off after a harsh scratch of feedback.

They approached the bar tentatively and Vance asked the barman for Grolt. Sprawled across the bar, next to them, was a little man with the complexion of a corpse. He dragged his face up from the wooden counter and snarled at the three of them, revealing a mouth full of black gums and very little teeth. Seckry was hit with the revolting stench of beer, cigarettes, peanuts and vomit.

"What in Gedin's name do you think you lot are doing in this part of town?" he said viciously, before retching out a mouth full of phlegm and gobbing it into an empty bowl on the bar.

Vance remained silent as the bartender called up the stairs.

"They all come here eventually," said the little man. "Grolt's the best in the business . . . but he ain't giving no business to the likes of rich scum like you."

A few moments later, a gigantic, heavily tattooed bald man

emerged from upstairs and glared at the group. It was like they were being sized up by an apex predator hungry for blood.

"We were sent here by a man named . . . Pawl Sevenstars," said Vance, seemingly unaffected by the behemoth's presence.

After a moment, Grolt simply nodded.

"You show 'em, Grolt!" the little man rasped. "Take an axe and cut their limbs off one by -"

Grolt gripped the little man's head with his sausage-like fingers and plunged his face into the bowl of his own phlegm before flicking his head to Seckry and the others, motioning them up the dimly lit staircase.

Seckry's heart was pounding as he took step after step, wondering if his dad would be at the top of them.

But as they emerged into the room, they found it empty aside from a surgical bed and a couple of other bits of mismatched furniture. The place looked like a torture chamber. There were numerous bloodstained blades, hooks, clasps and other weapons hanging from fixtures and scattered around the room, and racks of dirty syringes and scalpels.

"Pawl?" said Seckry. "Where is he?"

The big man shrugged his shoulders and pointed to a box in the corner of the room. It was a small, metal box with a white cable leading into it via a tiny hole. Grolt pulled a set of dirty keys from his pocket and unlocked a padlock that was keeping it secure.

Seckry slowly opened the box to see an old telephone, the one that the recorded message had to have been left on, and a tightly wrapped brown parcel. He unwrapped the parcel and folded out a faded, chequered shirt.

Vance reached down and picked up a note that had fallen out of it. He passed it to Seckry.

Seckry, I've had to leave this place but I am still in the city and I must meet with you. Lux is here in Skyfall, but he must not know your whereabouts. The only time I can meet with you is the 22nd June next year. Please come back to this room on that date and I will be here, waiting. Please give this shirt to your mum. I miss her. I miss you all.

Deep within Seckry's subconscious, he recognised the shirt. It was the shirt that Pawl had been wearing that day; the day they had been picking ellonberries in the fields of Marne, the day he had vanished from their lives.

"I really thought . . . I really thought he was going to be here," said Seckry, his voice cracking.

Eiya took a hold of his hand and squeezed it tight.

"He's alive and he's okay," she said comfortingly.

Grolt led them back down the stairs. But before they left the pub, Seckry said, "Where was Pawl staying? What was he like?"

But Grolt just shook his head.

"You won't get any words outta the big man himself," someone slurred from a table close to the window. "Had his tongue cut off by the Petrozelli family for talking too much."

Seckry sat in silence for the entire journey back. He couldn't believe he was going to have to wait until the beginning of summer next year to meet his father after the excitement of today.

"Seckry . . . your father is alive and well," said Vance. "Try not to be too disheartened. We tried what we could. And you can look forward to the twenty-second of June."

Seckry nodded, but June seemed like a long, long way away.

"I'll head to bed," said Eiya, as they opened the door to the flat. "You can have some time with your mum and your sister."

Seckry nodded gratefully and swallowed hard, clutching the shirt tightly between his fingers.

Coralle and Leena were happily watching Steelplank Street when he approached them, the shirt behind his back.

"You look as white as a sheet, love," said Coralle. "Still feeling sick from all the party food?"

Seckry stayed silent and motionless, trying to find the right words.

"Seck, you can be really creepy sometimes," said Leena. "What is up with you?"

"I wasn't . . . at Tenk's tonight," Seckry said, staring at the floor. "It's dad . . . he's . . . here in Skyfall." He slowly showed them the shirt.

Coralle got up from the sofa and drifted towards Seckry, her eyes locked on the shirt. She looked at Seckry, then the shirt, then at Seckry again. Then she took it gently out of Seckry's hands and put it to her nose, closing her eyes and inhaling the aftershave that was ingrained into it.

She stood for a moment, trembling, before tears started streaming from her eyes and she buried her face into the fabric.

Seckry wrapped his arms around her and told them what had happened. Leena said nothing, her expression unreadable.

"It's actually true," sobbed Coralle, squeezing Seckry tight. "What your teacher said . . . it's all true, about him and Lux being the Endrin lab babies . . . dear Gedin, he's alive . . . he's *alive*."

"But I still don't know where he is," said Seckry. "And we have to wait until the twenty-second of June next year to find out. That's nine months away."

Leena got up and, without saying anything, went to bed.

"It's okay, love," said Coralle, after sitting with Seckry for over an hour. "It's getting late. You head to bed. I'm gonna stay up for a little while, okay?" Her eyes were still wet, but Seckry could see that they weren't tears of pain.

Seckry nodded, exhausted, but when he did lie down, there was no way his mind was going to switch off and let him sleep. Instead, he phoned the barcode number and let the message play over and over again, savouring every word that his father spoke.

Chapter Six

The Student Exchange Plan

"Seck, you look terrible," said Tenk, as they rode the monorail to Estergate the next morning.

"It was an eventful evening," said Eiya.

Seckry spent the journey explaining everything to Tenk, who seemed almost unable to contain himself from the revelation.

"A secret message and a telephone number on the birthday card?" he exclaimed. "Dude! This is insane!"

Luckily, Eiya gave him a look that forcefully calmed him down a little.

"Yeah, that sucks that you have to wait so long to see him again though," he said. "But it does give you something to look forward to next year. The main thing I've got to look forward to is another family trip to the Gullmouth coast."

"I've seen pictures of that place, it looks beautiful," said Eiya.

"It might be beautiful," said Tenk, "but when you're stuck with a brother who insists on slapping you around the face with every fish that he catches, the scenic views are hard to appreciate."

When they arrived at Estergate, Seckry made a conscious decision to try to push all thoughts of his father to one side for the time being. He was going to have a lot of work to do this this year, and he didn't want to fall behind because he was daydreaming.

When they entered the building, the corridors were unusually alive with excited whispers.

"I hope it's Jobey Mobbins," Seckry overheard one girl

saying. "Will they be allowed to come to this year's ball? Oh Gedin, please tell me yes!"

Mobbins? thought Seckry. Why would Mobbins be coming to Estergate?

Tenk's eyes were wide with fury at the thought of Mobbins attending their annual ball, and was on the verge of grabbing someone and shaking some answers out of them. Luckily, Mr Usaki, the virology teacher, rounded them up, saying, "Emergency announcement in the main hall, please make your way there immediately. And how many times have I told you, Mr Huffings, your school tie is not to be worn like a martial arts headband."

As they made their way to the hall, Seckry stopped in fear. Snibble was walking straight towards him. Seckry's heart started hammering away in his chest as Snibble approached; he was sure the bully was going to throw a punch as revenge for what had happened before the summer holidays, but all Snibble did was smirk and shove Seckry's shoulder with his own.

"I don't get it," said Seckry. "I punched the guy right in the face. I mean, if he doesn't want to beat me to a pulp, then what does he want to do to me in return?"

"Mate, you never know," said Tenk. "Maybe, somewhere deep down, he actually knew he deserved it. An eye for an eye, I guess."

As they entered the main hall, they found Kimmy and Loca already seated, but they had no idea what the gathering was all about either.

When everyone was sufficiently hushed, Headmaster Gobbledee, looking flustered, began speaking.

"The Skyfall Board of Education have devised a student exchange plan. Each of the four high schools in Skyfall will swap two pupils for the duration of this year, in an attempt to build better relations between the schools."

Seckry was sure he heard the headmaster mutter the words, "*load of bloody nonsense,*" under his breath.

"The school we will be exchanging pupils with is . . . Norsegate, are they *kidding* me? Um . . . I mean, ahem . . .

Norsegate, yes."

It was no secret that Mr Gobbledee had once had a spat with the headmaster of Norsegate, and still held resentment for him. The fact that Norsegate were Estergate's arch-rival at Friction didn't help the relationship.

"The selection will be randomised by a computer," said Gobbledee, and a projector lit up the wall. A number of names began flashing across the screen in rapid succession, and Seckry thought he saw the name Eiya Tacana appear more than once. He closed his eyes and prayed to Gedin that it wasn't going to be her.

"The first pupil . . . that will be sent to Norsegate . . . is . . ."

A cheap sounding fanfare filled the hall.

"What?" shouted Loca, and the whole assembly turned to face her.

The name that the randomiser had landed on was Kimmy Kod.

"What a load of -" She muttered a couple of swearwords under her breath.

"Mr Kod," said Gobbledee. "Would you be so kind as to join me up here for a moment?"

Kimmy, looking absolutely distraught, stood up and hesitantly made his way to the front, glancing back at Loca several times.

Seckry heard Gobbledee mutter to Kimmy, "*I'm so sorry about this.*" Then, more loudly, "Right, on to the next one."

The name generator started flicking between pupils once more and Seckry closed his eyes, praying to Gedin once again that it wasn't going to be Eiya or himself.

When it stopped, there was a cry of, "You gotta be fippin kidding me!"

The name was Snibble Knotting.

"Mr Knotting!" said the headmaster, this time slightly more jubilant. "Well there's a turn up for the books."

Snibble made his way to the front, kicking a couple of other pupils and barging them with elbows as he passed.

Seckry's emotions were mixed. He was ecstatic that

Snibble would be out of his life for a whole year, but felt terrible for Kimmy, who would have to put up with him every day. Then again, Kimmy was a year older, so at least he wouldn't have to deal with him inside of any lessons.

"And now," said Gobbledee, "these are the two pupils we will be receiving in exchange!"

The random generator switched to a bunch of names Seckry didn't recognise, and stopped on a Gavanis Mendakar.

"Oh no she *doesn't*," bellowed their fellow Eastern Eidolons teammate Lessana Lubworth, who was sitting one row in front of them.

"*Does Lessana know her?*" Seckry whispered to Tenk.

"*Yep, and so do you, kind of. Remember that spider-like mecha that drowned at the beginning of last year's Meltdown?*"

"*That was her?*"

"*Yep. The thing is, Gavanis was the one who won the Meltdown for the Nightmare the year before you arrived. It was just her and Lessana left in the game at the end and she was the one who took her out. Lessana's had it in for her ever since. Damn, this is crazy. Kimmy and Gavanis are both Friction players. It's gonna screw things up so much.*"

"I would just like to ensure everybody," said Gobbledee, hastily, "that despite studying in opposing schools, these pupils will still represent their own schools in the Friction Mega Meltdown, and will train as normal with their existing teams."

"*Nobody gives a toss about all the travelling Kimmy will have to do,*" hissed Loca.

"Okay," said Gobbledee. "The second pupil we will be receiving is . . ."

The generator landed on the name Zovak McVorak.

Seckry opened one eye and peered around for any reactions. No one said a word. It looked like nobody had ever heard of him.

"Okay, that's the end of that!" said Gobbledee. "Please exit the hall in an orderly manner and return to the lessons you are supposed to be in. Snibble and Kimmy, come to my office with me, please."

The rest of the day was tainted by the news of the

exchange, and even though Seckry could kind of see the point the Board of Education were trying to make, he felt they were going about it in completely the wrong way. Poor Kimmy was going to be lost over at Norsegate.

Unsurprisingly, Loca wasn't taking the news well at all. She went to see the headmaster at lunchtime while the rest of the group ate in the canteen, but returned to them very shortly saying that Gobbledee was insistent he had no power over the situation.

When Seckry and Eiya arrived back at the flat that evening, Eiya made herself scarce once again because Leena was face-down, crying at the kitchen table.

"Are you okay?" Seckry asked quietly.

"Seck . . ." she said, lifting her head. "If all this stuff about dad really is true, then don't you feel disappointed in him?"

"Disappointed?" said Seckry.

"Seck, the man ran. He ditched us."

"No," said Seckry. "He was trying to protect us. He vanished because Lux was coming looking for him, and he didn't want Lux to find out that we existed, for our own safety. That's what I've been trying to tell you all this time."

"Seck, you don't understand," said Leena, exasperatedly. "Even if he did do it to protect us, try to imagine if you were him and you had a wife and kids. Could you leave them, even if it was for their own good? Could you just disappear one night and never return without even giving them an explanation or saying goodbye? How could you hurt the ones you love so much? He should have stayed with us and protected us, and if that Lux guy came looking for him, then he should have fought him."

Seckry was silent. He had never questioned his father's motives since Vance had explained everything to him.

"Seck, when you truly love someone, you don't leave them without an explanation, even when it's in their best interests to do so. You find another way to protect them."

Seckry made to defend his father once more, but he couldn't find the words. Was Leena right?

Seckry listened to his father's message again that night, but this time it just made him angry, and he hung up, his eyes soaking his pillow with hot tears as he buried his face into it.

Chapter Seven

The Notorious

The next day, after staying behind for a few minutes during a bionics lesson to finish his work, Seckry arrived late at the canteen to find a crowd of pupils clustered around the Ultimate Crazy Crane machine. Tippian was hanging off somebody's back, craning his neck to get a look.

"It's true!" he said desperately. "There's a Notorious in there!"

"A what?" said Seckry.

"What's it look like?" said Tenk, too excited to answer Seckry's question.

"Oh man," said Tippian, shaking his head. "It looks rancid."

"Seck," said Tenk, grabbing him by the arms. "The Notorious is the most foul, most disgusting, most nastiest Shocker you will ever know. There's like, only two of them in existence, or something like that. I can't even imagine what it tastes like."

"Tastes like?" said Seckry. "I thought that thing was full of gadgets and stuff."

"Most of the stuff, yeah, but they mix delicious snacks in there too."

"What do you reckon it is?" Seckry asked. "A gone off piece of meat or something?"

"Mate, you wouldn't even be able to tell. It'll be so rotten it'll just have morphed into some whole new abomination."

"Oh my Gedin, I think it's moving," said Tippian, who had now shuffled up onto someone's shoulders. It didn't seem to matter that he didn't know the boy; the whole school was too mesmerised and excited to care. Kids were clambering all over each other to get a peek.

Seckry was itching to see just as much as the rest of them, and so was Eiya, but before they had a chance to squeeze through, a butch dinner lady came bombarding towards them, scattering the crowd like a bowling ball knocking over skittles, and roaring threats about reports to the headmaster.

"It's gonna be catastrophic," said Tippian, tucking his school shirt into his trousers and plonking himself back in his seat.

"But surely if you won that thing you wouldn't dare to eat it," said Seckry.

"The first years will eat anything, Seck," said Tenk.

"Disturbingly, he's right," said Loca. "I saw one pick up a dirty sweet wrapper and shove it into his mouth before. I mean, you've gotta blame the parents really. Oh, look, there's the new guy."

A short, sweaty-haired boy with a scruffy, loose school tie and dirty trainers was being entertained by a group of girls at the entrance to the canteen, as if they had never seen a boy before in their lives.

"Those girls are lapping him up," said Tippian in disbelief, "but he's not exactly a stud."

Seckry didn't like to judge people on their appearance, but Tippian was right. The new boy wasn't a conventional heartthrob. In fact, Zovak McVorak's face was probably best described as resembling the leftovers from somebody's cooked breakfast; it was covered with patches of red, and shiny with grease. His shoulder length, black, curly hair didn't help much; it hung limply over his ears and forehead and was littered with dandruff.

As the group was gawping at the attention he was getting from the girls, Zovak caught Tippian's eye and excused himself before making his way towards them.

"Tippian Furst," Zovak said. "I hear you're Estergate's answer to me."

"Excuse me?" said Tippian.

"An inventor, I mean. I hear you're entering into the

Andersun Wellworth Young Inventor Award this year. I am too."

"Ah," said Tippian. "Well, good luck."

Zovak smirked.

"Oh, you don't have to wish me good luck," he boasted. "I'm going to win, there's no doubt about that. In fact, that's what I was going to say to you; it might be better for you to drop out of the competition this year and re-apply in four years' time when there's another one."

Tippian glared at Zovak, astounded at the boy's arrogance.

"I'm only giving you this advice because I admire you," Zovak continued. "I mean, I've heard about this voice changing thing from one of the teachers, and I'm sure in any other year you'd win the competition hands down, but it really won't stand a chance against my design."

"I'll be entering the Voicemaster this year, thank you," said Tippian sternly.

Zovak sighed and smiled apathetically, as if Tippian was a child who couldn't comprehend something.

"I guess I'll see you at the award ceremony, then," he said, and bid the group a farewell that left a bitter aftertaste in Seckry's mouth.

"Is that guy for real?" said Tenk.

"Don't worry, Tipps," said Loca. "I'm sure your Voicemaster is much better than anything he could come up with." She narrowed her eyes at Zovak's back and muttered, "Slimy piece of snot."

"What do you think he's making?" said Tenk.

"I'll find out," said Tippian darkly, stabbing a chip into a dollop of ketchup and twisting it like a knife in a wound.

"How's Kimmy doing over at Norsegate so far?" Seckry asked Loca.

"He sent me a text saying it's fine, but you know Kimmy, he sees the best in everything and everyone. I just can't believe that stupid Board of Education would do something like this to him. Oh, Gedin, here we go. Just to add insult to injury."

Seckry turned around to see a lanky girl strut into the

canteen with a confident swagger.

As soon as Seckry saw her face, he had flashbacks of last year's Meltdown. It had been very brief, but Seckry now remembered her scowling at him before climbing into her pod before the game. Seckry had been too focused and too nervous at the time to worry about it, but seeing her now brought that vicious expression right to the forefront of his mind.

Gavanis was probably twice the height of Seckry, and was all skin and bones, with pale blue eyes that poked out of their sockets a bit too much, and wiry blonde hair. She made her way over to the other side of the food conveyor belt, and as she passed them, she muttered something under her breath.

"What did you say?" snapped Loca.

"I said, 'Wow, one nil to Estergate already.'"

"And what's that supposed to mean?" said Loca.

"Come on," said Gavanis. "You guys get *me*, and Norsegate gets *that* waste of space, Kimmy Kod? Gotta hand it to you, you've scored."

"Waste of space?" spat Loca. "You better not be talking about my -"

"Oh Gedin!" said Gavanis, mock embarrassed. "I totally forgot he's your boyfriend now. Next time, think before you speak, Gavvy."

She strode off, chuckling to herself.

Seckry couldn't help but feel like Estergate had been screwed over. The initiative was supposed to help relations between the two schools, but sending over these two creeps was doing nothing to change his opinion of Norsegate. When the swap had been announced, Seckry had imagined that anyone would be a good trade for Snibble Knotting, but at least with Snibble you knew where you stood. These two slimy students were going to be a bit more difficult to suss out.

Chapter Eight

The First Patient

The rest of the week was pretty solemn. As much as Seckry thought he would be able to push his father out of his mind and concentrate on his schoolwork, it was harder than he had expected, especially since Leena's questioning of his love for them. To add to this, Zovak and Gavanis actually seemed to be making friends with Estergate pupils, and were putting on their sweetest act to gain popularity with the teachers too, which made Seckry and the group furious, since they could see underneath the saccharine bravado.

When the weekend finally arrived, Seckry was glad to get away from the place for a couple of days, especially since he and Eiya had made plans to meet with someone very important: Cartell Quinn.

When Seckry had received a video message from Cartell, one of the remaining innoya that hadn't been captured by Darklight in Skyfall City, they had agreed to meet up with him in the following few weeks to discuss Eiya's existence and other details about the innoya and their powers. But shortly after arranging the meeting, the man had delayed it indefinitely, and Seckry wasn't sure why. He knew that the innoya had been relocating after spending months in hiding from Darklight in an abandoned building down the Blacklear, but Seckry was sure that the move couldn't have taken them months.

Then, at the beginning of September, Cartell had got in touch, arranging to meet them at his new home in somewhere known as the Mechaner's Village, and apologising for the delay.

On Saturday morning, Seckry and Eiya looked up the location on his phone, and reeled at the amount of monorail changes they were going to have to make to get there. It was situated in the north partition and it was only then that they remembered that this was exactly where Sanfarrow's new super track ended. If it had been built, it would have taken them just minutes to get from Chronoway Crossing to where they needed to be, and Seckry suddenly appreciated the importance of Sanfarrow's grand project.

"It's one of the oldest parts of the city," said Coralle, standing over their shoulders. "They call it Mechaner's Village because it's where all the mechaners used to live during the industrial boom."

"Who were the mechaners?" Eiya asked.

"The bigwigs of the boom, basically," said Coralle. "The overseers, designers, and the directors of the big mechanical companies of the time. It's supposed to be a stunning area. I think there's some government incentive to stop the modernisation of the place because they want to keep the beautiful buildings intact."

"Seck, make sure you visit the Overhang while you're there and take a photo on your phone or something," said Leena.

"The Overhang?" said Seckry.

"It's this jut on the northern cliff that literally hangs over the rest of the city," said Coralle. "Sometimes you can see it at night, right in the distance."

"Seck, I think we could see that cliff from the rooftop," said Eiya, excitedly.

"They say that you get an amazing view across Skyfall from the Overhang," said Coralle. "It'd probably be a real tourist hotspot if the place wasn't so awkward to get to. I guess your friend Mr Sanfarrow is fixing that problem right now."

Seckry's gut reaction to anything related to the north partition was to dislike it, based on the Eidolons' rivalry with the Nightmare and Norsegate's arrogance over the last week, but in all honesty the Mechaner's Village sounded beautiful.

After a long and finicky journey, Seckry and Eiya finally arrived at the quiet Mechaner's Village Crossing and were met with the sound of sweet, chirruping birds, something that was a rarity in Skyfall. Unlike the majority of the city, which was like a scrap heap of metal, the Mechaner's Village immediately reminded Seckry of Marne, with its cobbled pathways, streetlamps, and assorted trees.

The address they were looking for wasn't far from the stop, and it only took them a couple of minutes of traversing the pleasant area to find it.

"Wow," said Eiya. "This is definitely a step up from the Blacklear."

Seckry and Eiya were standing in front of a huge mahogany structure with a stone archway that housed a set of beautiful, wooden double doors that were carved with intricate patterns.

A large, ornate sign read: *The Stonesoldiers' Guildhouse.*

As they approached the double doors, they were met with an ancient looking silver knocker in the shape of a bloodlion's head. Seckry had only ever seen bloodlions on nature documentaries, and he knew that they were native to the savannahs of the Harka continent, down south. They were vicious looking things, with puffy, red manes and a single horn sticking out of their foreheads. They also had a set of sharp teeth for hunting prey, and were known for baring them aggressively when they growled. This particular, shiny sculpture was baring its teeth at them in true to life fashion, clasping between them a large, circular knocking ring.

Seckry reached out to grab it and hesitated.

"It looks like it's gonna bite your hand off, Seck," said Eiya. Seckry had been thinking the exact same thing. It was so realistic it was scary. Seckry couldn't quite put his finger on it, but it was something about the eyes that seemed as though they were really looking at him.

Seckry laughed it off and gave the ring a few swings, banging on the old wood.

"Seckry, Eiya," said Cartell with a smile, as he pulled the

double doors open from the inside. "Please, come in."

The guildhall echoed as they followed Cartell through to the dining area.

"This place must be worth thousands of notes," whispered Eiya, scanning the architecture. "What do you think Cartell does for a living?"

Seckry shrugged his shoulders. When they had first met the man, they hadn't even thought about the innoya having jobs.

"I was a doctor for many years," said Cartell, who must have overheard them. "When all of this started happening with Darklight, I quit my job and devoted my time to protecting the innoya in the east as best I could. We had to band together, and we needed someone to take charge. I took it upon myself. Please, have a seat."

Cartell pulled out a couple of chairs at a long dining table that had been neatly made for three. As they sat down, Seckry caught sight of a pair of small hands clutching the corner of a wall in the distance, and a flash of red hair. Seckry recognised who it was immediately; Cartell's daughter, the one that had begged Seckry and Eiya to keep quiet when they had bumped into her at the Blacklear.

"This," said Cartell, loudly, "is Nilith. Come and say 'hi', Nilith."

Nilith poked her head out and smiled, embarrassed, but disappeared out of sight without saying a word.

"She's very shy," said Cartell. "The Darklight situation was confusing and upsetting for her. No child should have to live with the fear that they are being hunted. You'll have to forgive her, but she doesn't want to join us for lunch. I think everything's just a bit much for her at the moment."

"That's no problem at all," said Eiya, staring at the corner with sympathy. "I hope she can start to feel a bit better about things soon."

Before Seckry and Eiya had even had time to discuss things with Cartell, a cook entered the room, bringing them steaming plates of food that looked delicious.

"Thank you, Mrs Wurton," said Cartell.

As the cook was about to place Eiya's plate in front of her, she said, "Nilith helped me out with this one, Eiya. She's shaped your potato."

As the plate was placed on the table, Seckry could see that the potato had been intricately carved into the shape of an eiya flower.

Eiya put her hands to her mouth and looked as though she was about to cry.

"It's . . . it's beautiful," she said softly. "Tell her thank you . . . thank you so much."

After tasting the hearty, traditional lunch, Seckry decided to begin the conversation by saying, "There's something we should tell you about Eiya's existence."

Cartell placed his hand up slowly.

"I actually met with your teacher, Mr Jonn Vance, recently, and he has already explained everything to me."

"Really?" said Seckry. He had no idea Vance had been in contact with Cartell.

"Yes," said Cartell. "I was amazed at what he told me, I can assure you."

"The only reason I'm still alive is because you and the other innoya are here," said Eiya. "Apparently, if all the innoya die, then so do I, because I was created by innoya helitonium."

Cartell nodded and smiled gently.

"Well, you have nothing to fear, Eiya," he said. "I am still alive, and so are my fellow innoya who are living in houses nearby. And who's to say there aren't innoya out there in other cities, other countries? There could be none, there could be thousands, it's impossible to say. But as long as at least one of us is alive, then so are you, from the sounds of it. And we have no plans of going anywhere." He smiled and put his hand on Eiya's shoulder. "In fact, in five month's time, there will be at least another one of us. My good friends Yarrus and Nagala are expecting their first child."

After a moment, Seckry said, "I'm so sorry we couldn't save the other innoya, Mr Quinn."

"Seckry," Cartell said calmly. "You have nothing to be

sorry for. What you two and your friends did that night was courageous beyond belief. You did everything that you could, risking your own lives in the process. I cannot thank you enough." Cartell took a sip of water and leaned back. "We hadn't always been hidden away in that Blacklear building," he said. "For all of my life, myself and the rest of us have lived amongst general society. We are normal human beings after all. We possess no special powers, we are certainly not superheroes, that's for sure. We simply have an extra element, dormant inside our bodies. An element that one man was willing to kill for.

"We had suspicions that Darklight was planning some atrocity for a short while before he issued those Pro-Tek Chips, but we weren't sure what. I decided to gather up those of us in the east and move us into that abandoned building to be safe. My brother, living in the west partition, did a similar thing with a building over there."

"Who were they? The innoya that died in the Divinita chamber?" Eiya asked softly. "Did you know them?"

"They were families that lived in other partitions of Skyfall, mainly. Some of them I'd never met. Some of them I had. And one . . . one was the brother I just mentioned. When Darklight issued those Pro-Tek Chips to everyone in the city, claiming they were for our own protection, I knew something was up, and I stopped all of the innoya here in the east from attaching them to their wrists. But . . . before I had time to get a hold of my brother, he and the innoya he was looking after were gone."

"Just like that?"

"Darklight's men must have swarmed the place as soon as they saw the helitonium readings from their Pro-Tek Chips. It must have been within a matter of hours."

"I'm so sorry," said Eiya.

"I only hope that what has happened can only bring us more courage, and more knowledge."

"More knowledge?" said Seckry.

"Yes," said Cartell, his saddened face regaining some sort of hope. "Something interesting has emerged, and I have made an incredible discovery since the Darklight massacre. Helitonium can, in fact, be extracted from us without being fatal."

Seckry and Eiya exchanged looks of shock.

"We never thought it was possible, but using new technology, we have been able to extract a miniscule amount from one of us, once a day, and manipulate it to do what we want."

"Wow," Seckry said. "Which one of you has been the test subject?"

Cartell slowly rolled up his left sleeve to show them a purple bruise above his veins.

"There was no way I would let anybody else take the risk," he said kindly.

"Have you actually been able to control the helitonium?" Eiya asked. "Vance said that throughout history it has always been too volatile, too chaotic."

"Yes, we have so far been able to use it for our own will, and this may sound strange, but for that, we have to thank Darklight."

"*Thank him?*" Seckry spat.

"Okay, 'thank' may not be the best word," Cartell said gravely. "The man may have been a cold-blooded killer, but he was also extraordinarily intelligent. He figured out a way of controlling helitonium so that he could create that time portal. I have been in regular contact since the event with Jenniver Layne, and she kindly agreed to let me have copies of Darklight's scientific diagrams. I have basically copied his model. His designs are quite outstanding."

"So, theoretically, you could now create another time portal if you wanted?" said Eiya.

"Not quite," Cartell said confidently. "A portal that traverses time can only be created with the amount of helitonium that Darklight extracted, which was the entire amount from twenty innoya. To make another one, you would have to murder another twenty." He took a deep breath. "No, the amount extractable without killing the innoya is microscopic in comparison, but this does not mean that it is useless."

He placed his knife and fork down carefully and said, "Once you're finished, would you care to follow me?"

After scooping up the last bit of gravy, Seckry and Eiya let Cartell lead them through a couple of corridors until they emerged into what could only be described as a miniature hospital.

"This is why I had to delay our meeting," Cartell said apologetically. "I've been incredibly busy installing this new facility."

It was like they had stepped into a different building. The archaic, decorative structure had been replaced by whitewashed, clinical walls and sterilised plastic.

"Thanks to the Skyfall Science Committee, I have been able to get a hold of a selection of cells from animals that died of strange, incurable diseases. Have a look through this microscope."

Cartell led them towards one that was situated on one of the units, and Seckry and Eiya took turns to place their eye on the eyepiece.

"Those broken blobs on the left are the original cells that had been destroyed, and those on the right are ones that I have managed to modify using helitonium. They look in pretty good shape, do they not?"

Seckry had no idea what healthy cells looked like in the first place (he made a note to concentrate more in biology lessons) but he trusted Cartell's judgement.

"What this means," said Cartell, "is that we may very well be able to cure human diseases that we never thought were curable until now. People who have been told they will never get better may get a second chance at life using helitonium treatment."

He pulled down a wall chart, which consisted of an intricately planned architectural diagram.

"In six months' time, I want to open a clinic. It can be a place where people with incurable conditions can come for treatment. We may not be able to cure everyone, this technology is experimental at best, but we can try."

"This is amazing," said Eiya. "Where do you want to build it?"

"I've applied for permission to build the clinic on the site of Warehouse Twenty-Two on the riverfront."

"Wait," said Seckry. "The warehouse where Darklight kept the other innoya?"

Cartell nodded gravely.

"It's the perfect location," he said. "It's easily accessible for the disabled, and it's just the right size for my plans. They're knocking the structure down because it is so rusty it's unusable. And also because of what went on there. The government and the press don't know that the people that were being tortured there were special, but they do know that people were being tortured there, and so it makes sense to get rid of it and wipe that horrendous memory from the face of the earthia. Right now, I'm just waiting for a signature, that's all, and I can go ahead and start constructing this thing."

"But, doesn't it upset you, knowing what happened on that patch of land?" said Eiya.

Cartell smiled kindly.

"Of course it does. But . . . what could be more satisfying than creating a place to heal on top of a place that so many have suffered in the past? I guess in some way, it will feel like I am undoing what Darklight did."

Suddenly there was a loud rapping on the front doors that echoed through the old building.

"Strange," said Cartell. "I'm not expecting anyone else today."

Seckry and Eiya followed him back into the main hallway and Cartell opened the door to an old man holding the grips of a wheelchair in which a younger man sat, looking gaunt and vacant.

"I believe this is the residence of a Mr Cartell Quinn," the old man said hopefully.

"That's me," Cartell replied, and stuck his hand out.

"Wilbus Valenkar," said the old man, and shook Cartell's hand enthusiastically. "I'm afraid you don't know me, but I know a little about you, or at least the plans that you have."

"The clinic?" said Cartell.

"Yes, I heard news through the Science Committee, and I had to come to talk with you. It's about my son, Eryk."

They stared at the frail looking middle-aged man in the wheelchair, whose eyes hadn't left the same spot, and who was completely motionless.

"He has a condition known as Esterotopis," said Wilbus.

"Esterotopis?" Cartell said curiously. "I can't say I've ever heard of that."

"There's a reason for that," Wilbus explained. "Eryk is the first and only person to have the condition. Doctors say it is a degenerative disease that will take his life, and there is nothing they can do about it. I have come here today, Mr Quinn, to . . . offer you your first patient."

"Oh my," said Cartell, flustered but excited at the same time. "I mean, I haven't even . . . I don't have the permission . . . they haven't even signed the . . . it's all still in such an experimental stage, I only have a small set up here at the moment." He stopped talking and made eye contact with the man's son. "When was he diagnosed?"

"Four years ago," said Wilbus.

"And how long does he have left to live?"

Wilbus started to speak, but his voice faltered a little. "He has roughly two days, Mr Quinn. You can . . . you can see why I'm so desperate."

Cartell turned around briefly to make eye contact with Seckry and Eiya, before saying, "Quinn's Clinic has its first patient. Come on in."

They left Cartell's shortly after, allowing him to begin work on the old man's son immediately. As soon as he had accepted that his healing work had already begun, he had been in his element, determined to save his first life.

Seckry and Eiya were both buzzing on the journey back too at the thought of someone with no hope left suddenly getting a second chance.

That night, after falling asleep easily for the first time in a long time, he woke to the sound of laughter and found Eiya giggling uncontrollably in her sleep.

"*Eiya,*" he whispered. "*Eiya, what's so funny?*"

Eiya's eyes darted open and she burst out laughing.

"Gedin, Seck, was I sleeping?" she said, disorientated. "It was one of your memories again. It must have been. It was too vivid to have just been a normal dream."

Over the summer, Eiya had begun to have dreams that were direct memories from Seckry's subconscious. The first time had been a dream in which she had been running through fields of ellonberries and spotting the neighbour's cat before picking him up and carrying him back to her house, and the second time had been of being bullied by a group of boys back in Marne.

Seckry originally thought that he had to have told Eiya about these occasions at some point and she had been thinking about them before bed, but Eiya assured him that he had never mentioned them at all.

They had spoken to Sanfarrow over the phone at the time, and the scientist had seemed completely unsurprised by it. He told them that because Eiya had been created by Seckry's subconscious in the first place, it was quite understandable that sometimes her memories would blur with Seckry's own.

The strangest thing, however, was that the memories Eiya was experiencing were not always memories from before her creation. Sometimes she would relive things that had happened to Seckry in the last year, meaning that their minds were still somehow linked.

"I was in school," Eiya said, recalling the dream she had just woken from. "There was this teacher with bright red curly hair and . . . and she sat down at her desk and the chair snapped and she fell to the floor and then the wall clock came off its hook and smacked her on the head."

"Yep, that was Mrs Borgonvood," said Seckry, smiling fondly. "It was made all the more funnier by the fact that she was a dictator and everyone hated her."

"It's kinda cool, this idea that our minds are linked, isn't it Seck?"

Seckry smiled, but in truth, ever since Sanfarrow had revealed the nature of Eiya's creation, Seckry sometimes felt incredibly uncomfortable about it. He worried that Eiya was sad because she didn't have a real family, real parents, or a real history. He worried that she longed for a childhood of her own.

"Eiya . . ." Seckry said sheepishly. "How do you really feel about . . . you know . . . all this? Being created by my subconscious and all?" He looked down, embarrassed.

"Don't look so worried, Seck," she said affectionately. "It's kind of a nice thought, you know?" She smiled, and her dark brown eyes glistened in the lamplight. "You know what?" she said, "One of the biggest things I was worried about last year was, what if I did have a family somewhere? What if I couldn't remember them even when I met them? I would have had to have moved in with people who would have been strangers to me, and I would've been expected to love them. But the reason I couldn't remember a family is because I didn't have one, and you know what, Seck, I don't need one. It makes perfect sense. I only cared about you, and . . . I got to stay with you."

She sat up and hugged her knees to her chest.

"It's cool to think that I was at the back of your mind somewhere, waiting to be created," she said dreamily. "Remind me what I was doing in that dream you had."

"You were standing in a field of eiya flowers," said Seckry. "You were running your hands through the petals. I tried asking you who you were, but no words would come out."

"And it was definitely me?" said Eiya, curiously. "My face looked just like it does now?"

"Just like it does now," said Seckry.

"Did . . . my arms look like this?" Eiya said brightly, examining them as if they had just sprouted.

"Yeah, they did," Seckry said, smiling.

Eiya thrust her feet up into the air and curled her toes.

"What about my little toes?" she said. "Did they look like these ones?"

Seckry muffled a laugh with his quilt, careful not to wake

his mum and Leena.

"Well, I couldn't see your toes. They were somewhere beneath the flowers."

Eiya leaned her head on her left shoulder and gazed into his eyes silently, and Seckry could do nothing but return the gaze, mesmerised.

Chapter Nine

Tenk's Nan

On Monday morning, Seckry was feeling a little refreshed after the weekend, and felt like he was finally beginning to accept that he would just have to wait until next year to see his father again.

The only thing that spoiled the morning was the fact that they were due to have a triple helping of electronics with Cut Throat Cutson, and it was going to be the first time they had seen her since last year.

As expected, Mrs Cutson made their morning a living hell, ridiculing five pupils on six different occasions for not being able to answer questions, and forcing them all to fill half a workbook in the space of three hours.

At lunch time, they headed to the canteen, relieved to be done with her for the time being, and plonked themselves on an empty batch of seats lining the conveyor belt. But before Seckry could grab some food, Tippian shuffled up to him conspiratorially and said, "You heard about version seven point five, Seck?" His eyes remained focused on the wall as if he was some undercover spy.

Seckry shook his head.

"Friction's getting an upgrade, and it's going to be huge."

"Really? Wow, what are they changing?" Seckry said, intrigued.

"Shh," Tippian said desperately, though Seckry could see that nobody was interested in their conversation. "It's not been made official yet. I've only heard of it in the underground scene."

"Here he goes," said Tenk. "Has he ever told you about

the underground Friction scene he's involved in?"

"No," said Seckry.

"Well Tippers is part of this Friction network called Foof," said Tenk, but Tippian whacked him in the arm before he could continue.

"It's FIFE, not Foof!" he said "The Friction Independent Freedom Endeavour."

"They're a bunch of hackers that mess around with the programming to create custom games and stuff," Tenk explained, in a disapproving tone.

"There's nothing wrong with FIFE," Tippian said defensively. "Everything we do is within the rules."

"Yeah, that's why you've been shut down three times and had to move premises four," said Tenk.

"Okay, it's not . . . within the rules as such, but it should be. I mean, we're not affecting the official games at all."

"What are the changes?" Seckry repeated, anxious and excited at the same time.

"We've learned of three major ones at FIFE, but it's estimated there's going to be a whole list of them. The main one is the time reversal pockets. There are going to be these bubbles now that hold, like, a floating timer inside, and if you burst them, all time gets completely reversed for the amount that the timer indicates."

"So you mean, if someone got killed and then another person on their team popped a time reversal pocket, the dead player would come back to life?"

"Precisely," said Tippian. "Insane, ain't it? Imagine the possibilities."

"Why didn't Foof spot that environmental change last year, Tipp?" said Tenk, accusingly. "Remember all those players drowning? That could have been us! It's lucky Loca spotted that underground passage as quickly as she did."

"We heard rumours of it," said Tippian, "but nobody thought it was actually going to happen."

"See, Seck?" said Tenk. "Foof ain't all it's hyped up to be."

Their final lesson of the day was their second fringe

science with Vance, much to everyone's delight.

They spent the hour formulating the basic components needed for a teleportation device, and by the end of it, they had come up with a final design. When the bell rang, Seckry stayed behind once again to ask Vance about meeting Cartell.

Vance smiled.

"I was very keen to talk to an innoya after the events with the Divinita Project," he explained. "So I sought him out during the summer after you told me about him, and we discussed a lot of things. The clinic he plans to set up is an outstanding use of helitonium, if it works. I am one hundred percent behind him. I just hope that he gets permission to build it on the Warehouse Twenty-Two plot. It's the perfect location and size, with easy access for people with these disabilities. Up there on the Overhang is an incredibly difficult place to access until Sanfarrow's monorail restoration is complete, and even then it's out of the way."

"What else did you discuss with him?" asked Seckry.

"Well," said Vance. "Healing people isn't the only use that he's found for small amounts of helitonium." He opened a cupboard behind him and pulled out a tiny glass vial, swirling with turquoise vapour.

"Gedin . . ." said Seckry in awe. "Is that . . .?"

"Yes, Seckry. This is pure helitonium."

"What are you going to use it for?" Seckry asked.

"Seckry, do you remember me telling the class, during our first lesson, that there had been a small scientific discovery in Skyfall that changed my opinion on if teleportation was actually possible?"

"You mean . . . ?" said Seckry.

"That scientific discovery was Cartell's. It is helitonium that will allow us to warp reality in such a way that matter can disappear from one location and reappear in another. Of course, helitonium is just the raw power behind the thing. We still have a lot of work to do as a class to actually invent a machine that can achieve this."

Seckry didn't stay with Vance any longer because the others were waiting for him out in the corridor.

"You hungry yet?" said Tenk, as Seckry re-joined them.

"Yeah, sure," said Seckry, although in truth he was still fairly full from lunch.

Earlier in the day, Tenk had invited the group over for dinner, since his mum had made masses of special porridge, whatever special porridge was, and the group had tentatively said, "Okay."

They had been excited to get to know Richelle, since they had barely spent any time with her, but once again, she seemed to be off doing something with her own group of friends, and wasn't going to be joining them.

"Tenk," said Tippian, as they left the main gates. "We're not gonna be made to eat porridge as our meal are we? I mean, I like porridge as much as the next guy, but isn't it more of a breakfast thing?"

"Don't worry, nan's cooking the main meal," said Tenk. "Then my mum'll make us have the porridge as a dessert."

"What's so special about this 'special' porridge then, Tenk?" said Loca.

"I think she puts shrivelnuts in it," said Tenk. "Oh and a bit of shaved sourgrape too."

"Sounds delicious," said Loca, dryly.

When they arrived at Tenk's flat, they were greeted warmly by Tenk's mum as usual, but were given no pleasantries by his nan, who eyed each of them up silently before plonking a hand firmly on Tippian's head and saying, "Good grief, how old are you?"

"Um . . . sixteen," said Tippian, cautiously.

"Your mother obviously hasn't been feeding you properly," Tenk's nan replied. "Stunted your growth, no doubt. Well, you'll be fed proper tonight, don't you worry about that."

Tippian was used to being insulted for being shorter than the rest of them, but Seckry thought it was a bit out of order for Tenk's nan to be so blunt. It was the first time Seckry had ever met Tenk's nan, and despite the friendly looking floral cardigan and white perm, Seckry guessed she wasn't the kind old lady you'd find knitting by a warm fire.

"Right, take your seats," she ordered. "Come on, you're already late."

Seckry and the others did what they were told, and slops of slimy, green meat were thrown onto their empty plates before being topped off with canned vegetables and canned potatoes.

"Tenk!" Loca hissed. *"I told you earlier to text your mum and tell her I'm a vegan! You didn't forget, did you?"*

Tenk looked away sheepishly.

"What you two whispering about?" Tenk's nan blurted.

"I'm . . . a vegan," Loca said. "I'm really sorry, I can't eat this."

Tenk's nan glared at Loca as though the girl had suddenly started speaking another language.

"A what?" she said.

"She doesn't eat meat, nan," said Tenk.

"She doesn't . . . she doesn't eat meat?"

"*Or anything from an animal,*" Loca added quietly.

"Mum, there's loads of vegans nowadays," said Tenk's mum. "You need to catch up with the times, I'm telling you."

"Catch up with the times? In my day, if someone put a piece of meat down in front you, you bleedin' ate it, or you starved."

Tenk's nan grabbed Loca's plate and slid the sloppy meat on top of her own.

"I'll get you a clean plate, love," Tenk's mum offered kindly.

When Tenk's nan disappeared into the kitchen area for a moment to get the drinks, Seckry examined his plate of food.

"What . . . kind of meat is this exactly, Tenk?" he asked quietly.

"Gedin, I don't know," Tenk replied, looking even more queasy than the rest of them. "My nan probably doesn't even know herself. All I know is she doesn't believe you should pay more than one note for a piece of meat. She says the best cuts are the cheap cuts."

"Why does it smell so bad?" said Tippian, prodding it with his fork, creating an unpleasant squelch.

"Probably because my nan also doesn't believe in refrigerating meat," Tenk explained. "Back in her day people couldn't afford refrigerators apparently, and nobody got sick back then according to her."

"Back when life expectancy was at its peak, eh?" said Loca.

"Your nan doesn't believe in a lot of things, does she?" said Kimmy. "Is there anything she does believe in?"

"Capital punishment," said Tenk, after heaving on his first bite. "But that's about it."

After forcing the revolting meal down and telling Tenk's nan that it had been delicious, Seckry was actually looking forward to a bit of porridge. At least there was less chance of getting food poisoning from that, and he hoped it would wash away the remnants of gravy in his mouth.

However, when Tenk's mum proudly served it up, and Seckry took his first bite, he found that it clung to his teeth like cement.

"My jaw hurts," said Tippian, and he chewed slowly.

"Kids these days drink too many fizzy drinks," Tenk's nan accused. "Probably given you toothache."

But Seckry's jaw was hurting too. Even though the porridge was as bland and as flavourless as he had hoped after the disgusting dinner, it was almost impossible to chew, let alone swallow.

It took the group around half an hour to actually get through the stuff, and when they did, it was a relief. Luckily they were allowed to play video games for the rest of the evening in Tenk's room, but before they left the dining table, Tenk's nan said, "So who's girlfriend are you?" to Loca. "This little one's with the glasses?"

Loca spat some of her drink back into her cup.

"No, ma'am," she said.

"She's *your* girlfriend?" Tenk's nan pressed, nodding at Kimmy.

"Yeah," Kimmy said, his voice shaking. "We're an item."

"And Blondy is with the quiet girl over here. So where's your girlfriend?" she said to Tippian. "Don't tell me you ain't got one."

Tippian looked around, lost for words.

"Oh my Gedin, what's wrong with you? You better get out there, my son. I was married with my first child on the way when I was sixteen. I had a mortgage to pay, I had bills. You'll be middle-aged before you know it. None of you are getting any younger."

Tenk quickly ushered them all into his room before his nan could offend anyone else, but even though they tried to enjoy the evening, the damage had been done, and Tippian barely said a word all night.

Chapter Ten

Cut Throat's Cunning Plan

The following morning was met with another double helping of electronics with Cut Throat Cutson, much to their dismay, and by the end of it, Seckry and the others were absolutely sick of her.

"Gedin, I wish that woman would just leave us alone," said Tippian, as they filed out into the corridor, looking exhausted from the ordeal. Eiya ran to the bathroom because she had been too scared to ask to go during the lessons.

"She's got no intention of easing up," said Tenk. "The woman won't stop until she's reached the top."

"What do you mean?" said Tippian.

"She's been after Gobbledee's job for years," said Tenk. "She wants to become the new headmistress."

Tenk was right. Cutson had tried getting Gobbledee sacked last year by bringing up the Chlorocalm business to the Board of Education, but even though he was suspended, they thankfully let him come back.

"Can you imagine what it would have been like if Cutson had taken over as head?" said Seckry.

"I would have quit, mate," said Tenk. "I would have walked out of this school and never returned. And I'd probably have left a smelly wet fish in one of her office drawers as a parting gift."

"The horrible old hag would have loved the power," Seckry said, and was slightly surprised that the others didn't say anything in agreement. "What's the matter?" he asked, since Tenk and Tippian were both shuffling around uncomfortably and looking red in the face.

"What. Did you. Just *say?*" came a thin voice from behind that felt like it was piercing the skin on the back of Seckry's neck.

Seckry turned around slowly to see Cutson's haggard face, her narrow eyes burning with contempt.

"Come with me," she said quietly, and Seckry was led away from the guys.

As Seckry followed Mrs Cutson into the headmaster's office, Gobbledee wiped some coffee from his upper lip with a tissue and glared up at them from his desk.

"Mr Sevenstars here seems to think it's okay to walk around the corridors insulting members of staff," Cutson barked.

Gobbledee looked back and forth from Seckry to Cutson a few times, considering the situation carefully.

"I see," he said. "Would you like to tell me what happened, Seckry?" He took another sip from his mug.

"I called her a . . . horrible old hag," Seckry said. He tried not to sound too proud, but he guessed there was no point in denying what had happened. She had heard him loud and clear.

Gobbledee spat a short laugh into his coffee, then made a few coughing noises to disguise it. "Sorry, it . . . went down the wrong way, then. I . . . ugh . . . see. That is quite some comment."

"Well?" Cutson said angrily. "The boy clearly needs to be punished. If this was *my* school, Allon, this despicable boy would be expelled immediately."

Gobbledee took a deep intake of breath. "Mrs Cutson, I am sure Seckry understands that what he said was wrong, and regrets doing so, am I right?" He looked at Seckry and widened his eyes.

"Yes sir," Seckry said reluctantly. "I'm sorry Mrs Cutson."

"I think a simple detention will suffice," said the headmaster, and began shuffling through his paperwork as if that was the end of the conversation.

Cutson looked as though she were about to rip the little

man to pieces.

"Detention? Allon, this vile child has deeply insulted me."

"Yes, Cecilya, detention. And I would prefer it if you addressed me as Mr Gobbledee in front of the pupils from now on."

This really made Cutson take a step back.

Seckry liked this new Gobbledee. When he had first joined Estergate, the headmaster had seemed petrified at simply the mention of Cutson's name, but since the whole incident with Cutson trying to get him sacked, Gobbledee had almost become a new man.

After a few moments of silence, Cutson said, "Detention it is," giving Seckry an evil glare. "My room. Four p.m." Then she left the room furiously.

Before Seckry followed her out, Gobbledee put down his papers.

"Lesson of the day," he said. "Keep the names you come up with for her to yourself. I've got a list of them myself, but I'm careful not to say them out loud." Seckry caught the sliver of a guilty smile on the headmaster's face before he left the office.

As Seckry approached Mrs Cutson's classroom for his detention that evening, she joined him in the corridor and locked her door behind her.

"Mr Sevenstars," she said, pursing her lips as though saying the name put a bitter taste in her mouth. "I *was* planning to hold the detention here in my room, but I've just sprayed my classroom plants with GrowPro, and oops, I've just read the back of the bottle and it says that the fumes could cause irritation to humans if the area isn't well ventilated. We will have to hold the detention elsewhere." She quickly glanced down the corridor. "What a shame," she said in an overly theatrical way. "It looks like all of the other classrooms are locked." The left side of her mouth curved up slightly to form a sinister grin. "There's only one room left that we can use. The Pharyan studies room."

"Pharyan studies?" Seckry said suspiciously. "I didn't know

there was Pharyan studies being taught here. I've never had a lesson."

"Well the subject hasn't been taught for a few years," Cutson said, still grinning weirdly. "Follow me, please."

Seckry was led into the pneumatic pods in silence.

Cutson was fiddling around with something next to the control buttons that dictated which floor the pod stopped at. Seckry tilted his head and saw that Cutson had unclipped a small panel that read:

Maintenance and storage facility
DO NOT TOUCH

She pressed a red button and the pod began descending downwards.

"Where are we going?" Seckry asked.

Cutson didn't respond. She merely grinned with self-satisfaction.

Seckry had never seen the pneumatic pods go any lower than floor B, where Cutson's room was. He thought that it had been the lowest segment of the school.

Outside of the glass pod, the artificial, orb shaped lights that ran downwards, guiding the structure, had abruptly come to an end, even though the pod was still travelling downwards into darkness.

When it stopped and opened its doors with a hiss, they were met with a chilly, stagnant air. Seckry could almost taste the mould on his tongue.

"Welcome to floor Z," she said, and pulled a tiny battery-powered lantern out of her pocket. "Pharyan studies is just at the other end of the corridor."

"When was it last taught here?" Seckry asked, stepping out and coughing from the dust.

"Oh, what was it now?" Cutson said ponderingly. "Thirty years ago?"

Cutson unlocked the dirty looking classroom door and shoved the lantern inside, illuminating giant cobwebs and patches of festering black mould.

In the centre of the room was a single table.

"Right, here's your detention work," Cutson said, slapping a bunch of papers to his chest.

"You can't leave me down here," Seckry said angrily, taking them from her.

Cutson chuckled shrilly.

"Not scared of a little darkness are we?" she said. "See you in an hour."

She shoved him inside, slammed the door and locked it behind her. A pillow of dust wafted from the doorframe making Seckry wheeze. He slowly scanned the room around him as Cutson's footsteps echoed into nothingness.

She's just trying to scare you, he told himself reassuringly. *Don't give her what she wants.*

He pulled out his mobile phone to check for a signal, but as he expected, there was nothing. He was just going to have to get on with his work in the lamplight and wait it out. It was only one hour. How hard could it be?

Seckry sat at the table cautiously and read the questions she had given him. The only way to get through this was to not let his imagination run wild. There was nothing else in the room. It was just old and empty, that was all.

Before Seckry knew it, half an hour had passed. He had been so engrossed in his detention work he had almost forgotten where he was. Cutson had given him a diagram to dissect that was aimed at seventh year students, even though Seckry was only in year five, but the difficulty of it was only helping Seckry to concentrate more.

Then there was a scuttle.

Seckry froze, his heart hammering. But as his eyes locked on the object, he realised it was some kind of insect. If he could remember correctly from one of Butterkins' theory lessons, it was a fogopod; a common, small insect that lived in uninhabited urban structures, disguising itself with a speckled shell that could be mistaken for debris.

It casually strolled across the floor towards Seckry, and Seckry picked up the lantern to get a closer look at it. At the first sign of movement, the fogopod spread its stubby wings and fluttered over to the furthest wall, burrowing into a crack. But as Seckry stared at the wall, what at first seemed to be a crack began looking like something else. Something man made.

Seckry slowly extended his lantern and crept towards it. As he neared, there was no doubt about it. The fogopod had scuttled into a keyhole.

Seckry brushed his hand over the flaky wall, and a thick layer of dust smeared away to reveal a multitude of wooden planks, nailed over what had to be a door into another room.

As he scrubbed away even more dirt and grime, he began to see words written onto some kind of warning sign in the centre of the door. Seckry pulled away some of the rotten wood slowly, being careful not to catch himself on any splinters. It fell to the floor easily.

He lifted the lamp and read the text.

Due to tragic events, this room is no longer in use, and the subject will cease to be taught, in respect to the families affected.

Signed: Rendleworth Ruttcast, Headmaster, Estergate High

"What on earthia happened here?" Seckry said softly to himself.

He cleared more of the rot away from the upper half of the door so the subject name could be read.

Genesis Trinity Studies

He tried pushing the door, then pulling it, but even though the thing seemed to be rotting away, it was holding tight. He even tried picking the lock with an unfolded paperclip that he found in his pocket, but after prodding the wire into the hole and rummaging around a bit, he realised he had no idea how to actually pick a lock and gave up.

If he wanted to open the door he was going to have to get some help. For now he thought it was best to sit back down and complete his work. As much as he was intrigued by the secret room, he didn't fancy having to do another helping of detention as a punishment for not doing the first one properly.

Seckry had just enough time to do what he considered a decent job of the work Cutson had given him before she was unlocking the door. When she opened it to find Seckry happily gathering up his completed papers, she seemed astounded and offended that Seckry wasn't in tears, begging to be let out, and looked even angrier now than when she had first overheard his insult.

Seckry said nothing to her as they travelled upwards into daylight. Even though he was leaving school an hour later than usual, and with lungs caked full of dust, Seckry had the faintest glimmer of a smile on his face as he boarded the monorail home.

Chapter Eleven

The Hidden Classroom

The next day, after lessons had finished, Seckry wasted no time in excusing himself from the group and heading to Vance's classroom to tell him about the secret room he had found on floor Z.

"I had a feeling there were other nooks and crannies to this place," Vance pondered. "The school has been here for hundreds of years. They've completely redesigned it numerous times and built extras and knocked parts down, so I guess it's inevitable that there would be certain hidden rooms, but I had no idea Mrs Cutson had keys to one of them."

"Do you think she knows about the boarded up classroom too?" said Seckry.

Vance considered it for a moment.

"I imagine not," he said. "If the thing was completely covered in thick dust and you had to wipe it away, I doubt *anyone* that stills works here knows that it's there, never mind Cutson."

"What do you think happened in there? It said it was closed and the subject was to cease being taught in respect to the families that were affected."

"Well, there's an easy way to find out," said Vance, pulling a couple of torches and a huge hammer out of a drawer. "I knew this thing would come in handy one day. I've been looking forward to using it. Somehow, I always knew it wouldn't be for knocking in nails."

Before long, they were down in the Pharyan studies room

and Vance was swinging at the boarded-up door, smashing it to smithereens. Seckry stood a few yards away, shielding his eyes from splinters and coughing from the plumes of dirt.

Once there was enough space to squeeze through, Vance stepped over the pile of broken wood and Seckry followed.

The first thing Seckry noticed was that in the furthest corner, there were bunches and bunches of artificial flowers, yellowed from age. There were also crisp, dried up leaves and twigs; the remains of fresh flowers that had withered away decades ago.

"Somebody died here?" Seckry said quietly.

They approached the bouquets and Vance picked up a frail card that had been wedged into one of them.

"I hope this school burns to the ground," he read quietly.

"Wow," said Seckry.

Seckry would have guessed that if the school was to board up a room, they would have first removed everything from it, but as he waved his torch around, it was almost like a screenshot from the midst of a lesson, albeit without any pupils or a teacher. There were pencils and paper on desks, strange looking equipment and petri dishes scattered around, and plastic sculptures of DNA strands. The walls were covered in diagrams and posters, the largest of which seemed to catch Vance's immediate attention. Seckry followed him as he approached it.

At the centre of the diagram was a gigantic, strange looking, mostly circular symbol, split into three segments. The top was blue, the left lower segment was white, and the right lower segment was black.

Seckry's eyes immediately locked on the blue segment. It was labelled with the word helitonium.

"What on earthia . . . ?" Vance mouthed.

"They were teaching pupils about helitonium?" said Seckry. "After all that time we were trying to uncover the existence of it last year."

"Seckry," said Vance. "What is more baffling to me right now are the other segments either side of it."

Seckry scanned them. The white segment was labelled

Creogen and the black was labelled Exorophon.

"I've never heard of those," said Seckry.

"Seckry, I've been a science teacher for fifteen years, and . . . I have never heard of them either."

Vance suddenly made his way over to the teacher's desk and started flicking through the papers and notebooks that were on there. Seckry noticed that there was even a dirtied mug of coffee sitting on the desk that was stained with the remnants of the teacher's final dregs.

"Seckry, would you mind checking some of the pupil's desks?" said Vance, and Seckry happily obliged.

A few were empty, and a few, in true Estergate fashion, were filled with graffiti and bits of hardened chewing gum, but the fifth one he opened was filled with neatly arranged pens and pencils wedged against a perfectly preserved workbook.

Seckry opened it to the first page, which was titled with bubble writing that read:

The Genesis Trinity and its Origins.

"Sir, I think this might help us," said Seckry, and Vance took it from him carefully, spreading it out on the teacher's desk. They both leant over it, shining their torches on the pages.

The genesis trinity is the name given to the three elements that are thought to have been present at the beginning of time, and that were able to form the universe and the first molecules of matter. These three elements were:

Creogen - the element of pure creation, which created the matter.

Helitonium - the modifier that moulded the matter into different forms of life.

Exorophon – the element of pure destruction, that prevented the matter from expanding infinitely.

"Elements of pure creation and pure destruction?" said Vance. "I have never heard of such a thing in my life."

They continued reading, and ignored the gangly spinspider that crept over the corner of the page.

Until recent years, not much has been known about the current existence of the genesis trinity. Out of the three elements, only helitonium was ever present during the times of the Klaxion Empire. Creogen and exorophon were thought to be defunct after the initial forming of the universe, since they were no longer needed. Life had been successfully set in motion, and was able to exist and evolve on its own. For this reason, the fact that creogen and exorophon were never found on Earthia was never questioned, until the Pharyan Krakun drill finally breached the planet's crust and entered the mantle. The samples taken from the mantle actually contained small traces of both creogen and exorophon, revealing that these mysterious elements had never truly disappeared, but had been existing within the centre of the planet.

"Incredible," said Vance. "Do you know anything of the Krakun drill, Seckry?"

Seckry shook his head.

"Well it was the first drill to reach the earth's mantle, as this pupil rightly states . . . but . . . I have never heard anything of these creogen and exorophon samples. This is utterly bizarre."

The principles of the genesis trinity can be seen in every form of existence. Something is created, then it is modified, and then it is, ultimately, destroyed. The understanding of the genesis trinity may also be the key to understanding the nature of a human life cycle, and may help us discover new medicine to prevent the body's decay.

The genesis trinity has also been worshipped at times as a form of Gedin, since it was the creator of the universe. The Ancient Klaxions, even though they only knew of helitonium, worshipped it and feared it equally. They were also fascinated by it and used it in many scientific experiments.

Most famously, a Klaxion doctor named Incannah Innoya managed to successfully implant helitonic particles into human embryos, thinking it would give them some kind of special ability. Because of the dormant properties of helitonium, it had no effect on the humans whatsoever, but the element was present in their DNA, and the DNA of their offspring, with male carriers passing the gene onto male children, and female carriers passing the gene onto female children. These humans infused with helitonium, and their offspring for generations to come, were, and are still, known as innoya.

"Unbelievable," said Vance. "I had no idea that the word innoya was originally a Klaxion doctor's surname."

As they were reading, Seckry noticed that one of the booklets that Vance had pulled out of a drawer was labelled:

Journal – Professor Hovengart

Vance caught sight of it too and flicked through it.

"Have a sift through the rest of the stuff, Seckry," he said. "See if you can find anything else of interest."

Whilst Seckry was rummaging through papers and papers of undecipherable notes, Vance began reading from the teacher's journal.

"This is a new subject, for me and for everyone. I should be ecstatic at the pupils' progress. But something isn't right. There is something unsettling about the two brightest pupils, the two boys that are hungrier to learn than anyone else. They have become obsessed with the idea of acquiring creogen and exorophon particles, and I cannot get them to understand the dangers of this."

Seckry picked up a clipboard that was filled with a list of names with ticks next to them; a register of the class no doubt.

"Creogen and exorophon, if ever released from a controlled environment, could be catastrophic," Vance continued, turning a page of the journal. "Creogen could start creating matter randomly, and exorophon could start . . . destroying matter. The problem is, the boys seem to have no concept of how much of a threat this would be. They are over curious, and they are beginning to worry me. This subject was only ever meant to teach children about the history and the theory of the genesis trinity."

Vance stopped reading and said, "I wonder who these two boys were."

But Seckry wasn't paying attention. He was transfixed, staring at the class register.

Amidst the list of random names were two that Seckry recognised. Two that sent tingles down his spine.

Adelbert Endoman and Rikard Ringold.

Chapter Twelve

The Death of Yestelle Bookum

"I had no idea Adelbert and Rikard studied here at Estergate," said Seckry.

"Neither did I," said Vance. "I actually know very little about their upbringings. Were these the two boys Professor Hovengart was concerned about?" He flicked through a few pages. "There's one here titled, 'What Have I Done?'"

Seckry put down the register and listened carefully to Vance.

"I fear my most recent lesson," Vance read, "has ignited some deep desire inside Adelbert and Rikard. They are undoubtedly the brightest, most talented, and most enthusiastic pupils I have ever had the opportunity to teach, but as I have previously stated, they seem to possess a lust for power, and one of them has a distinct absence of any kind of morality. After learning that Incannah Innoya was successfully able to infuse embryos with helitonium, the boys were adamant that they wanted to infuse embryos themselves with creogen and exorophon. I fully explained to them that this is probably impossible, but if it were possible, the ramifications could be severe. Helitonium is dormant inside innoya due to the properties of the element, but creogen and exorophon would very likely be active, meaning that they could effectively give the human beings the ability to create matter . . . or destroy it."

Vance looked up at Seckry and they stared at each other, silently, until Vance continued reading.

"The boys also seem to have this idea that creogen and exorophon are enemies, and they have assigned themselves an element each to champion; Rikard to creogen and Adelbert to exorophon. Once again, I have tried to discourage this, but I have never encountered pupils so . . . intense and motivated in my entire teaching career. I told them that the trinity was not about choosing a side, but everything to them is a contest, a battle of some sort.

"Adelbert also seems to think that infusing something with exorophon would make it inherently evil, because of its destructive powers, and infusing something with creogen would make it inherently good-natured, because of its creational powers. But Rikard constantly disagrees with him on this, and argues that nurture and upbringing are the defining factors as to whether someone is good or evil, not their DNA."

Vance skipped ahead a few pages until he was close to the back of the journal and found an entry titled 'The End.'

"I am sorry for teaching this Gedin forsaken subject," he read. "If it hadn't been for my greedy fascination, then none of this would have happened, and Yestelle Bookum would still be alive.

"When Adelbert and Rikard first told me they had got their hands on creogen and exorophon particles from the Krakun drill, I laughed. I thought they were playing a trick on me, some kind of grim joke. But it was no joke. They told me they were going to infuse the embryos of two mumprats, one with each element, to see if they would remain dormant, or become active. Foolishly, I let them conduct this horrific experiment. Why? Because I honestly didn't believe that the particles they were in possession of were actually creogen and exorophon. I thought they were naïve boys whose imagination had got the better of them, and I was happy for them to conduct this experiment if it would finally get this idea of infusing embryos out of their system.

"But after the mumprats were born, I realised that the boys had not been playing games. The creogen-infused baby was squirming around, while bits of unidentifiable stuff, let's say, were popping out of nowhere around it. The exorophon baby was sat, doing nothing, until Adelbert began prodding it.

"This is where everything changed. Yestelle Bookum couldn't bear to see the animal treated like that. She snatched it from Adelbert and cradled it in her arms, protecting it. But I guess, all that the animal knew was that it was frightened and that it was angry and that it was under attack. Yestelle backed into a corner and held the animal tight, to protect it, and that is when it happened.

"I think it was her arms that began to break first. I remember the skin snapping open and revealing her muscle tissue underneath. It was horrific, like a scene from some macabre horror movie. She was screaming, but she still held the animal close, unsure of what was happening. I think the screams frightened the animal even more, and then things became horrendous. I could hear the bones snapping inside her fingers as they imploded in on themselves. Her hair completely disintegrated within seconds, and her clothes just ripped themselves into nothing as the rest of her vanished into oblivion, leaving nothing but spatters of blood on the floor and the walls.

"I grabbed a penknife from my desk and threw it at the mumprat, skewering it to the floor before it could kill anyone else.

"It's hard to remember exactly what happened during the next few moments; it was the closest thing to a living dream, or in this case, a living nightmare, that I had ever experienced. The only thing that I do remember was the awful, awful victory celebration from Adelbert. 'The trinity awakens!' he cried, his eyes wide with fascination. 'We've done it!'

"Everyone else was silent from fear and disbelief and utter horror, even Rikard. But Adelbert . . . he showed no remorse."

"'Somebody get the headmaster,' I remember shouting. 'This course, the trinity, everything . . . it's over.'

"My fear is not that I will spend the rest of my life in prison, which will inevitably be the result of allowing this to happen, but that Adelbert and Rikard will go on to realise their vision of infusing *human* embryos with creogen and exorophon. I daresay the plans they have already crafted for their futures are comprehensive enough to convince me they are deadly serious about it. They plan to set up their own scientific research entity named The End and Ring Company in order to get funding from the government. But the company will be a façade for their true goal; Rikard wants to infuse a human child with creogen, and Adelbert, a child with exorophon. I imagine in just a few years' time we will have the scientific knowledge to be able to create human babies in laboratories. This would mean that Adelbert and Rikard wouldn't even need to acquire embryos from anyone; they would simply be able to create new human beings from scratch. If they manage this, then they will create beings of immense power. One, the power to create matter, and the other . . . the formidable power to *destroy* matter."

As Vance stopped reading, he shook his head in disbelief.

"Gedin," said Seckry, softly. "My dad . . . and Lux. This is the reason behind their existence. This is why they were made in a lab. Adelbert and Rikard weren't creating sons for themselves because they were infertile and wanted children . . . they were creating . . . *weapons*."

Vance was silent, rereading the journal entry to himself.

"Sir, this means that . . . that my dad, and Lux, have . . . superpowers."

"Yes . . ." Vance said vacantly. "Yes, Seckry, I think you may be right."

Seckry was fascinated at the idea of his dad being able to create things at will, but as he thought of Lux, he became terrified. He had always imagined Lux as an unhinged man stalking the streets on a hell-bent mission to find his father and kill him with a gun. But Lux didn't even need a weapon. The man that wanted to kill Seckry's father, and himself, if Lux ever found out about his existence, had the superhuman power to destroy people with his mere mind.

"Seckry," said Vance. "I think you're forgetting one thing."

"What?" said Seckry.

"The most astounding thing about this whole revelation is that your father and Lux are most likely not the only ones to have these superhuman powers. If helitonium is passed from generation to generation through innoya of the same biological sex, then the creogen in your father's DNA . . . has most likely been passed on to *you*."

Chapter Thirteen

The Limiter

"Was this how I was able to create Eiya?" said Seckry. "Was it the creogen inside me?"

Vance considered this carefully, but eventually shook his head.

"No," he said, "it can't have been. No, Seckry, I don't think the creogen inside you was, or indeed is, active. If it were, then you would probably be creating matter here, there, and everywhere. No, according to Sanfarrow, Eiya was formed out of already existing particles of helitonium that night. No new matter was actually created. Your mind just morphed the helitonium into Eiya."

"When you say the creogen isn't active, do you mean you think it's dormant inside me?" said Seckry.

"No," said Vance. "I imagine Adelbert and Rikard invented some age-related limiter to stop your father and Lux having access to their powers as babies. Can you imagine the massacre? I'm sure the scientists learned their lesson from that mumprat. They probably had to wait until a certain age for their powers to awaken, and I would guess you are the same."

Vance flicked through the journal once again, trying to find any information on a timer, before saying, 'bingo.' He spread the page out for Seckry to read.

The boys are more serious about this End and Ring thing than I first thought. They have even planned an age of activation, so that the humans they infuse the trinity elements into won't be able to access their creative or destructive properties until they are old enough to control them. The current age they've decided on is around sixteen and a quarter. They have actually decided on a specific number of days into the sixteenth year but I cannot recall how many at this moment. The fact that they are being so precise about this scares me.

"I've just turned sixteen," said Seckry.

"Then, in the next few months, Seckry," said Vance, "you may become . . . something more than human."

Seckry sat down at one of the desks; his legs were almost too weak to stand. Everything he had been sure of had just changed again, and now his whole world seemed out of control. He knew that half of him had been created in a laboratory, and that he was different to most people in some way, but he had never expected this. He stared at his hand. What was going to happen to him? And would he be able to control it properly when it did?

"I think we should get moving," said Vance, before coughing heavily. "This place isn't going to do our lungs any favours. We should take as much information as we can with us, though."

Seckry nodded and began gathering sheets out of pupil's desks as Vance continued to rummage through the professor's desk drawers.

"Look at this," said Vance, pulling out a half-empty tube of sweets. "Doctor Sweetum's Fuzz Fumbles. Even *I* don't remember these."

"Ahem," came a sharp voice from behind them.

Seckry and Vance turned around slowly to find Mrs Cutson glaring at them through the gap in the crumpled door.

"Cecilya," said Vance, as if bumping into an old friend for the first time in years. "Good to see you."

Mrs Cutson said nothing, her eyes saying everything she needed to say.

"Care for a sweet?" said Vance, holding out the dirty tube. Some kind of dust beetle scampered out of the packet, jumped to the floor, and made a run for it.

"What in Gedin's name is this place, Jonn?" Cutson said accusatorially.

"Well, I'd like to ask you the same question, since you seem to be the regular visitor," said Vance.

"Regular visitor? I had no idea there was an extra room here. I knew there was something fishy going on when I let him out yesterday evening."

"Well I have to say you don't know your pupils well enough if you think you can lock Seckry Sevenstars in a stinking old room and not expect him to look for a way out."

"He was supposed to be doing detention. He should have behaved himself. Can't you see that this boy is feral, Jonn? He couldn't resist meddling in the affairs of Endrin last year, and now -"

"*Cecilya,*" Vance cut in, forcefully. "I would advise you to keep your opinions about what happened at Endrin last year to yourself, especially since you were so heavily involved in the influence they had in this very school."

"I was merely doing what I thought was right," Cutson said unconvincingly.

"That being aiding Kan Darklight, mass murderer and a child torturer?" Vance said, taking a slow step towards Cutson confrontationally.

"There was no way I c-could have possibly known . . . I would never have condoned s-such things had I been aware . . ." Cutson stammered. She opened her mouth to speak again, but closed it. Eventually, she said, "I'll be letting the headmaster know about the damage you and Seckry have caused to school property."

"And while you're there, you can explain to him your reasons for locking Seckry up down here in the first place," Vance said. "I'm sure he'll be very interested to hear your explanation."

Cutson gave them one final stare down before turning briskly and leaving them to collect the rest of the papers.

Chapter Fourteen

Tippian's Secret

When Seckry arrived back at the flat, he raced to his bedroom to find Eiya reading on her bed. She sat up as Seckry entered and gave him a sweet smile.

Seckry, unable to contain what was bursting inside of him, dropped to his knees, scattering the papers onto the bedroom floor and said, "Eiya, you're not going to believe this."

He spent the next hour explaining everything to her, and she listened with wide eyes.

"Seck . . . you're going to have, like . . . *actual* superpowers. Are you serious?"

"I don't even know," said Seckry, who had spent the entire monorail journey home trying to guess what the creogen awakening inside him would feel like, and how he would be able to use it.

That night, Seckry shuffled through the notebooks and papers he had taken from the classroom to see if he could find any clarity on the exact date that Adelbert and Rikard had decided was best for the infused elements to become active, but he couldn't find anything. Eventually he drifted off to sleep, the papers resting on his chest.

He dreamt once again that he was in the Divinita chamber with Darklight and Eiya, and Darklight had a blade to Eiya's throat, just like the Rabbit Man. Seckry screamed, trying to get to her, to save her, but his hands were tied to the wall behind him just like last time.

"Why don't you use your superpowers to do something?" said Darklight. "Oh, wait, you don't have them yet. That's a shame."

Just as Darklight drew blood on Eiya's neck, Seckry jolted awake to find Eiya kneeling on his bed, whispering to him that it was time to get up for school.

Seckry breathed a sigh of relief and Eiya giggled.

"It's exhausting, this sleeping business, ain't it?" she said.

Seckry smiled, but he decided to keep his dream to himself once again.

During lunchtime, Seckry managed to catch Vance on his own.

"I'm afraid I found no specific date, either, Seckry," he said. "But I still have a lot to go through. I had tests to mark last night so I wasn't able to give it my full attention. I assure you I will be reading avidly over the next few nights, though, so I will keep you updated."

When home time came, Seckry was itching to get back to the flat and have another read through the material he had gathered from the genesis trinity room, but Tenk and the others had organised an after school gathering at Tippian's house because his parents were out, and Seckry didn't want to offend Tippian by not turning up.

Seckry had decided to keep the revelations about the genesis trinity between himself, Vance and Eiya for the time being, until he was a little more clued up on what it all actually meant. As much as he wanted to tell the rest of the group, he wasn't quite ready to be quizzed about it.

It didn't take them long to get to Tippian's house, since he lived not far from Estergate. As soon as he let them all in, they were guided up to his bedroom. Seckry had been to Tippian's house once before; just before they had stormed the Divinita Chamber at the beginning of the summer. But he had been so caught up in the events that were going on that it had been purely business. They hadn't even ventured upstairs.

Unlike Tenk's room, Tippian's was immaculately clean with what seemed like hundreds of awards, trophies, and certificates scattered around the place. The centrepiece of the room was a giant, triangular shelf unit with about twenty square holes in it, each housing a different trophy.

"You got a new one," said Tenk, pulling one out of the pyramid that was shaped like a joystick wearing a pair of glasses. "The Video Game Appreciation Society Bespectacled Member of the Year," he read, with a frown.

"Yeah," said Tippian. "I think they had to meet some quota for the amount of trophies they were awarding that year and made one up. Still, I ain't gonna say no if they award me with something."

Loca was examining them too, and picked up a miniature sized golden cup with her thumb and forefinger.

"What's this one for?" she said. "The writing's not big enough to read."

"Oh, that's the Smallman award," said Tippian.

"Smallman, who's he? The guy they used before Andersun Wellworth?"

"No. Small *man*. I won it for being a small man."

"Oh," said Loca.

As Seckry was scanning the shiny array, he noticed that one of the shelves was empty; the one at the very top; the peak of the entire thing.

"Are you saving that spot for the Young Inventor Award?" he asked.

"Nope," said Tippian. "Even that ain't gonna cut it."

"What do you mean?" said Loca.

Tenk, who was a regular visitor of Tippian's house, shook his head mockingly.

"Don't get him started on that top spot," he said. "None of his trophies are good enough, and none of them ever will be."

"You might as well put something in there," said Loca. "It looks silly empty like that when all the others are filled."

"Might as well put something in there? *Might as well put something in there?*" said Tippian, flabbergasted. "This is the summit of the Tippian trophy pyramid. I'm not just gonna stick any trophy in there, I'm saving that spot for something truly special."

"And do you have something in mind?"

"No," Tippian said. "I'll just know when I receive it. It'll just feel right, you know?"

"Nothing's ever gonna be good enough. It's always gonna be empty, isn't it?" said Loca to Tenk, who nodded in certainty.

They spent most of the evening watching episodes of an animation called Battlebeast Ultra and drank three flagons of pop between them before Tippian scrambled out of his bedroom holding his crotch as though he was about to burst.

"He's tempting fate, leaving me in here unattended," said Loca. "He's gotta expect me to pry a bit. I'm a girl, and a nosy one at that. Let's see what he keeps in his bedside drawer."

Loca opened it and pulled out what seemed to be a woman's magazine, brand new and cellophane wrapped.

"No way," said Tenk, ripping it out of Loca's grasp. "*No way!*"

"What is it?" Seckry asked.

"Look at the name it's addressed to," Tenk said.

Seckry peered closer.

Dear Miss Tippitha Frost, please find your October edition of Glamourgirl enclosed. Stay beautiful x

"*It's Tippian's female alter ego, Tippitha!*" Tenk whispered excitedly.

"When in Gedin's name did Tippian have a female alter ego?" said Loca. "Did you know about this?" she asked Kimmy, who shook his head bemusedly.

The bedroom door reopened, but before Tippian had even taken one step inside, he saw the magazine and launched through the air, toppling Tenk over and crashing to the floor.

"They've all seen it, Tipps!" Tenk screamed, "It don't matter what you do now!"

Tippian wrestled to get the magazine back, but Tenk was bigger and stronger. Tippian eventually gave up and clambered onto his bed, but not before giving Tenk a firm thud in the ribs with his trainer first.

"I don't get it," said Tenk. "I ordered one issue of that

magazine to your home address under the name Tippitha Frost as a joke, years ago. It was a free sample offer. How come you're still getting them?"

"Well . . ." Tippian said hesitantly, "I wasn't just going to throw the thing away. I had a read of it, and then next thing you know, I'm hooked. I gave them my bank details and signed myself up for a subscription."

"What? And you kept the name Tippitha Frost?"

"Well, I can't sign up for a subscription to a girl's magazine with a boy's name, can I? They'd think I was some kind of freak."

"What era do you think we're living in Tipps?" said Loca. "You can be anyone you want these days. but I have to say, I never would have thought that for all these years you've been secretly reading some girl's magazine."

"It's not just *some* girl's magazine," said Tippian, defensively. "It's Skyfall's number one periodical for females aged twelve to eighteen, as voted for by the public."

"Did you take part in that vote?" said Loca.

"I might have."

"What's so good about it then?" asked Seckry, who wasn't sure if he was more amused or intrigued by the whole thing.

"Well, it's interesting, finding out how the female mind works. It might give me some heads up, you know, when I'm courting a lady."

"Wow," said Tenk, pulling out an insert. "Looks like you've got a fold-out poster of that actor Timson Smulder this month, Tipp . . . Impressive abs."

"Look," said Tippian. "I don't go keeping all this bumf that comes with it, especially not the pin ups of men, okay?" He ripped the poster out of Tenk's hands and began tearing it into neat squares. "It's just that some of the articles are . . . *enlightening*, you know? And it's got horoscopes. I mean, find me a magazine for men that has four full pages of horoscopes every month and I'll switch."

"What sign are you?" Loca asked, flicking through until she found the section.

"Zincar," Tippian said.

"Zincar . . . The month of October brings changes to a situation you've been stressing about in your life. Plus, that hot guy you've had your eye on these last few weeks? Natos aligning with Jusphere means that just a flutter of your eyelashes will have him swooning over you."

"Who's this hot guy then, Tipps?" said Tenk, winking.

"Look," said Tippian, who seemed like he was going to have a meltdown due to embarrassment. "I just reverse the genders, okay? If it says I've got my eye on a hot guy, then I just flip it to mean girl."

"There's a multiple choice personality quiz here that determines what you're gonna be like when you're older," said Loca. "Tipps, let's see what the future holds for you. Question one, how many boyfriends have you had? More than one, more than three, or zero?"

Tippian shifted uncomfortably.

"That would be zero, for girlfriends . . . *and* boyfriends," he added, giving Tenk a sharp glare.

After Tippian had answered all of the questions, which had included "How do you like to spend your evenings?" and "How many children do you want?" he waited for the result from Loca.

"Oh dear," Loca read. "If you're not careful, you're going to turn out to be a bitter old woman who scorns kids in the street for no apparent reason, who throws bricks at cats passing through the garden, and who is alone for the rest of her life."

"I'm gonna be a bitter old woman," said Tippian, looking as though he was on the verge of tears.

"Come on, Tipps, who on earthia comes up with these quizzes?" said Seckry, who could see Tippian was taking it to heart. "How can they say they know what you're going to turn into unless they know you in person? We know you better than that silly magazine does."

"Besides, Tipp," said Tenk, reassuringly. "You won't turn into a bitter old woman, you'll turn into a bitter old man, remember to flip the genders."

"Oh, that's helpful," said Loca, sarcastically.

"A bitter old man," said Tippian. "Oh Gedin, Seck, I'm gonna turn into that guy at your party - the one who was banging on your door and shouting at your mum."

"Mr Mulk?" said Seckry. "Tipps, no matter what this quiz says, I can never see you ending up like Mr Mulk."

For the rest of the evening, they played a board game, and Seckry hoped that Tippian would forget about the results, but between Tenk's nan offending him about being single, and now this quiz, Tippian seemed genuinely hurt. Seckry just hoped that the increased Friction training they'd be doing shortly would make him forget about it, and bring him back to his usual self.

When Seckry and Eiya arrived back at the flat that night, Seckry couldn't wait to get into bed and go through the papers. It was already approaching nine o'clock, so he scoffed down a quick bowl of cereal for supper and tucked himself under the covers whilst Eiya listened to some music on her earphones.

However, after an hour and a half of flicking through graphs, tables, charts and essays on the relevance of the genesis trinity, his enthusiasm began to diminish and he found himself drifting off, resigning to the fact that he wasn't going to find any information on a date.

Then, as his eyes were drooping, he caught sight of a number scribbled into the margin of a scruffy looking single sheet. It read:

16 years, 93 days

His eyes darted open and he was immediately wide awake again. He checked for a name at the top of the work, but there was none. Then, as he flipped the page over, he saw the initials AE printed at the end. There was no doubt about it; this was Adelbert Endoman's scrawl.

Seckry quickly loaded up the built in calendar on his phone and checked the date.

If this was truly the correct number, then the creogen

inside him was going to awaken the day after this year's Friction Mega Meltdown.

Chapter Fifteen

Polluted Veins

Seckry woke the following morning feeling elated. His concerns about Lux having superhuman powers had pretty much vanished, because all he could think about was that he was going to have superhuman powers too.

Seckry was now looking forward to this year's Mega Meltdown more than ever. Not only was he going to be able to compete once again for the Eidolons, but his powers were going to awaken the very next day.

After showering for school, Seckry showed Eiya Endoman's scribble, and Seckry asked her what she had been listening to last night.

Eiya smiled guiltily.

"Looking for Tomorrow," she said. "What is it about The Broken Motion that makes their tracks infinitely replayable? I've listened to every song on that album, like, fifty times, and every one of them still feels like it's the first time I'm hearing it."

Seckry laughed. "Yep, you were definitely made from my subconscious."

"Seck," said Eiya, her face becoming serious for a moment. "I was thinking about something last night when I was listening to 'A Time for Change' again and . . . the lyrics say 'Sanfarrow, Darklight, Kayne, the three, who'll unleash the dark heart, set the demon free.' The band told us they had found something about the trio creating some kind of monster, but we never got any more info about that."

Eiya was right. Seckry had forgotten about that lyric.

"Do you think the monster they were referring to was The

Rabbit Man?"

"There's only one way to find out," said Seckry, and began typing an email on his phone.

Since meeting the band last year, Seckry and Eiya had kept in regular touch with them. They had been especially interested to hear the details of the events that happened inside the Divinita chamber. Seckry had kept the information about what really happened a secret from most, but if there was anyone he was going to tell the truth to, it was the Broken Motion, who had helped them uncover Darklight's plans and set their entire thwarting in motion.

Within half an hour, Seckry's phone buzzed, a message waiting for him in his inbox.

Dear Seckry and Eiya

You know what? When we wrote those lyrics, we had just found the attached diagram, and we assumed that the figure on it was some hideous creation that the three of them were working on. We never found anything related to it afterwards so, to be honest, I think it was just some ditched idea. With Darklight gone now, I'd say there's nothing to worry about, but feel free to study it yourself.

Seckry opened the attachment.

It was a diagram of a man, naked except for some kind of loin cloth. His fists were clenched tightly and his skin was taut, and almost every vein was visible through his skin. But his veins weren't the normal blue colour of a healthy human being, they were jet black, as if pumping some polluted, tainted liquid through him. The eyes, however, were even creepier; they were as black as his veins, not just the pupil, but the iris and the whites too, just a deep abyss of nothingness, a hollow, empty void that seemed to suck life into it like a vacuum.

"I wonder what they were working on," said Eiya. "I don't like the look of this guy."

"You know, the great thing about being friends with Sanfarrow and Jenniver now is that we can ask them," said

Seckry. He stuffed his phone back into his pocket and made a mental note to show it to Sanfarrow the next time he was at the Chronoway construction site.

At lunchtime, Seckry couldn't keep the genesis trinity stuff to himself any longer and spilled everything to the rest of the group. Tenk, unsurprisingly, almost fainted into his plate of pasta.

"Mate, I told you, I told you!" he gasped. "You're some kind of fippin *deity!* You're not normal, I swear."

Seckry barely managed to eat anything because he was so caught up in answering everyone's questions, but the conversation changed when a group of guys shouted, "Hey, Tippitha Frost!" at Tippian.

Tippian turned and glared at Tenk.

"Tenk, you didn't? Did you?"

"How did that lot find out?" said Tenk, sheepishly. "I only told Joshwa Trap . . . and Benn Kingle."

"Tenk, you idiot," said Loca. "You think people in this school keep things to themselves?"

Tenk looked away ashamedly.

"Prepare to be taunted for the foreseeable future," Loca said to Tippian.

When the weekend finally arrived, Seckry decided to pay Ropart Sanfarrow a visit and show him the image from The Broken Motion, since he had been unable to get the dark-veined figure out of his mind.

Seckry and Eiya both agreed that it would be best for Seckry to go alone, since they hadn't heard from Sanfarrow since he had revealed that Kayne believed Eiya to be his dead wife, and Seckry was a little concerned about Eiya being in the same vicinity as the undead man. Seckry hoped that Sanfarrow had been able to talk some sense into him by now, but either way, he didn't want to take the risk.

When he arrived at Chronoway Crossing, he found Sanfarrow talking impatiently to someone on the phone.

"How is the construction going?" asked Seckry, when

Sanfarrow had hung up.

Sanfarrow took a few moments to speak.

"It's had its fair share of setbacks so far, Seckry, I can tell you that," he said grimly. "I've actually been wondering over the last few days if this renovation was the right task for me to undertake."

"But it'll be awesome for Skyfall," said Seckry, trying to be encouraging. "You said yourself that access to the Mechaner's Overhang would bring a lot of tourism."

"It would be fantastic," Sanfarrow agreed. "If it works. It just seems as though everything that could go wrong has gone wrong so far. We've had bits of the thing fall apart, two of my workers have been severely injured, and last week, it blew out the Metroban Bank's electricity. I'm beginning to question if . . . if I am the right man for the job."

"How is Kayne doing?" Seckry asked cautiously.

Sanfarrow closed his eyes and took a deep breath.

"He is starting to go a little stir crazy, as you can imagine. He spends every hour of every day in the room next to us, but he has to. If he left the building, he would be sighted and reported to the Patrol. And . . . even though I've managed to keep them at bay, if enough people report it, they might be left with no option but to arrest him."

Seckry stared at the closed door, still unnerved at the thought of the deformed man behind it.

"He's been asking to see Eiya," Sanfarrow said.

Seckry's stomach lurched, but it didn't come as a surprise.

"I've tried to explain to him that it's highly unlikely she is Elenya," said Sanfarrow. "But . . . I don't know, I think his mind is playing tricks on him. He's convincing himself to believe something improbable without even knowing he's doing it. Of course, I haven't contacted you or Eiya. I don't think him being able to see her will do anyone any good. It would just make him even more crazed."

If Seckry hadn't already been adamant on keeping Eiya away from Kayne, then he was now. He didn't want Eiya within a mile of the undead freak of nature.

"The reason I've come here," said Seckry, changing the

subject, "is to show you this."

Seckry opened the attachment of the dark-veined figure and Sanfarrow examined the screen, carefully.

"Dear Gedin, I daresay this has something to do with the genesis trinity," said Sanfarrow.

Seckry stepped back.

"The genesis trinity? Wait . . . you know about the trinity?"

"I have heard of it, yes, but I know very little, I'm afraid. I mean, I am aware of its existence, and I know that there was a theory at some point in time about it being the beginning of the universe, but we have a different theory today that doesn't involve those elements. Apart from that, I am pretty much clueless."

Seckry looked at the figure on his phone again and it sent shivers down his spine.

"This image was found at Endrin," said Seckry. "What has it got to do with the genesis trinity?"

"Well, Seckry, I'm afraid I can't answer that. Someone was studying the trinity at some point, and I imagine that was one of their diagrams, but that person wasn't me."

"Do you know who the person was?" said Seckry.

"Yes," said Sanfarrow, turning slowly to the adjacent door.

"Kayne?" said Seckry, and Sanfarrow nodded.

Seckry had originally had no intention of speaking with Kayne. He was simply going to get Sanfarrow's opinion and then leave without even saying 'hello' to the sheltered convict. But now, Seckry was reconsidering. If Kayne had been studying the genesis trinity at Endrin, then he may even have information on his dad and Lux.

Sanfarrow said nothing, reading the expression on Seckry's face. He knocked on the door.

"Seckry Sevenstars would like to talk with you, Kevan," he said.

"Let him in," came Kayne's deep reply.

Kayne's room was fairly spacious, which was useful, since the man's strange new form seemed to have grown a little since the last time Seckry had seen him; his hulking body visibly pulsating, and a particularly large muscle bulging out of his shirt, expanding and contracting seemingly out of Kayne's control.

Seckry didn't say anything, because he was unsure how to act around him. Instead, he just held up the phone.

"I haven't seen that image for quite some time," said Kayne's earthy tones. The mutation was obviously affecting his vocal chords too because he was getting deeper and huskier.

Seckry tried not to stare at the hideous defects as Kayne considered the image, but it was hard to ignore them.

"This is one of Adelbert Endoman's designs," said Kayne. "Are you familiar with him?"

"Yes," Seckry said. "Very familiar." He decided not to elaborate.

"Well, you probably know that Adelbert Endoman and Rikard Ringold were the founders of Endrin," said Kayne. "And they were the ones responsible for the infamous lab baby affair."

Seckry nodded, silently.

"This, Seckry, is what the project was truly about. It was about creating human beings infused with elements from the genesis trinity. And this diagram right here, is one of the humans infused with the destructive element, exorophon. Adelbert Endoman worked out beforehand that if the project was successful and the boys lived to see the day, their veins and their eyes would change colour when their powers were in use. Rikard's child, infused with creogen, would gain pure white veins and pure white eyes. Adelbert's child, would gain black ones, just like this."

Seckry turned the phone around and stared at it. It was no wonder it had been giving him the chills. This was a diagram of *Lux*.

"What do you know of the lab babies?" Seckry asked. "Do you know what happened to them?"

"Unfortunately not, I'm afraid," said Kayne. "I was reassigned to another project not long after I began looking into it. All I really have to go on are the same rumours that everyone else within the science community has heard; that Rikard's child locked Adelbert's in the labs and escaped because he thought Adelbert's child had gone mad. Who knows what happened to either of them? Is the one still trapped in those labs? Or did he finally escape?"

Seckry said nothing, motionless.

"Nobody has ever been able to locate the labs, of course," said Kayne. "Although we do know the name of them; Site Origin. For many years, people assumed the site was in Skyfall City somewhere. Somewhere out of sight, possibly underground. But during my short batch of research, I came across some interesting evidence to suggest otherwise."

"Really?" said Seckry. He had never really tried to guess where the labs had been located, but he had assumed that they had been in the city somewhere too, or possibly just outside, which was Vance's assumption.

"I was able to magnify some of the audio recordings that Adelbert and Rikard sent to confidences at the time, and there is a distinct howling of wind, and what could only be . . . snow, or sleet in the background."

"Snow?" said Seckry.

"Yes, as unlikely as it seems, I think Site Origin may have been a very long way away from Skyfall, somewhere far north of here, up in the vastness of the Frostpeak Mountains."

"Wow," said Seckry. "Why do you think they would have located there?"

"My best guess is invisibility. They didn't want to be found, and it was a place no one could interfere with. They seem to have done a good job of hiding themselves too, because I was never able to pinpoint a location. The Frostpeak Mountains are huge. I doubt anyone will ever come across it to be honest. It's a shame, though. I daresay it would be fascinating to find out if Adelbert's child was still alive, living there. And the scientific knowledge that could be acquired from the place would be monumental."

Seckry nodded and made to leave, since he had got all of the information he wanted out of Kayne, but the hideous looking man stopped him by reaching out a tentacle and closing the door gently.

"Before you leave, Seckry, can I ask you a question?"

Seckry gulped.

"Sure," he said.

"Are you . . . a religious person?"

Seckry was a bit taken aback.

"I . . . um . . . I'm still trying to work that out," he said. His mum had never pushed religion down his or Leena's throat, so he hadn't spent much time thinking about the existence of Gedin. In fact, the biggest conclusion he had ever made about Gedin was that he was happy not knowing. Too many wars had been fought over the years on the grounds of Gedin's existence for Seckry to get dragged into the debate.

Finding out that Seckraman, widely believed to be Gedin's son, was actually himself being inadvertently sent backwards in time, obviously affected things in his mind a little. But it still hadn't changed his views to the point that he was certain either way.

"I guess I'm okay with not knowing," Seckry said simply.

Kayne remained motionless, staring at the wall as if he could see something that Seckry couldn't.

"You know, I don't ever remember believing in Gedin," he said. "From as far back as I can recall, my brain just couldn't comprehend the idea of an invisible being or force that looked over us, controlled us. Becoming a scientist only served to enforce that belief. I studied organisms down to the finest detail, and saw nature at work; how things evolve, how human beings have changed over history, how we have originated from more primitive organisms. I've been utterly convinced for forty-seven years that Gedin does not exist, and with Him . . . any form of *afterlife*."

He pulled a small book out of his pocket and dropped it onto the room's single table. It was The Book of Gedin, the complete teachings of The Lord.

"It's amazing," said Kayne, "how a man's beliefs can be warped when he is staring death in the face."

"You mean . . . you're starting to believe?"

"I'm not sure if 'believe' is the correct word," said Kayne. "Belief is a strange concept to me. But the fear of nothingness; of ceasing to exist in any form beyond this brief second life, is terrifying. What I am trying to come to terms with is whether my mind is simply formulating a desperate, false hope; something to mask the formidable horror of non-existence, or . . . or if it is a sign from Gedin; a final message of His love . . . the love that I've rejected and dismissed all of my life until now."

Seckry's phone buzzed in his pocket. It was Cartell. He apologised to Kayne and answered the call.

"Cartell," he said lightly. "How's the clinic going?"

"Excellent, Seckry, excellent," Cartell said excitedly. "I actually have some fantastic news. The helitonium treatment is already working on Eryk Valenkar. I've been working on a device that will allow him to send signals from his brain to a computer that can output his thoughts as text on a screen. I'm going to test it today. I was wondering, if you have no other plans, if you would like to join us here at the guildhouse?"

"I'd love to," said Seckry. He was more than relieved to have an excuse to get out of this place and away from Kayne's morbid thoughts on the nature of existence. Plus, having the opportunity to see Cartell's patient being able to communicate with his father for the first time in years would be genuinely touching.

"Thanks for the information about the diagram," said Seckry, after hanging up. "I really have to go now."

"Of course," said Kayne, letting him open the door freely this time.

Chapter Sixteen

The Cursed Doorknocker

Getting to the Mechaner's Village on a Saturday was even more difficult than when he and Eiya had first ventured there. The monorails were so infrequent that Seckry had to catch a bus, which took a scenic detour around the entire western partition before finally entering the north.

Seckry arrived at the guildhouse feeling relief that he was away from the creepy Kevan Kayne, but there was something about the atmosphere that made Seckry feel like he was being watched.

He hesitated as he reached for the bloodlion doorknocker, because he was once again struck by how lifelike it was. Its eyes were piercing, and the snarling teeth that clenched the metal ring looked ready to bite his hand off. Seckry told himself that his imagination was getting the better of him, and closed his fist around it. But as he did so, there was a deafening crack and a flash of blue light.

Seckry crumpled to his knees in pain.

It was like he had been hit over the head with a hammer. He looked around wildly to spot his attacker, but even through his disorientated vision, he could see there was nobody there. As the ringing in his ears quickly faded, the only sound left around him was the gentle hum of traffic in the distance and a couple of chirrups from nearby birds.

His heart was pounding. Had he had some sort of seizure?

Seckry got to his feet, but nearly stumbled over again from dizziness and weakness. His limbs felt numb, as if he was semi-paralysed. As he used his left hand to steady himself against the doorframe, he winced in pain. He turned his hand over to see a gash gouged into his palm. A drop of fresh blood spotted the porch beneath him.

He stared at his palm, then at the glaring eyes of the doorknocker, then at his palm again.

Had the knocker really done this to him?

Scared of the same thing happening again, Seckry banged his good hand against the bulk of the wooden door, staying well away from the vicious wrath of the bloodlion.

Cartell pulled open the giant door with a smile that quickly disappeared when he saw the state that Seckry was in.

"Good Gedin, are you alright?" he said, reaching out and steadying Seckry, who was still a little dazed and wobbly on his feet.

"Uh . . . I'm . . . not sure to be honest," Seckry said truthfully. "The doorknocker, it . . . it stunned me," Seckry explained, though in truth, he couldn't put the sensation into words.

"You're bleeding," Cartell said. "Quick, come inside."

Luckily, being a doctor, Cartell had more than enough first aid equipment to patch Seckry up.

"It's absolutely bizarre," said Cartell, as he pulled the final thread of stitches through Seckry's palm and tied it tight. Seckry winced in pain. It was the first time he had ever had stitches.

"Luckily it's not that deep," said Cartell. "It looks a lot worse than it is actually is. That still doesn't explain what on earthia happened, though."

"There's something seriously . . . weird about that knocker," said Seckry. "Every time I look at it, it's like it's growling at me or something, like it's somehow . . . alive."

Seckry couldn't believe how silly it sounded, but it really did seem to be the only explanation.

There was a loud knock on the door.

"That'll be Wilbus," said Cartell. "Bear with me one moment, Seckry."

Cartell's footsteps echoed down the long entrance hallway.

"Mr Quinn," Seckry heard Wilbus say. He sounded out of breath.

"Mr Valenkar, are you alright?" said Cartell. "Dear Gedin, not you as well?"

Seckry stood up and rushed to the door.

"Did something happen to you when you touched the doorknocker?" he said.

Wilbus stared at Seckry for a few moments, seemingly dazed. "Yes . . . yes, there was this b-bang to my head . . . as though I was h-hit by something," he stammered.

"Me too!" exclaimed Seckry.

Wilbus lifted his hand, trembling, and a drop of blood dripped to the stone floor from a fresh slash across his knuckles.

"This is unbelievable!" said Cartell.

Without hesitation, Cartell grabbed the knocker himself, swung the ring back and forth, and examined it from all angles. He shook his head, perplexed, before rushing to get Wilbus's wound healed up too.

As Cartell was making sure the wound was clean, he seemed to be debating something in his mind.

"It can't be, surely?" he muttered to himself.

"Can't be what?" asked Seckry.

Cartell was silent for a few moments. "This . . . place . . . this guildhall . . . the guild who used to own this building were the Stonesoldiers."

"The worshippers of the underworld?" said Wilbus, frightened.

Seckry had never even thought to question who the Stonesoldiers were. He had never heard of them before seeing the sign outside the building.

"Well, the common belief is that they were worshippers of an underworld," said Cartell. "But in reality, they were simply a fraternity of mechaners who distanced themselves from the Gedeic religion. They were brandished as heretics, but I mean, I assumed they were simply non-believers; a group of people whose names were being tarnished. I didn't even consider the fact that this place had a history of heresy when I acquired it. I mean, worshipping demons? I'm not the greatest believer in the paranormal."

"And the bloodlion?" said Wilbus. "Was that a common symbol used by the Stonesoldiers?"

"Yes, I think so," said Cartell. "I just remember being impressed by how lifelike the knocker was, the first time I saw it. I didn't think to question its significance. I had someone come and clean the thing up. It was dirty and rusty when I acquired the place, but I didn't want to get rid of such an ornamental piece of craftsmanship. I can assure you, however, that the first thing I will be doing tomorrow morning is having that cursed thing removed. This clinic is supposed to be a place for healing, not maiming. Gedin, I'd kill more patients than heal them with that thing there to greet everybody."

After they were adequately bandaged, Cartell led them into the clinic, still completely baffled by the injuries. As they walked, Cartell assured them he would be looking into the history of the Stonesoldier fraternity that very evening.

When they entered the small clinic portion of the building, Eryk was sat in his wheelchair, being fed by a nurse that Cartell had employed. Eryk's face was pretty much expressionless because of his condition, and he was unable to even move his head or his eyes to focus on them, but as Wilbus entered the room, Seckry thought he saw the flash of a smile behind Eryk's eyes.

"I almost forgot," Wilbus said softly. "Before we activate the machine, there is one thing I know Eryk would love to have close to him."

"Of course," said Cartell. "What is it?"

"It's out in the car. Could you possibly give me a hand? It's a little heavy."

Cartell and Wilbus disappeared, leaving Seckry alone with Eryk, whose whole body began shaking rhythmically, no doubt from nerve damage that had got progressively worse over the years. It was uncomfortable to watch, but only made bearable by the thought that Cartell could one day heal him to some degree.

"Dear Gedin, Wilbus, what on earthia is inside this thing?" Seckry heard Cartell saying, amidst heaves.

The two men re-entered the room, lugging what looked like a giant ottoman that was securely fastened with a padlock.

"It's all of Eryk's most important possessions," said Wilbus.

"Are most of his possessions slabs of lead?" Cartell said light-heartedly. They placed it on the floor with a thud, and Cartell got to work, hooking Eryk up to the machine that would allow him to communicate via text for the first time in years.

When everything was in place, Cartell asked Wilbus if he was ready. It was no use asking Eryk, since he couldn't even nod in his current state.

After a silence in which Seckry thought he heard Wilbus mutter a brief prayer, Cartell activated the machine.

They waited, with baited breath, staring at the green LED screen on the machine.

Then came a single word.

Dad.

Wilbus whimpered and took a hold of his son's hand, squeezing it tightly.

"Yes, Eryk, it's me," he said.

Dad

I can

Talk

Again

Wilbus's eyes were welling up with tears.

"This is just the beginning," said Wilbus. "With the help of this wonderful man in front of us, Mr Cartell Quinn, we may be able to cure you."

Seckry could see the pride and excitement on Cartell's face.

"How do you feel, Eryk?" he said. "Any head pains at the moment, or any pressure in that area?"

I feel

Great

Thank you

Is

They waited for more, but there were no other words.

"Yes, Eryk?" said Wilbus.

Is she
Is Trixa
Okay?

Wilbus swallowed hard and turned his gaze downwards.

"Eryk, I . . . haven't seen her for a long time."

Wilbus turned to Cartell and Seckry and said, "Would it be okay . . . if I had a moment alone with my son?"

"Of course," said Cartell. "Of course."

Seckry followed Cartell out of the room and they waited until Wilbus asked them to come back inside. Eryk looked very weak from the mental strength required to output the text to the machine, so the nurse wheeled him out of the room into a separate area with a bed so that he could recover. Cartell followed in order to make sure Eryk's mind and body hadn't taken any damage during the experiment, leaving Seckry alone with Wilbus.

"It must be a wonderful feeling," said Seckry. "To be able to communicate with your son again."

Wilbus nodded, his eyes still watery.

"As I feared, though, Eryk is still longing for something he cannot have."

"What is it?" Seckry asked.

"The woman he loves," said Wilbus. "Trixa Turnfever was her name. They were together for four years."

"What happened to her?"

"She left him, for reasons I am unaware of."

"Just like that?" said Seckry.

"The thing is," said Wilbus, "Eryk was a normal man when he was with her. He knew he had this condition, but it hadn't started to affect him properly. When it worsened and Eryk lost feeling in his legs, Trixa upped and left."

Seckry felt terrible for Eryk. He couldn't imagine how it would feel to be dropped after becoming disabled.

"It's hard to say if she left because she didn't want the burden of looking after him, or if it was for other reasons."

"Do you think Eryk will ever learn to forget about her?" Seckry asked.

Wilbus smiled kindly.

"Have you ever been in love?"

Seckry stammered for a moment, caught off guard by the question.

"Um . . . yes," he said. "I'm in love right now."

"If she ever left you, do you think you'd be able to forget about her?"

Seckry tried to imagine a life without Eiya, but he couldn't. He would never be able to forget Eiya, no matter what happened.

"When you're truly in love," said Wilbus, "you never forget that person, and you never stop loving them, no matter what they do, or how much they hurt you."

"And Eryk hasn't seen her since the day she left?" asked Seckry.

"Not a word from her," said Wilbus. "I imagine she still lives in Skyfall somewhere, but we haven't seen her since. In truth, I don't know what has been killing Eryk more - his condition, or losing the woman he loves. You know, he kept everything she ever gave him, every card, every gift, and everything that even reminded him of her."

"Wow," said Seckry. "Does he still have them now?"

Wilbus turned and placed his hand on the large, padlocked, heavy ottoman. "Yes," he said. "They're right here beside him."

After Cartell had returned to tell them that Eryk was doing fine, Wilbus wanted to spend more time alone with his son. Seckry was ready to head back to the flat at that point, but his bus didn't arrive for another half hour.

"Want to see something spectacular while you're waiting?" said Cartell. "The Mechaner's Overhang is just around the corner."

"Sure," said Seckry. Leena had wanted him to take some photographs from the Overhang at some point, so this was as good a time as any.

Cartell shuffled on a tweed jacket and a scarf and led Seckry out into the crisp air, giving the doorknocker a suspicious glance as they left.

"Before I moved here, I never knew that this big, dirty city could look so beautiful," he said. "The view is stunning. You'll see exactly what I mean in a moment."

But as they turned the corner onto the path that led up to the Overhang, they were met with an unexpected sight. The entrance was bustling with Patrol officers and vehicles, flashing lights blinding their eyes.

Patrol tape barred off any access through.

"Sorry, no gawping at the view today, my friends," said a Patrol woman, firmly. "There's been an incident."

"An incident?" said Cartell.

"Part of the overhang has collapsed."

"Gedin, was anybody hurt?"

"Luckily not," said the officer. "As far as we know, anyhow."

"Any idea what caused it?" asked Seckry.

"We're looking into it. It may well be that the weight of it was finally too much, although there does seem to be some evidence of human interference, and a few of the residents around here say they heard angry yelling moments before the collapse."

"So that's what that noise was," said Cartell. "I remember hearing this low rumble shortly before you arrived, Seckry. I didn't think much of it at the time."

"Unfortunately," said the officer, "the tree that shelters the overhang was dragged over with it, and it hit the under-construction monorail track underneath, sending a lot of it crashing to the ground. Again, no one was hurt, but it did cause a lot of damage to industrial property."

"*Sanfarrow's track*," said Seckry. "He's going to be mortified."

Sanfarrow already seemed stressed enough as it was with the whole project. This set back was going to send him over the edge.

A male officer passed them and clambered into one of the vans, holding a cellophane bag that contained a large, broken syringe, wet with bright green liquid.

Something told Seckry that this wasn't simply a case of the

Overhang's weight causing it to collapse.

Chapter Seventeen

An Echo

The following few weeks were fairly uneventful in comparison to everything that had happened over the first couple of the new school year. Seckry's hand healed, and even though Cartell was now convinced that the injuries had to have been something to do with a curse made by the Stonesoldiers, he could find no mention of curses or enchantments on doorknockers, and neither could Seckry, even though he had done his own fair share of internet searching and library browsing. Cartell had since had the knocker removed and destroyed, despite it being worth an estimated seven thousand notes, and had replaced it with a simple, electronic bell.

As expected, Sanfarrow had been devastated by the news of the Overhang hitting the track. Seckry had phoned him the day after and the man had almost been in tears on the phone.

Seckry was anxious to find out what had caused the collapse, but nothing appeared on the news. The only information Seckry could get out of anyone was a rumour that there had been a spat between two rival gangs from rough districts either side of the Mechaner's Village. Seckry wouldn't have usually been so suspicious, but the image of that syringe with the bright green liquid had stuck in his mind ever since.

At Estergate, Seckry and Eiya were just about able to keep on top of their schoolwork, even though ancient history and anthropology seemed to be significantly more difficult than last year, and with homework at a manageable level as of the moment, Seckry was even able to fit in a few games of Friction with the rest of the Eidolons.

Gavanis and Zovak seemed to have settled right in, and had made friends with their own individual groups, much to Seckry's distaste. Nobody was more annoyed than Tippian, though, who was still offended by Zovak's arrogance, and who had been working extra hard on his voice changing device, determined that it would win the Young Inventor Award and prove the Norsegate sleazeball wrong.

In fact, Tippian had been working so hard on the device that he had become distant once again, and the group were beginning to worry about him, until one morning in the courtyard, when he arrived to school with eyes brimming with excitement.

"The Fearless Funfair is coming to Skyfall!" he yelled.

Tenk gripped Tippian by the shoulders.

"What did you say?" he demanded.

"You heard me, Tenk, it's coming to Skyfall at last! It's coming next month!"

"The Superdragon Three Thousand," said Tenk, releasing his grip and staring at the ground, lost in his own imagination. "I've waited years for this thing."

"What is it?" asked Seckry.

"It's a rollercoaster," explained Tippian.

"Mate," said Tenk, "the Superdragon Three Thousand is not just a rollercoaster. I've heard people describe it as a 'journey of epic proportions.'"

"A travelling fair has a rollercoaster?" said Seckry. As far as he knew, travelling fairs brought with them the usual carousels and dodgems, but he thought that rollercoasters were generally found in stationary theme parks.

"The Fearless Funfair is the exception to the rule, man," said Tenk. "Even though it's a travelling one, the Superdragon is classed as, like, the third best rollercoaster in the world. I've seen, like, hundreds of clips on the internet of it, it looks absolutely insane."

"I guess I already know the answer to my next question, then," said Tippian. "I'll get us all tickets on the weekend and you can give me the money."

Tenk slapped Tippian on the back, and nothing more was needed to be said. Seckry couldn't wait. It had been years since he had been to a fair, and the little ones that passed through the fields around Marne when he was growing up had been pretty tame.

That day, they had another lesson of fringe science with Mr Vance, which just topped off everyone's good mood, because they were now soldering things together and actually trying out designs for their teleportation device, and the class was alive with anticipation for when they would get one working.

When the final bell rang at the end of the day, the class were once again reluctant to leave, and Vance had to gently pry a soldering iron out of one boy's hand because he wouldn't let go. Eiya decided to head to the library for a bit to do a bit of reading on Elenya Kayne, so Tenk invited Seckry over to his flat for the evening to play some video games.

"Your mum isn't going to give us . . . um . . . any more of that . . . um . . . porridge, is she?" Seckry asked, trying not to offend anyone.

"Don't worry man," said Tenk. "We'll get a bag of chips from The Eastern FryFest on the way back. I told my mum you lot had bad stomachs afterwards because you must all be wheat intolerant, so she won't try to shovel that cement down your throats any more. I did try convincing her that I was wheat intolerant too but her reply was a thump around the head and 'don't you bloody try that on me.'"

Seckry relaxed, relieved.

"Oh, and you can meet my brother, too."

"Longo?" said Seckry. "I see Longo all the time."

"No, Raymus," said Tenk. "Remember? My eldest brother. He's been away at university in Bellaran. He's coming back for a whole year before going on to study for a VhP master degree in Cell Biology."

In truth, Seckry had almost forgotten that Tenk had another brother. He rarely heard Tenk, or the rest of them, mention him.

"Be warned, though, my mum is in a foul mood at the moment," Tenk said grimly. "Me and Longo have been beating each other up every day and she keeps saying she's sick of it and she's had enough."

"You guys *do* fight a lot," said Seckry.

"Well, it's him that starts it," said Tenk. "It's like, we're sitting at the table eating, and then all of sudden he'll kick my leg out of nowhere, and then when I throw a punch at him, it ends up being my fault."

When they arrived at Tenk's, they found that Raymus had only just arrived and was hugging his mum, with a huge trekking backpack still strapped to his back. He was even lankier than Tenk, and had the same, spiky, black hair.

"Gedin, it's so good to see you, love," Tenk's mum said as she hugged him. "Tenk, go and get Longo, will you? Tell him Ray's arrived."

Seckry followed Tenk as he entered Longo's room, but as soon as they stepped inside, Longo thrust his foot out and tripped Tenk up, causing him to smack his head on the bedstead. Tenk roared with anger and launched at Longo, sending them both smashing into a cabinet and knocking several things out of it, one of which smashed.

"Right!" yelled their mum, storming into the bedroom. "You can't even be civilised for your own brother on the day he comes back from uni. I've absolutely had enough!"

"Yeah, come on, boys," said Raymus. "Show mum a bit of respect. You have no idea how hard she works for us. The least you can do is behave around the house."

"They don't listen to a word I say anymore, Ray. They're like animals. Maybe you can teach them how to behave properly now that you're back, because I can't cope anymore."

"I know I used to fight with you guys when we were younger, too," said Raymus, "but we all should have grown out of it by now. When you guys move out and have to fend for yourselves, you'll understand, just like I did, how it's important to be responsible and treat people the way you want to be treated."

"Thank Gedin one of my children has a little bit of sense," said their mum.

Tenk and Longo got up from the floor, feebly.

"Sorry, mum," said Tenk.

"Yeah, sorry," said Longo. "It won't happen again."

"See, that's all they needed," said Raymus. "A little bit of common sense from their older brother."

When their mum had left the room, Raymus plonked his backpack down on Tenk's bed and began unzipping it.

"What you got?" asked Tenk. "A present for us?"

"You could say that," said Raymus, pulling out a small fire extinguisher.

"What's that fo-" said Tenk, but was cut off as Raymus aimed the nozzle at Tenk's face and blasted him, sending him flying backwards. Raymus continued to unleash the extinguisher, swinging its aim at Longo, sending him tumbling into the washing basket, then at Seckry, who dived for cover under Tenk's desk.

"Ha ha ha!" Raymus screamed.

"No way!" yelled Tenk. "You filthy liar! What about everything you just said to mum?"

"You really believed all of that crip?" said Raymus. "Geez, Tenk, when did you become so gullible. Longo obviously ain't doing the job of being an older brother properly. Well your big, *big* bro is back and he's gonna teach you both a lesson or two."

Suddenly, Tenk's mum burst into the room and Raymus threw the extinguisher at Tenk, who caught it.

"Mum! I told them not to go near it but they wouldn't listen!" cried Raymus. "They're even worse than I thought. It's like they've become feral!"

"I don't believe you guys!" Tenk's mum screamed. "After everything that your brother just said to you? Are you freakin' kidding me?"

"But . . . mum . . . it was . . . it was-" Tenk was waving a weak finger at Raymus, but his mum's glare told them that she wasn't going to believe a word that came out of his mouth.

Seckry couldn't believe Raymus had just done that, and

neither could Tenk, evidently.

"Looks like it's gonna take more than a talk to discipline these guys," said Raymus.

"I'm leaving them to you," Tenk's mum said finally. "Do what you want with them. I'm at my bleedin' wit's end."

As she left the room, Raymus leaned in closer to them.

"It's gonna be a fun year, boys," he said with a grin, before grabbing the extinguisher back and blowing another quick plume of smoke into their faces.

That night, Seckry returned to the flat to find Eiya lost in her own thoughts, solemn and unwilling to talk much. He tried to cheer her up, unsure as to what was wrong, but she decided to head to bed early.

Not long after Seckry had fallen asleep, he was jolted awake by the sound of Eiya sobbing. She was sat up in bed, cradling her face in her small fingers.

"Eiya, what's wrong?" Seckry said, concerned.

"Nothing, it's okay," she said, wiping away some of the wetness with her quilt. "I just . . . I had one of your memories come through again. And it was really powerful this time. Like, *really* powerful. The strongest and most vivid of the lot."

"Really? What was it?" Seckry had never seen her so affected by one of these strange recollections before.

"I was looking out, at like, some sort of big picture or landscape or something. It was around midday I think, and it was like, I knew someone was standing behind me, someone really important, and I couldn't bear to turn around for some reason, I was just frozen to this spot, looking straight ahead, and getting completely overwhelmed by all of these conflicting emotions. There was some kind of massive shape in front of me. It was . . . a word, disjointed somehow, but definitely a word. It was . . . the word 'echo.'"

"Echo?" said Seckry, racking his brain. As hard as he tried, he couldn't remember ever seeing a giant word 'echo.'

"I don't know who the person standing behind me was," Eiya continued, "but there was just all these strange feelings overtaking me. The person really meant something to me, but I don't know what it was. Just that they were really important, and . . . I loved them so much. The next thing I know, I've woken up in tears." She laughed at the ridiculousness of it. "What on earthia is that memory of, Seck? And who was standing behind you?"

Seckry was silent, staring at Eiya's tearful face.

"Eiya," he said gravely. "I have no recollection of that at all. That's . . . *not my memory.*"

Chapter Eighteen

The Wedding

They were both silent for a long time, searching each other's eyes, not daring to say what was beginning to creep into their minds.

Eventually Eiya said, "Seck . . . you don't . . . you don't think . . . ?"

Seckry laughed, but there was no humour in it.

"You mean . . . that the memory was from . . . Kayne's wife?"

"I never even considered it before now, but . . ."

"Eiya, it's impossible," said Seckry, determined not to get carried away. "Sanfarrow explained everything to us. You were made from my subconscious by the helitonium in the Cultivation Unit. There's no way you could be a reincarnation of Elenya. How would you explain all the joint memories we've had so far?"

"I don't know," said Eiya. "But . . . how do we explain this one?"

Seckry didn't have an answer. The memory certainly wasn't his. They were going to have to speak to Ropart Sanfarrow once again to get to the bottom of it. And, even though Seckry wanted nothing more to do with Kevan Kayne, he had no doubt that they were going to have to speak to him too.

That weekend, Seckry phoned Sanfarrow and arranged to meet at the crossing, and in spite of Seckry's fears of Eiya being within the same vicinity as Kayne, he knew she would need to come along to recall the dream exactly to the both of them.

When they arrived, the first thing Seckry noticed was that Sanfarrow's clean look was starting to fade, and he was beginning to resemble the unstable man he and Eiya had found sheltering in an underground lair last year. The stubble he'd been sporting a couple of weeks ago was now halfway to being a bushy beard, and judging by the faint odour of old socks in the room, he hadn't had a bath for quite some time.

"Four months," he said despairingly. "Four months of construction down the drain."

"Wow, did it really do that much damage?" said Eiya.

"It tore down half of the structure," said Sanfarrow.

"Do they have any more information about what, or who, caused it?" asked Seckry. "Me and Cartell saw a Patrol officer walking past with a massive syringe in a cellophane bag as evidence."

"Well, as far as I'm aware, the syringe was full of some kind of drug, and the whole thing is assumed to have been a clash between rival gangs on either side of the Mechaner's District. Both gangs are denying it of course."

Suddenly, the blinds began to close on the large window behind Sanfarrow.

"Kayne's coming out of his room," said Sanfarrow. "Do you still wish to stay?"

"Yes," said Eiya. "We need to talk to you about something. Both of you."

When Kayne emerged, he paused, his eyes locked on Eiya's.

"Seckry, Eiya," he said. "This is a nice surprise."

Neither Seckry nor Eiya said anything in return, and Kayne took a seat next to Sanfarrow at his desk.

"Anyway," said Sanfarrow. "I wasn't expecting to see you both so soon again. Not that you're not welcome, of course, I'm happy to share the track's progress with you, though I doubt it is the most riveting of information for a couple of teenagers. What did you want to ask us?"

Eiya paused for a moment, unsure of how to begin.

"You know I've been having some crossover memories with Seckry, where I can remember some of the things that have happened to him, as if they had happened to me?"

"Yes," said Sanfarrow, his expression serious.

"Well . . . last night, I experienced one of these memories, but . . . but Seckry has no recollection of it."

Kayne slowly leaned forward in his seat, the plastic cracking and stretching under the weight of his increasingly monstrous body.

"In the memory there's this big word ahead of me," said Eiya, "and I'm sure it's the word 'echo.' I'm staring at it, and . . . and it's like I know there's someone really important behind me and all these emotions are overwhelming me. It's like I really want to turn around and see who's behind me, but I'm so ecstatic and so petrified both at the same time, that I'm almost frozen, just staring at this big, massive 'echo.'"

Sanfarrow and Kayne looked at each other for a long time before Sanfarrow turned to Eiya and said, "That word 'echo,' do you think it could be part of a larger word, and you are just staring at a portion of it?"

"Possibly, yes," said Eiya. "It is kind of broken up, like, disjointed somehow."

Seckry could see Kayne's blood pumping fast through the inflamed muscles in his chest, and the intensity that was creeping into his facial expression.

"Eiya," said Kayne, and Seckry could see the distaste in his face at the act of calling the person he believed to be his wife by a different name. "For our wedding, Elenya and I hired a marquee from a company named Sechonia. Their logo was printed quite largely across it. Do you think the word 'echo' could have actually been the word Sechonia, obstructed on either side by something?"

Eiya thought for a moment.

"Yes," she said softly. "It very well could have been."

Kayne disappeared into his side room and reappeared a moment later with a rusty looking suitcase, which he dropped heavily onto Sanfarrow's desk. He clicked it open and began rummaging frantically through what seemed to be heaps of old photographs, before singling one out and smoothing it out on the desk.

Seckry and Eiya moved in close to examine it. The image showed a sunny day with flowers everywhere. It looked beautiful. Elenya was standing, talking to someone, and just behind her, facing away from her, was Kayne, a glass of champagne in one hand. On the far right was the Sechonia logo, half obscured by the wedding cake on the left, and half obscured by flowers on the right, making the visible letters 'choni.'

"Standing where Elenya was standing at that point," said Kayne. "Can you see how easy it would have been for this word to have read 'echo?'"

Seckry wished he could have argued, but . . . Kayne was right.

"Eiya, that memory is of our wedding day," said Kayne. "It was the most beautiful day of both of our lives. Eiya, the person standing behind you, the person that is overwhelming you with emotion . . . is *me*."

Seckry couldn't comprehend what he was hearing.

Kayne suddenly began trembling, and the deformed tentacles that were growing out of his body were writhing uncontrollably.

"Elenya," Kayne said to Eiya in barely more than a whisper. "Elenya, I've missed you."

Eiya backed away, petrified, her eyes wobbling with tears.

Seckry felt sick. How could this be possible?

"Kevan, please," said Sanfarrow, "I need time to look into this. We cannot come to any conclusions right now."

Something snapped within Kayne then, and he shoved the chair from underneath him.

"This is my wife we're talking about!" he roared at Sanfarrow.

"Kevan!" Sanfarrow shouted. "You're terrifying the poor girl. She's a teenager, for crying out loud." He turned to Seckry and Eiya. "I think it's best that you both leave for the time being so that I can research this more." He ushered them to the exit, hastily.

As Seckry was leaving, he turned to Sanfarrow and said, "This . . . can't be true, can it?"

Sanfarrow shook his head apologetically.

"It's very bizarre, I can assure you. But . . . There's no denying that that memory seems incredibly close to the wedding. I mean, if anyone should know, it should be me. I was Kevan's best man. Elenya was nervous and excited that day. The emotions that Eiya is describing match what I remember of Elenya on the wedding day exactly."

"But . . . it doesn't make sense," Seckry said. "Eiya's had other visions before which have come from *my* memories, I'm sure of it."

"What were the other memories?" asked Sanfarrow. "I didn't even think to question them at the time."

"The first one was of fields of ellonberries, and of finding a cat out in the fields. I grew up in Marne. We were out in the fields every day."

"Oh, Gedin," said Sanfarrow, his face grim. "Do you know where Elenya spent the first six years of her life?" Sanfarrow asked.

Seckry said nothing.

"It was Rithbarrow, just east of Marne. She would have played in those same fields. She could very easily have had a similar memory of finding a cat."

"But," Seckry said, dread filling his stomach. "There was another one . . . she had a vision of being in school and a teacher breaking her chair and a clock falling on her head. Elenya can't have had the same experience . . . surely?"

"Gedin, Seckry, I don't know. I'm so sorry. There is a possibility I may have been wrong in my first theory of you creating Eiya. I think we may just have to accept the fact that Eiya . . . could possibly be Elenya in some form."

Seckry barely slept over the next few nights. Everything he thought he knew about Eiya's existence had somehow been obliterated.

What was more disturbing was the idea that Elenya had to have been reincarnated for a reason, and that reason was probably to be Kayne's wife once again. The thought of Eiya being in love with someone else made Seckry's stomach cripple up with cramps.

Eiya spent most of the next few days doing more research on Elenya Kayne, and with every new bit of information, her face began to look more worrisome.

"Seck, this is why I've seemed upset . . . even before I had that vision . . . just the possibility of me being Elenya made me feel sick. The stuff I've found out about her at the library makes me want to vomit. She helped him, you know?"

"Who?" said Seckry.

"Darklight. She helped him get to the top. She knew about his plans for Project Suffer and she helped him. Before he turned against them all, Elenya was one of his biggest supporters. How can I ever have been someone who would condone such a thing?"

Seckry had no idea.

"Eiya, even if . . . even if you were Elenya in some form or another," he said. "You're not her now. You're Eiya, right?" He was saying it to convince himself as much as to convince her.

"I'm Eiya," Eiya said, but her eyes were still glazed over, her mind far, far away.

The following morning, Seckry had a phonecall from Sanfarrow.

"Seckry, I know this is all very confusing for everyone involved right now," he said, "so I am creating a test that will decisively identify whether Eiya's particles originated from your subconscious, or Elenya's dead body. Please, for now, try not to become consumed by stress. You have enough work to do at school. I will inform you of the results as soon as I get them."

"How will you be able to do that?" asked Seckry.

"I will take a sample of Eiya's blood, if that is alright with her, and I will also take a sample from Elenya Kayne's skeleton."

Seckry shuddered at the thought of having to dig up a dead body.

"Yes, it's an unpleasant thing, I can assure you," said Sanfarrow. "It would be unpleasant opening anyone's coffin to take a sample, but it will be even harder in that it is the coffin of someone I have known for many years."

"Where is she kept?" asked Seckry.

"The Blossom Hill cemetery in the west partition," said Sanfarrow. "When we found out that Darklight had buried her in the Endrin compound, we excavated her body immediately and gave her a proper burial."

Seckry thanked Sanfarrow and hung up, getting a tiny bit of satisfaction at the idea of a definitive answer. But as much as Seckry tried to keep an open mind, deep down, he already knew what the results were going to show; that Eiya, the girl he was in love with, was another man's wife.

Chapter Nineteen

The Burrowbeetle

Seckry spent the next few days in a kind of daydream, mulling everything over and over and never getting anywhere. He even managed to turn up to school one morning wearing two ties, one on top of the other, and couldn't remember putting either of them on, since he had been so consumed in his own thoughts as he had been getting dressed. He hurriedly undid the knot of the outer tie as soon as he realised, and stuffed it into his backpack, feeling embarrassed.

"Don't worry, man," said Tenk. "A couple of years ago when I was still half asleep one morning before school, I put on two pairs of trousers, one on top of the other, and I only realised when I got to the entrance. That's way worse than two ties."

"What?" said Seckry. "Didn't you feel the first pair on your legs as you were pulling the other ones over them?"

"Mate, I'm telling you, it was like I was still dreaming or something. Me and Longo had eaten, like, a load of cheese before bed the night before to see who could have the worst nightmares, but I just felt really out of it in the morning. The point I'm trying to make is, nobody even noticed. Even though my legs were noticeably thicker, nobody even took a second look. People are too busy thinking about themselves to care."

Tippian leaned closer to Seckry and whispered, "*He still doesn't know that for three weeks afterwards he was known as Two Trouser Tenk.*"

Over the next couple of weeks, the only thing that made

Seckry's life bearable was his growing conviction that Eiya was determined to be Eiya now, no matter who she had been in her past life. It had taken a lot of internal persuading, but Seckry had finally come around to the idea that Eiya having been Elenya changed nothing, and that she was still the same person he knew and loved.

After Eiya had given Sanfarrow a blood sample, it took her a while to regain her usual perky personality too, but eventually, thoughts of Elenya Kayne began to slip out of both of their minds while they waited for the results, and school life consumed them once more.

One day, to treat Eiya, Seckry took her to Softspoon's Bakery, to buy her whatever they were selling that had teraflower in it; whatever they had been smelling on the rooftop of the flats for the past couple of months. But when they enquired, the woman behind the counter looked confused.

"We don't sell anything with teraflower in it," she said blankly.

Now that Seckry and Eiya were inside the shop, the place did smell of lovely, warm, fresh bread, but they had to admit that they couldn't smell teraflower.

"Bear with me," said the woman, "I'll just check with Mrs Softspoon, in case I'm mistaken."

The place went silent for a few minutes as she disappeared into the back, before returning with a plump old woman with a scorn on her face.

Mrs Softspoon removed her baking gloves and placed them on the counter.

"Who told you we were using teraflower in our cooking?" she said accusatorially.

"Um . . ." said Seckry, scared by her tone of voice.

"Nobody," said Eiya. "We could just smell it. It smelled delicious."

There was another long silence.

"There was a woman who used to work here many years ago who brought her own special teraflower tart recipe," said Mrs Softspoon. "They were truly something, those mini tarts.

Best in the city, many of our customers used to say. We'd have people coming from all four partitions just for those things. But she . . . stopped working here, and she took the recipe with her."

"Oh," said Eiya. "Do you know where the woman went? Did she set up her own bakery somewhere else?"

"It . . . it's not something I want to discuss, I'm sorry," said Mrs Softspoon. "She doesn't work here anymore and we don't have the recipe so we're trying our best to relaunch the bakery with our new range. Is there anything you two would like to buy?"

Seckry and Eiya could tell that Mrs Softspoon didn't want to be pressed about it so they bought some chocolate and marmalade pastries and left swiftly.

As they were leaving, they heard the assistant whisper to Mrs Softspoon, "They're definitely clean, the machines. The smell of those tarts must just be ingrained into them."

Seckry and Eiya visited the rooftop quite a few times after that, wondering if they had just imagined the smell of teraflower that one time, but sure enough, the smell was as pungent and delicious as ever, making them wonder if the woman had set up a rival bakery somewhere close that they couldn't quite locate.

Even though they really fancied a teraflower tart, the rest of the selection in the bakery was delicious in its own right, and Seckry and Eiya visited a couple more times over the following few weeks, tasting each and every one of its pastries and pies. Mrs Softspoon grew kinder towards them every time they went in, and was very appreciative of the business, although one day, they found her on the phone to the council, complaining.

When she hung up, she sighed with exasperation.

"The building next door is empty," she said. "Has been for years. But some drunk, homeless guy is squatting in there and making a racket, singing at the top of his voice every night. I can't sleep with the noise. He does it in the day sometimes, too, and I'm sure he's putting off customers. Times are hard enough as it is. The council are going to ring me back about removing him."

The phone suddenly rang, and Seckry and Eiya decided to leave Mrs Softspoon to it, but couldn't hear a sound from the building next door as they walked past.

"The burrowbeetle," said Miss Butterkins, the following morning, which was bright and fresh and full of autumn crispness, "is one of the rarer species of beetle in our northern continent of Nakaria, and has been dwindling in population over the last decade due to a disease known as B-SAV Seven Two Four."

"But Miss!" one girl cried out, pulling her shirt up over her nose. "I don't wanna catch a disease!"

"Don't worry, Helly, the disease is not zoonotic, meaning it cannot pass to humans. However, burrowbeetles can give you nasty sting, so be careful!"

Butterkins handed a beetle to each and every pupil, and Seckry flinched a little as his started flapping violently between his fingers.

"Remember to hold them firmly by the tail!" she roared.

"Miss!" someone shouted. "Tobie's trying to stick a burrowbeetle down Lawra Fynn's top!"

Butterkins grabbed the offending pupil and yanked him into the air by his collar. She looked like she was on the verge of snapping the boy's neck, but luckily, only gave him a verbal warning.

Ms Butterkins, the pathology teacher, was not your average member of staff. It was only at the end of last year that Seckry and Eiya had learned that she had been living on the streets, homeless, until Mr Gobbledee had saved her from being attacked, and sent her to live with his sister while he did a stint of time in prison.

This explained a lot.

Butterkins' time on the streets had given her a quality that meant that you never quite knew if she was going to hug you or beat you to death, and she struggled slightly with determining what was and what wasn't normal social conduct.

She had been suspended from her job twice in the past; once for raising her fist to a misbehaving pupil, and another time for making a pupil drink wart ox urine as a punishment for bullying.

The remainder of the lesson was spent trying to get corks onto the burrowbeetles' stingers, then studying their exoskeletons for patterns that exposed if they were diseased or healthy, and by the time lunchtime came around, Seckry was starving, since he had exerted a tremendous amount of energy trying to catch his burrowbeetle when it had spread its wings and started buzzing around the classroom with the cork still attached.

As they queued up for a seat at the conveyor belt, Tenk did his ritual check of the Ultimate Crazy Crane machine to see if the Notorious was still there, and a couple of other pupils behind them followed suit. Ever since the Notorious had been spotted, the entire school seemed to be eager to see if some unfortunate, naïve newbie would be gullible enough to pop a coin in and have a go. Luckily, no one had taken it yet, since almost everyone now knew about the revolting capsule, but Seckry guessed that it was only a matter of time before some poor first year would turn up with no knowledge of what it was, and mistake the bubbling brown stuff inside the clear sphere for chocolate.

After a delicious seven chilli burger and chips, Seckry happily tucked into a marrowmallow dessert, but nearly spat it out when a high pitched squeal of despair rang out from the other side of the canteen.

He turned around to see a live burrowbeetle suddenly shoot into the air and buzz around wildly, flicking its tail aggressively.

The canteen exploded into uproar. Pupils were dive bombing over tables and ducking for cover, food was splattering everywhere, and one kid was scrambling up one of the indoor pipes.

"That thing was under a salad leaf!" screamed the girl who had unwittingly released it.

"Order! Order!" shouted one of the dinner ladies, but it

had no effect.

Seckry craned his neck to see where the burrowbeetle had wandered, but had to dive for cover when it zoomed past his head, its low-hanging stinger just inches away from his face.

Finally, it landed on a window above them, tapping the glass with its tail and trying to feel for a way out.

Putting his long limbs to use, Tenk climbed onto a chair, stretched out, placed his cap slowly over the bug, slid a dirty plate underneath it, then released the thing out of one of the open windows. A couple of cheers were thrown his way.

The canteen staff, who were now looking very embarrassed and ashamed at their carelessness, were trying to calm the screaming girl down.

The canteen emptied after that, and most of the pupils left their food on half, scared that some other bugs would be hiding in their salad, or cooked into a pie. The next day, Gobbledee announced that he would be looking very carefully into the hygiene standards of the kitchens, and that nothing like that would ever happen again.

Over the course of the next two weeks, despite Gobbledee's inspection, there were another two incidents involving bugs in pupils' food, and the headmaster was getting angrier by the day. Eventually, an external hygiene enforcement company descended upon the school to rinse the canteen out, and two dinner ladies lost their jobs.

Seckry did feel bad for them, but something had to be done to stop more incidents occurring before a pupil got seriously sick. He was also, for the first time, considering switching to bringing a packed lunch.

"Do you think it's someone playing a joke?" said Seckry to Tenk one lunchtime, examining the spaghetti hanging from his fork with precision before putting it into his mouth.

Tenk shrugged, shoving half a burger into his. If there was one person that wasn't letting the insect invasion stop him from enjoying his meals, it was Tenk.

"If it is, it's not a very funny one," he said, muffled through his bap. "And these domes are alarm triggered anyway so no pupils can tamper with them. You'd have to be a genius to get past the alarms to sneak bugs in. No, it's just the kitchens man, these dinner ladies need to be trained. I bet they've been taking scraps of lettuce from the animal supplies to cut costs, and that's how all this has happened."

Seckry ate his forkful of spaghetti, but found himself imagining he was chewing worms instead of pasta, and couldn't shake the image out of his head.

Around two weeks later, Seckry noticed a large patch of mould growing on the left wall of the canteen, and reported it to one of the kitchen staff, but they told him they'd been trying to scrub it away for days and it wouldn't disappear. Within three days the mould had doubled in size and was starting to let off a foul, musty smell.

"Guys, we packed-lunching it, starting tomorrow, or what?" said Tenk. "Even I'm fed up of this."

The rest of the group nodded, and Seckry was relieved. The canteen had gone downhill fast, and the thought of eating in there any longer made him feel queasy.

"Enjoy your last hot meal," said Tenk.

They ate reluctantly in silence, until Tippian muttered, "That guy makes me sick," and they realised he was glaring at Zovak, who was once again entertaining a group of girls a couple of seats away. "The girls are *still* all over him. I don't understand it. It's not like he's the new boy anymore, he's been here for months now. The guy's a total geek."

"Tipp, you're a total geek as well," said Tenk.

"I know, that's what I *mean*," said Tippian. "Why aren't they all over me too? What's that guy got that I haven't?"

"Gedin, that's Linzy Sweetcrust too," said Tenk. "Look at her."

Linzy Sweetcrust was the golden girl of Estergate Institute. She was envied by most of the girls, adored by most of the boys, and even had most of the teachers wrapped around her little finger. Seckry was sure the boys were just being blinded by the bright blondeness of her hair, or hypnotised by its myriad of intricate waves and curls, because he could see right through her saccharine façade, and he didn't like what he saw. In fact, Seckry had never even attempted to speak to her, and she had never shown any interest in speaking to him. The most interaction he had ever had with her was when she had glared at him once for brushing past her in a crowded corridor and displacing a portion of her immaculately styled hair.

"Your glasses are really cool," they heard Linzy saying in a sickly sweet voice. "Can I try them on?"

Zovak and the group of girls giggled as Linzy did a selection of poses wearing Zovak's specs.

"That girl would probably spit in my face if I offered her my glasses to try on," said Tippian, looking more jealous by the second.

"They're only all over him because he's something different," said Eiya, trying her best to make Tippian feel better. "Even though he's been here for a few months, he's still newer than everyone else."

"Yeah, but . . . I mean, back me up here guys, I gotta be better looking than him, right?" said Tippian, clutching at straws.

"Well . . ." said Tenk, hesitantly. Tenk wasn't the most tactful of people at the best of times, so Seckry was relieved that Loca cut in.

"Don't worry Tipps," she said jokingly, "you're a stud. And I mean, if those girls find a guy attractive who probably sprays them with sweat every time he turns his head and has more craters on his face than the surface of the moon, then I wouldn't want their attention anyway."

Tippian spent the remainder of lunchtime peering at Zovak from behind his bowl of soup, as if he believed it was somehow concealing his face, and Seckry couldn't help but watch the boy from a distance as well. It *was* fairly odd that he was getting so much adoration.

But as they were staring, Zovak shovelled a load of food into his mouth and then the girls around him began screaming.

Zovak's grin faded very slowly as everyone in the canteen

turned to face him. Seckry had no idea what was happening at first, until he saw something flicking around Zovak's mouth. Some kind of worm . . . or tail.

Zovak's eyes widened in horror as he looked downwards at the thing poking out of his mouth, then he heaved and spat out his mouthful of food, which included a giant mumprat that darted across the table, kicking cutlery everywhere in a frenzy, and scuttling into a narrow gap in the wall near some pipes.

Zovak vomited onto his plate and the girls fled from him, screaming even louder than before.

A few moments later, the headmaster appeared, his face bright red with anger.

"Right!" Gobbledee roared, as he strode into the canteen. "This canteen is officially closed! I have no other option than to shut the place down, since the standards of hygiene are evidently getting worse by the day, despite our best efforts to resolve the situation. Everyone, please make your way to the plaza! Your food today will be on the house."

Gobbledee tapped a code into a panel on the wall, assumedly deactivating the invisible barrier that prevented pupils from stealing.

Seckry was just as disgusted as everyone else at the thought of the hygiene in the kitchens, but he couldn't help but feel a little pleasure in the fact that, out of everyone, it was Zovak who had been the ultimate unlucky one. Seckry had never seen someone look so disgusted, so shocked, and so utterly humbled in all his life.

Chapter Twenty

Eidolons Forever

After that, Gobbledee stuck to his word, and the canteen was closed down until things were completely sorted out. It was the first time Seckry had switched to bringing a packed lunch, and he was enjoying the novelty of it. The only downside was that the autumn air was getting chillier by the day, so sitting outside in the grassy central plaza to eat wasn't as pleasant as he'd hoped.

As the weeks went by, Seckry and the others began training three times a week for the upcoming Mega Meltdown, since it would be upon them before they knew it. Since everything with Eiya possibly being Elenya in her past life, Seckry's mind had been clouded, but as soon as he was back in a Friction pod, running around the vast landscape of the digital world of Atoria, he felt truly happy and excited once more.

Despite being elated to be back training, their sessions this year were hindered by around half an hour every time while they waited for Kimmy to arrive by monorail from Norsegate. Loca, once again, complained to the headmaster that Kimmy's exchange was affecting the amount of training they could do for the Meltdown, but Gobbledee told her the same thing that he had told her at the beginning of the year; that he had zero control over the situation and nothing could be done.

They had originally planned to simply stay half an hour later each night, to pack in the same amount of training, but the janitor would kick them out so he could lock up at half past seven on the dot. Even though it made them frustrated, no one was taking the delay worse than Kimmy, who felt terrible for making them wait, even though it wasn't his fault.

One Wednesday, when school had ended, Loca and Lessana headed up to the training room to plan some tactics on paper, while the boys waited downstairs in the corridor for Kimmy to arrive. When he turned up, he was holding both hands on the top of his head and looked in pain.

"Dude, you okay?" said Tenk. "It wasn't Snibble was it? Did he hit you?"

Seckry couldn't believe it. If Snibble had hit Kimmy, he was going to be livid. Kimmy was one of the nicest, politest, most loveliest people you could ever meet. Only an absolute monster could have had the motivation to attack him.

"No one hit me," said Kimmy, sheepishly. "I had a bit of an accident . . . in the biochemistry labs." He slowly removed his palms to reveal a shining, bald patch in the centre of his short, dark hair.

"Wow," said Tenk, stifling a laugh.

"I mistook a vial of solonium for pyranide."

"And decided to pour the solution onto your head?" said Tenk.

"No, it kinda . . . exploded in my hands and I put my head down to shield my face. I actually wasn't the only one that got splashed. This girl, Jayra Honkins, got sprayed too, and she didn't duck."

"Oh my Gedin," said Seckry. "Is she okay?"

"Well, it turns out the mixture only disintegrates hair, and it kinda got rid of her moustache and unibrow, so she's come out of it quite well."

Kimmy placed his hands back onto his head. "I'll have to get myself a couple of hats tomorrow to cover this until it grows back."

"Here ya go," said Tenk, pulling off his own cap and shoving it onto Kimmy's head. "There's one to start you off."

"Thanks Tenk," said Kimmy. "I'll give it back to you tomorrow."

As Tenk was telling Kimmy not to worry, and that he could keep the hat, Seckry spotted a straggling girl peeping at them from behind the lockers. As soon as she realised Seckry had seen her, she went bright red and hurried away, disappearing around a corner.

"Did anyone else just see that?" Seckry asked, and the other three nodded.

"That was . . . weird," said Tippian.

"Yeah, what was that all about?" said Kimmy.

"What was that all about?" said Tenk. "I'll tell you what that was all about. She fancies one of us, that's what. That was typical fangirl behaviour."

"Fangirl?" said Kimmy.

"Yeah," said Tenk. "Looked like she was fangirling to me. Obsessing over one of us from a distance and then getting embarrassed about it as soon as she knows we can see her."

After a few moments of contemplation, Tippian said, "I hope it's me."

"It's got to be Seckry, hasn't it?" said Tenk. "After the Meltdown last year, and all this stuff in the news about taking down Darklight, you're like a minor celeb around here now, Seck."

"We were all in the news," Seckry opposed. "It could be any of us."

They hurried to meet with the girls in the training room after that, not wanting to waste any more of their precious time, and forgot about the fangirl. Then, after a heavy session of Friction, Seckry and Tenk said goodbye out in the courtyard, and parted ways with the others, ready to head back to Kerik Square, but stopped dead in their tracks when they noticed the same girl dart out from behind a lamppost and scuttle after Kimmy, unaware that anyone could see her.

"Looks like we've found out who the target of her affection is," said Tenk, pulling out his phone. Seckry watched as Tenk sent a quick text message to Kimmy.

Dude, I don't want 2 alarm u but she's behind u

"What a dark horse," said Tenk, as they ran to catch their monorail. "Always the quiet ones you gotta watch out for."

That weekend, Seckry and Tenk decided to go to the Friction Emporium to purchase a few upgrades for their avatars, and Eiya, who had never been to the place before, decided to join them out of curiosity.

"Have you spoken to Kimmy yet?" said Seckry, as they left the Square.

"Yep," said Tenk. "He reckons he was too scared to turn around when he saw my text and he just shoved his phone into his pocket and pelted away. He spent most of the time apologising to me, though, because he said he was running so fast the hat flew off, and he was too scared to turn back and get it."

When they arrived at the Emporium, the welcome girl, or Fewgy, as Tenk and Tippian liked to call her, gave them all an enthusiastic 'Hello' and handed them some free Friction keyrings. But Tenk put his head down with a stern expression and completely ignored her, much to the girl's confusion.

"Tenk," said Seckry, "what was that all about?"

"I can't talk to her!" Tenk hissed.

"Why not?"

"Why not? Because it'd be a bit inappropriate, don't you think? I mean, if Richelle knew about the chemistry me and Fewgy have, she'd never speak to me again."

"Oh yeah," said Seckry. "I forgot about your chemistry."

Inside the Emporium, the atmosphere was just as electric as it always was, and Seckry could feel his heart begin to race. Even the smell of the place was almost as good as a Friction event smell, as they were selling buttercandy popcorn and hotdogs from multiple stalls stationed around the building.

Seckry couldn't wait to purchase some upgrades for Anikam. He had gone into the Meltdown last year with just the default equipment that had come with his avatar when he bought him, and looking back on it, he couldn't believe he'd been so naïve. In sanctioned events, each player is allowed a maximum of three add-ons for their avatar, be it weapon enhancements, extra shielding clothes, or status changes, like immunities to certain elements and so forth, and having one of these equipped often meant life or death in a game as high profile as the Meltdown.

Tenk ran off almost as soon as they entered, so Seckry had fun showing Eiya around and watching her wide eyes take in the entirety of the place. After being given free mecha-shaped lollipops and getting entered into a prize draw to win a trip to the WePlay headquarters, they headed for the new avatars section to see the latest offerings.

There were around fifty new avatars since the last time Seckry had visited, and each one was unique. But Eiya was transfixed on just one.

"Seck," she said. "Is it just me or does this one look just like Anikam?"

It was a female, half human, half cheetah anima, sat on a rock, cleaning a long, thin, curved blade with a cloth. She tilted her head towards them and gave them a confident smile.

"Gedin," said Seckry, stepping closer. "You're right."

Beneath the avatar was its name, Alaria, and a logo, Plasmatel.

"It's the same company that made Anikam!" said Seckry, excitedly. "They've actually produced a new avatar."

While Eiya wandered off to browse some more of the new avatars, Seckry headed to the upgrades department.

After an hour of careful, excited deliberation, he finally settled on a large arrow quiver holster which would allow him to carry double the amount of arrows, a protective, invisible shield that would give him greater protection from bullets and other non-magical ammo, and immunity to fire. This last one was a strategic decision. After last year's underwater fiasco, he had almost been tempted to buy an upgrade that allowed him to breathe underwater, but he doubted the Overseers would pull the same stunt twice in a row, and figured there was more chance of some fire related obstacle this time around.

On top of his practical upgrades, Seckry even bought a few items of clothing for cosmetic purposes, like a flowing red scarf and a sleeker jacket. After getting his receipt and equipping them, Seckry grinned at the newly outfitted hologram of Anikam above his avatar cube, and he nodded to himself, satisfied. As if Anikam hadn't looked cool enough already, he looked awesome now, his arms crossed stoically, and his new scarf fluttering gently in the digital breeze.

When Seckry found Eiya, she was giggling to herself.

"I got sized up," she said guiltily, a teasingly cute grin on her face. "Do you think I'd be good at Friction?"

"I think you'd be awesome!" said Seckry, and he meant it. Eiya was a natural at video games, just like him.

As they were leaving, Seckry could see that Eiya wasn't happy about something.

"You okay?" asked Tenk, noticing it too.

"I just . . . I forgot something back there. I just need to go back and get it," Eiya said, letting go of Seckry's hand and sprinting back into the neon glow.

Seckry and Tenk stared at each other in confusion, but they didn't have to wait long for her to return.

"Boys," she said, beaming. "I would like to introduce you to . . ." she pulled out an avatar cube. "Alaria, my new avatar."

"Whoo hoo!" screamed Tenk. "Eiya's gonna play Friction!"

"Really?" said Seckry, shocked, but excited. He had no idea she had been serious about playing.

"Oh Gedin, Seck, what have I done?" Eiya laughed. "I don't even know the rules. I'm gonna get slaughtered."

"You'll be awesome," Seckry assured her, grinning. He couldn't wait to show her the sprawling valleys of Atoria and the many wonders hidden inside its digital landscape.

With the amount of training they were now doing for the Meltdown, Eiya didn't have to wait long before testing out her new avatar with the Eidolons, who were more than happy to let her practise with them. The only one who didn't seem pleased about it was Lessana, to nobody's surprise.

"Eiya, are you sure you've never played Friction before?" said Loca, as Eiya sliced through a bot with a clean swipe of her blade.

A grin crept across Alaria's feline face. "I think I would

have remembered," said Eiya. "I've only been alive for just over a year."

Loca's avatar looked away, embarrassed. She had obviously momentarily forgotten the nature of Eiya's existence. It was lucky Eiya took things like that so casually.

A few games in and it already felt like Eiya was a valuable member of the Eidolons, and they wished the maximum team number was seven instead of six.

One evening, after a day of mundane social science lessons, they decided it would be beneficial to increase the level of difficulty on the AI in their training session to over 700, the highest they had ever set it.

"We didn't win the trophy last year just to lose it again this year," Loca said breathlessly as she cranked the difficulty setting up. "The Nightmare won't recognise us by the time we're done training."

"What's the plan this time?" said Tenk.

"We have to work on our item collecting skills, because the Overseers are getting tricksier about where they're putting them. We all know we can collect items when they're just sat there, but collecting items in hard-to-reach places, especially when bullets are raining down upon us, is another matter."

Everyone nodded, and launched themselves into the game, spurred on by Loca's determination and passion.

The first half of the session was fairly straight forward, and Seckry had no problem taking out the sophisticated bots by using some advanced stealth, but quickly escalated into a gruelling scavenge amidst an onslaught of attacks that sent everyone bar Seckry and Tenk out of the game.

Finally, Tenk fired Basher's plasma canon at the last remaining bot, sending it smashing into bits at the other end of the tunnel, and they both caught sight of the final item, lodged between two stalactites hanging from the roof.

"Seck, it's too high to reach," said Tenk, "but you can knock it off with an arrow."

Seckry nodded, exhausted, and aimed his bow and fired.

Tenk thrust out Basher's chunky arms to catch the item,

but the arrow zoomed past the stalactites and clanked into the cavernous abyss.

Embarrassed, Seckry pulled another arrow out of his pack, aimed, and fired once more.

It missed again. But the worst thing was, he was even further away than the first time.

"It's okay Seck, I'll . . . uh . . . I'll get this one."

Seckry watched in shame as Basher clambered up the side of the cavern carefully and grabbed the item himself.

Before buying Anikam, Seckry had never used a bow and arrow. In truthfulness, he probably would have picked up the skills of a different weapon slightly quicker, but Anikam just seemed so perfect that the weapon choice hadn't even come into consideration.

It hadn't taken him long to learn the basic skills; a few practise sessions with his team, and he felt like he had been an archer all his life. But he had never been in such a difficult spot before. He had never had to fire at something so far away; something that required such precision.

Of course, there were other weapons he could buy at the Emporium, but Anikam had been built as an archer. His stats and everything were designed for it. Trying to adjust to a new weapon now would be even more work, and would go against Anikam's strengths.

"I'm really sorry about that, guys," Seckry apologised, as he and Tenk emerged from their pods.

"Seck, don't worry about it," said Kimmy. "It was really far away. Not everyone can make a shot like that."

The others agreed, but despite their encouragement, Seckry was, for the first time, beginning to feel as though he didn't belong on the team.

As Seckry, Tenk, and Eiya took the monorail back to Kerik Square that night, Tenk said, "Not every archer is gonna be as accurate as Kristian Surefoot, man, I wouldn't worry about it."

"Kristian Surefoot?" said Seckry. "Who's he?"

Tenk stared at Seckry for longer than was comfortable.

"Seck, come on. As an archer, you can't be telling me you've never heard of Kristian Surefoot."

Seckry was feeling as clueless as ever.

"I thought he would have been your greatest Friction hero," said Tenk. "Surefoot is the most famous archer to have ever played Friction. He won pretty much every Mega Meltdown he was a part of when he was in school, and then when he left school he went on to win loads of adult events."

"What's his avatar's name?" said Seckry, hoping he would at least recognise that.

"Lataki," said Tenk.

Seckry had never heard the name. He was feeling more unworthy of being on the Eastern Eidolons team now more than ever.

"Anyway, what I'm trying to say," said Tenk, "is that not every archer that plays Friction is gonna be as good as Kristian Surefoot. And it doesn't matter. As long as we work as a team, we can win this thing. Even if you're not amazing at archery like Kristian is, you're still a *good* archer."

Seckry was sure Tenk's intentions were to help and encourage him, but in all honesty, he was feeling a little offended. He was determined not to be just another average archer. He wanted to be the best. He wanted to never miss a shot again.

"Nobody will ever be as accurate as him," said Tenk. "I mean, the guy grew up in, like, a cabin out in the Lavawood Forest. They say he was hunting his own food with a bow and arrow from the age of six or something."

"What?" said Seckry. "Are you serious?"

"Yeah man, the guy was, like, a born killer. Imagine having to hunt for your food as a kid. Basically, if you weren't accurate, you didn't eat. It's no wonder the guy's so skilled now."

Seckry had relied solely on practise sessions with Anikam to improve his archery skills. He was really starting to doubt whether that was enough.

The following weekend, the Eidolons decided to take

some time away from Friction to recover from such an intense week, and no one was more relieved than Seckry, who had missed another three crucial shots during practise.

Instead, Tenk had planned a visit to the new chocolate factory chococorp, to buy their famous chocomelt bars.

The factory was located close to the city centre, and not far from the Endrin headquarters, so on Saturday morning, Seckry, Eiya and Tenk met up with the others at the entrance, only to find it heaving with people, mainly families with young kids.

"Gedin, this place has been open for months now," said Tenk, in despair. "You'd think the novelty would have worn off by now."

"Yeah, you have to be an idiot to be excited about it now," said Loca, dryly, staring at him.

"We'll be waiting for hours in this queue," said Tenk, and kicked a rubbish bin, weakly. "I can't be bothered waiting. Sorry guys, let's head back home."

"Well I'm not going home until I've eaten something," said Loca. "I'm starving now, after expecting chocolate."

"Let's grab some chips from Hatchbag's Chip Shop," said Tippian. "We can go down Gallica's Lane to eat them."

"Okay," said Tenk, dejectedly, giving the queue a scowl as they left.

"You ever been through Gallica's Lane?" said Tippian to Seckry and Eiya as they meandered through the streets of Skyfall.

"Nope," they replied in unison.

Tippian said nothing in return.

After buying a mound of chips, they turned a corner and Seckry nearly dropped his bag in shock.

"This," said Tippian, is Gallica's Lane, home to Gallica's Wall, the most graffitied wall in all of Skyfall."

"Wow," said Seckry. He couldn't even see the other end, and the entire thing was covered from top to bottom in multicolours of marker pens, paint, and spray. At one location, someone had even made a three dimensional face smoking a cigarette by attaching paper mache and painting over it.

"Don't the Patrol try to stop anyone?"

"Nah, the thing's become a tourist attraction," said Tippian. "They probably tried to stop people in the beginning, but now they just let people graffiti to their heart's content."

"Look, here's my contribution!" yelled Tenk, who had hurried halfway towards the other end.

Seckry followed him to find a small marking lodged between two doodles that read:

TENK WOZ ERE
TB
4
SS

(THAT'S SERRA SIMMONY, NOT SHAWNE STOPPART, FOR ALL YOU LOSERS OUT THERE)

"Had to clear that one up," said Tenk.

"Why didn't you just write Tenk Binko for Serra Simmony in the first place, instead of the initials?" said Seckry.

"Dude, I don't know," said Tenk. "It's just tradition, ain't it?"

There were a few others that stood out to Seckry; one that read, *IF U R READIN THIS U R N IDIOT*, and a defaced warning that originally read, *Graffitiing here is prohibited by the law*, but someone had added in a letter c to make it read, *Graffitiing here is against the claw*, and scribbled a giant crab claw next to it. But one piece, just a few yards away, had caught Eiya's attention, and she was staring at it, transfixed.

"Seck, look at this," she said softly, and put her hands to her heart. "It's so romantic."

Amidst the scrawls and profanities was a piece of large, elegant calligraphy that read:

I love you, Itraya Rosebloom.

"That's so cool," said Loca, also staring at the writing. "It's nice to know there are actually men out there with a bit of class. I bet Itraya Rosebloom's a lucky girl. I mean, there are a small amount of guys out there who would do something like this for a girl, and then there are buffoons like Tenk, who scrawl TB 4 SS."

"Oi!" said Tenk. "I bet if Serra Simmony ever came here, she'd be well impressed by my TB 4 SS graffiti. That's just as romantic in my eyes."

"Tenk," said Loca. "To Serra Simmony, who I imagine cares very little about your existence, it is probably about as romantic as giving her a wet fish, and to your current girlfriend, seeing as it is about another woman, it is probably about as romantic as a slap in the face."

"I can't help it that I wasn't with Richelle at the time," said Tenk.

As Seckry admired the graffiti, all he could think about was how much he wanted to say the words 'I love you' to Eiya, but was too embarrassed to do it.

"Come on, while we're here, let's leave a group message," said Loca. "When we're older, we can always come back here and remember this moment."

She pulled a marker pen out of her jacket pocket and very carefully wrote into a small gap:

EIDOLONS FOREVER

She paused for a moment, admiring her handiwork, and then continued underneath:

PROUD WINNERS OF THE 28TH FRICTION MEGA MELTDOWN

"Just a little incentive to us all," she said. "Now we gotta win this thing for a second year in a row, otherwise this graffiti will just be embarrassing."

"Are you trying to give us an incentive or jinx the bleedin' thing?" said Tenk.

"I don't believe in superstitious nonsense like jinxing," said Loca. "I believe in making our own success." She slapped Tenk on the back. Seckry wasn't sure if this was an encouraging gesture or if she just felt like slapping him.

"Come on, let's sign our names underneath," said Loca. "There's just enough room left."

As they each took their turn, Kimmy said, "Does anyone else feel guilty that Lessana isn't part of this? She is an Eidolon too after all."

"To be honest," said Loca, "I would rather Eiya's name next to ours any day. Lessana ostracises herself. Eiya's more of an Eidolon than she ever has been." She grabbed Eiya and squeezed her tightly. "If only there was room on the team," she said with a sigh.

After finishing their chips and pop, they left the lane via the other exit and passed a section of the wall that seemed dedicated to advertisements, posters and flyers. Most of them were scruffy and half ripped, promoting night clubs and events, but as Seckry was scanning the vast mess of attention-seeking text, he did a double take.

A single, clean little flyer with small, unassuming writing had caught his eye. It read:

Parafield Training Facility.
Martial arts classes
Stick Swordfighting
Archery Practise

Seckry carefully peeled the flyer from the wall, rolled it up, and stuck it into his jeans pocket. He was fed up of being just another mediocre archer who couldn't hit his targets one hundred percent of the time. Like Loca had said, things like luck and superstition weren't going to help them win the Meltdown. Hard work and hard training was. He was going to become as good as Kristian Surefoot, whether Tenk believed it was possible or not.

It was time to fire a real bow.

Seckry was itching to get to the training facility the very next day, but after checking the opening times in the small print, he realised they weren't open on Sundays.

As soon as Monday evening came around, it was time to practise once again, and Seckry accepted the fact that he would just have to carry on with a virtual bow until he had a free evening.

Lessana arrived even later than Kimmy that day, much to everyone's annoyance, and strolled into the training room smugly, holding two new upgrade chips, which she wasted no time before boasting about. The first was a shield against electrocution, and the second was some kind of ball and chain that was enchanted with explosive power so that it sent out a massive force wave on impact.

After listening to her talk for fifteen minutes about how her equipment was way better than the rest of theirs, they finally got into their pods and appeared in Atoria. But it wasn't long before Ogg's mouth was moving.

"I'm bored of this," she complained, before Loca had even started talking. "Who wants to go one-on-one? I will blast you to smithereens with my new kit."

The rest of the team were brimming with frustration. Even Seckry, who had learned to ignore Lessana's arrogance, was feeling just about ready to lash out at her.

"Just shut up and listen to my instructions, will you, Lubworth?" said Loca, her eyes fixed on the ground as if she couldn't bear to look at Lessana's ogre avatar.

"Alright, alright," said Lessana, mockingly. "I'm just saying. This thing is going to be a game changer, I'm telling you."

"Right," said Loca. "Tonight we're going to be working on our flanking skills. It's not always about simply getting the upper hand on an enemy, it's sometimes a better idea to attack from both sides, so that they don't have -"

Loca's voice was cut off as Lessana suddenly swung Ogg's ball and chain high into the air, and smashed it into the ground. A giant ripple spread out from her, destroying the area and shattering everyone's avatars into pieces. Seckry felt Anikam's skin being shredded by the force before he fell to the floor of his pod with a thud, and groaned from the impact.

He kicked the door of the pod open and clambered out, just in time to see Lessana fall out of her own pod, a guilty grin on her round, freckled face.

Loca calmly exited her pod and waited until everyone else was out.

"Lessana . . ." Loca said. "Get out."

Lessana burst into laughter.

"Come on, that was really funny! Did you see the power on that thing? It was crazy! I had to try it out at some point!"

"Lessana," Loca said again, very calmly. "You're done. Get out."

"I'm done?" Lessana said, breathless. "You're the ones who are done. Did you see tha-"

"You are no longer an Eastern Eidolon," Loca said, and this time, Lessana stopped chuckling. She looked at the others in turn. Seckry just glared at her. He was just as angry and fed up with her as the others.

"You're seriously kicking me off the team?" she said, astounded. "You can't do that. I fippin made this team. I was playing Friction before you lot had even heard of it."

"*I* am the team captain," said Loca, firmly. "And I. Have had. Enough. Of *you*." She took off her beanie hat and threw it at Lessana.

For a moment it looked like Lessana was going to start a fist fight with Loca, but then she turned around and stormed out of the training room, slamming the door shut behind her.

Tippian started clapping but stopped when he realised nobody was joining him.

"Looks like there's a free position going after all," Loca said to Eiya.

Chapter Twenty-One

The Superdragon Three Thousand

Eiya couldn't believe she was being given an opportunity to be an Eastern Eidolon, but she took it with open arms.

After throwing Lessana off the team, the new Eidolons had their best training session for a long time, and they were relieved to finally be able to practise without having to listen to her whine about Loca's leadership or moan that everyone was less skilled than her.

Eiya spent the week bursting into giggles of disbelief and asking Seckry if this was real, and if she was actually part of the Eidolons now, to which Seckry happily told her 'yes.' In fact, no one was happier that Eiya was now an Eidolon than Seckry. He couldn't wait to compete alongside her in the Meltdown.

When the week came to a close, Seckry had to be reminded by the others that it was the Fearless Funfair on Saturday. He had been so focused on Friction practise that he had completely forgotten about it.

When the morning arrived, he expected Tenk to be banging down his door, telling him to get a move on because he didn't want to miss a moment of it, but instead, Seckry found a text message waiting for him.

Hey man, don't call for me this morning to go to the fair. Loca will explain.

The only explanation Seckry could come up with was that Tenk had already left earlier than the rest of them because he couldn't wait a minute longer. The way Tenk had gone on about the fair for the last couple of weeks, it wouldn't have surprised him.

They had arranged to meet at Loca's house first, which was in the Kelcroft district of the east partition, before heading to the fair, so Seckry and Eiya caught the monorail.

When they arrived at Loca's, Tippian was running down the street behind them, his face brimming with excitement. In fact, he was so excited, he tripped over Loca's front door step and snapped the bridge of his glasses. Luckily, Loca's mum had plenty of masking tape in one of the kitchen drawers and was able to stitch it up for him temporarily.

Kimmy arrived a few moments later, wearing a padded helmet.

"Kim, what on earthia is that thing on your head?" said Tippian.

"My mum wouldn't let me go to the fair without it," he said miserably. "She's convinced that one of the rides is gonna break."

"Kim," said Tippian, "I think if one of the rides breaks and you get flung from a carriage, it's probably gonna be certain death. I don't think that helmet's gonna do you much good."

"That's what I said to her," said Kimmy, "but it made her break down in tears so I thought I'd wear it just to please her."

"Okay, guys," said Loca. "I've got some news to tell you about Tenk."

"Yeah, where is he?" said Tippian. "I thought he'd be first to arrive."

"Well," said Loca. "You're probably not going to believe this . . . but . . . he actually phoned me up last night and said he can't come to the fair because he's . . . wait for it . . . spending time with Richelle."

"What?" spat Tippian.

"That's exactly what my reply was on the phone."

"Are you serious?" said Eiya. "He's been excited about the fair for ages. Couldn't Richelle have come along with us?"

"Oh, she was invited from the start," said Loca. "But

apparently she wants to spend time with him *away* from us."

"Guys," said Tippian. "Is anyone else getting the impression that Richelle doesn't like us?"

"Yeah," said Loca. "The horrible cow. She only ever met us that one time at the stadium."

"Well, if she can't handle our awesomeness then that's her problem," said Tippian. "We're like, the most awesomest crew you could ever want to hang around with. Am I right? We *are* awesome, right?"

They glanced at each other, mostly lingering on Kimmy donned in his mum's protective helmet, and Tippian, staring at them through masking-taped glasses which were already hanging wonkily low on his left cheek.

"Okay, maybe not right now," said Loca, "but on the whole, generally, I'd say yeah."

As they headed for Featherduck Park, where the fair had been set up, Seckry still couldn't believe Tenk was going to miss the entire thing to spend time with Richelle. Riding the Superdragon rollercoaster had been, in Tenk's own words, his 'second most important lifetime goal.' Seckry couldn't remember exactly what Tenk had claimed his number one most important lifetime goal to be, but something was telling him it had been something to do with filling up a hundred loyalty stamp cards at Boggin's Burgers and getting a year's worth of free food in return.

As the pumping music became louder and the smell of freshly fried doughnuts wafted into his nostrils, Seckry began to brim with excitement. He had only ever been on small rides when a fair had passed through Marne a few years ago. At the time, he had thought it was the experience of a lifetime, but something told him the Superdragon rollercoaster was going to be on a completely different level.

As they reached the entrance, they waited behind a family who were being given welcome lollipops by a man dressed in a giant teddy bear costume, and Loca slapped her hands together.

"Nice," she said. "I need a bit of sugar to wake me up."

But when it was their turn, the bear walked away swiftly, disappearing behind one of the rides.

"Oi!" Loca shouted. "I want a free lolly! How rude was that?"

Tippian lifted his arms in turn, sniffing his armpits. "I don't *think* I smell," he said. "Saying that, my mum would probably tell you otherwise. Anyway, what we going on first? We hitting this Superdragon, or what?"

"Tipp," said Loca. "You don't go straight for the main attraction. Everything else would seem rubbish if we did that first. We gotta build our way up."

"So . . . the teacups, then?"

"Okay, maybe a little heavier than the teacups."

From where they stood, Seckry could see two log flumes, a house of mirrors, a carousel, bumper cars, a huge ferris wheel, a helter skelter, a pirate ship, and the largest rollercoaster Seckry had ever seen, which had to be the Superdragon. He followed the track with his eyes, but got lost when the thing disappeared into a tunnel.

Eiya was in a constant battle with her own excitement; she couldn't decide whether she wanted to play Hook a Duck, get a chocolate and toffee apple, ride the log flume, or play on the arcade machines, which were pumping dance music around the open field.

But before they could get on any ride, Tippian got distracted by a stall that was manned by a scrawny, unkempt looking man dressed in a very worn, striped, red and yellow suit, shouting, "Come and play Dimpy's coconut smash and win a giant gobstopper!"

Tippian handed over a couple of notes and was given three balls. He threw the first and missed completely, then he threw the second and just grazed the furry shell of one. Then, on the final one, he took aim slowly, recoiled his arm, and launched the ball directly at the centre of the middle coconut, hitting it hard. But it didn't budge.

"What?" Tippian yelled. "I hit it, square on!"

"Oh!" said Dimpy loudly. "So close!"

"So close?" Tippian said. "I hit the damn thing!"

"Didn't hit it hard enough," said the man.

"But . . . I . . ." Tippian was lost for words.

Loca squeezed one of Tippian's non-existent biceps. "You need to get to a gym, Tipp. You can't even knock a coconut off a stand."

Seckry noticed Dimpy licking his lips as he counted Tippian's notes into a tray of money that was overflowing.

They practically had to drag Tippian away from the tent. When they did, he peered around the back of it.

"I knew it!" Tippian hissed. "Look!"

Lined across the back were five giant bolts, screwed tightly to the canvas.

"The coconuts are bolted to the tent!"

Tippian grabbed one of the bolts and unscrewed it.

"Let's see what he has to say when I knock one down now."

There was no stopping him. The group could only watch as Tippian returned to the front, waving another two notes at the crooked man, who took them warily and handed Tippian three more balls.

Tippian took aim and hurled the ball with all his force at the centre coconut, smashing it off its stand and sending it flying through the air.

"Haha!" shouted Tippian, as Dimpy ducked for cover. "I got one! I want my gobstopper, please."

After regaining his composure, Dimpy stared at Tippian for a moment with sinister eyes, before grinning and clapping.

"Well done!" he shouted, so that every passer-by could hear. "The proud owner of a new giant gobstopper, ladies and gentlemen! You could win one too! Just two notes a try!"

Tippian snatched the prize out of the man's dirty hands and gave him an evil glare as they wandered off.

As they made their way through the busy rides, deciding which to go on first, Loca said, "Look, there's that wretched bear! I'm gonna get my free lollipop."

Seckry spotted the mascot in the distance, who was currently having his tail pulled by a couple of hysterical kids, while others were stealing sweets from his bucket as he was trying to shake them off.

The group approached him.

"Gerrof, you rabid kids!" came a muffled cry through the bear's fur.

"Wait," said Loca. "I recognise that voice . . ."

The bear looked in the group's direction, did a double take, then dropped his bucket of sweets and started running away from them.

"No way!" said Loca, and sprinted after him.

"Oh my Gedin, she's gonna kill the guy!" said Tippian. "That is some serious sugar craving she's got."

Loca caught up with the bear and dived on his head, wrapping her legs around his chest and toppling him to the floor.

"Aaaaargh! Loca, you're gonna kill me!" they heard the mascot scream from within the costume.

The others jogged to catch up.

"Tenk!" Loca said. "Why are you dressed as a bear at the Skyfall fair?"

"That's *Tenk* under there?" said Seckry in disbelief.

Tippian kicked him in the side.

"We thought you were with Richelle!"

"You weren't supposed to find out," said Tenk, heaving Loca off of him and ripping his bear head off, before shaking his hair, which was sodden with sweat.

"I don't get it," said Loca. "What's going on?"

"Look, I'm sorry I lied to you guys, okay? Richelle is actually spending the weekend with her friends."

"Okay, you lied to us about spending time with her, but . . . that still doesn't explain why you're dressed as a bear."

"My nan," said Tenk, miserably. "She thinks I should be starting to pay my way at home, give my mum a little bit of rent. She saw this advert in a shop window about becoming a fair mascot for one day and signed me up without even asking me. She think's it'll be good work experience for me."

"Why didn't you just tell her you didn't want to do it?" said Tippian.

"She would have had a fit," said Tenk. "Have you *met* my

nan?"

Tenk quickly shoved his bear head back on since there were a group of children passing by.

"Gotta keep it on at all times," he said. "The boss reckons it could traumatise the kids if they see there's a human under here."

"Tenk, I can't believe you're doing this," said Kimmy. "You've been waiting for this fair all your life."

"I know," said Tenk, miserably. "I won't even get a chance to ride the Superdragon." He gazed up at the epic rollercoaster, longingly.

"Surely you can get out of it somehow," said Tippian. "Just quit and don't tell her."

Tenk seemed to be genuinely tempted, though it was hard to tell, since the bear's face had a constant, slightly manic looking grin.

"I can't," he said, after much internal deliberation. "My nan would beat me to a pulp if she found out."

"Well, your nan's an old -" started Loca, but luckily Kimmy placed his hand over her mouth before she could finish her sentence.

"Your nan's a stern woman," Kimmy said tactfully. "It's probably best not to get on the wrong side of her."

"Look, I've gotta get back to work," said Tenk, brushing a few clumps of grass and mud out of his fur with his paws. "I'm on ice cream duty in ten minutes and I've gotta go get my equipment."

Reluctantly, the group left him to his job, but Seckry felt terrible watching him waddle away slowly.

"I actually feel a bit bad about toppling him over now," said Loca. "And it's very rare I regret maiming Tenk."

After riding something called The Gravitron, which spun them so fast it felt like they were floating, the group hopped into the front carriage of the fair's ghost train.

Apart from nearly choking on some fake cobwebs that dangled on them, Seckry was enjoying the cheap thrills that the ghost train was throwing at them. As a child, Seckry had been petrified of these things. Now, the camp props and pyrotechnics were almost comical.

But Seckry's grin was wiped off his face as their carriage was knocked off its track by a ghostly figure.

"This . . . is part of the ride, isn't it?" Tippian said. "Isn't it?"

Seckry gripped the hand rail in front of him as the carriage roughly sped through thickets of cobwebs into a pitch black cavern. Seckry wasn't sure if the carriage was on a new track or if the thing had completely derailed and was hurtling into an out of bounds area.

A few children in carriages behind them were screaming, and one began to cry. Then, a rough scrawl of ultraviolet paint on a mess of wooden planks appeared that read:

PATHWAY CLOSED

"Oh Gedin, we're gonna hit it!" shouted Tippian.

Eiya squeezed Seckry's hand as the train smashed through the wooden blockade (which now looked more like painted foam) and entered an icy cavern. It was then that Seckry nearly jumped out of his seat.

Hanging in front of them, above the tracks, was a giant, wooden symbol; a symbol Seckry was not expecting to see inside a ghost train.

It was the genesis trinity symbol.

"Seck, are you okay?" Eiya said. But Seckry couldn't speak. He was trying to work out what this meant. As they passed underneath the symbol, Seckry noticed that written across the walls were things like *DO NOT PASS*, *STRICTLY FORBIDDEN*, and *STRANGE ACTIVITY RECORDED AT THIS SITE*.

A moment later, their carriage began rocking back and forth, and undecipherable, evil sounding whispers echoed all around them. Then, Eiya screamed as a muscular, horned, demon figure rose from the snow on their left and reached a clawed hand out to them, just missing the tips of their heads.

Eventually, the carriage burst through another wall into

daylight, and they came to an abrupt halt in front of a very uninterested looking attendant.

"Unfasten your seatbelts, please," the attendant droned, flicking up their safety bars one-by-one.

"Seck," said Loca, doing a double take at his face. "I know that giant spider looked pretty lifelike, but come on, you weren't seriously scared in there, were you? You look as pale as a ghost."

"That sign as we went into the snowy area . . ." Seckry said distantly. "It was the trinity symbol."

Could it have been something to do with Site Origin?

Seckry caught the attention of the vacant ride operator.

"The symbol in there," he said. "The one with all the snow and the rocking of the train and the whispers and all that. What was that all about?"

The operator stared at him blankly.

"Mate," he said. "I just press start and stop. I have no idea what you're talking about."

Seckry scanned the booth and the exterior of the ride.

Choppy Chin's Amusements, read a small sticker on the booth's cheap plastic. The only thing he could do was take the name and try to find some contact details later.

After riding all of the small attractions at least twice, the group decided it was time to brave the big one: The Superdragon. As they were making their way to the queue, they saw Tenk handing out ice creams to a group of kids.

"He's gonna regret this for the rest of his life," said Tippian.

Before they joined the queue, they decided to see how he was getting on.

"Come on, Tenk," said Tippian. "Your nan will understand. They say it's the biggest and best rollercoaster Skyfall has ever see-"

"I know!" interrupted Tenk, desperately, as a snotty-nosed child ripped a tub of ice cream out of his paw without paying for it and ran away, squealing. "It's officially the third biggest rollercoaster in the world, and second to none in public votes for their favourite coaster. I've watched, like, fifty videos online of the thing. I've dreamt of going on this rollercoaster since I was seven years old."

"Well, screw your nan and come join us then," said Tippian.

"I can't." Tenk stared up at the ride and took a deep breath. "She thinks I'm a lazy good-for-nothing. I've got to do this."

"Hey, bear-man," said a mother, close by. "When you gonna stop chatting away to your mates and serve my son some ice cream, eh?"

"Sorry," Tenk said miserably, and started pulling out a vanilla tub.

"He doesn't like *vanilla,*" the mother said angrily. "He wants ellonberry flavour. With chocolate sauce. Lots of chocolate sauce."

The kid gave Tenk a look of disgust and kicked him in the privates. Tenk keeled over, nearly dropping the boy's ice cream onto the grass.

"Jaysin!" said the mother. "What have I told you about doing that to people?"

"Oww," said Tenk, weakly.

"Well you deserved it, to be honest," said the mother. "And don't you dare drop my child's ice cream."

Loca was about to attack the woman, but for Tenk's job's sake, Kimmy pulled her away.

"Come on, the queue's gonna get massive again if we don't hurry."

As they made their way to the coaster, Seckry kept glancing behind him. He felt terrible for Tenk. He had been looking forward to going on this rollercoaster his whole life, and now here was his chance, and he was stuck being abused by some vile woman and her son.

They waited just a total of ten minutes in the queue, and Seckry noticed that Tenk was still dealing with the same woman and child as they entered through the turnpike and took their seats.

"Bagsy front seat!" said Tippian, and clambered into the

first carriage. Each carriage held three people, so Kimmy and Loca joined him, while Seckry and Eiya took two of the seats behind them. There was an empty seat to Seckry's left, since no one in the queue wanted to be separated from their friends, and Seckry couldn't help but feel like Tenk should have been sitting there.

"Oh Gedin, Seck, I don't know if I'm excited or scared," Eiya said, her voice trembling.

Seckry closed his eyes, trying to prepare himself mentally, but they immediately shot open again when he heard Tenk's voice in the distance shouting, "No, you *can't* get a refund because your son thinks it's too sweet, and no, you *can't* get extra sprinkles on another one for free!"

Tenk threw his ice cream box to the floor, the melted stuff splashing all over the grass, then grabbed the horrible kid and pushed him over before racing towards the rollercoaster.

"Make way! Bear coming through!" he roared, shoving through the queue. He threw himself over the turnpike barrier and landed in the seat next to Seckry, pulling his safety guard down and locking it into place.

"Oh Gedin!" he said, as security guards started making their way towards them. "Start this fippin rollercoast – *aaaaargh!*"

They were propelled into the sky and Tenk's bear head flew off in the wind.

"Whoo hoo!" Tenk screamed, his arms above him. He held his palm out to high-five Seckry, but ended up slapping himself in the face when the rollercoaster took a sharp turn.

Seckry couldn't help but laugh in disbelief at what Tenk had just done. He was going to be in so much trouble, but he knew that for Tenk, the punishment would be worth it.

The ride was everything Seckry had expected and more. Never before had he felt such exhilaration and fear combined. Next to him, Eiya was screaming and laughing equally, gripping Seckry's leg so tight it felt as though her fingers were cutting into his skin.

After the initial drop, the coaster sped into a tunnel and started twirling like crazy before propelling them through seven gigantic loops. Then, a deep voice from the speakers beside each of their ears said, "Get ready . . . to get wet!" before the floor of the carriage beneath them dropped, and they were dangling, their legs swinging about beneath them.

"We're all gonna die!" Tippian screamed, as the rollercoaster plunged their legs into a lake of cold water, creating a massive spray that drenched them.

"This. Is. So. Cool!" yelled Tenk, who was now scissor kicking his furry bear legs wildly in excitement.

Just when Seckry thought the ride couldn't throw anything more at them, the track curved into a vertical climb that took them so high he was sure they had entered some low hanging clouds. As they tipped over the edge, he couldn't contain himself, and he opened his mouth in one long scream as they plummeted down to earthia, the whipping force drying them instantly.

When the rollercoaster finally slowed to a stop, Seckry could just about make out a group of people waiting for them through his dazed and giddy vision. Not only were there two security guards, but the fair manager as well, staring at Tenk as if he had just murdered a child.

"With me," said the manager. "*Now.*"

Chapter Twenty-Two

The Legend of Kristian Surefoot

"Yeah, turns out that little kid's mum is suing the fair because a member of staff assaulted her child," said Tenk, as they sat eating crisps in Tippian's living room the next day. "So I'm lucky I'm not getting sued personally I guess. The boss said he never wants to see my Gedin forsaken face again, and if he does he's gonna throw one of the fair's lemon pies at it."

"Did you get paid for working the day, though?" asked Tippian.

"Nope," said Tenk. "But I did manage to accidentally smuggle out all these sweets. I forgot I had shoved them all into my jeans pockets because the bear ones had rips in them." He emptied his bulging pockets and handed an array of multi-coloured packets out to each of them.

"Finally," said Loca. "My free lolly."

"What did your nan have to say?" asked Tippian.

"Everything I expected," said Tenk, staring into space. "That I'm a worthless, lazy bum who's got no work ethic and will never go anywhere in life, and who she's embarrassed to call her grandson."

"Wow," said Loca.

"Actually, thinking about it, it wasn't as bad as I expected. I thought she would have at least tried to get a cane out and thwack me with it, but she withheld any physical violence."

"Well, you may have lost the entire day's pay, and you may be a failure to your nan, but you did get to ride the Superdragon," said Tippian.

"Oh yeah, I don't regret it for one second," said Tenk,

happily.

When Seckry arrived back at the flat that lunchtime, Seckry called the number for Choppy Chin's Amusements to ask about the symbol in the ghost train.

"Jimbo speaking," said a gruff voice.

"Hi . . . um . . ." Seckry stuttered, "I recently rode the ghost train at the Fearless Funfair and I was wondering if you could give me a bit of info on the snow cavern portion of the ride."

Seckry was met with silence and a few chesty coughs, so he explained that he wanted information about the symbol and the writing on the walls.

"I guess nobody knows that story anymore," said Jimbo. "Yo, Thumper," he shouted distantly. "We need to change the ghost train. No one's scared of that thing anymore. We still got that bleedin' snow codswallop in there."

"What's the story?" Seckry asked.

"Well, there's this area up in the Frostpeak Mountain range that people have been afraid to go for years. I think some backpackers originally came across it. There's this big sign hanging above a crevice up there and nobody knows where it came from or what it means. Anybody that passes through that crevice doesn't stay for long. They say it's haunted, and they are tormented by the screams and whispers of the dead, and are assaulted by invisible beasts. It's assumed that the symbol is some kind of ancient, demonic rune or something, and has been hung there by the demons themselves. Who knows? Maybe it's a passageway to the netherworld. We built that ride about fifteen years ago when people were still talking about that place, but I guess people have forgotten it now. I don't think anyone's bothered venturing up there for a long time."

Seckry thanked the man and hung up.

Could it be?

Kayne had said there were sounds of snow and wind on some of the recordings from Adelbert and Rikard's phonecalls, and he had guessed that the labs were in the

Frostpeak mountain range somewhere, but it was too vast to know exactly where.

He phoned Vance immediately.

"Sir," he said, before Vance even had a chance to speak. "I think I may have uncovered the location of Site Origin."

After telling Vance all of the details, Seckry calmed down a little. It was exciting to finally pinpoint a location, but it didn't mean they were going to be heading there to investigate anytime soon. Vance had been excited too, but had reminded Seckry that Pawl had been very specific about meeting him in the Draindug District, and that they should be patient for now, and wait.

Shortly afterwards, Seckry received an enthusiastic message from Cartell, inviting him and Eiya to watch Warehouse Twenty-Two being knocked down, because the building of his new clinic was going to be commencing in just a couple of weeks' time.

Eiya seemed keen to go along, and Seckry felt a guilty pleasure at the thought of watching a building being demolished. It helped quite a bit that the building now represented so much pain and suffering.

But when Seckry and Eiya arrived at the site a few hours later, they found Cartell flicking through papers and shaking his head in dismay.

"What's the matter?" asked Eiya.

Cartell removed his glasses and squeezed the bridge of his nose with his forefinger and thumb.

"Apparently, it has come to the attention of the government that there is some small print in some silly document somewhere that's preventing the place from being knocked down."

Seckry glanced around at the demolition team. They were looking just as put out as Cartell.

"They told me three days ago that it was all going ahead," Cartell complained. "And then I arrive today to find some government intern handing me these."

He shuffled the papers and read aloud:

"It has come to our attention, blah, blah, blah, and that this property is protected under the act of blah, blah, blah, therefore, this property can only be dismantled after the protected period has expired, the only exception being extensive accidental damage of a nature in which the property is no longer salvageable."

Cartell slapped the papers to his leg.

"Even though I have purchased the land and the structure, I have no control over what I do with it."

"That's terrible," said Eiya. "Doesn't the government know what Darklight did here? You'd think they would be happy to see it knocked down and replaced with a modern clinic."

"To be honest, Eiya, I don't think the government really cares either way. All they care about is doing things by the books, even though the books are completely irrelevant and pointless to this situation. I mean, who will benefit from this derelict warehouse staying intact?"

After Cartell had taken a few deep breaths, Seckry asked him how his work on Eryk Valenkar was going.

"Fantastic, Seckry, fantastic," he said, his usual, kind smile reappearing for a moment. "With the right expansion and equipment, I believe I can one day bring him back to full health. I will have reversed the disease, and he will be able to walk and talk once again just like you and I."

"That's incredible," said Eiya.

"The one thing I can't do," said Cartell. "Is bring back the woman who left him when he became ill. But I can give him a new life, and I hope that he can forget about this Trixa, and find someone else to spend the rest of his life with. Someone who would never dream of leaving him if he became ill again."

"We doing this or not?" came an impatient, gruff voice from one of the bulldozers.

"I need to make some phone calls," Cartell called back. "I'm so sorry about this, you guys," he said to Seckry and Eiya. "I'm going to try to get this fixed and persuade them to override these documents. For the time being, feel free to have a look around inside the warehouse. Wear a thick skin, though. Darklight left some . . . traces of his handiwork behind."

Seckry and Eiya weren't sure they wanted to, but curiosity finally overcame them and they cautiously entered the building, their footsteps echoing.

"Oh my Gedin, Seck," Eiya said softly, staring at her own feet.

Seckry followed her gaze. Smeared into the floor were stains of splashes and smears of blood that had evidently been washed many times, but were stubbornly ingrained into the cement.

But the blood stains weren't the worst of the horrors. There were giant bird cages strewn around the place, and lines of crude handcuffs along the walls. As they wandered around, Seckry also noticed a few clumps of hair.

"Caged like animals," Eiya said, her eyes filling with tears. "Seck, I can't stay here any longer . . . can we go home?"

Seckry nodded, feeling the same way. The sooner Cartell managed to erase that place from the face of the planet, the better. But he didn't want to hang around thinking about it.

After a couple of engineering and politics lessons on Monday, Seckry pulled the Parafield Training Facility flyer out of his pocket and read the address. He finally had an evening in which the Eidolons weren't training, so it was time to get his aiming skills up to scratch with some practise using a real bow and arrow.

When Seckry arrived, he found the archery rooms almost deserted. The only people training were a frail girl who was too young to play Friction, never mind wield a real bow, and an older guy who looked even more clueless, holding his bow so awkwardly that Seckry was a little concerned he might injure himself.

Seckry watched them for a few moments, a little nervous about looking like an even bigger fool than the two of them combined. After a couple of failed attempts, the young girl left, looking quite upset and angry.

Seckry continued to watch the man struggle, missing his target every single time. He eventually started to feel relaxed, and convinced himself that even he could fire a bow better than what he was watching.

Seckry made his way over to the shelf of available bows and picked one up. It was much heavier than he had anticipated and felt unnaturally different from Anikam's. He strung an arrow, his hand wobbling from the tautness of the string, and fired.

Seckry smiled. The arrow hadn't hit the bullseye on the board, but at least it had hit the board somewhere.

Suddenly, Seckry had to duck because his fellow archer was swinging his bow around so wildly that Seckry was, frankly, fearing for his life.

"You can go a bit closer to the target," said Seckry, trying to be as helpful as he could without sounding patronising. "Try to work your way further backwards slowly."

The young man just smiled and said, "Thanks, I'm okay."

Seckry tried to keep himself to himself after that, but the man was firing arrows in all directions so recklessly that Seckry was concerned the staff would interfere soon and throw him out.

"Try holding the bow like this," said Seckry, who couldn't bear it any longer. It was lucky the facility was deserted because if the man had been firing arrows like this on a busy day it would have been a massacre.

Seckry strung an arrow into the bow and pulled it taut so the man could see his posture.

The man put his arm on Seckry's shoulder and leaned in close to him.

"If I had held my bow in the generic way you are holding it now, I would never have been able to hit the knots in the wood that I was targeting," he said.

Seckry slowly released the elasticity he had been maintaining and gawped at the mess of arrows on the facility's wall. He couldn't believe what he was seeing. Every single arrow was sticking out of the centre of a tiny knot in the wood.

"Now, if you don't mind, I have one knot left. See it? Just there, between target boards six and seven."

Seckry could just about make out the tiniest colouration in the wood.

"I think I need to up my game, though," the man said. "I think a flying shot should suffice. Stick your hands out, will you? I just need a boost."

Seckry, mesmerised, clasped his hands together as the man placed his left boot on top of them, and after a count of three, helped propel him into the air. The man spun, cartwheeling like an acrobat, and in mid-air, drew an arrow and fired it at such a speed that Seckry almost missed it, before landing on the ground with a forward roll and coming to a halt with one knee on the ground and his arms either side, steadying him.

Seckry couldn't believe it. The arrow hadn't just hit the knot, it was dead centre of the knot too. Who on earthia was this guy?

The man stood up with a grin on his face and put his hand out to shake Seckry's.

"Kristian Surefoot," he said. "Nice to meet you."

After gawping for quite some time, whilst being bright red with embarrassment at trying to give Kristian Surefoot archery advice, Seckry introduced himself.

"For the Eastern Eidolons?" Kristian said. "Of course, you're the one using Anikam right? I was there at last year's meltdown. Great event, I thoroughly enjoyed it. Kimmy coming back to save the day at the end with the gravity gun and all that was epic."

"You were there?" said Seckry.

"Of course, I'm at every Meltdown. Wouldn't miss them for the world. The Meltdowns were a big part of my life. They made me the Friction player I am today. Anikam was a good choice of avatar to buy. I actually had my eye on him for some time."

"Really?" said Seckry. "I didn't think anybody had even noticed him before me."

"Yeah, I remember his name appearing on my new avatar mailing list a few years ago. I looked him up and I actually wanted to nab him for my nephew, but they said he was being sent back for modifications at the time, and I'd have to wait a few weeks. By the time he was back on the shelves, my nephew had already picked another one."

"Modifications?" Seckry said. "What kind?"

"No idea," said Kristian. "Probably just some bugs they wanted to fix. The designers get a bit excited sometimes and release the avatars before they've been fully tested." He threw his bow back onto the rack. "Anyway, I'm done for the day. Hey, if you ever want any one-on-one training, give me a call." He handed Seckry a business card.

"Are you serious?" said Seckry.

"Sure," Kristian replied, and exited the facility, leaving Seckry staring in awe at the telephone number.

"You actually met Kristian Surefoot?" said Tenk, the next morning, astounded.

"Yep," said Seckry, gleaming.

"And he's invited you to his house for one-on-one training?"

Seckry nodded.

"Gedin," said Tenk, softly.

Seckry had spent just over an hour practising on his own at the facility after Kristian had left, but the entire time, he just kept imagining how much he could learn from private sessions with the master himself.

That evening, Seckry wasted no time in phoning Kristian and arranging a lesson for the following Wednesday.

When Wednesday came around, Tenk seemed even more excited than Seckry, and kept telling him to make sure he found out how many animals Kristian had hunted as a child, and what it had been like, killing just to survive. Seckry assured Tenk that he'd get some info, but in reality he had no intention of bringing the subject up at all in case Kristian got offended. And he was a little scared of what Kristian would do to him if he did offend him.

When he arrived at Kristian's house, which was located in a posh district in the south, he was surprised to see that it was a beautiful, expensive looking mansion.

Kristian had to have spotted him through the window because he came out to welcome Seckry before he could even knock.

"Seckry, Seckry," he said. "Follow me."

Seckry followed him into a gigantic room around the back of the house that was covered in posters of legendary players with illustrations of their avatars next to them. On the centre of one wall, the largest poster was of Kolda Kod, looking young and muscular. At the far end of the room was a single target board, and on a table was a single bow. But the most striking thing about the entire room was an elaborate, glass chandelier hanging from the ceiling.

Seckry wondered how the family had gone from living wild in a forest, to this life of luxury.

"This used to be the dining room," Kristian said. "I've been meaning to take that chandelier down for a while. Anyway, I've got some techniques I'd like to show you. Are you ready?"

Seckry nodded.

"I'm assuming you had plenty of experience firing real bows as a child, right?" said Kristian, throwing him the one that had been laid out on the table. "You're an intelligent guy. You wouldn't have picked an archer avatar without a bit of archery experience."

Seckry caught the bow and stumbled back a little from the weight of it.

"Uhh . . . actually . . ."

Kristian narrowed his eyes.

"Don't tell me you had never fired a real bow before picking an archer avatar," he said in disbelief.

Seckry shrugged his shoulders sheepishly.

Kristian approached him so slowly and accusingly that Seckry was sure the guy was going to punch him for his naivety, but instead, he placed his hand on Seckry's shoulder and said, "You wanna know a secret? *Neither had I.*"

"What?" said Seckry.

"It's true," said Kristian, a kind smile replacing his accusatory glare. "When I first saw Lataki at the Emporium, I didn't ask myself, am I a good archer? I didn't have to ask myself anything. I just knew, by looking into Lataki's eyes, that he was the avatar for me."

Seckry had felt exactly the same the very first time he had met Anikam. While the entire Emporium had been drowned by the vicious snarls of the Hammer Brothers and the roaring of the excited crowd, Anikam had met Seckry's gaze, and even though Seckry knew that he was just a digital creation, it was almost as if he and Anikam had held a mutual understanding.

"But, didn't you grow up hunting animals for food out in the wilderness when you were a child?" said Seckry.

"Seckry," said Kristian flatly, "I'm a vegan. I wouldn't hurt a fly, let alone an animal."

"What?" Seckry gasped. "I had visions of you smearing animal blood across your face and running through Lavawood Forest. My friend Tenk said you grew up in a cabin and you had to hunt for your own food, otherwise you'd starve."

"Seckry, Lavawood Forest covers a wide area, including the village of Herringhaven, which is where I'm from. I grew up on a council estate. I spent most of my childhood going to school and playing video games in my spare time. You grew up in a village, right? We probably had a pretty similar upbringing."

Seckry cursed Tenk under his breath.

"I moved to Skyfall just in time to start high school, and you know what? I had never even heard of Friction before moving here."

Seckry couldn't believe it. Kristian's story was so similar to his own, it was uncanny.

Kristian chuckled to himself.

"Don't blame your friend Tenk for telling you that stuff. It's quite a common misconception, to be honest. For some reason, people like to believe that I'm this strange guy with this crazy history of hunting. Some journalist probably came up with it at some point and the rumours spread like wildfire, but the truth is, Seckry, I didn't become a legendary archer because I was experienced. I became a legendary archer because I connected with my avatar, because I was hungry to learn, and because I used my head. Often, it's about finding a solution to impossible situations. Do you know how I famously won the Meltdown for the Warriors back when I was in school?"

Seckry thought for a moment, vaguely recalling something that Tenk had told him.

"Yes, I think so," he said. "Was that the year you managed to hit the trophy with an arrow from miles away? The one that was the longest shot anyone's ever connected?"

Kristian smiled wryly.

"That's how everyone remembers it, yes."

"You mean . . . that's not what happened?"

"As good an archer as I am," Kristian revealed, "I'm not so good that I can hit such a small target from that far away. I won that Meltdown not by using my hands, but by using my head."

Seckry frowned.

"The broadcast that was displayed on the screens of the stadium that year didn't catch what really happened. One minute the camera was focused on me, firing my bow, and the next it was on the trophy, hurtling across the rocks, away from the Slayers' grasp and into my teammate's hands. There was a large jut of rock just to the left and slightly in front of the trophy. It was one of these ones that narrowed at the bottom, as if it would break away from the ground if you pushed it. I considered firing at the trophy, don't get me wrong, but I would have had no chance of hitting it. So I fired at the larger rock beside it, which broke off and hit the trophy."

"So, when people asked you about it after the match, you lied to them and said you'd hit the trophy directly?"

"No," said Kristian, laughing gently. "I told them the

truth. To be honest, I think it's more impressive hitting that rock and then having it ricochet, but I guess the story of the single arrow striking its target from so far away was more appealing to the fans and the media, so over time they forgot about the truth and now everybody believes that's what happened."

After that, Seckry completely relaxed, and he had a new fire inside him. If Kristian could become a legend from passion, determination, intelligence, and hard work, then so could he.

For the remainder of the evening, Kristian showed Seckry several new ways to hold his bow, each for different situations, and taught him how to reload with super-fast efficiency, so that he could react better when he was surrounded by enemies.

When the lesson was over, Seckry felt like a new player. He couldn't wait to show off his new skills to the Eidolons.

Seckry thanked Kristian, assuming that that would be their one and only session, but Kristian offered to train him twice a week until the Meltdown, and Seckry gladly accepted.

Over the course of the sessions, Kristian taught Seckry numerous ways of outsmarting his enemies and even how to use a bow to strangle an opponent from behind. But when their final lesson before the Meltdown arrived, Kristian said he wanted to focus purely on aiming.

"I don't want you to think that having a steady shot isn't important," he said. "You still need to have exceptional aim to compete at this level of competition."

Seckry nodded as Kristian picked up the target board and dropped it a few metres further away.

It took Seckry a few shots, but eventually he hit the board. The problem was that every time Seckry landed an arrow, Kristian would move the target further away, until it was nearing the rear wall, and move Seckry back a step each time, to make the distance even greater.

Seckry fired shot after shot after shot, coming short every time. Eventually he dropped the bow to his side, exhausted.

"It's one step too far," he said. "It's impossible."

"You think I became the greatest Friction archer of the last decade by giving up when my hands got tired?" Kristian said sternly. "You give up now, you lose this year's Meltdown."

Seckry forced his arms to lift the bow once more and he took aim. But there was just no way he could hit it from this distance. He could barely see the board.

Kristian looked at his watch.

"We're staying here until you hit it," he said. "And in two minutes time, I'm moving you back another two steps, so you'd better hurry up."

"Further away?" said Seckry, aghast. "You've got to be kidding."

"Like I said, you've got two minutes. All you've got to do is hit it and we're finished. Simple."

Seckry's pain suddenly turned into a bout of anger and he pulled the arrow back aggressively. He was almost tempted to aim the thing right at the bottle of water Kristian was holding, and shoot the darn thing out of his hands.

"Come on!" Kristian shouted. "I want you to hit that board so hard it knocks the thing over!"

Seckry grimaced and looked up at the glistening chandelier, catching his breath.

The chandelier.

It was hanging directly above the target.

Seckry glanced at Kristian, who was looking at his watch again, no doubt counting down the seconds until those two minutes were up.

Seckry couldn't do this any longer.

He swung his bow upwards and fired, sending the arrow straight for the chandelier and slicing it from its fixture.

The weighty thing slammed into the board, obliterating it in a plume of dust and shattered glass.

There was silence aside from the tinkling of broken glass showering the wooden floor.

Kristian turned on him and glanced slowly back and for between Seckry and the carnage.

Seckry's anger vanished in an instant and was replaced by petrification. That chandelier could have cost hundreds, if not thousands, of notes. He was doomed.

"Kristian, I-I'm so sorr . . ." Seckry stammered.

But a huge grin began to creep slowly up the sides of Kristian's face.

"I thought you'd never work it out," he said.

"You mean . . . that's what I was supposed to do?" said Seckry.

"I lied about this place being the dining room," Kristian said. "The thing was made of sugarglass. I stuck it up there for the purpose of this training."

Seckry's mouth was hanging open.

"You used your intelligence to achieve the impossible. Welcome to the elite, Seckry," said Kristian, and held out his hand for Seckry to shake.

Chapter Twenty-Three

Lessana's Locker

"It was sugarglass!" said Seckry the next lunchtime as they were scoffing down sandwiches in the corridor. "Can you believe it?"

Tenk, who was sniffing his sandwich suspiciously, said, "I still can't believe the guy wasn't raised by wolves, to be honest with you, Seck."

"Guys, guess what?" said Tippian. "A bit of info's been leaked at FIFE. It turns out, one of the Western Warriors has a lightning bolt upgrade this year."

"Are you sure?" said Loca. "Because if that's true, that's pretty useful to know."

"I'm sure," said Tippian.

"Then we need to make sure at least one of us has got protection from electrocution," said Loca.

"I went to the Emporium as soon as I found out," said Tippian. "They've completely sold out of electrical shields."

"Wait," interrupted Tenk. "Didn't Lessana have an electrocution shield?"

"Oh, Gedin . . ." said Tippian. "This is gonna be messy."

Loca looked around shiftily.

"It's probably still sitting in her locker," she said.

"You're not saying we should steal it, are you?" said Tippian. "Lessana's bad enough when she's happy. Can you imagine what she would be like when she's mad?"

"No, I'd never steal anything off her," said Loca. "But, I mean, she's not exactly using the thing at the moment, is she? We could probably . . . borrow it, just for the Meltdown, and then put it back."

"No, it's not there," said Tenk. "Have a look for yourself. Her locker's empty. I saw her empty it the other day."

Loca grumbled.

"I bet she knew we'd be eying it up, and took it out of spite."

"Loca, we did throw her off the team. I know I'm not Lessana's biggest fan, but you can't blame her really."

"Someone's gonna have to ask her to lend it to us," said Loca.

"Are you mad?" spat Tenk.

"It would be really useful," said Tippian. "But do you really think she'd give it to us?"

Seckry's instinct was to agree with the two boys; he didn't think anyone in Lessana's situation would have been forgiving enough to lend them the electrocution shield, never mind Lessana, who was vindictive enough on a good day.

He was just about to oppose the idea when he thought of all the hard work and training he had been putting in with Kristian. If something of Lessana's could increase their chances of winning, even just by a little bit, then he was willing to do anything to get it.

"Who's gonna be the one to ask her?" he said reluctantly.

Tenk sighed and looked at the floor, shaking his head.

"This is gonna be bad, guys. Real bad."

"Come on, we can draw straws," said Loca. "I've got a ton of the things in my backpack." She pulled out a handful of bright blue straws and a pair of scissors before snipping the ends of them all at different lengths and shuffling them in her hands before squeezing them tightly in her palm and thrusting her closed hand out to the group.

"Why are you carrying all those straws around?" said Tenk.

"Tenk," said Loca. "Straws are just the tip of the iceberg. This bag's like a bottomless pit. There are things in here you've probably never even heard of."

They all took a turn in drawing a straw, and every one of them cringed as they peeled it out of Loca's tight grip. Seckry's stomach lurched as he pulled out what looked like the top half of one, but found that there was no second half of the straw to pull.

"Unlucky, Seck," said Tippian. "I'd suggest asking her after the final bell rings. You don't want to cause a fuss between lessons."

Seckry nodded.

"If I come to school with a black eye tomorrow, you'll know how I got it," he said grimly.

Luckily for Seckry, Eiya, Tenk and Tippian, Lessana was a year older than them, just like Loca and Kimmy were, so they never had to endure her wrath during lessons. Loca had given him the heads up earlier and told him that they were going to be in room S17 at the end of the day, so when the bell rang and everyone started evacuating the school, Seckry rushed to the seventh floor to catch her before she left.

He caught Loca and Kimmy's eyes as he approached Lessana. Loca silently mouthed him a 'good luck.'

"Lessana, I know this is probably a silly question but . . . could we . . . use your electrocution shield upgrade in the meltdown?"

Lessana shook her head lethargically and said, "Sure, go ahead."

Seckry opened one eye, surprised to see that there were no fists flying in his direction.

"Uh . . . thanks," he said uncomfortably, waiting for her to go get it.

"What, are you waiting for me to wish you good luck or something? I said you can use it, now get out of here."

"Can we have it now?" Seckry asked.

"You've already got it," Lessana said. "I left that one in my locker. I expected you'd want it."

Seckry frowned.

"You didn't take it?"

"No," Lessana said as if speaking to a child. "I left it in my *locker*."

"Oh Gedin," said Seckry. "Then I think we've been robbed."

"Look," said Tenk, as they arrived at the training room, "There's no way we could have been robbed. She's lying to us. She took it out of spite, she must have."

"Come on, Tenk, maybe she's being sincere," said Kimmy.

"Sincere? This is *Lessana* we're talking about."

"He's right, Kim," said Loca. "She's probably laughing at us behind our backs right now."

"I'm sorry, but Lessana can kiss my hairy butt," said Tenk, and pulled a marker pen out of his pocket. He walked over to the old whiteboard that was on the left wall and drew a caricature of Lessana kissing a pair of huge, hairy buttocks.

Seckry and the others couldn't help but stifle a laugh. Tenk was pretty good at cartoons.

"Wait," said Tenk, wiping out her body with his sleeve. "This is more true to life." He drew a plumper version with a cheeseburger in her hands.

"Oh, come on, Tenk," said Kimmy. "Don't make fun about her weight."

"Well, it's true," said Tenk. "I mean, if she really wants to compete at Friction again, she's gonna have to get on a treadmill. She was always holding us back because she was slow and out of breath."

He stepped back and admired his handiwork.

"Losing the weight wouldn't change her ugly mug though. It really does say something about a person when their ogre avatar actually has a more attractive face than them."

As much as Seckry disliked Lessana, he thought Tenk was getting a bit too personal, and turned around to put his backpack in his own locker, but he stopped as soon as he turned.

Standing by the entrance was Lessana, her eyes streaming silent tears.

Seckry opened his mouth to speak, but had no idea what to say. She had seen and heard everything.

"I . . . I just wanted . . . to give you guys the other upgrade . . . the ball and chain weapon."

Seckry stood static, bright red with embarrassment and shame.

"I'll give it to you another time," Lessana said, her voice completely stripped of its usual bravado, and exited the room. The others hadn't even noticed that she had come and gone. They were still too busy mocking her and laughing about her.

"Guys," Seckry said, feeling dreadful. "That's enough."

Before Seckry had time to accept it, the night before the Meltdown was upon them. Seckry and Eiya tucked themselves into bed and switched the light off at around 10 p.m, the earliest they had done for a long time. They had to be bright and fresh tomorrow if they wanted to stand any chance of winning.

But, hard as he tried, Seckry couldn't get off to sleep for nerves and excitement, and Eiya was even more alert, petrified at the thought of competing in her first Meltdown.

"Seck, I still don't know all the rules," she said, pained.

Seckry laughed lightly.

"Don't worry, I still don't, either. You'll be fine as soon as the game has started. It'll feel natural, just like any of our practise sessions. The main things to remember are that we need to collect all the items, and then we need to collect the trophy at the end. And if other players have any of the items, we need to kill them and acquire them before we can touch the trophy."

"But . . . there's all these changes too in the update, and . . . and . . ." She placed the rule sheets on her quilt. "I should sleep, shouldn't I?"

Seckry nodded, and she laid her head on her pillow.

Before long, Seckry had drifted into a troubled sleep in which he was sat in the front row of a wedding. Standing, waiting for his bride, was Kayne, his mutated body bursting out of his suit, and walking down the aisle towards him was Eiya, looking like an angel, dressed in an ethereal, white wedding dress. Seckry tried to call out, and to get out of his seat to stop her, but he had no control over his body. He was paralysed, frozen to the spot. Not even his jaw would open to let him protest. He was helpless. As Eiya passed him, she turned to look at him, but her beautiful eyes gave him a confused expression, as if she had no idea who he was, or what he was doing there on her special day.

He woke the next morning feeling groggy, and headed straight for the shower to wake himself up and shake the dream out of his mind.

Eiya barely spoke for most of the day, since she was glued to the pages of the new ruleset once more, analysing each and every change.

When five o'clock came around and it was time to leave the flat, he practically had to pry the sheets out of her little fingers.

As they exited the car into a sea of other families, Seckry was immediately hit with the warm smell of fried onions and ketchup, and the sweet stickiness of candy and syrup. There was also something else in the air; something that Seckry guessed was a hint of sweat from all of the nervous players.

Tenk was always saying you couldn't beat the atmosphere of a Meltdown, and he was right. There was something unique; some fizzing, nervous, excited energy about a Meltdown that you just couldn't find at any other time or at any other place.

Friction events were always filled with fans waving banners too, and this time, Seckry saw a distant child waving a banner that read "Go Sevenstars!"

Seeing his own name was surreal but invigorating at the same time, and only helped to fire him up and motivate him even more.

Finally, he caught sight of Tenk, who was approaching them with a massive grin on his face, wearing a fan t-shirt that read 'Eidolons Rule!' He turned around as he reached them, pulling the shirt tight. On his back were the words 'BINKO' and 'BASHER.'

"Tenk," said Loca, who joined them simultaneously, "as much as we *do* rule, those t-shirts are supposed to be for fans, not us. Take it off, it's embarrassing."

Tenk just turned around and puffed out his chest.

"Loca, I can be a fan of myself. What's wrong with that? Anyway, the guy let me have it for half price since my own name was on it. I couldn't turn down half price."

Kimmy was the last to join them, and Seckry couldn't help but notice how different he seemed from last time. Even the way he was standing was much more confident. Helping to win last year's Meltdown for the Eidolons had really given him the boost he needed, and from what Seckry had gathered from Loca, Kolda was now actually encouraging his son, rather than scolding him for not being good enough.

As they were getting prepared for battle, Kimmy did disappear to use the bathroom at one point, and Tenk followed him to make sure he wasn't being sick like last year, but returned a few moments later to ensure them that he was simply having a pee.

As everyone began to take their seats before the action began, Gavanis Mendakar and her mum wandered past and both gave the group a dirty glance. Gavanis's mum was just as lanky as her daughter, and had a hive of permed, narrow hair sprouting out of the top of her head, just making her even lankier.

"I can't believe you're being made to spend the entire year with these imbeciles," she muttered, her sly eyes scanning them up and down.

"Excuse me?" said Loca.

"The only reason you won the Meltdown last year was because the Overseers are biased, and they wanted an underdog to win for a change. Honestly, how did they expect my Gavvy to survive that underwater surprise last year when she's a spider mecha? It was a personal attack, if you ask me. And don't even talk to me about that Kod boy."

"What did you say?" said Loca, confrontationally.

"Please! He spends the whole time sleeping through the entire Meltdown, and then, all of a sudden, he turns up at the end and everyone thinks he's some kind of hero? Pathetic."

"Kimmy was unconscious," Loca said sternly.

But before Loca could attack the woman, the Friction

voice boomed around the stadium.

"Can all combatants please make their way to their pods, immediately."

Kimmy caught up with them, and the Eidolons hurried through the crowds into the central area, where four sets of six pods were clustered, each colour-coded to indicate the teams; red for the Northern Nightmare, blue for the Western Warriors, yellow for the Southern Slayers, and green for themselves.

To the left of the pods was the elimination stand; a large, empty stage that was where players went to watch the remainder of the event after being killed in the game.

Gavanis followed them down, and turned to Kimmy before joining her team.

"Come on, Kod," she said, outstretching her arms. "How about a good luck hug? We've both been handicapped this year having to travel to train."

A very unnerved and confused Kimmy gave the group a backwards glance before warily accepting her embrace.

"Yeah, good luck . . . after *this,*" Gavanis said loudly, and jabbed him in the base of the spine with something.

Kimmy yelled and recoiled.

Gavanis laughed and held up her weapon. It was a small syringe.

"Lenni's Limb Number," she said, in hysterics, as she backed away. "Hey, what's wrong, Kod? Got the Meltdown nerves again? You're shaking."

Kimmy's legs looked as though they were about to collapse.

"I can barely feel them," he said despairingly, clutching onto Seckry's shoulder for support.

"That sly, evil, ugly, stick insect pig!" Loca raged. "Where's the Overseers? This is sabotage!"

"Would all combatants please enter their pods," came the Friction voice once again, echoing around the stadium.

There wasn't any time to sort it out. Kimmy would just have to try his best.

On top of his pure rage and anger at Gavanis, Seckry felt

terrible for Kimmy. He had trained really hard, and all of his efforts were now wasted. He would probably be picked off in the first few minutes of entering the game.

As they were hauling Kimmy over to his pod, the commentators burst into life.

"Here we are, once again," said Mick Mannerim, "at the sold out Skyfall Arena for the twenty-eighth annual Friction Mega Meltdown, ladies and gentlemen! I believe the Eastern Eidolons have a new player replacing Lessana Lubworth this year, Jowe."

"Indeed they have, Mick," said Jowe Kingsfoller. "From what I know, she's very new to the game, and has only been training for less than a year. We'll find out tonight if that holds her back."

"Good grief," said Mick Mannerim. "There is something seriously wrong with Kimmy Kod. His teammates are actually dragging him into his pod."

"It could very well be a case of overtraining," said Kingsfoller. "It wouldn't be the first time it's happened, Mick. Especially after the win last year. Maybe he just wanted to make sure he would live up to everyone's expectations and pushed himself too hard in the build-up."

"He's been drugged!" Loca screamed at the commentator's booth, but Seckry knew they wouldn't be able to hear her.

Once Kimmy was inside, the rest of them quickly entered their own pods, Eiya taking a deep breath before stepping into hers.

Seckry placed his Anikam avatar into the slot when the Friction voice prompted him to, then his dark pod suddenly came alive, and swooping footage of green hills and forests played all around him.

"Heroes of Atoria," said the Friction voice. "A group of Desertic bandits recently attempted to steal the highly valuable necklace collection of Princess Omotep of Greenwillow. The bandits were caught, but the necklaces were lost during the capture, and are now believed to be scattered across Greenwillow. King Tockenhep has promised fame and fortune to any group who can retrieve his daughter's precious necklaces and deliver them to the sacred Head of Koshka. To aid heroes in their quest, he has placed many power-ups across the land."

Chunky text appeared that read:

FIND ALL SIX NECKLACES AND DELIVER THEM TO THE HEAD OF KOSHKA FOR THE WIN

The horn that signalled the start of the match blared through the stadium, and Seckry felt his feet lift off the floor of the pod as the gravity disappeared.

Chapter Twenty-Four

The Twenty-Eighth Annual Friction Mega Meltdown

"Here! We! Go!" screamed Mick Mannerim.

Seckry felt his weight return, and he hit the earthy floor of a forest. He scanned around him hastily and noticed Eiya's avatar standing right beside him, holding her sword ready for action.

"You okay?" Seckry asked her, but Eiya had no time to respond, as a flaming axe hurtled towards her. Seckry pulled her to the ground as the axe thudded into a tree behind them, scorching the bark.

Their attacker, a humanoid barbarian, swiftly hid himself behind a tree a few yards away, but Seckry could see a protruding elbow.

Seckry rolled to his knees, aimed carefully, and took a shot before the avatar could hurl another axe at them. There was a cry of pain as the arrow thudded into the elbow, knocking the avatar from his hiding spot. Seckry wasted no time in firing directly at the humanoid's bare chest, and he crumpled into a heap on the mossy floor.

Seckry lowered his bow and turned to Eiya, but Alaria's face was manic.

"Look out!" Eiya shouted, and dived on him as a laser blast zapped the spot where he had been kneeling, frazzling the shrubbery.

"Let's go, let's go!" Seckry said quickly, and they both scrambled to their feet, running into the safety of some nearby trees.

When they were sure they were out of sight, Eiya leaned back against a huge oak, breathing heavily.

"This is so brutal," she said. "We were almost toast."

Seckry suddenly swung his bow up as an anima burst into their clearing, but he lowered it as he recognised the pink fur of Kittya, Loca's avatar.

"Guys, you okay?" she said, and they both nodded. "Great. I just spoke to Tenk and Tippian. I've sent Tippian to look for an entrance into the underground because there's almost always a high-tech underground facility in Greenwillow levels, and it'll most likely require someone with hacking skills to get in."

"What about Kimmy?" Eiya asked.

"I'm going to look for him now," Loca said, Kittya's face wrinkling with concern. "He didn't spawn close to me. Have you guys seen him at all?"

"No, it was just us two," said Seckry.

"Okay, you should split up and try to find one of the necklaces each. If we all find one and meet at the head, we're sorted."

"What is this Head of Koshka?" Seckry asked. "What does it look like?"

"Don't worry, you won't be able to miss it," said Loca. "Ive got to go." With that, she sped off into the woods to find Kimmy.

Seckry readied his bow and scouted the area. His archery lessons with Kristian were already paying off, as he felt like he was holding the bow much more confidently and strongly than last year, and he knew his reaction speed had doubled. Once he was sure the area was clear, he looked Alaria deep in the eyes and said, "Welcome to your first Meltdown, Eiya."

Alaria's feline mouth curved into a nervous grin, and Eiya laughed with a slight disbelief at the fact that this was actually happening.

"Three players are already out!" Mick Mannerim roared, as Seckry darted through the trees in the opposite direction of Eiya. "Two from the Warriors and one from the Slayers. The Eidolons and the Nightmare still have all members intact."

"Yes!" Seckry muttered to himself, quietly. That meant that Kimmy was still in the game somewhere.

But his joy was short lived. As he reached another clearing, a mecha was stood with its arms outstretched, rotary canons built into each of its fists.

Seckry dropped to his knees and shuffled behind a giant toadstool, aiming an arrow at the player inside the cockpit of the machine; a girl that Seckry recognised as one of the Southern Slayers.

But the mecha had to have had some kind of scanning upgrade attached, because it immediately turned to face Seckry, its robotic legs stamping on the ground as its body rotated.

Seckry pulled the arrow back quickly, but a metal lid slid over the cockpit, protecting the player.

Seckry sprinted out from his hiding place immediately as the guns began spraying bullets into the toadstool, spattering chunks of fungus everywhere.

There was no way Seckry could take out the player with that metal shield covering her, but he had to do something before she relocated him and caught him in her bullet storm. He dived to the left, aiming instead for her fists, and fired an arrow straight into the connecting tubes between the mecha's forearms and fists, slicing off both metal hands in succession, sending them smashing to the floor and leaving the mecha completely weaponless.

The protective lid dropped from the cockpit, and Seckry could see the girl inside, fuming with rage.

Seckry pulled an arrow back, and aimed it directly at her.

But before he could let go, the girl pressed a button and a thin layer of semi-translucent, digital fabric materialised, forming a wall between them.

Seckry gripped the arrow tightly, just before it could slip through his fingers. He had seen this type of barrier in one of the official guidebooks. It was a reflection sheet. Anything fired into it would come straight back out in the opposite direction. He froze, trying desperately to think of a solution before the player could come up with a way to kill him. But, if he let go of the arrow, it would come racing back to him, causing a self-kill.

"Go on," the girl laughed through the mecha's tinny voice. "Fire one. I dare you."

Seckry's heart was racing. There was no way he could penetrate the sheet. He had to somehow get his arrow to be reflected in the mecha's direction. He only had a few seconds before the player would get tired of this taunting and come stampeding towards him.

Then it clicked.

Seckry glanced up into the trees and shouted: "Fire! She's vulnerable from the top!"

There was nobody there, but the mecha didn't know that. She looked up, scanning the treetops wildly, before creating another reflection sheet floating above her in case of any downward fire.

Seckry seized the moment.

He aimed for the narrow gap between the sheet facing him and the one facing the sky, and fired.

The arrow shot into the underside of the sheet above the mecha at a ninety degree angle and was reflected back out of it, straight into the cockpit, smashing through the glass and destroying the player. The lifeless beast collapsed to the ground and the two reflection sheets disintegrated into a cascade of small, binary numbers.

Seckry raced around the fallen player, heading for the trees once more. He had no idea where he was going, but the only way he was going to find anything was by exploring.

He stopped a few times, listening to the words of the commentators, trying to work out which players were close by, and which players were already eliminated. Sometimes the commentators could be a hindrance, revealing hiding spots and other things, and sometimes they could be a blessing. This time, there was one thing Seckry was listening out for; Eiya's name. He couldn't help but worry about her, as if this wasn't just a video game, and that she was in real danger.

But all he heard were the names Haveld Barkar and Donnis Camb, who seemed to be in the midst of an epic battle inside a hollowed-out, giant tree trunk somewhere.

Eventually, Seckry found an exit out of the dense forest, and skidded to a halt as he realised the grassy floor beneath him suddenly gave way to a gigantic chasm. It was like the programmers had literally ripped a rough chunk out of the digital ground. The strangest thing was that there was a jut of land in the centre of the deep chasm, like a tall, thin island, and on top of it was a glowing necklace, hovering slightly and spinning on the spot.

For a millisecond, Seckry considered making a sprint and jumping, but thankfully, common sense overtook before he could act upon it. The island was much too far away to reach via a jump; he would have fallen to the bottom of that rift and his game would have been over.

He quickly hid behind a tree as another player, (a chunky humanoid from the Northern Nightmare that Seckry recognised as Beng Rots), came jogging into the clearing. The avatar spotted the necklace, grunted greedily, and launched himself off the cliff. It was a good attempt, Seckry had to admit. The player nearly reached the edge of the island, but instead, clawed the wood desperately as he fell to his death with a heavy thud.

There had to be another way of reaching it.

Seckry scanned the treetops above him. Over to his left there was something strange about one of the trunks. It looked like it had been carved into, making rough steps. It was hard to see what was going on at the top of the tree because there was so much foliage, but Seckry wasn't about to wait around wondering.

He glanced around him quickly, making sure there were no bullets flying in his direction, and made a dash for it. He scrambled up the trunk, digging Anikam's sharp claws into the wood to help him.

But about half way up, Seckry felt a hand grip the back of Anikam's jacket and he was wrenched away from the tree, falling to the ground and crashing to the floor in a cloud of dead leaves.

Even though the simulated pain within the Friction

universe felt slightly different to real pain, it was still excruciating to hit the ground with such force. He opened his watery eyes to see Jobey Mobbins' avatar glaring down at him evilly.

"That's for last year!" Mobbins shouted, before scrambling up the trunk himself.

Seckry forced Anikam's body to move, and began chasing after Mobbins, wincing as he did so. He managed to grab Mobbins' right foot at one point, but the muscular humanoid just kicked his hand away.

After a great deal of climbing, Seckry realised that Mobbins had reached some kind of treetop wooden platform. He heaved himself up to find Mobbins grabbing a hold of a zip wire. Seckry's eyes followed the line of the wire. It ended just after the chasm. Mobbins was going to whizz down there and let go above the island, landing directly on top of it and seizing the necklace for himself.

Seckry had just moments to think of a plan. In those few moments, his eyes scanned around him wildly and he noticed two things; one, that there was something strange sitting in the bottom of the chasm; something shiny and metallic that looked suspiciously like a hoverbike that he had seen once before in an over-eighteens match, and two, that there was something directly to his right; a floating pickup of some sort in the shape of a glowing, purple jacket.

A piece of text appeared on his heads up display as he focused on it.

Gravity Protection Suit

You will be able to fall from any height and the impact will do no damage.

That was it. Seckry had a plan. The protection suit had to have been placed there for a reason, and he was going to use it.

He gripped the spinning suit and it vanished, making the whole of Anikam's body flash purple.

Gravity Protection Suit equipped

Seckry flung himself through the air, just as Mobbins kicked off the platform, and he wrapped himself around the hulking humanoid, sending them both hurtling down the zipwire at a breakneck speed.

Mobbins wriggled violently, trying to shake Seckry off, but Seckry dug Anikam's claws into his bare skin, attaching himself and making Mobbins yell out in agony.

Seckry was waiting for the right moment to unleash his plan, but it was hard to judge where they were in relation to the chasm because they were moving so fast and branches and leaves were whipping them as they sped.

Then the trees cleared, and the chasm was beneath them.

Seckry slashed his claws across Mobbins' knuckles, and the humanoid let go of the zip wire, sending them both free-falling through the air in a spinning tumble. Mobbins roared as they plummeted into the seemingly bottomless abyss.

"See you next year!" Seckry shouted, just before they crashed into the base, sending shards of rubble, rock, and stone spattering everywhere.

"Genius!" screamed Jowe Kingsfoller. "Seckry Sevenstars just pulled off a massive trick, Mick! He saw that gravity suit and he acted accordingly. This is why I love Friction!"

"You and me both, Jowe. What a treat for the fans!"

Seckry picked Anikam's body up after one of the strangest sensations of his life. He had felt the impact of hitting the ground, but there was absolutely no pain. It had almost felt fun.

He had no time to relish in the joy of his new pickup, though. He had to get the necklace before another player figured out an easier way to swipe it for themselves. He jumped over Mobbins' lifeless avatar and plonked himself onto the hoverbike.

It took him a moment to get used to the controls; he crashed into the chasm's walls a couple of times before working out how to move upwards, as well as backwards and forwards. When he finally grasped it, he gripped the handles and thrust upwards, floating into the fresh Friction forest air once again before swerving over to the island and grabbing the item.

"Yes!" Seckry said to himself, as the fourth necklace in the corner of his heads up display lit up, this one with a green glow, signalling that it was in possession of the Eidolons. But his celebration was cut short when a blue forcewave thumped into him, flipping him over three times and throwing him off the bike. He grabbed one of the handles desperately and hung on, dangling below the vehicle as it spun through the air. He heaved and wrenched himself up, back onto the seat, just in time to see another forcewave racing towards him. He swerved the bike out of the way and focused on the attacker.

It was an anima down in the forest.

There was no way he could ready his bow whilst trying to manoeuvre the bike, especially since wave after wave was being fired at him and he was constantly dodging the blows.

No, he had to think of another way to take out the player.

He drew an arrow out of its sheath and held it like a spear, then he revved the hoverbike's engine and propelled towards the attacker at full speed.

The abruptness of the move made the anima drop his weapon in shock and confusion.

Seckry held out the arrow as though he was jousting, and plunged it into the anima's chest before skidding to a stop a few yards further on.

"Oh, Gedin," said Seckry, unable to contain the massive grin that was spreading across Anikam's face. He would never have had the guts to try something like that last year. He couldn't believe he had actually pulled it off.

As he sat, catching his breath for a moment, he listened for more info on the other players.

"And Tippian Furst takes down Carrum Dago, acquiring the third necklace for the Eidolons! Impressive play, Jowe. He waited in hiding while Dago deactivated the dome around the item, and then sprung on him after the technical work was done. Intelligent move, intelligent move!"

Seckry cheered internally, but he still hadn't heard any mention of Eiya. Where was she? Had she been eliminated? And Kimmy, too. He had to have missed the commentators' comments on him during the action.

He checked his heads up display for an update. The Eidolons had three out of the six necklaces, the Northern Nightmare had two, and the Southern Slayers had one. All of them had been found, and the Eidolons were in the lead, but they needed to acquire all six and deliver them to whatever the Head of Koshka was before they could win the trophy.

He used the hoverbike to float upwards, so he could get a better idea of where he was and where he needed to go next, rising through the thick leaves and emerging into the sky.

The landscape was like a sea of green cloud, and up there, Seckry could see the huge, orange, digital sun, now sinking swiftly into the horizon, leaving the players in a cool twilight.

But it didn't take long to find his next destination.

Far off in the distance to his right was a giant, stone head, and Seckry could see a cluster of players gathered around it, like tiny insects from where he was, and the distant flashes of magic and gunfire.

That had to be the Head of Koshka.

He kicked the hoverbike into full speed and zoomed in its direction.

It took Seckry around five minutes to reach the building, and he had heard the commentators announce another two eliminations as he was travelling; Amelya Kiggins from the Western Warriors, and Tippian. He had no idea who was left. He had completely lost track. He also heard the commentators say something about Gavanis using an electrocution shield effectively, which explained the stolen upgrade.

As he pulled the hoverbike to a halt, he looked up in awe. The stone head was a monstrous-looking thing the size of several houses, its hollow eyes and wide-open mouth spilling out an ominous red light.

Seckry ducked as a laser beam from a faraway opponent shot past Anikam's head.

He had no time to waste. He had to pick off the remaining enemies and capture their necklaces.

He jumped off the bike and ran into the open area, diving behind some mossy rocks for cover. He strung his bow and edged out, scoping for players.

Closest to him was Tenk's avatar, Basher, caught in a furious grappling match with one of the Southern Slayer humanoids, both of their weapons lying on the ground. The Slayer suddenly pinned Basher down before punching him in the face three times. Then, as he raised his fist to go for the killer blow, Seckry let loose his arrow, piercing the avatar in the ribcage and sending him out of the competition.

Seckry darted out from his hiding place, rushing to Basher to see if Tenk was okay.

But as he reached him, a blast of fire engulfed them both, and Seckry saw Basher's skin disperse into cinders. He turned to the attacker; a robed alchemist female humanoid with a staff, who looked shocked that Seckry was still alive, unaware of his fireproof upgrade, and fired a quick arrow, hitting her in the forehead.

But the arrow disintegrated on impact. She had to have some kind of protection from bullets and arrows. Seckry was useless against her.

The alchemist then raised her staff once more, and the glowing fire that was licking the tip morphed into a freezing blue. She was going to blast him with an ice attack, and Seckry had no protection whatsoever against that.

He was done for.

But as she swung the staff into the air, there was the roaring of an engine and a futuristic tank sped across the rough ground, pummelling into the alchemist and smashing her avatar into pieces.

Seckry scrambled for cover, but grinned in surprise as Kimmy's avatar waved at him from the driver's seat.

"I've got just enough feeling in my legs to press accelerate and brake!" he yelled, but before he could say any more, a rocket collided with the tank, exploding both the vehicle and Kimmy.

Seckry shielded his face as flaming debris panged around him.

He quickly located the offender through the smoke; a Mecha with dual rocket launchers on each shoulder, and fired an arrow at the cockpit, but it bounced off.

Then, just as Seckry was about to run, a high-pitched scream sounded around the clearing, and Eiya's avatar, Alaria, pounced out of one of the treetops behind the Mecha, landed on its head, and pierced her sword through the glass cockpit, directly into the player's chest. The mecha fell forwards heavily and Eiya jumped off, running into Seckry's arms.

Seckry squeezed her tightly and laughed incredulously.

"I thought you were out of it!" he panted.

"I'm just as amazed as you, Seck," she said.

They listened momentarily as the commentators went wild.

"We're down to the last six players!" Mick Mannerim yelled. "Seckry Sevenstars, Eiya Tacana, and Loca Thumbsuckle for the Eidolons, and Rikky Rasseton, Leller Umsworth, and Gavanis Mendakar for the Nightmare! And more importantly, the Eidolons are now in possession of all six necklaces, meaning they just need one player to enter the head for the trophy to appear!"

Seckry and Eiya both glanced at each other for a split second, and then Seckry saw Loca dart out of a hiding place and made a run for the head, dodging a few flying projectiles from the remaining Nightmare players. As she entered the head's mouth, there was a flash of golden light and the trophy appeared, but it wasn't simply sitting on the head's tongue; it was hanging from a rope attached to the roof of its mouth, like some giant tonsil.

"The trophy is right there for the Eidolons to take!" shouted Jowe Kingsfoller. "They are moments away from their second win in a row!"

But Seckry could see that there was no way up for Loca, and one of the remaining Nightmare players was heading towards her, about to take her out with a spear. The trophy would need to be cut down so she could catch it.

This was it. This was where all of Seckry's training with Kristian was going to come into play. This was his moment of fame. He darted out, pulling his arrow back to the point where it was nearly snapping the string.

"If Sevenstars can sever that rope it'll be a miracle, Jowe!" said Mick Mannerim. "We know that Sevenstars' skills with a bow are good, but that's one hell of a distance!"

"Well, I hear he's been training with Kristian Surefoot, Mick, and we all know what he's famous for, don't we?"

"Remember this moment however you like," said Seckry, and tilted his bow to the left, aiming for a much larger target than the rope; the head's third tooth.

The arrow whizzed through the air and hit the tooth, smashing it into shards of stone that severed the rope behind it, releasing the trophy.

"This is it!" screamed Mick Mannerim, as the trophy fell towards the outstretched arms of Loca's avatar.

Suddenly, there was a sub-atomic boom, everything turned black and white, and the Friction voice said, "Time reversal pocket activated!"

Anikam's body began involuntarily moving backwards. Seckry lost control of everything; he couldn't even turn his head or move his eyes. The shards of tooth that had sliced the trophy off its rope were now fitting back together and locking into the god's gum, and the arrow that had hit it was now hurtling backwards, soaring in reverse towards Seckry, before slotting back into his bow, the hilt slipping into his poised grip.

This couldn't be happening.

Colour flooded back into the world around them and the Friction voice said, "Play!"

Seckry had no time to get to grips with what had just happened. He aimed quickly, firing the arrow at the exact same spot on the tooth.

But this time, the Northern Nightmare knew exactly what he was going to do.

The other remaining player launched sideways through the

air, snatching Seckry's arrow mid-flight.

"Jowe! Did you just see that!" screamed Mick Mannerim. "I can't believe my eyes! Thumbsuckle practically had the trophy in her hands! The Eidolons had it in the bag, and out of nowhere, Gavanis Mendakar pops the time reversal pocket!"

"Unbelievable, Mick! What an incredible turn of fortune for the Northern Nightmare. Excellent play!"

Seckry drew another arrow and aimed again, desperate to repeat the move that was going to win the game.

But it was too late.

As he readied his bow, the avatar that had caught his previous arrow threw it at Anikam's neck.

Thud.

An excruciating pain rippled outwards from Seckry's neck and the Friction universe burst into a mess of binary numbers before changing into the shiny interior of his pod. He hit the ground, kicked the door open and slid out.

The crowd was deafening.

He looked up at the big screens and saw Gavanis's spider mecha stab Loca through the chest. A few moments later, Loca burst out of her pod and joined Seckry as he raced to the elimination stand.

It was just Eiya left for the Eidolons. And there were three Northern Nightmare players. Nobody would be able to survive a three-on-one onslaught.

"Eiya!" screamed Loca, as two of the players raced towards her, one holding a spear, the other a trident.

"I can't watch," Loca cried, but remained glaring at the big screens.

Seckry's heart was pounding.

Please don't let it be painful for her, he thought.

But as the one player drew back his spear to plunge it into her, Eiya charged at him with her sword and thrust it into his stomach before he had a chance to strike. Then she pulled it out swiftly and spun it at the same time, decapitating the player that had been charging at her from the other direction.

Loca jumped so high, Seckry thought she might fall off

the stand.

"Eiya! You legend!" she screamed.

Seckry couldn't believe it. He felt like his chest was going to burst with pride.

"Just two players left!" shouted Mick Mannerim. "Gavanis Mendakar for the Nightmare, and the newcomer, Eiya Tacana for the Eidolons. Just remember, one team has to be in possession of *all* necklaces AND the trophy to end the game and capture the win."

Eiya wasted no time in racing to the fallen necklaces that were now floating above the lifeless avatars that had been eliminated, while Gavanis seemed to be reloading the guns on her mecha's body and heading into the mouth of the head.

"It looks like Mendakar is going to allow Tacana to retrieve all of the necklaces in order to get them all in one place, then attempt to take out Tacana when she goes for the trophy," said Jowe Kingsfoller, and Seckry knew he was right. As Eiya entered the head and collected the sixth necklace from where it was floating above Kittya's body, Gavanis fired a blast out of one of her legs, but Eiya rolled out of its path, missing getting hit by a fraction.

"She's going to do it! She's going to do it!" Loca screamed next to Seckry.

"Tacana has all the necklaces!" screamed Jowe Kingsfoller. "She just needs to get past Mendakar and grab that trophy!"

Eiya swung her sword up and charged at Gavanis's avatar, screaming all the way. Gavanis fired shot after shot at her, but she dodged them and deflected them with the blade. As she reached the mecha, she swung the blade with all her force and sliced off one of the legs.

But as she made to swing for a second leg, Gavanis swiped one at Eiya, knocking her out of the mouth and tumbling away from the head.

As Eiya dragged Alaria to her feet, she saw Gavanis's avatar exiting the mouth to come for her, but as the mouth became unoccupied, something strange happened. There was the rumbling sound of stone moving, and the bottom of the mouth began rising, closing shut.

Gavanis's avatar stopped prowling and turned around, then she scuttled back to the head quickly and pounced on its cheek, using what had to be suckers to clamber up into one of the hollow eyes.

"Clever move!" shouted Mick Mannerim. "Tacana won't be able to reach her, and Mendakar can just fire shots at Tacana from there until she finds her target. The mouth has now fully closed shut so there's no way Tacana can get through to the trophy. Once Tacana has been eliminated, Mendakar can pick up the necklaces and then climb through one of the hollow eyes to get the trophy. I think this may be the end for the Eidolons, Jowe!"

Seckry grabbed hold of the railings as he watched the final moments of the match, his eyes unmoving from the screen above him.

Eiya ran to the mouth, trying desperately to find a way in, but as she scrambled, a rain of blasts hit the ground all around her. She had just seconds before she was picked off. Eiya jumped, scratching her claws on the head's stony surface, trying to climb the thing and reach the other hollow eye-socket, but it was no use. She slid down.

"We all played well," said Kimmy, in defeat. "Fair play to the Northern Nightmare this yea-"

But before Kimmy could finish his sentence, Eiya did something that nobody in the entire stadium was expecting.

She reached for her waist and pressed her evacuation button.

"Oh my goodness!" yelled Jowe Kingsfoller, "What on earthia is Eiya Tacana doing? She is evacuating her pod. I don't understand this. I mean, there was very little she could do in that situation, but she was still in the game. Is she actually quitting?"

Seckry watched from the elimination stands incredulously as Eiya burst out of her pod and began running into the audience. The six necklaces were hovering on the ground at the point where she exited, there for Gavanis to take.

"You know what, Jowe? Sometimes, Friction just gets too much for some people. The pressure can affect your mind -"

"Wait!" screamed Kingsfoller. "It can't be . . ."

Over the tannoy, Seckry heard a ruffling of paper.

"The eight-point-five changes! Wait! Yes! Oh Gedin, she's pulling off rule four-one-five! That's Lessana Lubworth she's grabbing!"

"Jowe, you're gonna have to explain this to the rest of us," said Mick Mannerim.

"Rule four one five," Kingsfoller read. "A team is now allowed one player substitution swap at any time."

Suddenly Lessana was sprinting through the crowd and down to Eiya's pod.

Seckry looked up at the big screens. Gavanis was almost back on the ground. They were moments away from losing the trophy to the Northern Nightmare.

Lessana jumped into the pod and slammed the door shut, and Ogg materialised on top of the necklaces, collecting all six in one go.

Gavanis looked down in shock and confusion.

"Lubworth?" she hissed, and her voice sounded throughout the stadium. "You were thrown off the Gedin damned team!"

"Aren't you pleased to see me?" said Lessana, through Ogg's gruff ogre voice, and without hesitation, swung her ball and chain, slamming it into the closed mouth. The ball detonated on impact and the stone erupted, creating a giant hole through which Ogg scrambled.

She swung her chain upwards, snatching the trophy from the deity's tonsils just as Gavanis was aiming for her, and it dropped directly into Ogg's chunky palm.

The Meltdown victory music burst into play around the stadium and the crowd went wild.

"That's it!" screamed Mick Mannerim, his voice just audible over the music and the mayhem. "For the second time running! The winners of the Friction Mega Meltdown, ladies and gentlemen . . . the Eastern Eidolons!"

Through the deafening crowd, Seckry could just about hear Gavanis's screams of rage as she ripped herself out of her glowing red pod, untied her headband, and threw it at one of the screens.

"I can't believe it!" Jowe Kingsfoller was screaming. "Just when it seemed like they were out of it, the Eidolons pull off the most spectacular comeback! I can assure you, ladies and gentlemen, that what Tacana just did was one hundred percent legal in the new Friction ruleset! Outstanding, absolutely outstanding!"

"I never thought I'd say this," Loca shouted at Seckry. "But I've never been so pleased to see Lessana!"

Chapter Twenty-Five

A Distant Flash

"I guess it paid off spending two days reading through those rule changes," Eiya said, grinning.

They were back at Estergate's Friction training room, scoffing their faces with jam-filled doughnuts that Tenk had picked up from one of the stalls at the stadium, and swigging back copious amounts of fizzy Fructofruit, which had been one of their prizes for winning.

"Eiya, you're such a . . . such a freakin' legend," said Loca, wrapping her arms around her. For a moment, Seckry thought she was about to kiss her.

"Thanks for . . . helping us out," Kimmy said to Lessana.

"Well," said Lessana. "I was mad at you guys . . . but I couldn't let that skinny scumbag take the trophy."

"We appreciate it," said Seckry.

"So," said Lessana, after a few moments of silence. "What's the situation? Am I an Eidolon or what?"

"You're an Eidolon," said Loca. "I don't know how it's going to work with the numbers now, but we'll work something out substitution-wise."

Lessana nodded, content, and everyone relaxed after that.

An hour into the evening, Tippian received a text message, and his face lit up as he read it.

"It's Kalem from FIFE," he said excitedly. "The Overseers caught Gavanis on camera, jabbing Kimmy with that limb number. She's been immediately dropped from the Nightmare, and she's suspended from playing Friction at all for two years!"

"Wow," said Seckry. "How are they going to stop her

playing?"

"It'll recognise her as soon as she steps into a pod," Tippian explained. "The Friction voice will tell her to get out."

"I hope it tells her to do more than that," said Tenk.

Over the next few hours they recalled each and every moment of their individual battles with other players, and relived the excitement of the event. By the end of the evening, everyone was feeling ecstatic from a mix of adrenaline from the win, and sugar from all the junk food. Tippian was still so fired up he ended up running around the training room pretending to dodge bullets before grabbing the real golden trophy that they had won (a replica of the in-game trophy) and filling it with an entire bottle of Fructofruit, then downing it, like drinking from a goblet, spilling it all over his t-shirt.

When the janitor finally came around to kick them out for the night, Seckry was exhausted, and he and Eiya headed back to the flat, their eyes drooping.

Before getting into bed, Seckry stood at the windowsill gazing out across the streets of Skyfall. Eiya shuffled up next to him and took a deep breath.

"You were amazing," Seckry said to her, softly.

Eiya gave him an innocent smile, two little dimples forming in her cheeks, and Seckry wanted nothing more than to kiss her right there and then.

Seckry swallowed, about to lean in, but before he could, Eiya turned her head to look out of the window, and her eyes glazed over, as though she were lost in her own thoughts, no doubt about the Elenya Kayne situation once again.

She jumped into bed a few moments later and was out like a light, so Seckry did the same, and fell into the deepest sleep he had had for a long time.

When his alarm went off at seven thirty in the morning, the first ray of cold sunlight was already creeping up over the monorail track and shining into the bedroom. Seckry fumbled for his phone to switch it off, but as he picked it up, he realised he had a text message waiting. It was from Vance.

Seckry, please come to my classroom at 9am in the morning. If you feel any tingling sensation in your fingers, please resist the urge to try anything until you're here. We don't know how these powers are going to work, and safety is paramount.

Seckry jolted upright.

His powers.

With Friction having consumed his life for the past several weeks, he had almost forgotten about the genesis trinity and the creogen in his DNA.

He got out of bed, being careful not to wake Eiya, who was still sleeping like a baby after the exhaustion of the previous day, and hurried to the bathroom. He wanted to obey Vance's caution, but he couldn't help staring at his hands as he stood at the bathroom sink, imagining something coming out of his fingertips; some incredible, mysterious force. Thankfully, nothing strange happened as a result of him simply imagining it, and he dressed himself quickly before leaving the flat and pulling the front door shut quietly.

When Seckry arrived at Estergate, the place felt a little eerie. Being a Sunday, the usually heaving front courtyard was now empty, the only remnants of pupil occupation being scraps of litter gently fluttering over the barren concrete.

Seckry had expected to have a half hour wait for Vance, since he had been up and out of the flat so early, but to his surprise, Vance's car slowly pulled into the parking lot just ten minutes later.

"I assumed you'd be here a little earlier than I'd suggested," said Vance with a smile, clicking his car's lock into place with his keys. "If I was told I had superpowers and they were awakening today, I'd be pretty eager too."

They took the stairs, since the pneumatic pods had been taken out of service for maintenance over the weekend, and entered Vance's classroom. Vance locked the door behind him.

"So," he said. "Nothing yet, I assume?"

Seckry shook his head. "Feels like a normal day."

"I was actually half expecting you to turn up floating or something this morning," said Vance. "I imagine you'll be able to create particles of air underneath you to push you upwards at some point."

Seckry smiled.

"If I knew how to, I would have."

The idea made him salivate with excitement, but the truth was, he hadn't had any indication by his own body that there was anything different about it yet.

"Congratulations, by the way," Vance said. "That was an incredible night of action."

"You watched it?" said Seckry.

"Of course. I had marking to do, so I couldn't be at the stadium, but I saw it on TV. That gravity suit stunt you pulled off was fantastic."

"Thanks," said Seckry. He had never imagined Vance watching Friction before. He felt a surge of pride, knowing that most of the pupils and staff had also been tuned in to watch him and the others compete for the school.

"Okay, I guess the first thing to do is just try this thing and see what happens," said Vance.

Seckry sat down at one of the desks, cautiously.

"What do you think I . . . do to make it work?" Seckry asked.

"I have absolutely no idea," said Vance, but seemed quite happy that he didn't know.

Seckry looked at his fingers for a moment and tried to imagine something coming out of them; some kind of string of energy. But nothing happened.

"Why don't you try imagining a specific object or material," said Vance, pulling up a chair so he was sitting opposite. "How about water? That could be an easy one."

Seckry closed his eyes and concentrated hard, trying to imagine the form of a floating droplet of water; the blueness and wetness and frailty of it. But nothing happened.

"I've been thinking about this over the last few days,"

Vance said, "and it's hard not to suspect that Adelbert and Rikard would have created some specific method of controlling the powers."

"What do you mean?" asked Seckry.

"Well . . . do you remember the teacher explaining how the mumprat infused with creogen was creating random bits of material around itself? The boys probably learned in that moment that they had to give humans some way of limiting that creational power with the mind, otherwise they would be creating things here there and everywhere."

"You haven't come across any instructions in the stuff we found in the genesis trinity room, have you?" Seckry asked him.

Vance shook his head.

"Unfortunately not. I guess the boys hadn't decided on that before they left school."

Seckry dropped his hands onto the table.

"This is going to be pointless, isn't it?" he said, deflated.

Vance took a deep breath and rubbed the stubble on his jawline thoughtfully.

Seckry attempted to concentrate hard once again over the next fifteen minutes, imagining plastic, then metal, then wood. But as hard as he tried, nothing materialised in front of him. Also, according to Kevan Kayne, when the creogen inside of a person was working, their veins would turn white, but Seckry's veins had remained their usual pale blue just under his skin, and showed no signs of changing.

"Do you think there's a possibility the creogen didn't get carried down to me from my dad?" Seckry asked, but before Vance could answer there was the glimmer of a distant flash through one of the windows. Vance pelted towards the blinds and flicked them shut, before sticking his fingers through them to create enough space for him to see out of. Then he quickly pulled a pair of binoculars out of one of his drawers and stared, transfixed.

"What was that?" said Seckry.

After a few moments, Vance pulled his fingers back through and turned around worriedly.

"It was the flash of a camera over in the library. There was a . . . man in a black hood. He vanished as soon as he saw me."

"He was . . . taking a photo of . . . us?" said Seckry.

Vance said nothing.

"A camera couldn't pick up something from that far away, surely?" said Seckry.

"It was a telescopic lens from what I saw," said Vance. "Something that would have a powerful zoom."

"Who'd want to take a photo of -" Seckry stopped himself as realisation dawned on him. "You don't think . . . that it was . . . Lux, do you?"

Vance said nothing for a while, lost in his own thoughts. Eventually he said, "Your father is convinced that Lux is still unaware of you and your sister's existence. It could just have been a tourist taking a photo of the school."

Seckry nodded slowly, but even the smallest suggestion that the crazed, murder-bent Lux knew who he was and where he was gave him the chills.

"I think we should forget about these powers for the moment," said Vance, his tone of voice serious and stern. "I will do my best to uncover some instructions. I think it's pointless until we have them. For now, I want you to have something."

He disappeared into his storage room and reappeared a few moments later holding a gun and a futuristic looking metal helmet.

"*Gedin*," Seckry muttered, taken aback.

"You probably won't need to use this," Vance said reassuringly, "but it wouldn't hurt to be prepared. Don't worry, this isn't a pistol, it's a stun gun that I've modified slightly. It won't kill a man, but it will paralyse him effectively. It fires a pellet of tranquilliser into a person's bloodstream and it works almost instantly. The charged coating of the pellet will provide the initial takedown via an electric shock, and by the time that wears off, the tranquilliser will have kicked in, giving you at least ten minutes before they can start moving again. That should be enough time for you to get help, should you need it."

Seckry breathed in and out slowly. The thought of carrying any type of gun around with him made him extremely anxious, but what was even more worrying was the helmet that Vance was holding in his other hand. Did Vance really expect him to walk around the streets wearing that thing? He'd be the laughing stock of the entire city.

"Oh, yes, the helmet!" said Vance, and threw it to Seckry.

Seckry caught it, surprised at how heavy it was, and stared at it, horrified.

"Sir . . . I . . . u-um," he stammered.

"Don't look so worried," Vance said with a smile. "It's something I was working on last year when we assumed Eiya's memory had been lost. It was designed to stimulate those parts of the brain that hold subconscious memories. I imagined it could help her recall her past."

Seckry sighed with relief.

"Of course, there's no need for it now," said Vance. "But I thought I'd give it to you anyway. If you ever forget where you've left your keys, feel free to try it out."

Chapter Twenty-Six

The Andersun Wellworth Young Inventor Award

Seckry spent the next few days exhaustively looking behind him whenever he heard the faintest of sounds, and gripping the base of Vance's stun gun inside his pocket whenever anyone so much as glanced at him in the street, in case it was Lux.

The only person who seemed even more anxious than Seckry was Tippian, who had only a matter of days to finish his invention before the Andersun Wellworth Young Inventor Award.

When the evening of the award ceremony came around, Seckry, Eiya, Tenk, Loca and Kimmy all met in Estergate's courtyard, and were guided by Mrs Furrowfog to the canteen. It seemed a strange choice of place to hold the event, especially after all of the issues with closing it down because of the hygiene, but apparently it was tradition, and Seckry had to admit, they had completely transformed the place. It had been given a full, elegant makeover, with royal blue drapes hanging from the walls, and stone statues of famous inventors dotted around. Thankfully, the awful, mutating mould that had been growing on one of the walls was concealed by the largest drape in the room, right behind the stage that had been set up. Seckry assumed it was still there, hidden, because he overheard teachers almost every day complaining about it.

While they were waiting for the ceremony to begin, Tenk amused himself by trying to guess the names of the inventors.

"That one's definitely Jupitus Kengo, he said, proudly. "Inventor of the light bulb. Definitely. I'd swear my life on it. See? I'm more knowledgeable than people give me credit for."

A girl who was sitting in the row in front of them turned sharply around and said, "It's Jutticus Farrencio, you twit. Jupitus Kengo is the guy from the washing powder ads."

Tenk was silent after that, except for the odd whisper of, "*I was almost right. Still pretty impressive, I think.*"

When everyone was quiet, the host, a winner from several years ago, talked a bit about the history of the award and then a little bit about their sponsor, Andersun Wellworth. When he finally introduced the first inventor onto the stage, the group sat up with full attention, as it was Tippian, looking petrified.

Go on, Tipps, you can do this, Seckry thought.

"The Voicemaster," Tippian said to the audience, and paused, taking in deep breaths, "is a device that allows you to capture someone's voice and recreate it, effectively allowing you to talk just like them."

There were a few murmurs of intrigue from the audience, but Seckry heard someone mutter, "My daughter's invention is *so* much better than this."

Tippian shuffled uncomfortably.

"You're probably wondering where the device is," he said, and then unbuttoned his smart shirt.

"The Voicemaster is designed to be discreet," he said. "It can attach to the collar of your shirt with a clip, or you can wear it around your neck on a chain, like I'm doing today, and it will be close enough to do the job. Nobody will ever know that you're using someone else's voice."

Seckry squinted, and could just about make out a little bead on a chain around Tippian's neck. He had to admit, he was impressed. When Tippian had first shown them the prototype of the Voicemaster on his birthday at the flat, it had been an ugly piece of circuitry the size of a television remote.

Tippian reached into his pocket and pulled out his set of

keys, pressing a button on a small keyring that must have switched the Voicemaster on wirelessly.

"Allow me to demonstrate," said Tippian, except that his voice was now that of a gruff, burly, middle-aged man.

There were a couple of gasps from the audience and Tippian said, "Stole this one off my uncle Boffer."

There was a raucous applause, and Tippian, for the first time, seemed to relax. He continued by showcasing a range of other voices from his family that he had captured, including his nan's, which had people crying on the floor with laughter. Then, the crowd had a whale of a time volunteering their own voices to Tippian, who got them to recite his selection of required words, before talking back to them as themselves.

By the time Tippian was leaving the stage, the audience was cheering like mad, and Seckry and the other Eidolons were whistling and stamping their feet, with Tenk even shouting, "Go Tippers!"

After watching the next four inventions, Seckry was sure Tippian had secured the award. There had been a couple of interesting ideas, but none with the sheer scope and appeal of the Voicemaster. After that, the place went downhill into complete chaos, as one girl accidentally let off a gas explosive that had everyone gasping for air and mothers screaming, herding their children out into the corridors. Eventually everyone returned to their seats, but the jovial mood wasn't restored by the next entry, who produced a device intended to suck up dirt, and was promptly escorted off stage whilst the host explained to her that the vacuum cleaner had been invented quite some time ago.

Finally, Zovak McVorak was introduced onto the stage to polite applause, although Tenk booed him discretely.

Seckry had no idea what invention Zovak was going to unveil, but he was sure it wouldn't stand a chance against Tippian's.

"I present to you today, ladies and gentlemen," said Zovak, running his fingers through his black, greasy hair, "the Purika formula."

A projector flickered on above the audience, projecting a mathematical formula onto the drapes at the back of the stage. It was three lines long and looked incredibly complex. Even the host, a former winner, looked completely baffled by it.

"I'm going to need a volunteer for my presentation today," Zovak said, scanning the crowd. His eyes met Seckry's.

Not me, not me, Seckry thought, hoping that he was telepathically sending out a signal.

"Seckry Sevenstars," he said. "Would you be so kind as to help out on this one?"

Seckry wanted no part in helping Zovak in this competition. What would Tippian think? He felt like a traitor, but he couldn't refuse in front of the entire audience. He reluctantly got up and made his way down to the stage.

"Thank you, Seckry," said Zovak. "Now, I can assure you, ladies and gentlemen, that Seckry was unaware that I would be calling him down here today. This is no magic trick."

Zovak rummaged around for a moment in a box that had been placed on a table for him, before pulling out a giant syringe.

Seckry stepped back instinctively, saying, "Whoa, what's going on?"

The crowd gasped as soon as they saw the needle.

"This won't hurt a bit," Zovak said with a grin, approaching Seckry forcefully, grabbing his arm, ripping up his sleeve and plunging the needle into his bicep.

Seckry was in complete shock. What on earthia had he just been injected with?

Someone in the crowd screamed.

Seckry tried to yank himself away but Zovak held his arm firmly.

"What are you *doing?*" Seckry said.

"Mr Sevenstars," Zovak said, loudly. "You have just been injected with a substance called pyroproxymatil monocalsilate, otherwise known as venomicin."

Seckry vaguely recognised the name from a chemistry

lesson, and his heart started pounding. "The *poison?*" he blurted. From what he remembered, venomicin was one of the fastest acting poisons there was, and turned a person physically green before their organs exploded inside of them.

"Yes, the extremely toxic poison," Zovak confirmed.

The crowd was now becoming a complete bustle, with a few cries of outrage and a few boos. Seckry saw that Eiya had left her seat and was halfway down to the stage, but was being held back by a security guard.

"Please! Please! Do not fear for our friend's life, ladies and gentlemen," said Zovak, smoothly. "You see, the Purika formula will completely eradicate every single ounce of the poison from his system."

"*He's turning green already!*" someone yelled.

Seckry looked to his left. Even the host seemed as though he was about to burst onto the stage and intervene. If Zovak was telling the truth, then he only had around ten minutes before he would be dead.

Zovak pulled a small, white tablet out of his box and held it up between his forefinger and thumb.

"I proudly present to you," he said, dramatically, "the Purika pill. Open wide, Seckry."

In any other situation, Seckry wouldn't have followed a word of Zovak's instructions, but his life was on the line. He opened his mouth and Zovak dropped the pill onto his tongue. Zovak handed Seckry a glass of water and he swallowed the tablet as fast as he could.

As the crowd went silent, waiting to see what would happen, Seckry felt an overpowering wave of happiness surge through him. He closed his eyes and the entire canteen seemed to disappear around him. He had never felt so relaxed, so content, and so blissful in all his life. All thoughts and worries about the poison had completely vanished.

"As you can see, my friends, the Purika is already destroying the unwanted particles in Mr Sevenstars' body," said Zovak, and Seckry opened his eyes, still riding a wave of euphoria.

The audience calmed a little, and one of the judges who

was sitting close to the stage said, "This isn't just some invention, this is a medical miracle!"

"What Seckry is feeling right now," said Zovak, "is a sense of purity; a sense of complete and utter wellbeing that he has never felt before. And do you know why? Because my invention has also eradicated all of the other impurities and toxicity from his body. Toxicity from things like junk food. Did you have any junk food yesterday, Seckry?"

"I had some crisps in the middle of the night," Seckry admitted.

"Crisps! In the middle of the night!" Zovak shouted. "It's no wonder this invention is making you feel great. All that deep fried oil in your stomach. I've just cleansed you of it completely."

As much as Seckry wanted to hate Zovak at that very moment, he couldn't because he felt too euphoric.

"Purika's possibilities are endless," Zovak continued. "Being underage and all, I wouldn't know what a hangover feels like, wink, wink, but I've heard they're pretty grim. Well, with the Purifier, I can safely say that hangovers are now a thing of the past. All you need to do is take one of these Purika pills in the morning, and every single toxin will be eradicated from your system within minutes. No more headaches, no more sickness, no more anything. Just complete and utter wellbeing."

A host of parents burst into applause, and Seckry was sure he even saw one father at the front of the audience shed a tear of joy.

After that, Seckry was ushered off stage and back to his seat, where Eiya squeezed his hand tightly and stared at him, worried.

"And do you know what the best thing about Purika is?" Zovak asked the audience. "It never fully leaves your system, so the more you take, the more you become a toxin fighting machine. If you took enough of this stuff, you would self-cleanse."

He paced the stage for a moment, letting this sink in, and there were a few claps.

"And finally," Zovak announced. "Purika can also be used to cleanse problematic bacteria externally."

He grabbed the drape at the back of the stage and yanked it hard, so it came off its hooks and fell to the floor, heavily, revealing the massive patch of mould that had caused the canteen to close shop months ago.

The audience gasped at the sight of it, and Seckry heard a few parent's cries of outrage about the cleanliness of the school their child was attending. Seckry hadn't been in the canteen since it had closed, so he was surprised to see that the mould had doubled in size and looked even more dense and revolting than ever.

Zovak pulled a disinfectant spray out of his box and held it up for everyone to see.

"Purika for the home," he said proudly, and sprayed several patches of the mould with it. Within a matter of moments, the black fungus was shrivelling up and disappearing, and before long, they were staring at a white wall that looked like it had just been freshly painted.

The audience gave a standing ovation, and Seckry could do nothing but look to the rest of the Eidolons in amazement, and they could do nothing but give him the same look back.

"I'm really sorry, Tipps," Seckry said, as they left Estergate.

"Yeah, who could have predicted Zovak was gonna invent a cure for all diseases?" said Tenk.

Tippian said nothing, hanging his head low. To nobody's surprise, Zovak had won all three of the judge's votes and had taken home the award; a giant trophy made out of the famous Wellworth metal.

"Don't worry, Tipps," said Tenk. "The trophy wasn't even that great. Like you said, it still wouldn't have been good enough for the top spot of that trophy pyramid in your bedroom."

"Yeah," said Loca. "You'll win another award at some point that'll be way more important than that one."

"Cheers guys," said Tippian, but it was clear to see that he was heartbroken.

Seckry spent the next week reading through the papers he had taken from the genesis trinity classroom, fervently looking for any information about how to use the creogen inside him, but found nothing, and as time went on, he became ever more anxious. He carried Vance's stun gun around with him wherever he went now, but even that seemed slightly pointless. If Lux truly knew who Seckry was and wanted to kill him, he could just use his exorophon powers to disintegrate the gun with a swipe of his hand. And then, with another swipe, he could disintegrate Seckry too, as easy as that. No mortal weapon or armour would be able to defend against that.

On the Friday night of that week, Seckry lay on his stomach on top of his quilt, staring blankly at the papers that he had laid out across his pillow, as Eiya lay reading a book in her own bed. But after reading the same sentences over and over again, they started to sound like nonsense, and he dropped his head into the array of papers, puffing out a deep breath of frustration.

Then his phone began buzzing. It was Vance.

"Hi sir," said Seckry.

"I'm guessing you haven't found any more information about the activation," said Vance.

"No," said Seckry. "Any luck with the other documents?"

"Nothing at all," said Vance, and Seckry's heart sank. "But I do have a proposition for you."

Vance was silent for a moment, and Seckry waited patiently. He would listen to any suggestions on how to figure this thing out.

"Seckry, how would you and Eiya fancy a vacation of sorts over the Seckramas holidays?"

"A vacation?" said Seckry, looking sideways at Eiya, who was placing her book on her lap very slowly.

"Okay, a vacation is probably stretching it a little bit. It would be more of a trip . . . or . . . an expedition."

"Wait . . . you're not serious?" Seckry switched his phone

to speakerphone so that Eiya could hear everything too.

"We know the location of Site Origin," said Vance. "I mean, the amount of information we could retrieve from the place would be invaluable. I would say it's pretty much a given that we would somewhere find instructions on how to use your abilities."

Seckry could barely contain his excitement.

"Gedin, yes, yes! Let's do it!" he said.

"Before you get too excited," said Vance, his tone becoming serious, "I want to warn you in advance that it will be a difficult trek in parts. It'll also be pretty cold, and by that I mean so cold your little toes might drop off."

"Well," said Seckry, "if we find out how to use my powers, I could just grow new ones."

Vance chuckled down the line.

"Very funny, Seckry . . . also probably quite true. Do you think Eiya would want to be a part of this too?"

"Hell yeah!" shouted Eiya, who was jumping up and down on her bed in excitement.

"She said y-"

"I heard her," said Vance, merrily. "There's one other thing I would like to ask you both. Expeditions like this can be dangerous for a small party, in case something were to happen. It is always better to have strength in numbers. Do you know anyone else who might be interested in coming along?"

A massive grin spread across Seckry's face.

"I think I can muster up a few people," he said.

Chapter Twenty-Seven

The Journey North

"It's gonna be awesome!" Tenk yelled.

As Seckry had expected, it hadn't required any persuasion to get Tenk, Tippian, Loca, and Kimmy on board. Seckry hadn't actually spoken to Kimmy, but Loca had answered for him, saying that he was coming and he didn't have a say in the matter. Seckry told Tenk to invite Richelle too, which he did, but unsurprisingly, she wasn't interested.

Over the following few days, the trip was all any of them could think about, and they spent most of their final lessons before the Seckramas holidays whispering excitedly to each other, much to the displeasure of most teachers, who reminded them that the holidays hadn't started yet.

The group met with Vance a couple of evenings, and he briefed them on some of the dangers they could face out in the wilderness, along with giving them each a list of clothing and gear they needed to buy.

When the holidays finally arrived, Seckry and Eiya arranged to meet with the others out in Kerik Square to discuss their journey and make sure they were ready for leaving the very next day.

But as Seckry was staring out of the living area window at the rusty fountain below, waiting for the group, his phone started buzzing.

Seckry barely recognised Vance's voice on the end of the line.

"Seckry . . . I'm afraid there will be no trip north . . . I seem to have caught a rare Pharyan bug."

Seckry said nothing for a moment, his heart sinking.

"Um . . . are you . . . alright?" Seckry asked.

"Oh, I'm alright," said Vance. "That is, if you can call almost incessant vomiting, a swollen neck, and bizarre hallucinations alright. I'll survive, at least, but a trek into the mountains is, unfortunately, out of the question now."

"How did you catch a Pharyan bug in this country?" Seckry asked.

"I was doing an advanced biology lesson with some of my sixth formers during the week, and it seems that one of the yaktak livers we were dissecting wasn't as locally sourced as the packaging stated."

Seckry lay back on the sofa and stared at the ceiling, completely and utterly deflated.

"I hope you get better soon," he said to Vance, before saying goodbye and dropping his phone onto the coffee table.

"The guys are just arriving," said Eiya, "we'd better give them the bad news."

"Guys," Seckry said, miserably, as they went out into the crisp air and joined the others at the fountain, "the trip's cancelled. Mr Vance is ill."

Tippian's mouth dropped open and Tenk slapped the rim of the fountain in anger.

"I bought a phrasebook and everything," said Kimmy. "I've been learning Kringa in case we bumped into any wandering locals up there."

After a long bout of moping and lamenting all the things that would have been awesome about a trek into the mountains, Tenk stood up straight, his face defiant.

"Do we really need Mr Vance?" he said. "I mean, I know I'm no Humblebert Horris, but I think I could just about survive out in the snow."

"Who on earthia is Humblebert Horris?" said Loca.

"Only, like, the most famous explorer there ever was!" exclaimed Tenk, astounded that she'd never heard of him.

"He did an internet search for famous explorers yesterday," explained Tippian. "He had never heard of him before that, either."

"Always belittling me," said Tenk under his breath. "I am quite a knowledgeable guy, you know?"

"But, seriously," said Loca. "Tenk's right, we could actually do this. It'd be one hell of an adventure."

"An adventure, or a deathwish," said Tippian. "I mean, I was just as excited as you guys when Vance was gonna be leading us, but on our *own?*"

"Come on, Tipps," said Tenk. "It'll be like walking to school when it snows and they take the monorails off, only there'll be a lot more snow . . . and maybe the odd snow monster or two."

"Are you guys actually serious about this?" said Seckry.

"Deadly serious," said Tenk. "I mean, what about all this trekking gear? It wasn't cheap. It'd be a waste of my money."

"A waste of your mum's money," Tippian corrected.

"A waste of my mum's money," Tenk confirmed.

Seckry looked to Eiya, who's eyes were glistening with intrigue.

"You really need to find out what you can about your dad . . . and your powers," she said.

Seckry thought long and hard about it for the rest of the day. One minute he was dismissing it, thinking they would all be mad to go trekking on their own with no prior experience, and then the next moment he was thinking how much safer he would feel having access to the creogen inside of him, if Lux ever were to come hunting for his blood.

At around eight o'clock at night, Seckry took a deep breath and clicked Vance's contact on his phone.

"Sir," said Seckry. "We're gonna do it alone."

It took Seckry around half an hour to convince Vance that it was a good idea. Vance began by completely dismissing it on the grounds of it being too dangerous, but eventually began to give in to his curiosity.

"Do you realise how difficult this will be?" he asked Seckry.

"Sure," Seckry replied, although in all honesty he knew he probably had no idea.

"And your friends are all committed to this one hundred percent?"

"One hundred per cent," said Seckry. "I mean, Kimmy's been learning the language and everything."

Vance chuckled lightly, but then burst into a fit of coughing and vomiting. Seckry held the phone uncomfortably, unsure whether to ring back in a few minutes, but Vance returned to the line.

"I doubt he will need any Kringa up there," he said. "The walk to the location we've pinpointed doesn't cross any villages or settlements. It'll be a pretty grim and barren trek through dense snow in a straight line from the final train stop."

"Well, we're all prepared, we've got all the equipment and gear you told us to get . . . and . . . and . . . I need the instructions for these powers for if . . . if Lux really *is* coming for me."

Vance was silent for a long time, aside from the odd cough.

"Your mobile phones won't work up there," he said, eventually. "You'll need an emergency transmitter, so that you can send out a distress signal to satellites if you're in danger. I would ask you to come here and collect one from me, but this bug is highly contagious, so I recommend Pepperbee's Supplies over on Semworth Street."

"Thanks," said Seckry, all the excitement he had felt yesterday rushing back.

Seckry decided not to mention Vance's sickness and their small change in circumstances to his mum. It had been hard enough persuading her to let him and Eiya go when Vance was going to be leading them. If she knew that they were going alone, she would have downright refused to let them leave the flat. Tenk and the others followed the same plan; as far as all parents knew, this was an official school trip led by their fringe science teacher.

According to Vance's plans, the trip would take them three days in total; one day travelling, one day exploring the labs, and another day of travelling to get back. If they left in the morning, they would arrive back two days before Seckramas.

After an excited, restless night, Seckry and Eiya said their goodbyes to Coralle, who waved them off with a suspicious glare, and met up with Tenk before boarding a monorail to Skyfall National Train Station, where they were meeting the others.

When they arrived, Loca, Kimmy and Tippian were already waiting for them, and Loca raised her eyebrows, staring at the top of Tenk's head.

Seckry and Eiya hadn't mentioned anything on the monorail out of tact, but Tenk's bobble hat more closely resembled a tea cosy, patterned with frilly, pink flowers.

"Don't start, Loca," he said. "I argued about it for the last hour and a half before leaving. My nan knitted it. She said I was wearing it no matter what, and if I took it off once more, she was gonna staple it to my head. It's the only one I've got now. Plus, she was extra mad this morning because dad had accidentally dropped her best cardigan into the paper shredder."

"How do you accidentally drop a cardigan into a paper shredder?" said Loca.

"I don't know," replied Tenk. "It looked like it was pretty shoved in there, to be honest."

After they had gone through their checklists to check for one last time that they had everything they needed, they queued for their tickets and Seckry took in the vastness of the place.

Since he had arrived in Skyfall last year, Seckry hadn't left the city, so this was the first time he had been to Skyfall's main train station since that first journey from Marne, and he had forgotten how busy it could be. It was heaving with commuters and they could barely hear themselves over the hustle and bustle, the hissing of pistons, and the grinding of metal against metal.

Most of the trains passing through were nothing like the little monorails that snaked through the buildings of the city;

they were monstrous looking beasts that could carry thousands of people, and as their train pulled to a stop, they realised that it was the largest of the lot.

Seckry would have loved it if this smooth running beast ran all the way to the Frostpeak mountains, but it was only taking them as far as the northernmost city of Solstaven, where they would need to change.

The journey to Solstaven only took around two hours, since the train was hurtling through the Nakarian countryside at what seemed like the speed of light. The second half of their train journey, however, was not quite as smooth. After Tenk had almost made them miss the train because he had been distracted by a stall selling something called Solstaven Treacletart, they boarded the tiny carriage to find it dank and stale and empty aside from an attendant with one eye and a creepy twitch.

It was another three hours from Solstaven to the Mountainbase stop, even though the actual distance was shorter, and as every hour passed by, Seckry could see the landscape beginning to change from grassy plains to icy cliffs, and small, crystal clear streams.

Around an hour before they were to arrive, they opened their heavy backpacks to have their first meal of the journey, which mostly consisted of protein bars and dried fruit for sustenance. It was the first time Seckry had eaten a protein bar, and he vowed that once the journey was over, that would be the last; they had the flavour of cardboard, and the texture of a rubber boot.

Tenk, who exchanged a look of disgust with Seckry, opened his flask of water to wash the chewy stuff down, but found the water had been replaced with Fizzler Frothpop, which erupted all over him and soaked into his trousers.

"Raymus!" Tenk shouted, between clenched teeth.

"Is your brother serious?" exclaimed Loca. "This is our survival on the line!"

"It's okay," said Kimmy, trying to calm everyone down. "We've got plenty of water, and there'll be more than enough snow to melt and boil up there."

"How's it been, living with Raymus, anyway?" Seckry asked Tenk.

"A nightmare," Tenk replied, trying to squeeze the sticky liquid out of the material and back into the flask. "This is nothing. He replaced my toothpaste with freshly mixed cement last week. That was worse."

When the train finally slowed to a halt, Seckry had to rub a circle in the condensation of the window beside him to see out of it, and found that his breath was steaming it up again almost immediately.

They heaved their backpacks off the old carriage onto a wooden platform that housed a lone, unmanned ticket booth sprouting a red flag, and was surrounded by pure, white snow that seemed to stretch for infinity in all directions.

They watched the train slowly pull out the station and rattle away in the direction they had come, until it sank into the mist and left them in complete silence apart from the gentle whisper of the frozen wind.

Somehow, until now, the journey hadn't felt real to Seckry, but all of a sudden the reality of it hit him, and he felt vulnerable and scared.

"It's a long trek from here," said Loca, pulling out her compass. "North is this way. Follow me."

They trekked through the deep snow for what seemed like forever, with Tenk asking if they were there yet several times. They eventually saw a thicket of snow-covered pine trees and headed towards them. Their plan was to skirt the edge of the forest until they reached the coordinates where the labs were supposed to be, and then they would camp outside the labs to give them a whole day of exploring the following day.

But as they exhaustedly pressed forward, the cold sun began to sink behind the trees on their left, and the biting cold began to get even colder.

"I don't get it," said Loca, "We've already reached the coordinates. We should have come across the labs already."

"Let's carry on walking then," said Tippian. "They can't be far." But his voice was drowned out by the wind, which seemed to be getting stronger by the minute.

"No, we've got to head into the forest," said Kimmy. "We need to get a fire going as soon as we can so we don't freeze."

Seckry and Eiya nodded, relieved at the idea of some kind of warmth, and exhausted from all of the heavy walking. Loca, after studying her map for another five minutes, reluctantly agreed, and they headed west.

Once they had gathered enough firewood from fallen branches, they made a stack in the centre of a clearing and used Seckry's lighter to get it going. The heat was immediate, and Seckry closed his eyes, every one of his muscles relaxing as the stiffness evaporated.

Before long, Tenk had fallen asleep on the open ground and Tippian kept jolting awake after dozing off in a sitting position, so Seckry, Eiya, Loca and Kimmy got the tent set up, and gently ushered the two boys inside before settling down themselves.

Wrapped up in his thermal sleeping blanket, Seckry suddenly felt at ease. They couldn't be far from the labs, and they had the whole day the next day to find them and explore them. So far, everything was going to plan.

As he was sinking into a fuzzy half sleep, he felt Eiya's blanket shuffle ever so slightly closer to his, and he could feel her warm breath pluming softly out of her little nostrils.

When he eventually sunk into a deep sleep, he dreamt that Eiya was unzipping her blanket and wrapping her arms around him, before pressing her cold lips against his, sending shivers of warmth down his spine.

Then, when he was dreaming that she was running her fingers through his hair, there was the snap of a branch outside the tent and Seckry jolted awake in a cold sweat. Everyone else was fast asleep around him, apart from Tippian, who was sat upright, just like Seckry.

"Seck," Tippian whispered, his eyes petrified, narrow slits. "Look to your left."

Chapter Twenty-Eight

Ringold Blood

Without moving his body, Seckry turned his head, and he took a sharp intake of breath, forcing himself to remain still.

Outside the tent, illuminated by the firelight, was the outline of a figure. It was the size of a human being, standing on two legs, but had horns that curved in a downwards spiral.

Seckry slid his palm silently under his pillow and slowly closed his hand around the handle of Vance's stun gun.

"Seck," Tippian whispered again. "Is it me . . . or is it getting closer and closer?"

Seckry swallowed hard. He couldn't even answer. His jaw was locked tight in fear.

"We won!" screamed Tenk, suddenly, sitting up and raising his arms in celebration, knocking the gun out of Seckry's grip.

Seckry reached down and grabbed the gun again as quickly as he could before swinging it up in front of him.

The sound of Tenk's sleeptalking woke up Loca, who saw the gun and screamed before quickly covering her own mouth with her hand.

Seckry's eyes stayed locked on the shadow, which slowly disappeared into nothing.

"What's going on?" said Kimmy, his eyes flickering open. He switched their battery powered nightlamp on.

"No!" hissed Tippian, and switched it off again. "Everyone quiet!"

"The noise has scared it off," said Seckry, through clenched, clattering teeth.

They spent the next half an hour in almost silence, waiting to see if the thing returned, but there was no movement outside apart from the flames licking the withering firewood.

"It's just an animal. It'll leave us alone if we leave it alone," said Loca, but it hadn't looked like any of the animals Seckry had seen in his guidebook to Kringa.

The others, one by one, fell back asleep, but Seckry didn't sleep for the rest of the night. It would have been impossible even if he had tried.

When the cold, bright morning arrived, Loca raised her head, her eyes puffy and her mouth downturned into a repulsed frown.

"You know what?" she said. "The snow I can deal with. The freezing temperature I can deal with. The threat of wild beasts hunting us I can deal with. What I can't deal with is another night sleeping next to Tenk's manky feet."

"They ain't manky!" said Tenk, offended.

"Tenk, the surfaces of your feet have got more craters on them than the moon. What on earthia is wrong with them?"

"I just sweat a lot, that's all," Tenk said, defensively. "Can't help it. The sweat makes them blister."

"Well, someone else is gonna have to top and tail next to you tonight because I can't deal with those manky things next to my face."

There was silence for a short while afterwards, until Tenk mumbled under his breath: "*They ain't manky*," and unzipped the tent, clambering out.

A few moments later, he came running back, shouting, "Guys, you've gotta come see this!"

Loca sighed.

"Tenk, I told you yesterday, I don't want to see you peeing your name into the snow. It's really not that impressive."

"No, seriously!" said Tenk. "Get out here, all of you."

Seckry and the others scrambled out into the fresh, biting air, and followed Tenk to the edge of the forest. About fifty yards north, they were blockaded in by steep mountain cliffs, and straight in front of them was a cave with a giant, circular, wooden symbol attached to the rock above it; the symbol of the genesis trinity.

"We were here the whole time," said Loca. "It was just too dark to see. I knew we should have carried on walking."

They wasted no time in packing up their belongings, and before long, they were heading into the cavern.

It was longer and more claustrophobic than Seckry had anticipated. At one point, they had to crawl on hands and knees to get through, and Kimmy's backpack got caught on a stalactite, causing a few brief moments of panic.

When the glimmer of white snow appeared ahead, Seckry sighed with relief.

They emerged into an open area, and Tenk shouted, "There it is!"

Standing in the centre of the open space was a vast collection of dome-like structures, interconnected with linking corridors, and a large, tube-shaped thing that had to have been an electricity generator that was making a low hum.

Tenk rushed forward, but Kimmy suddenly shouted, "Tenk! Stop!" and threw his arms out to stop any of the rest of the group moving.

"I can see digital tripwires ahead of us," said Kimmy. "The place is filled with them."

Seckry squinted, but couldn't make out anything. But as he scanned around, he noticed that, in the very far distance, on either side of them, were some kind of thin, curved towers. They were eerie things; unnatural metal poles jutting out of the snow and encasing the group like a giant ribcage.

Kimmy took off his bobble hat and threw it in front of him to test the tripwires. Before it could hit the ground it was sucked away to their left, and blasted with a flurry of invisible hits before landing on the ground with a pat.

"It's the towers," said Kimmy. "They must be blowing out and sucking in these really precise pockets of air whenever one is triggered."

"How do we get past them?" said Tippian, squinting behind his glasses. "The place is riddled. I can just about see them now."

"We could try running," suggested Loca. "We don't know how fast those towers can blow out those pockets of air. We could try to outrun them."

"Rather you than me," said Tenk.

"Loca," said Kimmy, concerned, "I'm not sure, they seemed pretty fast just then."

"Well, there's only one way to find out," said Loca, before sprinting into the invisible wires.

"Loca!" screamed Kimmy, as Loca was bombarded by invisible punches, sending her flying in one direction then spinning backwards in the opposite direction, taking an absolute beating before coming to to a stop in the snow and lying there, groaning.

"Oh my Gedin, she's hurt," said Kimmy and ran to help her, but he too, was thrown into the air and smacked with around ten or eleven blows before landing heavily into a heap beside his girlfriend.

Seckry, without thinking, had edged forward in concern for both of them.

"Seck," said Tenk, and pointed towards Seckry's feet.

Seckry looked down, and saw that his left ankle was directly intersecting with one of the tripwires.

He prepared himself for the worst.

But nothing happened.

He shook his leg around, tempting fate, but again, no pockets of air came. He reached down and waved his hand through the laser.

"They're not affecting me," he said in disbelief.

He got up and ran to Kimmy and Loca, skidding to his knees. Tenk tried to follow him but got knocked back at the first wire.

"Guys, are you okay?" said Seckry.

"We're fine," said Loca. "A little bruised, but fine."

"Okay, just stay where you are, lying down." Seckry could see one of the lasers hovering precariously close to Kimmy's chest. "Try not to move at all."

"How are you managing to walk through them without getting hit?" said Kimmy.

"I . . . I have no idea," said Seckry, truthfully.

"Seck, why don't you make your way to one of the towers

and see if you can deactivate them somehow?"

It was a great idea.

Seckry jogged to the towers on their left. As he approached one, he could see a small, circular hole which he guessed was releasing the air, and underneath it, a panel with a diagram of a handprint on it.

Seckry carefully pressed his hand to the handprint, and a red circle of light appeared around the tip of each of his fingers, before all turning to green.

A word appeared above the panel:

Ringold

"*Gedin*," said Seckry, aloud.

The towers knew that he was family. That had to have been why they weren't attacking him. The lasers were able to pick up that he was a relative of Pawl.

Alongside the name was a power symbol. He pressed a free finger to it and there was a gigantic mechanical sigh, as each of the towers powered down in succession.

The others had to have heard the noise too, as they began running around and hugging each other in celebration.

"Woo hoo!" he heard Tenk shouting. "Way to go, Seck!"

He ran back to them and explained the handprint, before they headed, single file, towards what looked like the main entrance to the facility.

As they reached it, Seckry noticed a heap of sharp shards of metal on the ground. He bent down and brushed his fingers over the broken metal. It had to be the remains of the lock that had kept Lux trapped inside; the lock that had made his dad's xinary watch turn red when it broke.

Seckry stood back up, took a deep breath, and heaved open the heavy door, which screeched from disuse. Then he gave the group behind him a quick glance before stepping into the building where his father had been made.

Chapter Twenty-Nine

Site Origin

The interior of the building was a strange mix of industrial factory and homely comfort. Rooms were decorated with wallpaper and ornaments, but had pipes riddled across their ceilings and electronic panels dotted around the walls.

Seckry and the others spent the first hour just wandering around, taking everything in. They found a large room which must have been the living area, a kitchen, two bathrooms, storage rooms, and many rooms that they couldn't identify, filled with strange machinery and objects none of them had ever seen before. One room was even filled with eerie, empty animal cages, and Seckry guessed that his father and Lux weren't the first experiments the scientists had conducted at the facility. Eventually, they travelled down a long corridor to a locked door with another hand symbol on it, just like the one on the wind towers outside.

Seckry placed his palm to it, and there was a click.

They opened the door and filed onto a platform that jutted out over what could only be described as an abyss in the ground.

"Oh. My. Gedin," said Tippian softly.

In the centre of the abyss was a humongous, cylindrical drill.

Seckry leaned over the bars and followed the line of the drill as it pierced downwards, so far that it eventually disappeared into darkness.

"This must be where they extracted the trinity elements for my dad and Lux," he said, staring into the abyss. A stagnant iciness prickled his cheeks. "I guess the samples they had from the Krakun drill weren't enough to infuse into human beings."

"Guys, look behind you," said Loca.

Seckry turned to see two glass panels either side of the door they had come through that were windows into small compartments embedded into the wall. In the centre of each room stood a stand holding a petri dish. But the two rooms were very different.

In the left compartment, the entire floor was alive with grass, mushrooms, and insects, and there were strangely-coloured, randomly shaped bits of material everywhere.

In the right compartment there was nothing, but it wouldn't have been right to call it empty. The emptiness and the nothingness that existed behind that glass seemed so devoid of any life that it was almost thick with death and decay, and the walls were cracked and flaked and riddled with rot.

Above each compartment was a diagram of a human head and torso. The first had pure white veins and white irises and pupils, and the second, just like the Broken Motion's diagram, had jet black veins and jet black eyes.

The image affected Seckry then just as much as it had affected him the first time he had seen it. It sent shivers down his spine, and the threat of Lux with chaotic, destructive powers suddenly seemed immediate once again.

"Seck, this is gonna be you," said Tenk, staring at the white-veined figure. "I mean . . . everything that happened last year with you going back in time and being Seckraman and all that, and basically being the messiah, you were saying that it was all coincidence and that there was no messiah, but . . . I don't know man, I mean, you're like the angel of light or something, you pretty much *are* some kind of deity."

Seckry made to disagree a few times, but couldn't come up with any cohesive sentence.

"Tipp, what on earthia are you doing?" said Loca.

Seckry broke out of his trance to see Tippian flailing about and slapping his own body repeatedly.

"There's bugs everywhere!" he shouted. "Look at 'em!"

Seckry hadn't noticed before now, but as he raised his own arm, he could see tiny, glowing specks settled across it.

"These are smelter flies," said Kimmy, curiously, examining one that had settled on the back of his hand. "I've never seen one in real life before. They're supposed to be native to the jungles of Emriel, down by the equator . . . not up here in the snowy mountains."

As another one floated towards Seckry and settled on his forearm, he realised they were almost identical to the glowflies that were native to Skyfall, except, instead of a bright, neon blue, they were a fiery orange and red.

"What on earth are they doing here?" said Tippian, shaking a few more off his body and squirming.

"I don't know," admitted Kimmy. "That creogen compartment looks sealed to me. I don't think they're coming from there."

He exited the cavernous room, following one of the flies as it lazily floated through the corridor. The others watched him in silence.

After a few moments, there was a muffled cry of, "Gedin! You all need to see this."

They followed his voice around a few corners, filing through the narrow corridors one after the other, and found him standing at a circular entrance to a room that was overgrown with vegetation.

Kimmy entered, and the others followed him in, slowly.

Seckry stepped over a spongy root and waded through some leaves, snapping a few stems as he went, and specks of warm moisture dabbing his skin. The place was like a giant greenhouse that had been left to its own devices; overgrown and overrun with all sorts of strange looking plants and flowers. The vegetation was even covering most of the ceiling. Where there was a gap in the leaves, thin shafts of light were flooding through.

Loca reached up and gripped a few vines, ripping them away from the domed ceiling. Seckry had expected to see a glass roof, with sunlight pouring in, but instead they found a mess of fluorescent tube lighting behind the glass, some popping and clicking and stuttering on and off.

"Artificial sunlight," said Loca. "I guess that solves the problem of the dark, northern winters."

"Vance did say they were growing their own food here in the labs somehow," said Seckry, taking in the vastness of the place. "A completely self-confined existence."

They wandered around the greenhouse for a while, admiring the exotic plants with equal curiosity and wariness. When they reached the far western corner of the room, they found a gigantic flower whose petals were giant flaps that were as furry as an animal.

"I just want to stroke it!" Loca squealed, but as she put her fingertips to it, the petal seized up and retracted, making her jump and scream.

As they explored further, Tippian prodded a spotted, bulbous flower, but it reacted by sneezing a spray of spores directly into his face, covering him with little green dots.

Tenk, however, had been completely enthralled by something else; a tree of some sort that was bearing fruit the size of melons, except that they were a silver colour and were covered in thick, stumpy spikes.

"I have to take one of these things back with me," he declared. "Man, they should serve these beauties at Graveturner gigs. Can you imagine? This is the most heavy metal fruit I've ever seen."

"Tenk, we need to be careful," said Loca. "I wouldn't eat anything from here. It could be poisonous."

"Seckry's dad grew up eating this stuff, and he turned out alright, didn't he? Why would they grow fruit that wasn't safe to eat?"

Tenk had a point, but even Seckry had to agree with Loca. They had no idea what these things were or what they would do to someone's body if eaten.

"Okay, I won't eat one," said Tenk, "but I gotta at least take one back to show it off."

Once Tenk had carefully picked one of the spiky fruits off its branch and stored it safely in his backpack, they left the greenhouse to do some more exploring. Seckry was getting anxious to find the instructions for activating the creogen, because even though they had all day to explore, a part of him worried that they weren't going to be simple to find.

It didn't help that the facility was like a maze, and they found themselves backtracking more than once after going around in circles.

Then, they took a left turn into an oddly wallpapered corridor and found themselves standing outside two adjacent, wooden doors. Hanging on a plaque outside the one door was the name *Pawl*, and hanging on the other was the name *Lux*.

Seckry took a moment to mentally prepare himself and slowly opened the door to his father's old bedroom.

There was a single bed on one side, neatly made, and a bedside table with a lamp on it. There was also an acoustic guitar leaning against one wall, and an old television and games console.

"No way . . ." said Tenk.

Seckry followed Tenk's line of sight to see a poster tacked to the wall. A poster of the old Friction logo.

"Seck . . ." Tenk continued. "Your dad was a Friction fan . . . no wonder you're so good."

Seckry couldn't believe what he was seeing.

"But . . ." said Tippian. "I thought they were completely isolated up here? How did they even know about Friction?"

Seckry thought for a moment. He had always assumed the same thing, but there had been televisions in a few of the rooms, including this one. They had to have been aware of the outside world and the things that were going on elsewhere. His dad had probably watched Friction on the sports channel.

"How did they get a poster here?" said Loca. "Didn't they shut themselves off from society?"

"I'm sure the two scientists made trips back and forth to the closest cities sometimes," said Kimmy. "They must have done. They were bound to need to shop for some things."

"Seck, would you like a moment on your own?" said Loca, and Seckry was grateful for the offer.

As the others left the room and their footsteps disappeared, Seckry sat gently down on his father's old bed. He was suddenly overwhelmed with emotion. His father's room was so similar to his own it was uncanny.

"*Dad, I can't wait to see you again*," he whispered to himself softly, and focused on their meeting at the beginning of the summer next year, so that he wouldn't feel upset.

When he had composed himself, he carefully went through the bedside table drawers, the cupboard, and another set of drawers, searching for information, but felt incredibly uncomfortable doing so, as if he was intruding. All he found were clothes; clothes that would have fitted him today. Pawl would have been sixteen when he escaped from the facility, the same age as Seckry.

When he was ready, he called to the others and they met outside the bedrooms.

"Do we want to enter Lux's bedroom?" said Loca, hesitantly.

"Course we do," said Tenk. "Right, Seck? Why wouldn't we?"

Seckry nodded.

"Of course," he said. "We need to search every room for any clues on how to activate the powers." But secretly, he felt sick at the idea of entering the bedroom of the crazed man who wanted to murder him, his sister, and his father.

Loca opened the door, but before anyone could step inside, she recoiled in horror.

Seckry stood, frozen to the spot, staring through the door at a room that had been completely trashed and destroyed, with the words 'I AM LUX' in all capitals scrawled across the walls in numerous places in a red and black substance that Seckry could only guess was blood.

"I don't think anyone he was living with would have been in any doubt of what his name was," said Tippian. "There were only four of them here. What in Gedin's name is this all about?"

"Like Seckry said," offered Tenk. "The guy went crazy. He killed Adelbert and Rikard and then went after Seckry's dad, too. You can't exactly try to explain the mind-set of someone like that. If the words 'I LIKE BAKED BEANS' or something had been written across the walls, I wouldn't have been surprised."

Eiya, who had been squeezing Seckry's arm tight, slowly released her grip and took a hold of the hanging door plaque that said the name 'Lux.'

"Something was scratched out," she said.

"Hmm?" said Loca.

"Look at Pawl's plaque and then look at this one."

Seckry examined it closely. Eiya was right; the wood had been heavily scratched and damaged, and the word 'Lux' had been painted on neatly rather than printed on.

"Are you saying that he erased the original name and painted the same thing on top of it?" said Tippian. "That doesn't make sense."

"Tipps," said Tenk. "You're not getting it, are you? The guy was crazy. *Craaaazy*."

"Unless . . ." said Eiya. "Unless the name underneath . . . *wasn't Lux*."

Chapter Thirty

A Name, Erased

Seckry stared at the writing on the walls once more.

I AM LUX.

Could it be that Lux was announcing his new name? That Lux hadn't been the birth name Adelbert had given to him, after all?

"If Lux wasn't his real name, then what on earthia was it?" said Loca. "It has to be documented in this building somewhere."

"Lux," said Tippian, ponderingly. "He decides to give himself a new name, and he chooses Lux. You'd think he'd choose something a bit grander, wouldn't you? What does Lux even mean, anyway? I've never heard of anybody else with that name."

Tenk took a deep breath, but Tippian caught him before he could say anything.

"Okay, Tenk, I get it, I get it. The guy was crazy."

"Come on," said Loca. "Let's look around to see if we can find out what his real name was. I doubt we're gonna find anything in here. There's nothing left except broken wood and ripped bedsheets."

"Seck, your dad said Lux was in Skyfall city, didn't he?" said Tenk, as they searched the facility for any corridors they hadn't yet ventured through. "If he's using his original name, he could be anyone. He could be somebody we know!"

"Tenk, if he was somebody we all knew, then why would he have kept it a secret all this time?" said Tippian. "If he knew who Seckry was and where he was then he probably would have . . . tried to kill him by now. And he went to all this trouble to erase his name and reinvent himself as Lux. Why would he go back to using his original name?"

"I think Tenk's right," said Kimmy. "Lux could very well be disguising himself in Skyfall by using a different name, and since nobody knows what his original name was, it would be a perfect disguise. I don't know why he hasn't come after Seckry yet, but maybe he's waiting for something."

"Waiting for what?" said Tippian, but nobody had an answer.

Eventually they found a room which looked like an office of some sort, with several blinking computers still running, and paper strewn everywhere.

Seckry picked up one of the pieces of paper and scanned it for names, but all he could see was technical jargon about ratios and formulas. The others followed suit and examined some of the papers, before Loca yelled, "Here's some names!"

"Let's see," said Tippian, but Loca screwed up her face.

"It just says Pawl and Lux," she mumbled, dejected, and peered closer. "This is different ink, too. It's thicker. He's actually erased the real name from this as well and put 'Lux' over the top of it."

"That's ridiculous," said Tenk. "He can't have done that on everything where his name was written. Let's go through the rest."

They spent the next hour and a half overturning paper, some ripped and some scrunched up, and some untouched in wads and in wallets, but every instance of the boys' names had been modified.

"He really *was* crazy," said Tenk, seemingly only just believing it himself.

"This is pointless," said Seckry. "We need to concentrate on looking for instructions for the powers, it's already gone midday."

"We need to eat first," said Tippian. "Am I the only one who's starving?"

"I'm hungry," said Tenk, "but not for the cardboard we brought with us. Are you sure I can't eat that spiky fruit,

Loca?"

Loca gave him a glare that answered his question without needing to speak, and everyone opened their backpacks.

Seckry was just as unenthusiastic as Tenk at eating the protein bars and meal replacement drinks they had brought, but that was the last thing on his mind right now. If they didn't find the instructions he needed, the whole trip would have been a waste.

When they were ready, they began filing through the rest of the multitude of documents and files that were in the office, this time specifically looking for instructions, and discarding anything that didn't look helpful, to save time.

After another couple of hours, Seckry was getting even more anxious, and told everyone to split up and search every other room for any info. Another hour of fruitless searching went by before Tippian called, rallying everyone together next to a storage cupboard.

"It's not the instructions," he admitted. "But I think you might find this interesting."

He slowly handed what seemed to be an old, children's painting to Seckry. Seckry turned it around.

There were four stick figures in the painting; two adults, and two children. The one child had a splash of yellow paint atop its head, and Seckry guessed that had to have been his dad's blonde hair. The other child had a splash of brown paint on its head. But there was something strange about the second child. Whereas Pawl had two lines for two arms, Lux only had one, his right.

On the bottom of the painting there was a scribble of just about readable words.

BY PAWL AGE 5

"That could have just been a mistake," said Tenk.

"No, there's more," said Tippian, and handed them other paintings. Some were by Pawl and some were by Lux, but all of them depicted Lux with just his right arm.

"All the stuff I was just going through makes sense now,"

said Loca. "There were all these references to an accident when the boys were little. It must have been this. It was something to do with one of the machines here. He must have got his arm caught."

"I've got something for you guys, too," said Kimmy, holding up a sheet. "Looks like Lux wasn't so careful with this one."

Seckry looked closer and could see that where Lux had removed the original name with paint or bleach or whatever he had used, there was still the faint outline of the first letter. It was an F.

"Oh my Gedin," said Tenk. "Lux is Frederiko Featherfull over in the third block, Seck. I knew there was something dodgy about that guy."

Tippian laughed.

"You're not still mad at that guy for accidentally eating your helping of peachpear pie at the Seckramas dinner two years ago, are you?"

"Frederiko's got two arms, anyway," said Seckry.

"It could be a prosthetic," said Tenk, but didn't look like he believed himself either.

"Well, this does really narrow it down," said Loca. "We know he has just one arm and his real name begins with an F. There can't be that many people in Skyfall who fit that description."

"You're right," said Seckry, elated and scared at the idea of identifying Lux and possibly what he looked like and where he lived.

After that, they split up once again, desperate to find any kind of advice on how to activate Seckry's creogen, but more hours passed, and they had still found nothing. The only thing Seckry found that seemed like it might be remotely useful was what seemed to be a touch screen, electronic diary, but when he tried to access the entries, he found them to be password protected.

"It's getting late," said Loca, returning to find Seckry in a heap of documents that he had already been through once. "This is unbelieveable. You'd think there'd be some information somewhe-"

She was cut off by a series of bangs from the direction of the greenhouse.

"Was that you, Kim?" she called.

"It was chunks of snow hitting the building, I think," Kimmy replied, joining them. "The wind has gotten really strong out there. I can hear it."

Loca made her way to the entrance and shrieked.

"Guys," she said, desperately. "We have to go. We have to get out of here, right *now*."

Chapter Thirty-One

The Red Flag

Seckry ran to see what was happening, and saw through the glass that snow had piled up outside so high that it was up to the height of his shoulders, almost blocking them in.

"We have to climb through that gap before we're trapped for good," Loca said, heaving the door inwards to reveal the white wall.

"But we haven't found Seckry's instructions," said Tenk.

The same thing was going through Seckry's mind, but if they didn't leave right there and then, who knew how long they would be trapped for?

"Why don't we stay here overnight," said Tenk. "The snow might melt during the night, and we can travel tomorrow."

"Tenk, we have no idea how long this snowstorm is going to last," said Loca.

"Loca's right," said Kimmy. "I read that these things can go on for weeks."

"We need to go," Seckry said reluctantly. "We need to go now. We've searched everything anyway. There's no instructions."

He looked at the electronic diary he was still holding, before shoving it into his backpack as a last ray of hope for any real information.

"We're gonna have to make our way back into the forest and camp there," said Loca. "The trees should shield us from the wind a bit."

Seckry nodded and tried to suppress the memory of the demon-like shadow he had seen outside the tent, before they began climbing out into the whipping wind.

The trek to the forest was horrendous. The snow on the ground was so fresh and deep that it was like wading through quicksand at points, and the cavernous pass they had to climb back through had to be dug out, making it an even more claustrophobic experience than the first time.

When they finally reached the shelter of the trees, they dropped their backpacks to the ground and fell to their knees, exhausted.

"Who wants to gather firewood?" said Loca, who was met with silence.

They eventually got a fire started after all chipping in and gathering a few bits of bark, and set up the tent before clambering in and falling straight to sleep. Seckry had no idea if the demon shadow returned that night, because he slept right through until sunlight was casting sharp shards of light through the gaps in the leaves above them.

They set off first thing, thankful that the howling winds seemed to have come to a halt, and traced their steps back to the little train station. But after half a day of travelling, the station was nowhere to be seen.

"I'm sure it was around here somewhere," said Loca.

"I don't remember seeing that on our journey," said Tenk, pointing to a small, red flag that was jutting out of the snow a few yards in front of them. "Do you think someone's been travelling here too, and stuck it in the snow as a beacon or something?"

He waded over to it and gave it a yank, but couldn't remove it.

Then, as Tenk was heaving, Seckry's stomach suddenly tied into a knot. He had seen that flag on their outward journey. It had been sticking out of the roof of the station's ticket booth.

"Tenk . . ." Seckry said. "I don't think that flag's gonna come out."

"Why not?" said Tenk, kicking the pole in anger.

"Oh no," said Loca, coming to realisation. "Oh, Gedin,

no."

There was silence as everyone turned their eyes slowly towards the snow beneath them.

"It can't be . . ."

"The entire station and the track is under all of this *snow?*" Tippian said in disbelief.

"The station, the tracks, and any possible train to get us out of here," said Kimmy.

"We're stranded. We're actually stranded," said Tippian.

"Look, the worst thing we can do right now is panic and deplete ourselves of all of our energy," said Loca. "We need to calm down and wait it out. Seck, you've got that emergency locator transmitter thing, right? We're gonna have to use it, and wait for a rescue team from Skyfall or Solstaven. It could take them a while to get here, though, especially in these conditions, so we're gonna have to go all the way back to the forest and trigger the signal there. We've got plenty of supplies to last us another night. We won't starve."

"My mum is gonna kill me," Tippian said. "She is actually gonna rip me to pieces with her bare hands."

"That's if we're not ripped to pieces by that demon before we make it back," said Tenk, looking like he was on the verge of tears.

They had no more time to waste contemplating it. They headed back to the shelter of the forest, exhausted once again and in desperate need of a real meal of some sort. Seckry's feet were pounding, and he wouldn't have been surprised if his toes had gone black and blue inside his boots from the cold.

When they finally got back to their spot in the forest, Seckry triggered the distress signal, and they waited silently, as though a helicopter was going to magically appear out of nowhere. But after hours of sitting in silence while the night crept in, they once again set up their tent and settled down for the night.

When morning came, Seckry rushed out of the trees, hoping that he would see some form of human life, but there was nothing but the barren wasteland of white for miles all around. The wind seemed to be coming and going in strong bursts again, and even more thick snow was falling from the sky. Seckry wondered if emergency vehicles would even be able to get to them in these conditions.

Panic suddenly crept over him. They had just enough food for around one more day, but that was it. After that, he had no idea what they would do. And starvation wasn't even the worst of his fears. His main concern was his mum and Leena, and everyone else's parents, plus Richelle. It was Seckramas eve. They were supposed to have returned home yesterday. His mum would be absolutely frantic, fearing for their safety, and he had no way of contacting her to tell her they were okay.

He returned to the tent to find the others awake, and shook his head, slowly.

As the hours crept by, the group became quieter and quieter and Seckry had no doubt that everyone was thinking the exact same thing as him; no one was coming.

When twilight finally signalled the end of the day, Seckry could do nothing but stare at his feet in shame and fear and helplessness.

That night, Seckry fell into an uneasy sleep, his stomach growling, and dreamt once again that he was back in the Divinita chamber with Eiya, but instead of Darklight threatening to kill her, it was Kevan Kayne who was in the room, holding Eiya in his mutated, pulsating arms.

"Get off her!" Seckry screamed, disgusted at the sight of Kayne's tentacles touching Eiya's skin.

"She's my wife!" Kayne roared. "I'm protecting her. Protecting her from you, which is more than you've ever done for her."

"What?" said Seckry, softly.

"That's right," said Kayne. "When she needed you most, you couldn't protect her. You couldn't save her. You *failed.* When you could have stopped Darklight from killing all of those Innoya, you didn't. You weren't strong enough. Eiya only survived by chance. You were ready to let her go. You were ready to let her die with them!"

"No!" Seckry screamed, trying to run towards Eiya, to rip her out of Kayne's embrace. But he couldn't. He was trapped, just like in his previous dreams. His wrists were clasped to the wall behind him.

"Eiya!" he pleaded.

"Why don't you use your superpowers to escape?" said Kayne. "Conjure up a knife to cut yourself free."

"I . . . I . . . can't," Seckry said, helplessly. "I don't know how."

Seckry stared into Eiya's eyes and saw the disappointment in them.

"Eiya," he said again, before opening his eyes.

Seckry sighed with relief when he realised he had been dreaming, but was struck with panic when he saw that Eiya wasn't sleeping next to him.

The tent was open, the material flapping gently in the wind.

Seckry darted up, but found Eiya outside, gathering a small collection of wood.

"I was just . . . just getting . . . some extra . . . in case . . . we . . . ran out," she said, her whole body trembling and her teeth chattering.

The sight of her in such a state overwhelmed Seckry and he found that warm tears were filling the corners of his eyes. He tried to say something to her, but he had a lump in his throat.

What had he done? He should never have brought Eiya, or any of the others to this place. It was all for his selfish desire to activate his powers, if he really had any, and he was still without the instructions he had brought them here to find. Kayne had been correct in the dream. He was helpless to protect her. He couldn't save her from Darklight, and there was nothing he could do to save her now.

"I should have done this thing on my own," he said.

"Seck," Eiya replied, as comfortingly as she could through clattering teeth, "I would never have let you . . . come here alone. Wherever you go . . . I go. Your dad . . . means the world to you."

It was true; the idea of his father had almost consumed Seckry over the last few months, but he realised right then that, no matter how much his father meant to him, nobody could ever mean as much to him as Eiya.

He reached out and wrapped his arms around her, burying his face into her neck. He had never felt such an utter longing for her; a longing to be close to her, so close that he couldn't be any closer, where every particle that he breathed in smelled of her, rich and sweet, and dizzying.

Seckry held Eiya so tightly that he was almost worried he was hurting her, but she squeezed him back just as passionately.

When he finally relaxed his arms, Eiya put her tiny, frozen nose to his cheek and inhaled.

"Seck," she whispered in his ear, her lips barely parting for her to make a sound. "Kiss me."

Seckry wanted nothing else in that moment. He reached up to the side of her face and laid his palm gently on her pale skin. Eiya brushed her nose over Seckry's cheek until it was touching his own, and she opened her eyes; her big, beautiful brown eyes that were glistening with warmth from the reflection of the campfire.

But just as Seckry's lips were about to touch Eiya's, he reeled back in shock.

He couldn't believe what he was seeing.

Eiya's skin had become translucent.

Chapter Thirty-Two

Translucency

"Seck?" Eiya said desperately. "What's wrong?"

"I . . . ugh . . . I -" Seckry could barely string together a sentence to describe what was happening. "Eiya, I can see . . . right *through* you."

Eiya's forehead scrunched into a frightened confusion.

"I must be losing my mind," said Seckry. "It's the cold. It's making me see things, it must be." He hoped to Gedin that this was the case. They had been out here in the freezing cold for way longer than any of them had ever had to endure before; it was inevitable that their brains would have a hard time dealing with it. Seckry told himself that it was just some crazy hallucination, and lifted his hand, slowly, to touch Eiya's cheek once again.

"Oh, Gedin," he said, feeling sick to the stomach.

Eiya's skin didn't feel like human skin any more, it was like touching a fine layer of silk. He pulled away, scared of damaging her.

"Seckry, you're . . . really freaking me . . . out, right now," Eiya said, her voice trembling even more now than it had been from the cold. She pulled off one of her gloves and stared at her own hand.

She let out a breathless whimper. Her hand was just as transparent as her face.

"Seck," she said softly. "What's happening to me?"

They both stood there, petrified, having no idea what to do, and scared to even move in case Eiya vanished completely. After a few minutes, Eiya's skin slowly regained its opacity and relief flooded through Seckry.

He threw his arms around her and held her even tighter than before.

"Eiya, I can't lose you, I -"

He cut himself short as he realised Eiya's neck was fast becoming translucent once again.

He sprang back, horrified.

"Eiya . . . oh Gedin, it's *me* . . . it's when I touch you."

They stood silently for a few moments as Eiya's skin returned to its normal colour.

"Are you sure?" said Eiya. She held her hand out, and Seckry tentatively took a hold of it. Just as he expected, a wave of translucency spread from the point of contact.

"Seck," Eiya said, agonised, as Seckry let go. "I don't understand. How is this happening?"

"Okay, we need to test a few things," Seckry said, trying to keep his composure. "I'll touch one of the other guys to see if the same thing happens to them, and you touch one of them too, to see if the same thing happens to you."

They clambered back into the tent and Seckry shook Tenk awake.

"Tenk," he whispered, "I know this sounds really weird, but . . . I need to touch you."

After a couple of blinks, Tenk, his expression unfaltering, said, "I know I always claim that sooner or later everyone wants a little bit of the Tenkmeister, but I thought you were content with Eiya, to be honest, Seck."

"I've just got to touch your arm or something for a moment," Seckry said, not in the mood for playing games, and gripped Tenk's left arm.

He waited.

Nothing happened.

"Now Eiya's got to do the same," Seckry said.

Eiya held Tenk's arm gently, and her skin remained completely opaque.

The others sat up in succession, roused by the commotion.

"What's going on?" said Loca. "Eiya, are you alright?"

"Can I touch you for a moment?" said Eiya, and took

Loca's silence as a *yes*.

Once again, Eiya remained completely normal. Seckry did the same, and Loca remained exactly the same. After both trying Kimmy too, Eiya thanked them and turned to Seckry.

"What? Nobody wants to touch me?" said Tippian. "Why am I being left out?"

Kimmy reached over and touched Tippian's forearm.

"Thanks, Kim," said Tippian, happily.

"Guys . . ." Seckry said. "When I touch Eiya, her skin . . . her skin becomes see-through."

"Really?" said Tippian. "That's so cool. I wanna see this."

"Tipps, I'm not messing around here," Seckry said, more sternly than he had ever spoken to Tippian before.

He explained what had happened to them out in the clearing.

"Seck," said Tenk, gravely. "I know exactly what's happened."

"You do?" said Seckry.

"So do I," said Tippian.

"Somebody has screwed you over and messed you up," said Tenk.

"What?" said Seckry, perplexed.

"The same person that screwed me over," said Tippian. "Zovak McVorak. He messed with you on stage, giving you that Purika stuff, and he's probably done some permanent damage."

"I think they could be right," said Kimmy. "I'm guessing only Eiya is affected because she's different to the rest of us. You know, molecularly? The helitonic particles that she's made up of must be fading if they come into contact with you for too long because the Purika stuff is recognising them as . . . unpure."

"Seck . . ." Eiya said, softly. "They're right . . . it's cleansing the world of . . . *me*."

Seckry couldn't believe what he was hearing. If what they were guessing was true, he would never be able to touch Eiya again, and right now, he felt like he couldn't survive without holding her close.

They talked about the situation for a few hours after that, but eventually, everyone except Seckry and Eiya fell back to sleep, one-by-one.

"I just have to go to the toilet," Seckry said, and made his way out into the woods, but really, there was something else he needed to do.

He took one of his extra shirts out of his backpack, and when he was far away enough from the tent, he scrunched it up into a ball and shoved it into his mouth, before collapsing to his knees and letting out a gigantic, long, guttural yell, muffled by the material. It was the only thing he could do to relieve the pain and frustration that was engulfing his whole body right now.

He let the shirt drop out of his mouth and he knelt there for a long time afterwards, just breathing heavily and watching the steam of his breath vaporise into the icy atmosphere as warm tears trickled down his frozen cheeks.

Then, there was a sharp thud in the base of his neck.

His hand shot up and he felt something sticking into his skin. He pulled it out and found himself staring at some kind of dart with a black feather pluming out of it.

Seckry turned around slowly.

Standing there in front of him was the demon figure, and Seckry only just about had time to feel petrified at seeing its horns and its terrible, beastly face, before his vision blurred and his consciousness slipped away.

Chapter Thirty-Three

Caged

Seckry opened his eyes. It took a while for him to focus, but when he did, the first thing he saw was the rest of the group scattered around him, all coming into consciousness along with him.

He breathed a sigh of relief as he saw Eiya beside him.

"Seck . . . the demon . . . it got us . . . it tranquillised us," she trembled.

They were in a giant cage that was within some kind of log cabin. Their backpacks, sleeping bags, and tent were all there too, outside of the cage, piled up in one corner of the room.

Eiya gripped Seckry suddenly, as the morning sun coming in through the window on the opposite side of the cabin was ousted by the demon figure. It moved forward slowly, and with every step, Seckry began to realise that the demon's features were completely human apart from its head. Then it reached up, grabbed its own horns, and pulled upwards.

The demon they had been unable to identify was actually a woman of around sixty, who had been wearing the head of a dead animal as a kind of helmet.

Her face was tough, leathery and full of scars, and she had short, wiry, dark hair.

"Naluk! Vinaka zetupay," the woman said, throwing the animal head to one side and pulling a machete out of a sheath on her belt. "Ne nisha na'lahuk!"

"Gedin, what is she saying?" said Loca. "It sounds like she's going to kill us!"

"Kim," Tenk said desperately, "where's your phrasebook? We could really use it right now."

"It's in my backpack over there," Kimmy said in distress. "Wait, I remember a few things. Naluk . . . it means . . . 'why?' and . . . zetupay, I'm sure that's 'location' . . . paired with 'vinaka' . . . 'you' . . . she's demanding why we are here."

"Tell her we're not her enemy!" said Tippian.

"Belinga!" said Kimmy, his voice faltering. "Belinga . . . ni commasar."

The woman slammed her machete on the bars of the cage, making the whole thing vibrate with a clang.

"Nituk!" she said. "Morteka na gendru."

Everyone looked to Kimmy, but he shook his head.

"I have no idea what that means. We don't speak Kringa," he said pleadingly. "Do you know any Unilan? That's the only language we know."

"We are not your enemy," Tenk said. "We're friends!"

The woman was silent for a moment, before saying: "Are you . . . people of . . . *him?*"

"People of him?" said Loca. "People of who?"

"Are you . . ." the woman repeated. "Follow of the revolution?"

"The revolution?" said Loca.

"Look, we're not followers of anyone or anything," Seckry said. "We're . . . just visiting." Even though this wasn't strictly the truth, Seckry was sure she was mistaking them for another group of people, maybe some rival mountain clan.

Seckry got up and stepped forward to try to calm her down, but the woman thrust her free arm into the cage, gripped Seckry, and pulled him to her so that his back slammed into the bars. She slid the blade of the machete up to his throat.

Eiya screamed but cut herself off as she realised the noise was making the woman press the blade even firmer on Seckry's neck.

Seckry swallowed and felt his Adam's apple cross the point of the blade.

"Followers . . . must . . . be . . . stopped," said the woman, but then paused for a moment before drawing a big intake of breath through her nostrils. She muttered some indecipherable exclamation to herself, then breathed in again, before pressing her nose into Seckry's hair and sniffing like an animal.

She slowly relieved the pressure of the machete and pulled her hand back through the bars before placing the blade back in its sheath. Then she turned Seckry around so that he was facing her.

She grabbed his face and pressed her fingers all over it, as if moulding a clay model, all the time her eyes darting across his features in what seemed to be excitement and disbelief.

"You . . ." she said. "Just . . . like . . . . *Pawl.*"

Chapter Thirty-Four

Leftovers

"Do you know my dad?" Seckry said desperately, his heart racing.

"Pawl," the woman said again, grabbing a tuft of Seckry's hair and examining it.

"Pawl is my dad," Seckry said, deliberately slowly. "My father."

"Father," the woman repeated, understanding. "Pawl . . . has child?"

"How do you know him?" Seckry asked, although he was doubtful she could understand what he was asking.

The woman didn't respond, but pulled an old, rusty key out of one of her pockets and opened their cage with a screech.

They filed out slowly, still slightly wary of what was going to happen to them.

When they were all out of the cage, the woman spat into her hands, clapped them together, then slapped her own face twice, once with each hand.

"Oh Gedin, she's gonna kill us," said Tenk.

"No, it's the traditional Kringa greeting," said Kimmy. "She's welcoming us. She's saying 'hello', and indicating that she's a friend. It's considered very rude in Kringa culture not to return the gesture, I think."

Kimmy spat into his own hands and copied her, giving himself a firm slap on either cheek.

"We've all got to do this?" said Tippian. "I've got very sensitive skin, I'll end up as red as a beet-"

"Tipps, just do it, man!" said Tenk, hurriedly. "Do you want to get out of here alive, or what?"

Tippian spat a few times, but only managed to get the tiniest speck of spittle.

"My mouth's too dry from the nerves," Tippian said.

"Here, you can have some of mine," said Tenk, and spat a mouthful of phlegm onto Tippian's open palms.

Tippian, looking as though he was about to be sick, reluctantly slapped himself before wiping the remainder of Tenk's spit into his trousers.

Seckry, Eiya and Loca followed suit.

"Me," said the woman, patting her chest. "Kalandra."

The group introduced themselves in turn.

"Baruck?" Kalandra said, waiting for them to answer.

"Baruck?" said Kimmy. "I think . . . I think that's the word for meat."

"Meat?" said Tenk. "Oh Gedin, she's saying we're dead meat, isn't she?"

"No," said Kimmy. "I think she's asking us if we want meat. She's asking us if we're hungry."

"Baruck, yes," said Loca. "Yes please."

Kalandra nodded firmly and gestured for them to sit around the round table that was at the centre of the cabin.

"Pawl . . . was friend," she said, as she ladled massive scoops of a revolting looking stew from a huge pot into bowls for each of them.

Seckry listened intently.

"Pawl . . . hide here . . . I protect him."

"Protect him from what?" Seckry asked. "From . . . Lux?"

Kalandra hissed.

"Do not speak," she said, a pain entering her voice. "Do not speak name."

Kalandra raised her left hand slowly, and it was only then Seckry realised that she had two missing fingers. Then she pointed to the largest scar that ran from her forehead all the way down to her chin.

"Oh my Gedin, Lux did this to her," said Loca.

"He must have come here first when he broke out of the

labs," said Seckry. "He must have come here looking for my dad."

Kalandra plonked a bowl of stew down in front of each of them, and even though it was a muddy colour and smelled like fermenting fungus, Seckry was grateful for it. He gulped down a few mouthfuls, trying not to let it linger on his tastebuds for too long, but as he did so, he began to realise that the stew tasted incredibly delicious. It was chock full of a mix of strange, tender meat from what had to have been mountain game and birds, and flavoured with several types of mushrooms that each had its own distinct, nutty flavour and texture. It was finished with a generous amount of creamy butter, which made the stew melt in his mouth, and warm his stomach in a way that he had been longing for out in the snow.

By the look of things, Seckry wasn't the only one who was enjoying the taste. Before Seckry had even taken his fourth mouthful, Tenk was scooping the bottom of his bowl and tipping the last drops into his mouth.

Kalandra, for the first time, smiled. She patted Tenk roughly on the back, making him wobble in his seat.

"More?" she said. But Tenk didn't even have to answer before she was pouring ladles into his bowl until it was full to the brim, almost spilling over the sides.

Tenk still managed to finish his second helping even before anyone else had finished their first.

When Seckry had finished, he thanked Kalandra for such a satisfying meal, and asked her, "When was my dad here?" But Kalandra just stared at him, not understanding.

"What was my dad like?" Seckry tried, but once again, Kalandra just shrugged her shoulders, not familiar enough with the language.

"He must have found this place when he first escaped from the labs," said Loca. "And then, at some point, made his way south, and eventually met your mum and settled in Marne."

"And then, years later," said Kimmy, "when your dad's xinary thing turned red, and Lux escaped, he must have found this place too and demanded where your dad was."

"I guess Kalandra didn't want to cooperate," said Tenk.

They sat in silence for a while, taking everything in.

"Can you believe it's actually Seckramas today?" said Tippian. "Our parents are gonna be going mental back home."

"Merry Seckramas," Tenk said to Kalandra, but Kalandra didn't return the greeting. Instead, she waved her hand impatiently and said, "Na, na. Nack." She shook her head. "Seckraman, Gedin, nack." She placed her hand on Tenk's shoulder, leaned in to him, and then pointed very slowly at the sky through the window of the cabin.

"This," she said, as the sun emerged through the clouds and the leaves of the treetops. "This. My Gedin." Then she pointed to the ground and said, "This. My Gedin," once again. Then she turned around and cupped her worn hands in her sink, forming a puddle of water. "This," she said once more. "My Gedin."

"Worshipping the things that keep her alive," said Loca. "The sun, the soil, water. Pretty sensible."

Kalandra suddenly jumped up and ran to the window, staring up at the sky through the snowy treetops.

Seckry had no idea what she was doing at first, but then he heard it; the distant chopping of helicopter blades.

"The rescue team!" shouted Tenk.

Seckry jumped up and ran to the window, joining Kalandra in searching the sky, but he couldn't see anything because of the amount of leaves above them.

"We have to go," Seckry said to Kalandra. "Thank you so much for the food."

Kalandra looked at Seckry, then at the window, and nodded in understanding.

As the others were quickly grabbing their backpacks and the tent, Kalandra took a hold of Seckry's forearm and said, "Pawl . . . is . . . okay?"

Seckry honestly didn't know the answer to that question. The only contact he had had from his father in the last nine and a half years was the recorded telephone message and the note they had found at The Axe and Cleaver Inn.

"He's okay," Seckry said forcefully, to convince himself just as much as Kalandra.

Kalandra breathed a sigh of satisfaction before dipping one of her remaining fingers into a pouch of bright blue powder on her belt and drawing a circle of strange, foreign symbols on his wrist.

"What is it?" Seckry asked her.

"This . . . sign . . . good luck," she said, and kissed the base of his open palm.

Seckry lifted his arm to look at the symbols she had painted, and a wave of emotion overcame him, triggered by the resurgence of a long forgotten memory. These were the same symbols that he had found inscribed on his father's mysterious watch the day he had disappeared. They had been a good luck wish from Kalandra, etched onto the surface of the xinary.

"Seck, we have to go! Come on!" shouted Tenk.

Seckry thanked Kalandra once more and grabbed his backpack before racing out into the forest to join the others.

Surprisingly, the forest's exit was not far from the cabin, and they passed their camping spot just before running out into the open. It was no wonder Kalandra had tranquillised them and caged them, thinking they were attackers; they had unwittingly been camping right outside her home.

As soon as Seckry bolted out of the trees, he saw the helicopter. There was just one, facing them, and slowly lowering to the ground.

"We're saved!" Tenk shrieked manically.

They shielded their faces from the whipping wind and upturned snow as the helicopter landed and its propellers wound to a stop.

The door was kicked open and someone jumped out; someone Seckry was not expecting.

It was Vance.

"Sir?" said Seckry, astounded.

"Thank Gedin you're here," Vance said. "Are any of you hurt?"

"We're fine," Seckry said. "But what . . . when . . . how do you even know how to fly a helicopter?"

"I was given some vouchers for flight lessons a few years back," said Vance. "A gift from the Science Committee. Didn't think I was going to be putting my basic skills to the test so soon, though, I can assure you. The Skyfall mountain rescue operations team wouldn't fly in such bad weather. They said it would be putting themselves in too much danger, and you would have to wait it out until the conditions were better."

"Charming of them," said Tenk.

"I protested, of course," said Vance, "but they weren't interested. So I took matters into my own hands. I borrowed this helicopter from them."

Seckry looked at the others.

"Borrowed or stole?" he said.

"Well," said Vance. "I *am* going to give it back."

Before they could talk any more, Vance urged them all to clamber inside.

"I was worried you wouldn't be in the same spot as you were when you triggered the alarm signal," he said, as he slammed the door shut.

"Are you still feeling ill?" Seckry asked him.

"Bright as a button, now," Vance said. "Nothing a bit of Lenylin Plus couldn't cure."

As Vance fired up the propellers once again, he said, "Site Origin . . . did you find it?"

"Yeah," Seckry replied. "Yeah, we did."

Vance lifted off, and Seckry spent most of the journey telling him everything that had happened, from the tripwire-triggered poles, to the revelation about Lux's original name not being Lux, to getting captured by Kalandra.

The journey was bumpy in places because the storm seemed to be the worst between Solstaven and Skyfall, but once they were out of it, the ride was smooth and the views were stunning. Skyfall was like a giant disc of flickering lights, intertwined by the snaking monorails that ran between its high rise buildings.

"The snow hasn't even reached Skyfall yet," said Vance. "You'll probably find it very mild here now after what you've just been through."

"Do our parents know we're safe?" asked Tippian.

"They will do very shortly," said Vance.

"They're going to know that we went on our own, aren't they?" said Tenk, fear in his voice.

"Oh yes, they already do," said Vance accusatorially. "None of them took the news that I was still in Skyfall too kindly. It was a bit of a shock to me, since I was under the impression they all knew you were heading up there alone."

"My mum is gonna kill me," said Tenk. "She's actually gonna kill me. And my nan, she's gonna - oh no . . . oh no, there they are!"

As the helicopter slowly descended onto the landing pad of the mountain rescue grounds, Seckry saw that Tenk's mum and Raymus were there waiting for them, alongside his own mum and Leena, and Kimmy's, Loca's and Tippian's parents too.

As Vance opened the door and they began filing out, Tenk was met with a firm slap on the arm from his mum that turned into multiple slaps and shouts of, "What were you thinking? . . . lying to me . . . you could have died!"

Seckry prepared for the same from his mum, but Coralle just let out a deep sigh of relief and wrapped her arms around him, crying gently into his puffy clothing.

"I'm so sorry, mum," he said, overwhelmed with emotion himself.

"It was about your father, wasn't it?" Coralle said, and Seckry nodded slightly.

Coralle said nothing more after that, aside from, "Let's go home, it's Seckramas."

"You missed the feast, bro," said Raymus to Tenk.

"You're lucky we saved you a load of food," said his mum, before giving him another couple of slaps. "And we don't even have the phone number of your girlfriend. Does she even know you're alive?"

"I'll talk to her as soon as we get back," said Tenk.

Before everyone left, a mountain rescue member approached the helicopter and threw his arms out.

"Are you going to explain yourself?" he said to Vance.

"I'll explain myself as soon as you explain yourselves in regards to why you were ready to let these teenagers freeze to death in the Frostpeak mountain range."

The rescue man almost responded, but was met by the evil glares of everyone's parents, and took a few gulps before telling them all to leave the premises, then disappearing back inside.

After everyone had thanked Vance for the fifth time, they all split up, returning to their homes, and Seckry and Eiya were driven back to the flat by Leena, who had recently got her driving license after several failed attempts.

When they arrived back at Kerik Square, all the residents had finished eating and had returned to their flats, but the great table still stood in the centre, next to the old fountain, piled high with leftovers.

"Love," Coralle said to Seckry. "I know how much your father means to you. We're all still confused about him leaving and everything with the lab babies, but . . . you can't keep getting yourself into these dangerous situations. I don't think my nerves can take it."

Seckry had to tell her what he really felt.

"Mum," he said, his voice cracking. "Dad wasn't just a normal human being. And . . . neither am I. There is someone out there who wants to kill dad, and me with him, and I have to be prepared."

Coralle began crying once more, and Seckry hugged her tightly.

"I don't understand any of this," she sobbed, before excusing herself.

As soon as they had arrived back at the square, Tenk had run to his bedroom to phone Richelle, but was now returning to the great table, telling them that she was fine, and she sent her Seckramas wishes to them all.

Before they tucked in, Tenk's dad and brother Longo joined them too.

"Glad you weren't eaten alive up there, son," said his dad. "Gedin knows why anyone would want to go for a holiday to somewhere even colder than here, though. Next time, head in the bleedin' opposite direction and get some sunshine down south if you want a break from Skyfall."

Suddenly, Longo gave Tenk a firm thud in the arm.

"What was that for?" Tenk cried.

"Mum made me eat all of your helpings of her food as well. She kept saying it wouldn't keep, and she hadn't spent three days cooking just for Mrs Rooby to take it all home for her cats at the end of the meal."

"Surely someone else would have eaten it?"

"Tenk," Longo said dramatically. "She garnished the fish heads with *extra* fish eyeballs. Mum's lucky people weren't throwing up just watching *me* eat the stuff, never mind eat it themselves."

Seckry was as relieved as Tenk to find out that the leftovers waiting for them didn't contain anything cooked by Mrs Binko, and was actually stunned at how delicious leftovers could actually look.

If he was being truly honest, he was still feeling satiated from Kalandra's stew, but as soon as a few silver lids were lifted from pots and platters, he started salivating once more.

There were crumbly pies and jars of preserved fruits alongside slices of fresh meat and fish and things Seckry couldn't even identify but looked delicious. There was even a giant mound of sandwiches stacked so high that they had to be skewered through the top to prevent them from toppling over, and Seckry was sure he counted eight layers of filling between the bread.

"Yes!" exclaimed Tenk, picking up a tin-foil-wrapped parcel that had his name written on it in marker pen. "Mrs Bumkin remembered my crispy bits. She keeps them for me every year." He unravelled the foil to reveal a collection of oil-drenched scraps of burnt batter.

"What are those?" asked Eiya, fascinated.

"It's the scrapings from the bottom of the deep fat fryer when she's cooking all those battered cobeyfish she always does every Seckramas."

"I call them the heart attack snack," said Tenk's dad. "Keep me a few, will you?"

After they had scoffed their faces, and drunk copious amounts of ellonberry juice, Seckry and Eiya returned to the flat, and were careful not to upset Coralle any more than she already was, keeping themselves to themselves and mostly staying in their bedroom.

Before long, Eiya fell asleep on her bed, exhausted from the ordeal of the trip, so Seckry pulled the digital diary that he had found at the labs out of his backpack.

He switched it on and was met with the same login screen as he had been two days ago. There was no username field, just one for a password, so the device had to have been used by just one person. But Seckry had no idea what the password could be.

He tried a few obvious choices, like each of the scientist's names, then each of their names with a number next to it, then words like helitonium, creogen, and exorophon, but none of them worked. He spent the following hour trying different combinations, but eventually dropped the thing onto his bedside table in frustration.

It was only then that he realised a text message was waiting for him on his phone.

It was from Tippian.

Want me to run my homemade hacking software on that digital diary, Seck? It hasn't failed me yet.

Seckry sent a quick message back.

YES PLEASE!!

While he waited, he wondered what else Tippian had hacked into over the years.

A few moments later, Seckry received a reply with an executable file attached.

Open this program on your phone and then press the phone to the diary. Oh, and keep both away from your head. The radio waves might mess with your brain.

Seckry warily opened the file and did as Tippian instructed, squeezing the phone and the diary together in one, outstretched hand.

Nothing happened initially, but then the monotone screen of the diary started to flicker, and the text started to break up.

Seckry continued to squeeze until he began to feel hot, shooting pains in his fingers, and he dropped both to the floor.

When he picked them up, the diary now read:

Welcome, Adelbert.

Chapter Thirty-Five

Broken Segments

The first thing Seckry did was use the diary's built-in search function to search for the word *activation*, and sure enough, it returned a collection of results, the first being the entry, 'Instructions for Activation.'

Seckry pressed the entry with his finger, his heart racing, and was met with two symbols, each broken in half by a split down the middle. One was white, and of a swirling angel figure. The other was black, and of a swirling demon.

Underneath, there was an explanation.

We needed a way for the boys to be able to control their powers. We decided upon the locking together of broken symbols. We gave Pawl the symbol of an angel, to signify his creogenic powers of creation, and Lux, the symbol of a demon, to signify his exorophonic powers of destruction. We have altered their brains so that they will be able to conjure up a vivid image of their chosen, broken symbol, and by pushing those two broken segments together, they will activate their respective powers. To deactivate them, they will need to separate the segments in their mind again.

The first thing that Seckry noticed was that Lux had actually gotten into the diary and even changed his name digitally. But he was too excited to think about it any longer.

He phoned Vance immediately.

"I've got the instructions, sir," he said as soon as Vance picked up.

"Excellent," Vance replied. "I'll be at Estergate first thing tomorrow morning. You can meet me there to test it out. I imagine you'll be tempted to try the instructions tonight, but for your own safety, and Eiya's, I highly recommend waiting until you're in my classroom."

Seckry agreed, and just hoped his anticipation wouldn't get the better of him.

That night, Seckry and Eiya pulled their quilts onto the floor and sat playing their favourite beat 'em up video game. It was Seckry's idea to move to the floor in between their beds, so they could pass the controller to each other easily, but the reality was that he just wanted to be closer to her.

Before either of them realised it, they had fallen asleep on the floor, the game still running quietly on the television.

It was only when the voice over shouted, "K.O. You lose!" that Seckry jolted awake.

His instinct was to wake Eiya up so they could get back into their beds, but she was sleeping so peacefully that he couldn't bring himself to do it. Instead, he lay awake for a while, just watching her sleeping, and longing to be even closer to her.

As Seckry lay there, Eiya whimpered a couple of times and reached out sleepily, finding Seckry and digging her fingers into his pyjamas before pushing her head up into his side and breathing him in.

Seckry quickly scrambled away from her silently, knowing that if he had let her touch him for just a moment longer, she would have begun to evaporate. His heart was pounding. What if he had still been asleep when she had reached out to him? She might have put her arm around him without him knowing, and . . . she may not have been there when he woke up.

Eiya's eyes opened groggily and she focused on Seckry's petrified face.

"Seck?" she said softly. "What's wrong?"

"You were . . . you were, um . . . your arm touched mine."

Eiya sat up silently, understanding the gravity of such a small thing.

"We need to sort this out asap," said Seckry. "I need to talk to Zovak. Have you got any idea where he lives?"

Eiya shook her head.

"In the north partition somewhere, but aside from that, I have no idea."

"I'll see if any of the other guys have his address," said Seckry.

"Don't worry, Seck," Eiya said affectionately. "It's all gonna be okay. We'll wait until we go back to Estergate and we'll ask him for an antidote. If he's smart enough to design that Purika stuff, he must be smart enough to be able to design an antidote. That's if he hasn't already done so."

"Yeah . . . you're right," Seckry said, but as much as he tried to convince himself that Zovak would be able to help them, there was something in the back of his mind telling him it wasn't going to be as easy as it sounded.

"And in the meantime," said Eiya, standing up and yawning, "we'll make sure we don't fall asleep next to each other on the floor again." She smiled and let herself fall backwards onto her bed.

After a troubled second sleep, Seckry woke to the first sliver of sunrise beaming into the bedroom. Being careful not to wake Eiya, he crept out of the room, had a quick wash in the bathroom, threw on some clothes, and left the flat for Estergate, clutching the digital diary.

"Has your mum forgiven you?" asked Vance, as Seckry took a seat in his classroom, placing the diary in front of him.

"I'm not sure she's ever really going to forgive me for any of this stuff to do with my dad," Seckry replied. "She says it's turned her into an emotional wreck, but . . . but I can't stop trying to find out the truth. I just wouldn't be able to live with myself."

Vance sat down opposite Seckry.

"Of course," he said. "This isn't just about uncovering the truth about your father, it's also about uncovering the truth about yourself."

Once Seckry had shown Vance the diary entry, he closed his eyes and tried to clear his mind of everything aside from the two segments of the angel symbol. As much as he tried, flashes of things in his immediate memory kept distracting him and he had to open his eyes again and start over. After the third time, he leaned back in his chair, taking a deep breath.

"Don't worry," said Vance. "I know how hard it is to clear your mind, especially for someone who has lived in a city as big and manic as this one for the last year and a half. I've lived here all my life and all I see and hear when I close my eyes at night are speeding monorails, construction cranes, and neon lights. Just relax and keep trying. It'll come to you eventually."

Seckry leant forward and closed his eyes once more. He found himself thinking of his father's chequered shirt and Eiya's translucent skin, but he kept his eyes closed anyway, and continued to take deep, long breaths, until eventually, all of his conscious thoughts seemed to drift into the distance.

Then, suddenly, something changed.

Seckry's mind cleared completely, and a sense of ease and cleanliness and purity overcame him. It felt too, like he had somehow stopped time around him, and he was existing in his own kind of time warp.

With his eyes closed, Seckry had been able to see mostly darkness with bits of squiggly flashes of colour now and again up until now, but this had all vanished and had been replaced with a completely blank canvas of colourlessness, so blank and empty that it was almost encouraging Seckry to paint something onto it with his imagination.

Carefully, Seckry thought of the swirling angel symbol, and amazingly, the two broken halves began materialising in front of him, so vivid and so sharp that he felt like he could almost reach out and touch them.

As the drawing of the segments completed, Seckry no longer knew if his eyes were still closed or if they were open. The picture was so clear that he wouldn't have been surprised if his eyes were open wide and the two halves were right there, floating in front of him.

The next step was to push the halves together so that they

locked into place.

Making sure not to panic or rush anything, Seckry gently imagined the two pieces drifting towards each other.

But nothing happened.

He waited patiently, giving the two segments enough time to move, but they sat, not moving an inch. After a few moments, Seckry nudged them with his mind once again, firmer this time, so that they forcibly shifted a little. But as they did so, they sprung back into place, sitting well away from each other.

Seckry took a moment once again, trying to keep as calm as possible, before using his mind to push the segments, this time with as much force as he could muster.

The pieces squeezed inwards, but the closer they got, the harder Seckry had to push, as if they were repelling each other like opposing magnets.

Seckry tried three more times, the third time concentrating so hard on pushing them together that his head started to pound with pain.

But they wouldn't lock together.

Suddenly, the pain in Seckry's head became so acute that it wiped the symbol away, and the canvas with it, and the classroom came back into his vision.

"I don't get it," Seckry said, as Vance's hazy face became slowly clearer.

"What did you see?" Vance asked. "Your eyes suddenly opened at one point and you were staring at me, but I waved my hands in front of you and there was no reaction. Could you see me?"

"No," said Seckry. "Not at all."

He continued to explain everything that he had felt, and the fact that the two segments wouldn't fit together.

"I imagine these things could take time to master," said Vance. "I would suggest taking a breather for a moment before trying again."

Seckry nodded and took Vance's advice.

Over the next hour, Seckry managed to clear his mind and enter that strange zone of timelessness another three times, but every single time, the segments would stay locked in place, refusing to move towards each other, and the harder Seckry pushed with mental force, the more they refused, causing him searing pain.

After a fourth failed attempt, Seckry couldn't contain his frustration any longer and he kicked his chair out from underneath him, turning away from Vance and the diary and pacing around the classroom.

After a minute or two of trying to calm down, he said, "I'm sorry, sir."

"It's quite alright, Seckry," said Vance calmly.

Seckry couldn't believe that, after everything he had put his friends and Eiya through, nothing was happening once again. He almost felt as though he was going mad, and that this entire thing about having creogen inside him was just some strange hallucination formed by his dementia. Was he really expecting to have super powers? Before finding the hidden classroom, Seckry would have laughed at the idea. Now he had become deadly serious about it.

"Seckry," said Vance, comfortingly, putting a firm hand on Seckry's shoulder and squeezing it. "Go home and enjoy the rest of the Seckramas holiday as much as you can, okay? It's very unlikely that we're going to figure this out today. Unfortunately, I have an incredible amount of work to do before the beginning of term, so I won't be able to see you again until then, but when school does start, you can come to my class every morning before lessons begin, and we can work on getting these powers activated, okay?"

Seckry nodded and he began to feel terrible with guilt.

"Sir, I'm so sorry about everything," he said.

"Sorry?" said Vance. "What have you got to be sorry for, Seckry?"

"For taking up all of your time, for insisting on going into the mountains without you, and then for you having to come and rescue us when we got stranded. I bet you sometimes wish you'd never met me, the amount of trouble I've caused."

Vance chuckled deeply, a kind warmth imbued into it.

"Seckry," he said. "Somehow, I think our paths were

always meant to cross."

Seckry tried at least twice a night after that, despite Vance's concerns about him testing it in his own home, but each night, he would become more frustrated than the previous night. It seemed that the more and more he tried to push the pieces together, the less willing they were to budge from their opposing positions, and he had a hard time even getting them to quiver now, never mind moving towards each other.

When the holidays ended and it was time to return to Estergate, Seckry was elated to finally get a chance to confront Zovak about the purifying substance inside of him, and it was a relief to have something to take his mind off the creogen.

After a mundane triple period of calculus on their first day back, Seckry spotted Zovak surrounded by his usual harem of girls at lunchtime by one of the vending machines.

"Zovak, can I talk to you?" he said sternly.

Zovak eyed him suspiciously, and without moving his head he said, "Sure."

"I'd like to talk to you alone," said Seckry.

Zovak glared at him for a moment before telling the girls to meet him in a few minutes out in the plaza. When they were out of earshot, Seckry turned to Zovak and said, very firmly, "I want you to get rid of this stuff in my bloodstream immediately."

"Excuse me?" said Zovak.

"Everyone was impressed by that Purika stuff, even me, but injecting me with poison was completely out of order. And whatever that Purika stuff is that cleansed it, it's still in my system, and it's causing me problems. Big problems."

"What kind of problems?" said Zovak, curiously.

Seckry had no intention of going into detail about Eiya's existence with him; he didn't trust Zovak one bit, and even though Seckry could think of no reason why Zovak shouldn't be aware of her unique composition, Seckry had decided beforehand that the less Zovak knew, the better.

"It doesn't concern you," said Seckry. "I just want this stuff out of my body completely."

"Well," said Zovak, "I hate to tell you this, but the Purika probably left your system a couple of days after the awards ceremony, so I don't think that's your problem."

"You said that everyone who took a dose of it would feel the effects to some degree for the rest of their life," said Seckry.

"Yes," said Zovak, "but . . . but only a, um, small amount would stay in your body. Not enough to cause any . . . trouble. What trouble did you say it was again?" Zovak was pale enough as it was, but his face seemed to be draining of even more colour now, leaving him looking quite ill.

Seckry was still reluctant to divulge any information with Zovak about Eiya.

"There's enough left in my system that it's purifying things that I don't want to be purified," Seckry said sternly.

"Look," said Zovak. "I was lying when I said it'd stay in someone's system forever. It won't, okay? It'll eventually disperse and you'll be back to normal again."

"After how long?" said Seckry.

"I'd say um . . . I mean . . . um, only a couple more weeks . . . months possibly."

Seckry glared at Zovak.

"What about an antidote? There has to be something that can rid this stuff from me immediately."

"There's nothing," said Zovak. "Look, I have to go, I've got to get to-"

"There must be something you can do," Seckry cut in, but Zovak just shook his head and left Seckry standing in the middle of the corridor.

Seckry had very little time to think about the Purika in his body over the next few weeks because they were given a mountain of homework for literature and physics, and Mr Grimsback had said that if anyone handed in an unfinished piece like Konny Lakle did last year, he was going to seize their backpack and shave his beard into it. As unlikely as this sounded, Mr Grimsback's beard was usually full of rotting food and spittle, so even the slightest doubt was more than enough to motivate them to do their best.

But after a month of waiting for the Purika to leave his system, Seckry still couldn't touch Eiya's fingers without transparency bleeding up her arm. Aside from being fed up of nothing changing, he had no idea what long term damage he was doing to Eiya every time he touched her. He was still petrified that one day he would place his fingers upon hers, and she would vanish completely.

When Seckry couldn't take it any longer, he cornered Zovak in the corridor one day, after the final bell had rung.

"Nothing's happening," he accused. "Nothing at all. This stuff is still inside me. It's still affecting me."

Zovak, this time, looked furious and shoved Seckry backwards.

"You've got no right to intimidate me," he said. "It's all in your mind. You need to leave me alone."

Seckry was a little shocked. He had never been accused of intimidating anyone in his life. His mind flashed back to the unassuming, innocent boy he had been when he had walked through Estergate's doors for the first time last year, and he thought of himself now. Had he really become an intimidator?

"I'm sorry," Seckry said. "It's just . . . it's just really important to me. I didn't mean to be so aggressive."

"Well you can stay away from me from now on, Sevenstars," Zovak said. "You need to shut up about the Purika still being in your system because I don't care. Frankly, I don't know why you wouldn't want it in your system anyway. What's so important to you that's being purified by it? The purifier eradicates toxic substances. Whatever it's getting rid of is something dirty and diseased anyway, so you're better off without it."

Seckry held his tongue. Whatever Eiya was, she certainly was not dirty and diseased.

"If there's no antidote to clear this thing completely from my body, can you please give me the ingredients list of Purika so I can get Mr Vance to help me out with creating an antidote?"

"The ingredients are top secret," said Zovak.

Seckry closed his eyes to calm himself down.

"Please, Zovak, I can't stress how important this is."

"I'm done with you, Sevenstars," Zovak said. "If you come near me again, I'll report you for harassment."

Zovak left Seckry feeling at an utter loss. He couldn't understand why Zovak was being so defensive. Eventually, Tenk and Tippian re-joined him in the corridor.

"Okay, this Purika stuff is even fishier than we thought," said Tippian. "I found out last night that Zovak isn't even allowing the Science Committee to commission it. That's usually part of the deal. If you win the Wellworth award, your invention goes into production. But he's keeping it all to himself."

"Why would he do that?" said Tenk.

"Well, he doesn't want Seckry seeing the ingredients, and he doesn't want the Science Committee seeing the ingredients. There has to be something in there that he doesn't want people to know about something . . . dangerous."

Chapter Thirty-Six

Tippian Two-Point-Zero

As more weeks went by, Seckry felt like he was going crazy with helplessness. He tried getting Tenk and a couple of the others to approach Zovak individually and persuade him to hand over the ingredients, but Zovak reacted by accusing the entire group of bullying, and reported them to Mrs Furrowfog, who was the school's anti-bullying chief. The group were called in to her office one afternoon and quizzed about the situation before being made to swear that they would never approach Zovak again.

Seckry spent the remainder of the term feeling utterly miserable. Not only was he forced to keep his distance from Eiya, the person he felt he couldn't get close enough to, he had now been brandished as a bully, the one thing he never thought he would become. On top of this, he had pretty much given up any hope of being able to use his powers, because as hard as he tried to shift the imaginary segments every night before bed, and once a week in Vance's classroom, they refused to budge, leaving both him and Vance perplexed.

Eventually he had to stop himself from trying because it had consumed him so much that he was falling behind in nearly all of his lessons, and he had even been given detention by Mr Splinicky for such a poor grade in his human biology coursework. Luckily, Mr Splinicky wasn't a complete sadist like Mrs Cutson and had only kept him for fifteen minutes before taking pity on him and letting him go with a mild telling off, but Seckry, nonetheless, had to clear his mind of the powers for the time being if he wanted to stay afloat at

Estergate.

Without realising it, weeks went by and the bitter winter air mellowed into the soft breeze of spring. Homework began piling up even more than usual and the schooldays felt long and tiring, with the only fun coming in the form of Vance's fringe science lessons, in which they seemed to be making good progress towards the completion of a teleportation device.

Between lessons, Tenk was still having fun showing off his morningstar-shaped fruit to anyone and everyone, which, amazingly, didn't seem to be withering, as though it was imperishable.

Seckry and Eiya waited for the results of the DNA test from Sanfarrow, but had, strangely, received no contact about it. Seckry almost called Sanfarrow a few times, but stopped himself because he was too anxious about what the results would say. Besides, Eiya had seemed to have almost forgotten about the whole Elenya Kayne thing, so Seckry didn't want to bring it to the forefront of her mind again if he didn't have to.

In March, Seckry visited Cartell to see how he and his daughter were doing, but found the innoya doctor highly frustrated and still locked in legal woes with the acquisition of the warehouse grounds. The only thing that seemed to be keeping him happy was the fact that his healing work on his first patient, Eryk, was still going well, and he predicted that he would be completely wiped of his crippling condition in just a couple of months' time, and Seckry was elated for Cartell, Eryk himself, and his father.

The only thing that was bittersweet about it was that the poor man was still desperately missing the woman who had left him when his condition had worsened, and nobody knew where she was. But when Seckry and Eiya visited the library one evening to find some books on ionisation trails to help them with their meteorology homework, they heard a familiar name being called in the distance.

"Miss Turnfever," they heard. "Can you get a duster and

make yourself useful instead of standing around like a lemon?"

Seckry turned to see that the regular Mrs Parsonpot, who ran the library, had a new assistant; a timid looking woman with downcast eyes, who nodded immediately and went to fetch a cloth.

Seckry recognised the surname straight away and approached her when she started dusting the fiction shelves.

"Hi," he said hesitantly. "Can I . . . can I ask you your first name?"

The woman looked up and blushed, embarrassed.

"Trixa," she said, and then scanned his face, probably wondering what on earthia he wanted.

"Do you . . . do you know a man named Eryk?" Seckry said, unsure what her reaction would be.

Trixa lowered her duster, and her fearful eyes turned to ones of fascination.

"Eryk?" she said. "Is he . . . do you . . . do you know where he is?"

"Yeah," said Seckry. "He's being healed by a man named Cartell Quinn. He's going to be pretty much back to full health soon. He'll be able to walk and talk and everything."

Trixa whimpered.

"What?" she said. "Are you . . . serious?"

Seckry nodded.

"He . . . he still loves you," Seckry said, and Trixa's eyes welled up with tears, an unbelieving smile on her quivering face.

"I . . . still love him, too," she said.

Seckry gave her the address of the guildhouse and went back to studying. Deep down, he couldn't understand how she could have left him in the first place if she had truly loved him, but maybe she regretted it, and hadn't been able to contact him since. All Seckry knew was that Eryk had already forgiven her, and to see her would make him ecstatic.

As the weeks went on with Seckry being unable to approach Zovak about the Purika antidote at school, and still being baffled by the broken segments, one of the only releases for his frustration was the friendly Friction matches he would play with the rest of the Eidolons every Thursday. He enjoyed taking down hoards of AI opponents, and had fun experimenting with different tactics, now that the pressure of the Meltdown was behind them until next year.

The only person that didn't seem to be enjoying Thursday evenings that much was Kimmy, whose stalker seemed to be getting progressively worse. One time, Tippian caught her peering through the Friction common room door window, and another time, a couple of them saw her sneakily blow Kimmy a kiss before darting around a corner in the corridors.

"Does anybody even know this girl's name?" said Loca.

"Nope," said Tenk. "I think she's a year younger than us, though."

"I have to do something about this situation," Kimmy said. "It's getting really uncomfortable."

"Kim, be grateful, man," said Tenk. "I'd give anything to have my own stalker."

"What?" said Loca. "You would actually *like* to have a stalker?"

"Too right I would!" said Tenk.

"Tenk, you *do* realise these stalkers are quite strange people. Would you really want someone like that following you around?"

"I wouldn't care if they were weird. Maybe I just like pleasing people, but it'd be awesome. My stalker would be the happiest stalker ever. I would go out of my way to deliberately give them what they wanted."

"What, like your head on a plate?" Loca said dryly.

"No, I'd just show them a little bit of flesh on accident slash purpose now and again."

"You mean pull a moonie?" said Tippian.

"Nah, a moonie is insulting," said Tenk. "But I'm sure they'd appreciate the subtle beauty of an accidental builder's bum from time to time."

"How would Richelle feel if some girl was following you and blowing you kisses when she wasn't looking?" said Loca.

Tenk just shrugged his shoulders.

"Never really thought about it."

"Yeah . . . well think about it," said Loca, looking uncharacteristically upset.

A couple of weeks later, when they were getting some upgrades out of their lockers in the Friction common room, a note fell to the floor.

"Where'd that come from?" said Loca.

Nobody answered, but it was sitting beneath Kimmy's locker, so there wasn't much doubt in anyone's minds.

Kimmy hesitantly picked it up and read out loud.

"I know we haven't spoken, but I just want you to know how much I think about you. I took a photo of you on my phone when you weren't looking and I've printed it off and I sleep with it under my pillow every night. I didn't think you liked me back, or even knew of my existence, but my heart melted when you winked at me right before you got into your pod at the Mega Meltdown. I mean, especially since you have a girlfriend and everything. I actually think it was the best moment of my life."

Kimmy lowered the note, looking utterly horrified.

"This girl is insane," he whimpered. "I didn't wink at her! I didn't even know she was there!"

Nobody knew what to say in response, so Tenk tried to get everyone into their pods for a game, but Loca excused herself, saying she suddenly didn't feel too good.

On the monorail back to Kerik Square that night, Seckry said, "Do you think Kimmy would actually do that?"

"Who knows?" said Tenk.

"But . . . Kimmy was falling about because Gavanis injected him with that limb number stuff. The last thing he must have been thinking about was winking at his stalker in the audience."

"Yeah, you're right," said Tenk. "He probably winced in pain from the needle and the stalker took it as a wink to her."

"Or she could just be completely deluded," said Eiya.

"This may have happened entirely in her own head."

In the days that followed, Loca seemed distant and quiet, which was not a usual trait of hers, and when she did talk, she seemed irritable and snappy.

The following Thursday, as Kimmy met them at Estergate for Friction practise, he gathered them closer as Loca went to use the bathroom.

"Guys, I think I'm gonna take Loca on . . . a proper date," he said sheepishly.

"A proper date?" said Tenk. "Like skydiving or something?"

"Skydiving? No, I was thinking more of a meal at a restaurant. Something . . . romantic."

"What for?"

"Well, she's been really upset about this whole stalker thing, and I'm sure she thinks that I'm encouraging it, even though I'm not, and I just thought it'd be nice to do something . . . special for her, you know?"

"That sounds really sweet," said Eiya. "I'm sure she'd love that."

"You've got a girlfriend, Tenk," said Kimmy. "Can you recommend a place?"

"Mate," Tenk replied, slapping his hands together. "It's gotta be Myke's Meathouse in the central restaurant quarter. They do this thing where, if you can eat a whole chicken to yourself in under half an hour, they give you, like, two racks of barbecue ribs for free."

"What?" said Seckry. "I'm not sure you should listen to him, Kimmy."

"Why would you even want an extra two racks of ribs after eating a whole chicken?" said Tippian. "I'd be sick by that point."

"I've never managed it myself," said Tenk. "But my dad did it once, and he said those ribs were the best ribs of his life. He said the only thing better than Myke's Meathouse ribs was free Myke's Meathouse ribs. Saying that, he was pretty ill that night."

"Can you take the ribs home if you're full after the chicken?" asked Tippian.

"No, Tipp," said Tenk, as if it was the most ridiculous question he'd ever been asked.

"I don't think I'm gonna take her to Myke's Meathouse," said Kimmy. "But thanks for the suggestion, Tenk."

Before they could decide on a place for Kimmy to take Loca, Loca re-joined them, and the group went silent.

"We were um . . . just, um . . . just discussing restaurants," said Kimmy. "I was thinking maybe I could take you on . . . a proper date sometime," he said, as quietly as he could without being completely unheard.

Loca stared at him for an uncomfortably long period of time.

"I'm sorry, Kim, I'd rather not," she said, and excused herself from practise once more, leaving Kimmy mortified.

"If you'd told her you were taking her to Myke's Meathouse, she might have said yes," said Tenk. "Just saying."

As the smoggy atmosphere of Skyfall warmed and the corridors of Estergate began to hum of heated plastic, hinting at the summer that was just a month or two away, posters began appearing advertising the annual ball.

"It's later on in the year than last time," said Seckry, reading the date.

"Yeah, they decided to shift it to right before the summer holidays this year," explained Tenk. "I heard Gobbledee saying something about pupils seeing the ball as an end to the hard work, and everyone slacking off afterwards, so they've pushed it along."

"Can Richelle come to the ball?" Seckry asked. Richelle was a pupil of Westergate, so he wasn't sure how it would work with them.

"Yeah, since we're together we can choose which ball we want to attend. We're coming here, of course. Couldn't miss the Estergate ball. It's a tradition."

In some ways, Seckry was excited about the ball this year; he would be able to officially ask Eiya to be his date this time, something that Natania had robbed him of last year, but it would be a bittersweet night because he knew he wouldn't be able to touch Eiya, not to kiss her, or even hold her hand.

The only person that seemed even more concerned about the ball than Seckry was Tippian, who had gained an inferiority complex since Tenk's nan had insulted him, and the quiz in Glamourgirl magazine had predicted his future to be a lonely one.

"Who are you asking to the ball this time?" Tenk questioned him one lunchtime, as they sat in the newly reopened canteen, slurping noodles with sugarshrooms.

"I don't know," said Tippian. "I was banking on Curly Hetchings again, but I asked her yesterday and she said no."

"Really?" said Tenk. "Did somebody get there first?"

"No. That's the worst part. She just straight up refused. Did I do something wrong last year?"

Seckry thought about it. From what he recalled, most of the night went fairly smoothly for Tippian, but Seckry had been too caught up in everything that was happening between himself and Eiya last year to remember much else.

"I mean," said Tippian, "I puked in the bathroom not long before kissing her because I was wrecked from that Whistlebloo stuff, but I don't think she found out."

"I think she kind of cottoned on," said Tenk. "She did ask you afterwards why your breath smelled like a mix between gasoline and rotting carrots. That's probably what did it."

Three days later, Tippian plonked himself down on a seat at the canteen conveyer belt, removed his glasses, and slammed his head onto his folded arms on the counter, shaking it.

"What's wrong with you?" said Tenk.

"No one will go with me," came Tippian's muffled voice. "I asked six different girls today, and they all said no."

Seckry and Tenk exchanged glances silently.

"The worst thing was," said Tippian, "after the fifth one, I kind of got a bit manic, and I don't know what came over me, and I turned around, and Linzy Sweetcrust was there with all her friends, and I panicked, and I just . . . I just came out with it. She was the sixth one. I asked Linzy Sweetcrust to the ball."

"You actually asked Linzy Sweetcrust?" gawped Tenk.

"Oh my Gedin, Tipp, if she had said yes then you would have been a legend."

"Well, of course she didn't say yes," Tippian lamented. "Although she didn't say no either. I think she was too horrified to even respond. She just kind of whimpered in disgust and almost started crying."

Tippian shook his head, unable to believe what he had done.

"Well, it's officially settled, anyway," he continued miserably. "I'm not coming to the ball this year. You guys have fun, and don't drink too many slipshakers."

"Come on, Tipps," said Tenk. "You know what these things are like. Everyone turns up with a date, and half of them split up before the end of the night. There'll be loads of single girls waiting for someone to approach them. It'll be your perfect opportunity."

"But how will I get in?" said Tippian. "You know the rules. You have to turn up with a date. The bouncers will rip me to shreds if they catch me sneaking in."

"Tipps," said Tenk, dryly, "the bouncers are Mr Mumble, the ethnobotany teacher, and Mrs Jopson, the special needs teaching assistant. They'll most likely give you a pat on the hand if they catch you."

"I saw Mr Mumble yank a plant out of the ground with his little finger before. He's surprisingly strong," said Tippian.

"A plant?" said Tenk. "I was there that day. It was a blade of grass."

"Yeah . . . well . . . you try pulling a blade of grass out of the ground with your little finger. It does require a lot of strength."

"Look, they ain't gonna do anything to you if you get caught," said Tenk. "They'll most likely feel sorry for you and let you stay anyway."

Tippian went silent after this, lost in his own thoughts.

"And I'd recommend getting a large tub of chococorp chocolate ice cream on the way home tonight," Tenk continued. "It's my staple pick-me-up food for when I'm feeling down. It really does make you feel better."

Tippian's feelings of rejection, however, weren't helped when they spent one evening that week at Tenk's flat. Tenk had tried to sneak them into his bedroom without his nan catching them, but as soon as she spotted them, she blurted, "Got yourself a girlfriend yet, Tiptooth?"

Tippian looked around him, confused.

"Mum, his name's Tippian. Get it right, will you? Tiptooth is the name of your denture liquid."

"Is it?" she said. "What kind of name is Tiptooth for a denture liquid? That's ridiculous. Well, Tippytum, are you gonna answer my question or what?"

Tenk's mum shook her head.

"Mum, Tippytum is the name of that digestion aid stuff you take."

"Oh, for Gedin's sake!" the old woman cried. "Has the boy got himself a girl or what?"

"No," Tippian said meekly. "No, I haven't."

"Mum!" said Tenk's mum. "Just leave it, okay? Remember that talk we had the other night about treating Tenk's friends with a bit of respect?"

"What?" Tenk's nan said defensively. "I'm helping the boy out. If I don't give him a kick up the backside, who will?"

The following week, on top of looking depressed, Tippian seemed to be developing large bags under his eyes, and was constantly yawning. When he fell asleep during a philosophy lesson, Seckry thought it best to bring it up.

"I'm just addicted to this TV show, that's all," he explained. "I've been making my way through all of the box sets."

"What TV show?" quizzed Tenk.

Tippian pulled a chunky box out of his backpack. The cover was of a muscular man with a huge, curly moustache and a cheesy grin on his face, leaning against a sports car with a cigar in one hand and a pistol in the other.

"Showdown? You're watching the entire series of *Showdown?*" said Tenk, aghast.

"Hey," said Tippian. "It's a popular show."

"Yeah, popular with my mum," said Tenk. "It's like, twenty-odd years old. My mum remembers it from back in her day. Besides, nobody ever used to watch that thing for the story, all the women just gawped at Buck Bodstock and his fake tan and tight pants. What are you getting out of it?"

"Inspiration, that's what," said Tippian. "There hasn't been a guy since him that's ever got that much female adoration. He was a legend. I'm taking some tips from the master."

On the Friday of that week, Tippian didn't even turn up to school, so Seckry, Tenk and Eiya went straight to his house when the bell rang to see if he was okay.

They found him in his bedroom, slumped in a mound of discs and open cases with about ten cans of crushed, empty energy drinks littered around the place.

"I wasn't watching this thing just for inspiration," Tippian said through chattering teeth. "I was searching for something . . . and I finally found it."

He raised his TV remote and clicked play. Buck Bodstock appeared on screen, chasing a robed Arivelian guy through a parking lot. The Arivelian stopped when he hit a wall overlooking a river, and Buck strolled up to him with a confident swagger.

"Better luck next time," he said, in a deep, manly, cheesy voice, before booting the guy over the wall so that he fell into the water below with a splash. The camera then zoomed in to Buck's face, and with a twinkle in his eye, he said; "Take that, you filthy junikrapogswash!"

Tippian zapped the TV off and raised a weak arm in triumph, before pulling the collar of his t-shirt to reveal his Voicemaster invention, and clicking it on.

"Guys," he said, in Buck Bodstock's voice. "Say hello to Tippian Furst Two-Point-Zero."

Chapter Thirty-Seven

The Estergate Ball

As school wound down before the summer holidays, Seckry found himself finally accepting the fact that he couldn't activate his powers using the instructions in Adelbert Endoman's diary, and he was okay with it. The main thing that was on his mind was that it was almost June, the month in which he would be meeting his father, and he would be able to tell Seckry everything he was doing wrong. Some nights, Seckry lay awake thinking about him; what he would look like now, how he would act around Seckry, how Seckry would act around him. It was going to be a strange experience, but one Seckry knew was going to be one of the defining moments of his life.

Lessons at Estergate began to descend into madness, with pupils high on the dizzy summer air and caffeine-filled pops, and teachers letting them do what they pleased because they were too exhausted to argue.

The only exception was fringe science, in which all of the pupils, including Seckry, were eager to finish their teleportation device before the end of the term. By the time it was their penultimate lesson, they had all the circuitry in place of two small discs, each about the size of a person's palm, the sender and the receiver. All they needed was Vance's special ingredient before they would be able to finally test them. But just as Vance was getting the vial of helitonium from his cupboard, the end of lesson bell rang.

"Sir, we have to stay and finish them!" one pupil yelled.

"We're so close!" wailed another.

"I wish I could keep you," said Vance, honestly, "but you

have lessons to go to, and I have another class on their way."

Just as they were about to protest, helplessly, Cutson pranced into the classroom. She was carrying a heavy cardboard box full of sheets of paper.

She scanned the classroom and then eyed the two teleportation devices suspiciously.

"Here are the completed tests," she said.

"Thank you, Cecilya," said Vance, calmly. "Just pop them down on my desk."

Cutson eyed the desk, leaned over, and let the box slip through her fingers, directly onto the unfinished teleporters.

The entire class yelped.

"Oh, I'm ever so sorry," Cutson said with fake innocence. "This left wrist of mine, I've been having terrible trouble with it lately."

Vance lifted the box of test papers up to reveal the mess of circuitry underneath.

"I hope that wasn't anything important," Cutson said smugly, and there was silence as she turned around and left the classroom.

"That . . . that . . . horrible . . . vicious . . . malicious pile of . . . of . . . yaktak dung!" spluttered Tenk, as they headed for economics with Mrs Wesserfeld.

Seckry said nothing, but felt exactly the same way Tenk did; livid about Mrs Cutson's deliberate 'accident.'

After Cutson had left, Vance had assured them that all was not lost, and that they would be able to rebuild the devices next year. But after expecting to be able to test them in a couple of days' time, the class were heartbroken.

Mrs Wesserfeld spent the lesson bewildered and lost for words as to why half the class were raging like rampaging rhinotaurs, and the other half were crying into their workbooks, and looked like she was about to burst into tears herself.

By the time lunchtime came around, Seckry had half accepted it. Tenk, on the other hand, was still trying to find the right words to describe Cutson, although couldn't seem to settle on anything. At one point he almost settled for, "the stinking butthole of a constipated haghog," but dismissed it as too tame a moment later.

After a lunch that none of them could really bring themselves to enjoy, Tenk announced, "Right, that's it! I'm going for that Notorious."

Seckry and the others glared at him.

"Are you insane?" said Tippian.

"Tipps, I'm not gonna eat it," said Tenk. "I just can't see something that epic get left in there for the cleaners to throw away at the end of the year. I'll keep it as a memento."

"You are sick," said Loca. "Actually sick."

Tenk approached the Food Grabber machine, and as soon as he did, a crowd began gathering and the canteen was filled with excited chatter.

Tenk stuck a coin into the slot and manoeuvred the crane, taking his time to get the positioning just right. Then he pressed the grab button and the crane snatched up the plastic ball containing the Notorious and dropped it into the funnel for Tenk to collect.

He reached in, ripped it out, and held it up to a host of cheers and the chants of, "Eat it, eat it, eat it, eat it!"

"No chance, suckers!" Tenk yelled back, and shoved it into his backpack, zipping it up tight.

A few moments later, Gavanis and a group of girls she had befriended strolled into the canteen.

"What's all the fuss about?" she demanded. "You're not showing off that stupid fruit again, are you, Binko?"

"No, I'm not," Tenk said. "And it ain't a stupid fruit, it's the best fruit anyone has ever seen in their life, and you're jealous that you ain't got one!"

Gavanis approached Tenk slowly, as if she was going to say something to him, but instead, snatched his backpack out of his hands and ran backwards, shouting, "I stole your stupid fruit! I stole your stupid fruit!"

Tenk ran towards her, but she backed away, unzipping the bag.

"If it's that amazing, then it should be eaten," Gavanis

said, and plunged her hand inside. She fumbled around for a moment and Seckry heard a clicking sound. Then Gavanis pulled her hand out, holding a black and green, furry piece of solid mould.

"Gedin, this does look weird. Looks disgusting actually."

"Gavanis, no!" shouted Tenk, running towards her. "That's not the fruit, that's the -"

But Gavanis, seeing that Tenk was about to rip it from her hands, stuffed the whole thing into her mouth.

Tenk stopped.

The entire canteen drew an intake of breath.

"Wait," Gavanis said through the side of her mouth. "This tastes. . . oh my Gedin." She slowly looked around at the canteen, then the Food Grabber machine, before horrified realisation dawned upon her. As the crowd erupted into howls of laughter and gasps of shock, Gavanis dropped to the floor, spitting out the remainder of the Notorious and heaving.

"She's been hospitalised," said Tenk, the following day, although there was very little concern in his voice. "She won't be coming to the ball, that's for sure."

It was their final day in school before the summer holidays, and the ball was at 7pm in the evening. It was also the day of their final fringe science lesson of the year, and the class were still devastated about Mrs Cutson's sabotage.

Vance, however, met them with a motivated grin, and looked at his watch as soon as everyone was seated.

"We have one hour," he said. "One hour to rebuild these things. What do you say?"

Everyone gasped excitedly.

"You think we can actually do that in one hour?" someone shouted.

"Not if we waste any more time talking about it," said Vance. "Get your lab coats on!"

The following hour seemed more like ten minutes to Seckry, who, by the end of it, was sweating like everyone else. When Vance had suggested it, Seckry had doubted whether they could actually repair all the damage that Cutson had done, but when the bell rang for their next lesson, the teleporters looked miraculously okay.

"We've gotta test them before we go!" yelled Gemella Garrot "We can't leave now!"

"Who do you have for your next lesson?" asked Vance.

"Cut Throat Cutson," someone spat.

"Ah," said Vance. "Well, in that case, you're in luck, because I have the next hour free, and Mrs Cutson has gone home."

"Gone home?" said Eleria Laskin "Why?"

"She was very upset," said Vance. "Someone had replaced the Supergrow in her watering can with ultra-strength acid, and it killed all of her precious plants."

"What?" blurted Harvie Bump. "Who did tha-"

The class was silent as they saw a glint in Vance's eyes and the glimmer of a smile on his face.

After a few celebratory hugs, the class was ready to put all of their hard work to test, and they gathered around the teleporters as Vance placed a coin on top of the sender.

He pressed the button they had built into it to activate the teleportation, and the small vial of helitonium that was lodged inside began to tremble and crack before turning a bright orange and red, and leaking into the classroom as a swirling, fiery vapour.

"Is it supposed to do this?" said Tenk.

But before Vance could answer, the coin disintegrated into a pile of burnt ashes, and the orange vapour dispersed in the air.

After a few moments of silence, Vance said, "I think we may have missed a couple of connections in our haste."

They tried several more times during the hour to teleport different things, but each of them turned into dust. It was a disappointment after their renewed hope of getting something working, but the class finally accepted that they weren't going to be doing any teleporting until next year, and once they had said their goodbyes for the summer to Vance, everyone's minds turned to the ball.

When Seckry and Eiya got back to the flat, they began getting ready for the ball straight away. Seckry had bought a new suit with a red bow tie, and before he'd even had time to look at himself in the mirror, his mum was almost in tears of joy.

"I'm so proud of you, love, you know that?" she said, smoothing his shoulders down. "You look like a man. You look like . . ."

"Like what?" asked Seckry.

Coralle took a breath.

"Like your father," she said.

Just then, Eiya called Seckry to the bedroom.

When he entered, he stopped, taken aback by the sight of her. She was wearing a strapless, white dress that flowed down her body naturally, with sparkling bands around the waist and the top that Seckry soon realised were made up of hundreds of little, shiny butterflies, and her hair was loose and straight this time, gently brushing her naked shoulders.

He opened his mouth to say something but nothing came out. He felt like his heart was melting.

"Can you get the last button for me?" she asked softly, "I can't quite reach it."

Seckry swallowed as she turned.

"I can't touch you," he said, pained.

"You don't have to touch me," Eiya said. "Just be careful, and you won't come into contact with my skin."

Seckry took hold of the button with petrified precision, and squeezed it through its hole.

"Thanks," Eiya said gently, and stayed where she was for a moment. Seckry closed his eyes, the wonderful smell of her sweet perfume making him dizzy.

When Eiya turned around, she squeezed her hands together and gave him one of her signature smiles; an innocent, mesmerising smile with her head tilted slightly to the right, her eyes glistening in the lamplight.

"How do I look?" she said.

"You look . . . beautiful."

Seckry felt nervous and uncomfortable being so honest with Eiya, but there was no other word to describe her; she was the most beautiful girl he had ever seen.

They took a taxi to Estergate and met the others out in the courtyard.

"Where's Richelle?" Seckry asked Tenk, noticing that Tenk was stood alone.

"We've already had this conversation," said Loca. "The cow has ditched us again . . . I'm sorry Tenk, I shouldn't have called her that, but I mean . . . come on."

"She decided she couldn't be away from her girlfriends over in Westergate and changed her mind last minute to go to their ball," Tenk explained. "She said her friends are single and they wanted to go as a group. They don't have date restrictions over there."

Seckry couldn't believe it. He thought the ball was going to be their long overdue chance to get to know Richelle, but she was avoiding them once again. He felt terrible for Tenk, too, although Tenk seemed to be strangely unfazed.

"Yep, I'm supporting my buddy Tipps over here tonight," Tenk announced. "Neither of us has got a date, but we're defying the system and going to the ball anyway."

There was silence for a moment before Loca said, "You know . . . there is an easy way -"

"Loca," Tenk cut in, "as much as I love Tippian, we're not going as a gay couple."

Tenk and Tippian managed to sneak past Mr Mumble and Mrs Jopson with the help of Kimmy, who distracted them by fake tripping and pretending to hurt his knee, and once they were inside the hall, Seckry was awed by the transformation. This year, the place had been decorated with thousands of fairy lights, and ornate drapes hung from the ceiling, making a blanket-like sky, lit up with artificial stars.

Once they had got themselves a drink each and started dancing in a group, Seckry caught sight of Kimmy's stalker, beaming at them from behind a table.

Loca saw her too, and said, "Right! That's it! I'm putting an end to this, now."

"Come on, Loca," said Tenk. "Don't be mean to her. She's not causing anyone any harm." But Loca had already stormed after the girl. The others ran to catch up with her and prevent her from throwing any punches.

The stalker girl tried to escape in time, but Loca caught her arm.

"Who are you?" Loca demanded.

The girl tried to rip her arm away but Loca squeezed it tight.

"My name's Cally," the girl said, almost sobbing.

"Well, Cally," said Loca. "I don't know what you want from my boyfriend, or what you think you're doing, following him around like some little creep, but it needs to stop, okay?"

"What?" said Cally. "I'm not . . . I'm not interested in your boyfriend."

Loca laughed.

"We've all seen you. And we all saw the note you left in his locker, lying about him winking at you. I know my Kimmy would never do that. I'm sorry to be so harsh, but you need to find your own boyfriend, okay?"

Cally looked confused and shook her head.

"You've got it all wrong. I don't even know your boyfriend's name."

Loca slowly let go of her arm and the girl ran away, straight out of the building.

"Straight up denying it," Loca said in frustration. "Hopefully it'll scare her off, anyway."

Seckry nodded but felt terrible for the girl. And the strange thing was that she actually seemed to genuinely believe what she was saying.

Shortly after that, the music disappeared and Mrs Furrowfog got up on the makeshift stage they had made at the end of the hall and asked everyone to take a seat. All the pupils at the ball looked as confused as each other, since nothing formal had been planned.

"When are you gonna start using your Voicemaster to pick

up girls then, Tipp?" asked Tenk, as they took their seats.

"Nobody's broken up with anyone yet," Tippian complained. "Everyone's all happy couples. What's wrong with them?"

"Okay, for the first time in the history of the Estergate ball," Mrs Furrowfog announced. "We are crowning a ball prince and a ball princess."

There was excited chatter amongst the pupils and a few whistles and claps.

"We have had a hard time deciding this evening, because you all look absolutely gorgeous," Furrowfog continued. "Yes, even you, Bogger Bratvast. But there is one couple who did stand out in our eyes and we are proud to present these crowns to . . . Linzy Sweetcrust and Troye Travus!"

"Are you kidding me?" Loca blurted.

Linzy made her way through the crowd with a massive, fake smile on her heavily painted face, her date following close behind. But as she passed Tippian, she stopped and leaned down before patting him twice on the cheek, patronisingly.

"Never humiliate me in front of my friends again, you hear, sweet cheeks?" she said in her saccharine tone. "You want a date? Here's my first bit of advice. Don't wear a necklace. Necklaces are for girls. Pretty girls like me. In fact, I think that one would go perfect with this blue dress."

"No -" Tippian objected, but Linzy had unclipped the chain holding the Voicemaster and attached it to her own neck, looking pleased with herself. As she made her way up to the stage, Tippian looked mortified.

"She's stolen it," he said in anguish. "The Voicemaster was my only chance at getting a kiss when they play 'With me Tonight.'"

The others couldn't believe what Linzy had just done, but there was nothing any of them could do about it. She was already accepting her bouquet of flowers and tiara, and taking her place by the microphone.

"Before I start," Linzy said, flicking her bleach blonde hair over her shoulder, "I would just like to thank a certain someone for my jewellery tonight." She sniggered a few times and pretended to hold back laughter. "Tippitha Frost!" she announced.

Tippian looked around at the others, his face going bright red, and then turned back to the stage, his face defiant.

"It's *Miss* Tippitha Frost to you," he said quietly, and reached into his pocket, clicking the wireless keyring that activated the Voicemaster.

Chapter Thirty-Eight

The Jump

"I'd also like to thank everyone here," Linzy said, her deep, male voice silencing the dancefloor. "Ahem," she coughed, trying to clear her throat. "I'd like to thank . . . ahem, ahem. There's something wrong with this microphone," she bellowed, and tapped it, giving everyone an eardrum-popping screech of feedback. "Um . . . I'd like to thank my date tonight . . ."

Troye Travus looked horrified, and Seckry was sure he saw him searching for an exit out of the building.

"I knew that girl had been smoking all these years," Seckry overheard Mrs Jambert, the photography teacher, say to one of the other teachers. "Listen to her. Ruined her for life."

"Her voice sounds really familiar," said the other teacher, Mrs Underfoot, if Seckry remembered correctly. "Wait . . . she sounds just like Buck Bodstock. Oh, Gedin, it all makes sense. Her mother was always travelling, meeting celebrities all the time. I bet the poor husband doesn't have a clue."

"What are you saying?"

"Well, Buck was quite irresistible back then. Hell, a 'tache like that? It would have been hard to say no, know what I mean?"

Linzy tried to speak a few more times, but eventually collapsed to the floor in tears in front of everyone, letting out deep wails mixed with guttural, smoky coughs, before being ushered off.

As the music began playing once again, Tippian turned to the rest of the group and threw out his hands.

"She gave me no choice," he said.

Seckry tried not to think about the fact that he couldn't touch Eiya, and he had fun dancing around with the rest of them for the rest of the night, and mixing drinks at the bar with Tenk, Tippian and Kimmy to make the ultimate fizzing pop.

Tippian spent most of the time, however, staring at a girl named Ivara Zaskin, who Seckry vaguely knew from the seventh year, and who looked like an Arivelian model.

"Tipps," said Tenk. "Maybe you should focus your attention on someone a bit . . . less . . . um–"

"Someone who's single," Kimmy cut in, motioning to Ivara's date, who was a muscle-pumped beast from a different school that seemed ready to burst out of his suit.

But several slipshakers later, and the couple seemed to be in a heated argument at the bar, before the guy walked away and left the ball with another girl hooked onto his arm.

"Tippian Furst," said Tenk, dramatically. "I think the stars have just aligned in your favour."

"What?" said Tippian, still lost in a mesmerised stare.

"The guy's just left with another girl! Man, this is your chance!"

"What? No, Tenk, I'm not approaching any girl without my Voicemaster. That was my only hope, and Linzy Sweetcrust ruined it for me."

"Tipps," said Tenk. "I didn't want to say anything before now, but that voice sounded ridiculous on you. I really don't think that would've helped. You just gotta go for it."

"Tenk, she looks like she just stepped out of the front cover of Glamourgirl. Do you seriously think I stand any chance of getting a kiss off her?"

"Okay, I admit, at the beginning of the night, nobody thought you had no chance with her more than I did, but her date has just left with another girl! This is your perfect opportunity. She's looking for someone to sweep her off her feet and tell her everything's gonna be okay. That someone could be you!"

"Tenk, I . . ."

"And when I say sweep her off her feet," interrupted Tenk. "I don't mean a martial arts sweep. I don't mean kicking her feet from underneath her."

"Yeah," said Tippian, blinking very slowly. "It's alright. I understood that one."

It took Tenk another ten minutes of arguing with Tippian before Tippian finally gave in and agreed to at least approach the girl, who seemed to be tipping a clear liquid from a little flask into her drink under the table.

The group watched out of the corner of their eyes, trying not to make it too obvious, as Tippian got her attention. They couldn't hear a word he was saying because the music was too loud, but after five minutes, they were impressed that she hadn't told him to go away. In fact, the girl seemed incredibly animated, and Seckry was sure he overheard her complaining about her date.

Then, the lights dimmed even further and 'With me Tonight' began playing.

Seckry turned to Eiya and took a deep breath. All he wanted to do in this moment was take her in his arms and brush his nose against hers, feeling the softness of her skin under his palms and tasting the sweetness of her lips. But he couldn't do anything. He felt incredibly sad looking into her eyes and seeing her there, just standing there on her own, an angel in white, just holding her own little hands together. A girl that beautiful should never have had to stand there alone, without someone to hold her hand.

As much as he felt bad for Tenk that Richelle had ditched him for her own ball, Seckry was kind of glad to have someone with them who wasn't going to be kissing anyone, or looking to kiss anyone, either. So, instead of lamenting the fact that he couldn't touch Eiya, Seckry watched Tippian, to see if there was any way he would be able to win a kiss off the girl he'd been drooling over.

"He left it too late to approach her," said Tenk. "He's got no chance. She ain't gonna kiss him after talking to him for fifteen minutes. Oh no . . . here's her date! He's back in the building and he's coming for her!"

Tenk cupped his hands and shouted through them.

"Tipps! Tipps! Abort mission! I repeat, abort mission now!"

But Ivara, seeing her date, suddenly grabbed Tippian by his shirt and yanked him towards her, slapping her lips upon his and giving him a big, long, passionate kiss, just as the words "I close my eyes and kiss you," sang through the speakers.

All Seckry, Tenk and Eiya could do was watch, their eyes transfixed on Tippian as his arms dropped to his sides and hung limp like a ragdoll's.

The girl's date smashed his drink on the dancefloor and stormed out of the building in rage.

Once the girl had let Tippian go, she excused herself and left the ball, leaving Tippian to wander back to Seckry and the others, who were still gawping.

"Guys," he said, out of breath and with a giddy grin. "If I die tonight, I will die a happy man."

When the music began to wind down and the floor was a mess of plastic cups and sticky liquid and even the odd forgotten shoe, Tippian leaned against the bar, staring up at the lights rotating on the ceiling, grinning happily.

"Tipps," said Loca, "I hate to break it to you . . . but she only did that to make her date jealous."

"So?" said Tippian. "She kissed me. On the *lips!*"

Loca and Kimmy then said their goodbyes and headed off.

"We'd better head back too," said Tenk. "Richelle's coming over to the flat to see me once she's finished with her friends."

Once they had said goodbye to Mr Bibbons, the business studies teacher, who slurred that he loved them like they were his own children, they got in a taxi and dropped Tippian off at his house before heading back to Kerik Square.

As Tenk headed for his flat and Seckry was fumbling for his keys in his tight pockets, Eiya said, "Seck, I don't feel like going back just yet. There's something I want to do."

Seckry paused.

"I think they cemented up the entrance to our disused reactor," he said, remembering their expedition last year.

"Not the reactor," Eiya said, smiling. "Follow me."

"Henrei's?" said Seckry, as she led him into the arcade.

The arcade was open all hours, seven days a week, with a spotty-faced student manning the place for Henrei during the nights. Tonight, however, the student was slumped over the desk with a load of paperwork around him, snoring.

"Fancy some Friction?" Eiya said, giggling.

"Are you serious?" said Seckry.

"Yeah."

"Friction . . . now?

"Trust me, Seck. I don't want to shoot anyone or swing my sword tonight, I just want to be in there with you."

"But . . ." Seckry said. "What about your dress? You can't run around inside there wearing that, can you?"

"I'll strip down to my underwear once I'm inside," Eiya said simply. "No one will be able to see me once I'm in there."

Seckry obeyed, and stepped into a pod, closing the door behind him and placing his Anikam avatar into the required slot (he never went anywhere without him).

"I'm just loading up a private session of the Atoria overworld," said Eiya, through the internal chat system. "No one will be able to join or modify our session."

A few moments later, the rolling hills of Atoria spread out before Seckry, all lit by the blue light of the world's huge moon and the dazzling stars in the digital sky.

As soon as Eiya's avatar, Alaria, appeared in front of him, she ran to him, throwing her arms around Anikam and squeezing him tightly, burying her cat-like face into the fur of his neck.

"Gedin, Seck, you don't know how long I've wanted to do this," she said.

It was only then that Seckry understood, and he squeezed her back, passionately. This was a loophole in which they could touch each other, albeit in bodies that weren't their own.

"Even though it's Anikam I'm holding, it still feels like you in a way, you know?" Eiya said, running her paws across Anikam's face. Then she closed her eyes and pressed her nose against his, and they stayed like that for a while, just breathing each other in.

"This is kinda weird," said Seckry, and Eiya giggled. "But kinda nice too."

"It is kinda nice," Eiya said softly.

After another few moments, they turned their gaze to the hills in the distance.

"Let's do some exploring!" Eiya said excitedly. "I think I'm still on a sugar rush from all those slipshakers."

"How many did you have?" Seckry asked.

"I can't remember," Eiya said. "Basically, so many that I can't even remember. So quite a lot."

"Have you ever been to the top of the highest cliff?" Seckry asked her, and Eiya shook her head.

Seckry grabbed her left paw and began running.

"Come, on, the view is beautiful," he laughed.

It was a long climb up to the top of the largest cliff in Atoria, but Seckry had done it once before, and he knew a bit of a shortcut that cut out a portion of the climbing.

When they reached the top, they stepped towards the edge, panting slightly and admiring the views. In the distance, they could see the mechanical mayhem of Section 52, and to the right, the rocky peaks of the Golboro land. Straight in front of them was the forest that they had been placed in for last year's Meltdown, and Seckry could just about see the tip of the stone head poking out of a clearing in the middle.

"It's stunning," Eiya said happily. "I can't believe I'm playing Friction now, can you?"

"I can't believe it either, but it seems so natural and so right."

After watching the moon slowly travel across the night sky, and a myriad of strange, AI birds swoop through the valleys, Seckry and Eiya finally decided to call it a night.

"It's so tempting to just jump off this cliff, isn't it, Seck?"

Eiya said as they were about to exit their session. "I wonder how much pain the programmers would have added to the impact."

"Probably quite a lot," said Seckry, laughing. But then a thought occurred to him. He loaded up his heads up display and selected the gravity protection suit he had picked up in the Meltdown, asking for more info. As he scanned the text, he found the information he was looking for.

The suit can be also be simultaneously assigned to any ally that you are in contact with, if you switch this setting on in the options.

Seckry found the option and checked it, before suddenly letting out an incredulous laugh at what he was about to do.

"What?" said Eiya.

"Nothing, I just . . . Eiya, are you ready for the experience of a lifetime?" He leaned over the cliff cautiously and felt a surge of vertigo. It was a long way down.

"Seck, you're not . . . you're not actually thinking of doing it, are you?"

"Hold my hand," Seckry said, and squeezed hers tightly.

"No, wait, Seck, this is crazy! I was only jok-"

"This is going to be amazing," Seckry cut in, and launched them both off the clifftop.

Eiya's screams soon turned into hysterical laughs as they plummeted in an exhilarating freefall, Seckry squeezing her paw tight as the wind whipped through their fur.

They landed heavily in a meadow of wild Atorian flowers, sending cascades of purple petals and digital butterflies fluttering into the night air.

The impact was like a hit of warm, fuzzy euphoria that rippled through Seckry.

"Oh my Gedin, Seck!" Eiya cried. "You're insane!"

"It felt good though, didn't it?" he laughed.

"I want to do it again!" Eiya cried, clambering to her feet and jumping on the spot.

When they eventually stumbled out of Henrei's arcade,

giddy and giggling, Eiya thrust her finger out towards Tenk's flat.

"You know what, Seck? I think we should go and say hello to Richelle."

"Um . . . they probably want a bit of privacy," said Seckry.

"I don't care," said Eiya. "She's refusing to hang around with us and I demand to know why. Okay, maybe I won't demand to know why. Maybe we could just say goodnight to them both instead."

They crept around to the back of the flats, and Eiya picked up a small stone to throw at Tenk's bedroom window. But as she readied her aim, they both stopped and stared.

Tenk was sat at the window, gazing out teary-eyed at the city, with a giant spoon in one hand, and a tub of extra-large chococorp chocolate ice cream in the other.

Chapter Thirty-Nine

Bottled Sand

When Tenk saw them standing there, he simply drew his blinds slowly, without even acknowledging them.

"What on earthia has happened?" said Eiya. "We've got to talk to him. Tenk!"

"Please guys, I really don't want to talk right now," came Tenk's muffled voice.

"Tenk, are you alright?" said Seckry. "We're worried about you."

"I'm fine . . . I just . . . I just," Tenk trailed off into what seemed to be quiet sobbing.

"Tenk, please let us in," said Eiya.

After a few moments, Tenk unclipped the latch of his window and let down the rope ladder that he used sometimes to get into his bedroom without going through the front door. Seckry and Eiya climbed up it and clambered into the warm bedroom.

"Did Richelle break up with you?" asked Seckry, as softly as he could so as not to upset Tenk anymore than he was.

"Yeah she did," said Tenk. "About six months ago."

"What?" said Seckry.

Eiya looked just as confused as he was.

"I've been lying to you guys this whole time," said Tenk. "We literally went out with each other for a few weeks and that was it. She broke up with me on her birthday back in the summer. I've got no idea why."

"So this is why none of us have seen her," said Eiya. "We thought she hated us."

"I don't get it," said Seckry. "Why have you been lying to

us about it? Why didn't you just tell everyone what happened?"

"I don't know," said Tenk. "I just . . . really liked her, you know? Remember how much I used to go on about the chip and milk girl? That was her! I found her. It was like I had found my soulmate. I thought we were going to be together forever. And then . . . boom. One day, she's just like, that's it. I don't want to see you anymore. I couldn't face telling anyone. I had been boasting about having a girlfriend since the moment she agreed to go on a date with me. How embarrassing would it be for me to tell everyone that she dumped me just a few weeks later."

"Tenk," said Eiya. "We would have all been here for you, right Seck?"

"'Course," said Seckry. "Tenk, you really didn't have to hide it from us."

"Thanks guys," he said weakly. "But my nan's another matter. It was just easier to lie to her. You've seen how she is around Tippian, telling him he's worthless for not having a girlfriend and that there's something wrong with him and he needs to hurry up. Imagine what she would have been like to me, her own grandson."

"How did you hide it from her?" asked Eiya. "Didn't she wonder why she had never met the girl?"

"It's been hard, believe me. I've just been making up excuse after excuse, but I've finally run out of excuses, and she must be starting to cotton on by now."

"I think it's time you told your nan the truth," said Seckry. "If she really loves you then she won't care if you've got a girlfriend or not. I know I don't have a nan, so I can't speak from experience, but I'm sure a nan should be proud of her grandchildren."

"I'll pluck up the courage soon," said Tenk, miserably.

They stayed with Tenk for a few hours until he fell asleep. Seckry and Eiya pulled a blanket around him and left discreetly through the bedroom window.

The following morning was Saturday, and the first day of

their holidays. It was a bright, breezy day, and Loca had arranged for the group to meet at the Friction Emporium to celebrate the start of summer by treating themselves to some upgrades.

On the journey there, Tenk looked just as upset as he had the previous night, but Seckry hoped that the Emporium would take his mind off Richelle.

"Look, it's Fewgy," said Seckry as they entered, but Tenk, for the first time, seemed uninterested.

"You filthy liar," said Loca, as she joined them at the entrance. "I can't believe you led us on this whole time."

"As I said to you on the phone, Loca, I don't want to hear your jip today."

Tenk had obviously confessed to the others already.

"Okay, I won't give you any more hassle for lying to us," she replied. "But I'm intrigued to find out why Richelle dumped you. It'll benefit you in the long run if I find out. Then you'll know what mistakes not to make next time."

Tenk didn't seem convinced.

"Anything major happen around the time it happened?" said Loca. "Any fights?"

"Nothing," said Tenk. "We were having a lovely time. It was her birthday and -"

"Wait," cut in Loca. "It was her birthday?"

"Yeah, she dumped me on her birthday."

"What did you get her? What kind of present?"

"Why?" said Tenk.

"Just tell us. What did you get her?"

"A bottle of sand with her name written into it," said Tenk.

"Oh my Gedin, it's worse than I thought," said Loca.

"What?" said Tenk.

"Tenk, are you kidding me? Like, one of those cheap, tacky things you can get at the Skyfall market?"

Tenk was about to say something, but instead turned around and told them he was going home.

Loca sighed.

"I didn't mean to upset him," she said. "But he's even

more of an idiot than I thought. And I thought he was a pretty big idiot to start with, so that *really* is saying something."

"I don't get it," said Tippian. "A bottle of sand sounds like a good gift to me. I thought girls love that kind of thing."

"We do," said Loca. "When we are *seven years old*."

Seckry and Eiya didn't stay at the Emporium for long because they felt bad for Tenk. But when they knocked at his flat, his mum said he didn't want to see anyone and turned them away. They tried again a bit later, but Tenk still didn't want any company, so they decided to wait until he was ready.

That night, Eiya was standing at the bedroom window, looking out at the twilight cityscape. Seckry joined her and leaned on the windowsill, but immediately jumped away when he realised he was making Eiya's arm disappear.

"I wasn't even touching you that time," he cried.

Eiya watched as her arm slowly became opaque once more.

"Eiya, this is crazy," Seckry said. "It's getting worse, not better. And I'm tired of waiting. I'm tired of waiting for something that may or may not go away."

Eiya said nothing, silently agreeing.

"There has to be a way to reverse this thing," Seckry continued. "And if Zovak won't give me a sample, or the ingredients list, then . . . then I'm gonna have to take it by force."

"By force?" said Eiya, shocked.

"I'm going to break into his house and take a sample," said Seckry.

Eiya stared at him, her large, beautiful eyes alive with a mix of worry, excitement and fear.

"I'm not going to sit around waiting for years to be able to touch you again, Eiya. I can't. I can't do it."

Eiya let out something that was half a disbelieving laugh and half a cry. "Seck," she said. "If you're going, then I'm coming with you."

It didn't take Seckry long to find out Zovak's address the next day. It was in an area of the north partition called Bemora, or The Beat, as it was more well known, because it was generally populated by out of work artists and bohemians.

After taking a short monorail journey, they arrived at the house to find it bizarrely painted in black and white stripes.

"This looks like something out of a creepy fairytale," said Eiya.

They hid behind the front garden wall for a while, poking their heads out to see if there was any activity in the living room, but there was nothing. There didn't seem to be a television running, and nobody was going in or out.

"There's a driveway too, but no car," said Eiya. "I think everyone's out."

"Perfect," said Seckry, and they followed the wall through a gulley between the houses before jumping into Zovak's rear garden. As soon as they landed on the grass, Seckry noticed the kitchen window was slightly ajar.

Very carefully, they crept up to it and peered inside. There was no sound and nobody in sight, so Seckry pulled it open further, gently, before clambering inside and helping Eiya through.

But as soon as Eiya dropped to the kitchen tiles, a thin man in pinstripe trousers and braces burst into the kitchen and dived on them, knocking them both over.

"Thieves!" he shouted. "Zovak! Call the Patrol! Call the Patrol!"

Zovak ran into the Kitchen.

"Sevenstars? Tacana?" he said. "Dad, get off them!"

"They broke into our house!" screamed his father.

"Leave it, dad, it's okay, I know them."

"They're your friends?"

"Um, not exactly. Just leave it, it's okay."

As the man released them, Seckry realised it was the same man that had tried to con Tippian at the Fearless Funfair. Dimpy, if Seckry remembered his name correctly. As Dimpy stepped back, he shrugged his jacket at them as if to say that there was more of where that came from.

"What in Gedin's name are you doing in my house?" Zovak demanded.

"Your dad is Dimpy?" said Seckry, avoiding the question.

"The one and only!" said Dimpy, proudly.

"Look, you guys," said Zovak. "I'm guessing this is still about the Purika stuff, right?"

Seckry put his hands out to say, *Of course.*

"Well it ends here today. I'm fed up of you hounding me. I'll tell you the truth, okay?"

"The truth?" said Seckry.

Zovak took a deep breath.

"The reason . . . the reason I haven't given you the ingredients for the Purika is that . . . the Purika doesn't . . . purify anything."

"What are you talking about?" said Seckry.

Zovak sighed and pressed the bridge of his nose with his thumb and forefinger. When he released them, his eyes looked tired.

"The whole thing was one big illusion," he said. "Just an incredibly big optical stunt. That poison I injected into you? It wasn't poison at all. It was that stuff." He pointed to an old bottle sitting on one of the kitchen units. It read:

Green Skin Fancy Dress Party Injectable Temporary Dye.

"I just injected you with a tiny bit of that. Just enough to wear off after two minutes. And the Purika pill? It was an energy capsule from the local pharmacy, made of sugar and caffeine. You were just experiencing a rush from that."

"But . . . but what about . . . what about the giant patch of mould the Purika destroyed." Seckry stammered, not quite believing what he was hearing.

"That did take a lot of work, I have to admit," said Zovak. "Getting them to shut down the canteen. Phew, I thought they would have closed the thing after the first incident. Then they carried on after the second, and eventually I had to stick that bleedin' rat in my own mouth to get them to do something about it."

"Wait, you were the one behind all that?" blurted Eiya.

"Like I said, the whole thing was one big optical illusion. The mould wasn't mould at all. I kept sneaking in there and spraying this stuff onto the wall."

He opened a cupboard under the sink and pulled out a spray can with the words *Mutant Fungus* written across it in a B-movie style font.

"I got it from a practical joke wholesaler," said Zovak. "It's pretty much indestructible unless you've got the right solution to get rid of it. They give you the solution when you buy the can. I just sprayed that onto it at the ceremony."

"Why?" said Seckry. "Why did you trick everyone like that?"

"Because!" said Dimpy, proudly. "That's what we do, me and my boy, Zovey! We're illusionists. Best in Skyfall City!"

"More like con artists," said Eiya.

"So this is why you wouldn't let anyone commission it," said Seckry. "There was nothing to commission. You robbed Tippian of the award. He would have won that thing hands down. He *should* have won it."

"I know he should have," said Zovak, uncharacteristically anguished. "It was a great invention. And it was real."

"Pah! Real," said Dimpy. "Don't listen to them, son. Who needs real when you can do what we do."

"They're right, dad," said Zovak, staring at the ground. "I'll turn myself in tomorrow. I'll be stripped of my award and it'll go to the next highest deserving entry, which will be Tippian, I'm sure."

Seckry and Eiya left after that, completely shocked. As they exited through the front door, they passed a huge bookshelf in the living room full of guides on hypnotism and how to seduce girls. Suddenly, Seckry understood why Zovak was so popular with the female population of Estergate.

But even though they were relieved that Zovak wasn't going to call the Patrol on them for breaking in, Seckry and Eiya were far from content after all the revelations. If Zovak wasn't the cause of Eiya's dissipation, then what on earthia was?

When they called at Tippian's the next day to tell him about Zovak's deception, he took his glasses off and threw them onto his bed.

"I knew it!" he shouted. "Well . . . actually . . . I had no idea . . . but it doesn't surprise me!"

"Looks like you're gonna get the Andersun Wellworth award after all, Tipp," said Eiya.

Tippian did a bit of rearranging on his pyramid of trophies to make room for it at the number two spot.

"Still not worthy of the top spot, then?" said Seckry.

"Honestly," said Loca. "Like I said before, nothing will ever be good enough for his top spot, I guarantee it."

Everyone was at Tippian's except Tenk, who was still upset about Richelle leaving him, and offended by Loca's ridiculing about the present he had gotten her for her birthday, but the heat of summer was starting to make them itch for being outdoors, so they made their way to Featherduck Park to play with a drone that Tippian had designed from scratch.

They had fun playing with it, but the atmosphere just wasn't the same without Tenk.

Then, as Loca was hovering it close to an ochal fruit on one of the trees, trying to chop it off using the propellers, she suddenly stopped controlling it and stared at a group of girls who were walking past, leaving the drone crashing to the grass.

"Be careful!" yelped Tippian.

"It's her," Loca hissed. "It's Richelle!"

It had been so long since Seckry had seen her, he doubted he would have recognised her if Loca hadn't pointed her out. But she was right.

Richelle glanced at them and continued to walk past.

"Richelle?" said Loca.

Richelle turned, looking confused as to who the group were.

"Oh, hi," she said.

"We'll meet you in a minute by the lake," said one of her

friends, and left Richelle alone.

"Richelle," said Loca. "We're really sorry Tenk's such a . . . a . . . douchebag."

"Oh, you're Tenk's friends!" she said, relaxing a little. "I knew I recognised you from somewhere. Wait. He wasn't a douchebag."

"Really?" said Loca. "Isn't that the reason you dumped him?"

"No, of course not," said Richelle. "I wish I'd given him a better explanation at the time but . . . I just didn't want to get into a relationship, you know? I thought it would be best for me to focus on school."

"But that dreadful bottle of sand from the market," said Loca. "That must have contributed to it. I want to apologise on his behalf for tha -"

"Oh Gedin, that was the sweetest thing ever," interrupted Richelle. "I can't believe he did that for me."

"Excuse me?" said Loca.

Richelle sighed.

"I grew up in Oceaton over on the coast, and they have this really beautiful sand there, it's almost pink. We lived right on the beach, and I used to play in that sand every day. When I moved to Skyfall when I was ten years old, I was really homesick for a long time, and the one thing that I missed the most was that sand. I remember wishing, if only I had bottled some of it and brought it with me, it would have been like a taste of home, you know? It might have just taken the edge off that homesickness just a little." She laughed affectionately at the thought of it.

"I was telling all of this stuff to Tenk on one of our dates," she continued, "but I had no idea he had been listening so intently. And then for my birthday . . . he actually gets in touch with my uncle over in Oceaton and has him send over some of the sand. Then he gets someone to bottle it and write my name in it. It was the best gift I've ever been given. I felt like crying when he gave it to me. Especially since I was just about to dump him. I nearly postponed it until the following day because of that, but I guess it would have just prolonged the inevitable."

Richelle looked as though she were about to break into tears. "Look, I'm sorry, guys, but I've gotta go. I hope Tenk is doing alright." She waved and left them gawping, silently.

Chapter Forty

A Good Luck Wink

That evening, the group decided to call at Tenk's and make amends.

"Who knew Tenk was such a secret romantic?" said Tippian, as they knocked the door.

Longo answered, and tried to stall them from entering by telling them there was a new secret codeword, and with every wrong attempt, they'd each get a dig in the arm. But Loca gave him a glare that said something like, *If you lay a finger on me, the rest of your life won't be worth living*, and he sheepishly moved aside.

They found Tenk in his bedroom with his quilt wrapped around him, playing a handheld video game.

"I don't want to see any of you," he said, not even looking up at them.

"Tenk," said Seckry. "We're really sorry."

"We had no idea you'd gone to so much trouble with that bottle of sand," said Loca.

"Mate," said Tippian. "I didn't think there was anything wrong with a bottle of sand from the market in the first place. But what you did was incredible."

"It's okay, I forgive you guys," said Tenk. "It's Loca who stamped on my metaphorical manhood. I'm not talking to her."

"Tenk, come on, I am genuinely sorr -"

"Is someone talking?" blurted Tenk. "Must just be a whisper of the wind."

After a few moments of awkward silence, Loca sat down on his bed.

"Tenk," she said. "If it makes things any better I can . . . I can start calling you The Tenkmeister."

This got Tenk's attention.

"What about King Tenk, Ruler of All?"

"Okay, don't push your luck," said Loca.

Raymus suddenly opened Tenk's bedroom door and let himself in.

"Tenk, there's a weird girl hiding in the bushes outside your bedroom window," he said. "She's been there for over an hour."

Tenk got up and glared through the glass.

"It's Kimmy's stalker," he said.

"Are you kidding me?" yelled Loca. "After I gave her that talk at the ball? Wait . . . that doesn't make sense. Why has she been outside your window for over an hour? We've only just arrived. How could she have known Kimmy was coming here?"

"I'll leave you guys in peace," said Raymus, before farting loudly and wafting the fumes towards them. "Cheese and pickle sandwiches and mudbloat pie," he said. "Enjoy."

As everyone was choking on the stench, they tried to work out why Kimmy's stalker would be stationed outside Tenk's.

"I mean," said Loca. "It definitely is *Kimmy* she's stalking, isn't it?"

"It's hard to tell," said Tippian. "We're always in a group when she's staring from a distance."

"Well it was definitely Kimmy she was following home that night," said Seckry. "Me and Tenk saw her."

"Yeah," said Kimmy. "I remember it vividly because I ran away so fast that my hat blew off, and I lost it, and felt really bad because it was Tenk's hat."

He paused for a moment, staring into space.

"It was Tenk's hat," he repeated.

"She wanted the hat!" said Loca. "It all makes sense now!"

"But, wait," said Kimmy. "What about that note that was in my locker in the Friction training room?"

"Did you see it actually fall out of your locker?" asked Seckry.

"No, I just remember seeing it on the floor beneath it. I just assumed it had fallen out of mine."

"Who's locker is directly next to yours, Kim?" said Loca. "Tenk's!"

"But . . . all that stuff about winking at her at the Meltdown," said Kimmy. "Did you wink at her, Tenk?"

Tenk was wide eyed.

"The wink," he muttered. "Why didn't I work it out before now?"

"You did, didn't you!" said Loca.

"What? No!" said Tenk. "I wasn't winking at *her*! I was winking at . . . um . . . nobody."

"What do you mean, nobody? Who were you winking at?"

"Oh, Gedin," said Tippian. "It was Mrs Rutterworth wasn't it? I knew you always had a thing for her."

"Tipps! Don't be disgusting! It was nobody, okay. Just leave it at that."

But after several minutes of them hounding him for an answer, Tenk looked like he had had enough.

"Okay . . . look . . . I wasn't winking at Mrs Rutterworth and I wasn't winking at Miss Henderford, and I certainly wasn't winking at Tippian's mum. I was winking at . . . *myself*."

When nobody responded, Tenk continued.

"The stalker girl must have been sitting right by the commentator's booth, and that thing is really big and shiny and reflective. Well, I saw Romsworth Bandle getting a good luck wink from his girlfriend before the match, and well . . . I could see my own reflection in the booth, and, you know, I was still feeling a bit down from the whole Richelle dumping me thing, and I needed someone to give me a good luck wink too."

"And that someone was yourself?"

"Well, nobody else was going to give me one! And it worked," Tenk said matter-of-factly. "I felt great getting into my pod."

"The next thing we know, he'll be giving his reflection a goodnight kiss in the mirror before bed," said Loca.

"Oh, he's already done that," said Tippian.

After that, Tenk's depression seemed to vanish completely, and Seckry was glad to see him back to his usual self. In fact, it was hard to get him to stop talking about his new stalker, Cally.

"She likes you, you like her," said Tippian, a couple of days later. "Why don't you just get together?"

"I don't think you understand the way a stalker's mind works, Tipp," Tenk replied. "As soon as the stalkee shows any affection back, the attraction is gone. She'll move on to someone else. No, I gotta pretend I couldn't care less about her existence. That's how it works."

That evening, Seckry looked at the calendar on his phone, before closing his eyes, his heart starting to beat a little faster. In just one week's time it would be the date he would meet his father.

He was broken out of his trance by his mum's voice, calling from the kitchen.

"You couldn't pop around to Softspoon's for me, could you, love? I just need a loaf of that super soft bread they do, but my hands are full, and I think they close in about fifteen minutes."

"Sure," said Seckry, grabbing his keys from his bedside table. Eiya was busy reading, so he headed out on his own.

When he entered the bakery, he found Mrs Softspoon packing up for the night.

"You're lucky," she said. "I was gonna close early. It's been a quiet one today, I can tell you."

"I'm sorry to hear that," said Seckry, paying for the loaf before she shut down the till. "Are you still having trouble from the homeless guy? Is he still squatting next door?"

"You bet," said the owner. "And his drunken chanting has gotten worse. I swear he's trying to conduct some spiritual summoning in there. I've contacted the Patrol numerous times, but they just say they're too busy and they've got more important things to do. I mean, I do kinda feel sorry for the guy in a way, especially since he's only got one arm. Must be tough living like that. But it's really affecting business."

"One arm?" Seckry said, swallowing.

"Yeah, no idea what happened to him. Maybe he was born like it, or maybe it got chopped off when he was a kid."

Seckry was silent for a few moments.

"Do you . . . do you have any idea . . . what his name is?"

"I think he calls himself Flynt," said the owner.

Seckry's chest began to rise and fall rapidly. The man next door had one arm and his name began with an F. Seckry was suddenly aware that he still hadn't managed to activate his powers, and he would be useless against Lux if he were ever to meet him.

"Th-thanks . . . for the bread," Seckry stuttered, and left the bakery, intending to walk very briskly past the house next door.

But as he stepped out, he realised the front door of the house was hanging wide open. There would have been no way he could have walked past without peering in. As he took a few steps, he turned his head slightly, staring into the dark corridor, and what he saw made his legs involuntarily stop moving.

Plastered roughly across the walls of the corridor were photographs. Photographs of a single person.

Photographs of *Seckry*.

Seckry turned back to the street, filled with fear, but found himself facing a man; a man with one arm, his eyes a piercing, vivid blue, and his hair black, hanging shabbily down to his shoulders.

"I've waited a long time for this moment, Seckry Sevenstars," he said.

Chapter Forty-One

The End of a Life

Instinct took over.

Seckry whipped Vance's stun gun out of his pocket and fired.

The pellet slammed into the man's chest and electrocuted him, making him seize up and fall backwards onto the concrete pavement.

Seckry stood, frozen to the spot, having no idea what to do next. He hadn't expected it to work. He thought Lux would have been able to disintegrate the gun with a swipe of his hand before Seckry even had a chance to fire. But Seckry had got him. He was down.

"Please . . ." the man begged, his mouth foaming. "Please . . . spare me."

"I know who you are," Seckry said, his voice shaking. "I know you're the one who changed his name to Lux. And I know you want me and my dad dead."

"N . . . no . . ." the man stammered. "You have answered my . . . .calls . . . my prayers . . . you have revealed to me that you are the One, my Lord."

My Lord?

"What?" said Seckry.

"I am sorry I doubted you . . . but I had to check," the man continued, still semi-paralysed on the ground. "I've been praying to you, worshipping you for a long time, asking you to come to me if you hear my prayers, if you truly are the One. I should never have doubted you. I should have known you would come. Please forgive me, my Lord."

Seckry had no idea what was happening.

"You're . . . not Lux?" he said.

"No," the man replied. "My name is Flynt Farcroft, and I've travelled all the way from Phary to seek you out. I had no money when I arrived so I had to squat in this abandoned building. It was close to you, but not so close as to be obvious. I began praying to you, summoning you when I arrived, but it didn't work. I doubted myself a few times, but I was convinced you were His son, and I knew I was doing something wrong. I realised then that simply praying to you wouldn't be enough. I needed a shrine. So I followed you a few times and took some photographs."

"It was you who snapped me in Vance's classroom?" said Seckry, not quite believing what he was hearing.

"I made the whole building a shrine to you," Flynt continued. "And I prayed to you every day and every night, asking you to help me, to come to me."

"I'm . . . I'm really sorry," Seckry said. "But I'm not the son of Gedin. Why . . . do you think that I am?"

"Was it not you who saved this world from the Great Meteor? Aren't you the Immortal One? I first heard rumours on the internet, and then I did my research and found the oldest ever painting of Seckraman. There is no doubt about it . . . it is *you*."

"Wow . . ." said Seckry to himself. "Um . . . okay . . . yes, that painting is of me, and yes, I did save the world from the meteor but . . . but I'm not the son of Gedin. It's . . . a complicated story."

"But you finally answered my summoning," said Flynt, looking devastated. "You're here. You came to me. Have you not come to heal me?"

"Heal you?" said Seckry.

"That's what I have been asking of you all this time," said Flynt. "I have been praying that you will give me back my arm. The arm I lost in the Pharyan civil war."

"I'm really sorry," said Seckry, "but I was just getting this loaf of bread from Softspoon's. That's it. I had no idea you had been . . . summoning me."

The paralysis was wearing off, so Flynt groggily got back to his feet.

"I'm sorry for shooting you," said Seckry. "I thought you were someone else."

"Are you saying you don't have the power to heal me?"

"I'm sorry, I don-"

Seckry cut himself off, thinking for a moment.

"You know what?" he said. "I can't heal you right now. But . . . one day I might be able to."

He was going to be meeting his father in a week's time. If Seckry was taught how to push the segments together and activate the creogen inside him, he may very well be able to regrow the man's arm.

"If you have the power to heal, then you must be the son of Gedin!"

"No . . ." said Seckry. "I can assure you . . . look . . . there's someone that can look at your arm and talk to you about prosthetics and stuff for the time being. His name's Cartell Quinn and he's doing amazing things with science. I'll give you his address, but I can't do anything to help you right now."

Seckry waited while Flynt went to get a pen and paper. He would have followed him inside, but would have probably freaked out seeing the walls plastered with photos of himself.

"You're . . . not the son of Gedin?" Flynt said once more, as he returned.

Seckry shook his head apologetically as he wrote down Cartell's address, and the owner of Softspoon's stepped out of the bakery, pulling the door shut.

"Oh," she said, startled to see them both there. "Having a word with him for me, are you? Hope you have better luck than me." She gave Flynt a dirty look. "Like talking to a brick wall."

When Seckry arrived back at the flat, his legs still felt like jelly. He couldn't believe he had actually fired Vance's stun gun. And never did he dream that he would meet someone who worshipped him. He should have expected it though, really. After nobody talking about the time travel thing or asking him about it, he had assumed that no one that he didn't want to know knew, and had become complacent. But of course there would be rumours about what happened that day.

He burst into the bedroom, about to tell Eiya everything that had just happened, but found her hugging her legs to her chest, her eyes streaming with tears.

"Eiya?" Seckry said, quietly but desperately. "Are you alright?"

"Seck," she sobbed. "It was the 'echo' thing again. I must have dozed off while you were gone. I thought I wasn't going to experience it anymore, but it was so intense this time . . . it was just like this voice in my head telling me that I had to remember it, that I needed to remember that day and that feeling because it was so important. It was like . . . the feelings for this person behind me were so strong it was just making me want to cry."

Seckry sat down on the edge of her bed, slowly.

"Seck . . ." Eiya continued. "I think it's Elenya's way of trying to remember who she used to be, who she . . . used to love."

Eiya was interrupted by the buzzing of Seckry's phone. It was someone Seckry hadn't spoken to in a long time. Ropart Sanfarrow.

"Ropart," said Seckry, although he still would have felt more natural calling him Sanfarrow.

"Seckry," replied the scientist. "I am very sorry I haven't been in touch with the results of the test, but . . . I do have them."

Seckry's heart was pounding.

"The truth is, Seckry," Sanfarrow continued. "The results of the test came back a long time ago, but . . . I just . . . couldn't bring myself to contact you."

Seckry could hear Sanfarrow's erratic breathing on the other end of the line.

"Seckry . . . I can confirm that Eiya . . . Eiya was indeed created from Elenya Kayne's consciousness. She was not, as I originally predicted, created from you."

Seckry said nothing in reply. He just stared at Eiya, holding the phone to his ear, and Eiya stared back, understanding what his expression meant, fresh droplets wobbling in the corner of her eyes.

"The reason I am telling you now," said Sanfarrow, "is that . . . Kevan . . . Kevan is passing. He is passing in a matter of hours. His body has finally come to the end of its second life, and, if my calculations are correct, he will be gone before midnight. What I need to ask Eiya is . . . will she come to visit him? Just to be with him in these final moments."

Seckry felt sick, but how could he deny a dying man the chance to see his wife one last time, even if it was a wife who couldn't remember their life together. He passed the phone to Eiya and agonisingly watched her face as Sanfarrow explained everything.

When Eiya ended the call, she just stared at the duvet.

"I have to see him," she said vacantly. "I'm his wife. I'm his wife, and I've ignored him for all this time. Deep down I knew that the results would come back like this . . . but I tried not to think about it. I let him rot away without ever going to see him."

"But," said Seckry. "You're Eiya now, right? We said, no matter what the test results show, you're Eiya, and you always will be from now on, no matter who you used to be in a previous life."

"Yeah," Eiya said distantly. "Seck . . . this thing with me disappearing every time you touch me. Do you think it's to do with this? Maybe I have been brought back to life like this for a reason. Maybe . . . my body is rejecting you . . . rejecting us."

Seckry couldn't bear to think about it.

Eiya suddenly got up and started getting her things together.

"I have to go. I have to go now."

"I'm coming with you," said Seckry.

"No, Seck," said Eiya. "Sanfarrow was adamant on the phone that you couldn't be there. He said Kayne has been traumatized by the fact that I've been with you all this time.

He said he wanted to see me alone."

"But," Seckry said. "Eiya, what if -"

"It'll be fine, Seck," she reassured him. "Sanfarrow said he's going to be there too. I won't be completely alone. Sanfarrow will make sure nothing happens to me and that I'm completely safe."

Seckry wanted to find an argument for her to stay because he was too worried about her, but he didn't have time because Eiya was already leaving the flat.

"I've got my phone in my pocket," she said. "And I'll be back before midnight."

Seckry watched her climb down the grated stairs and leave the square, a sinking feeling in his stomach. Even though he had guessed the results too, the reality of them made everything suddenly feel warped and wrong.

As he went back into the flat, his mum said, "Where's she gone, love? I'm just about to serve up."

"Um . . . she's gone to a friend's house from school . . . a girl needs some support from another girl."

"Oh," said Coralle, staring at him suspiciously.

After an awkward tea, Seckry went back to his bedroom and collapsed onto his bed, feeling utterly sick. The thought of Eiya and that . . . freak of nature made him want to vomit. He had to think of something else to stop his mind from wandering. He opened his bedside drawer, looking for a book. What he found, however, was Adelbert's electronic diary, which he hadn't looked at since finding the instructions for activating his powers. He pulled it out, deciding to have another read. He doubted he would find any new information, but at least it would distract him for the evening.

He located the section with the instructions and read over them again, scrutinising every bit of text and every detail of the diagrams, but he found nothing new that would help him, so he flicked through, to see what else was on there. Eventually he came across a section called The Trinity Awakening, but it was locked with extra security. Even Tippian's hacking software hadn't been enough to get rid of the password protection.

Seckry pulled out his phone and loaded Tippian's app before pressing it to the diary once again. But after squeezing them together, the section still hadn't been unlocked. Some of the screen was now showing strange, random symbols, but that was it.

He tried again, squeezing them together more tightly, but dropped them onto the bed after a hot, sharp pain seared through his palm.

He picked up the diary to find the section finally unlocked, and began reading.

The Trinity Awakening

After 16 years and 93 days, the time finally came for the boys' powers to awaken. Words cannot describe the emotions I felt this morning, knowing how powerful my child would be.

But Rikard . . . he did the unthinkable. He ruined everything. Everything. And he's known since the day they were created.

Rikard tells me the boys cannot know the truth. But to me, the entire project is now over. I will never forgive Rikard for what he has done to all of us. I will never forgive him for

Seckry jumped in shock as his mobile buzzed on his bedsheets. It was Vance. He dropped the diary and answered it.

"Sir," said Seckry.

"Seckry, I'm sorry to call you so late," Vance said loudly, over a heavy bustle of chatter.

"Where are you?" Seckry asked.

"Oh, it's the Science Committee annual banquet," said Vance. "Originally intended to be a place for heated discussion about the topics of tomorrow, but in actuality an event where a lot of old men get together in smart suits to complain about the fact that they're not allowed to smoke pipes in the building. Listen, Seckry, there's something really important I have to tell you."

"What is it?"

"Ropart Sanfarrow," said Vance. "Do I recall you telling

me something before about him feeling like he couldn't repay Kevan Kayne for saving his life?"

"Yeah, Sanfarrow fell into the river when they were both young," said Seckry. "He said he's had to live in guilt since Darklight turned against them because he didn't save Kayne's life in return. He said he has never been able to repay Kayne. He said that Kayne will die before he has a chance to repay him for saving his life all those years ago, and it torments him every day."

"Seckry," said Vance, sounding grave, even above the background noise. "I managed to get hold of a copy of the results sheet from Sanfarrow regarding the test to determine whether Eiya was from yours or Elenya's consciousness, and there was something very strange about it. At first, everything seemed completely legitimate, but the more I studied it, the stranger the name Elenya Kayne looked on that page. I used some equipment to scan the document and take a closer look, and there is a definite pixilation on those words."

"I don't understand," said Seckry. "What are you saying?"

"Seckry, the name Elenya Kayne has been pasted over a different name using some kind of image editing software. Elenya Kayne isn't the name that was printed on those results."

"You mean . . . ?" said Seckry

"I believe Sanfarrow is finally repaying Kayne by giving him his dying wish," said Vance. "He is convincing Kayne that Eiya is his wife, even though the results were that she was created from you."

"Oh my Gedin," said Seckry.

"Seckry, is Eiya safe with you right now?" said Vance.

"No," said Seckry. "No she's not."

Seckry ended the call and shoved his phone into his pocket, along with Adelbert's diary. He didn't have time to find out what Rikard had done to upset Adelbert so much. Eiya was in danger, and Sanfarrow evidently no longer had her safety in his best interests.

Seckry didn't even have time to explain to his mum before he raced out of the flat. He sprinted down the first few steps before leaping over the railing and landing heavily on the ground in a rough tumble, then tearing out of the square as fast as his legs would allow.

There wasn't even time to catch a monorail. They were so sporadic at this time of evening that Seckry would make better time on foot.

When he eventually reached Chronoway Crossing, he was gasping for air, but found Sanfarrow's office door wide open. He raced in to see Sanfarrow sat at his desk, his head hanging low, and his eyes glazed over.

"You were quick," Sanfarrow said, not looking up. "I thought it would be a few more hours before you came looking for her."

"Where is she?" Seckry said furiously. "Where has he taken her?"

Sanfarrow, his eyes still locked on the floor, sighed in exhaustion.

"Kayne isn't in this building anymore, and he hasn't been for months. His body was becoming . . . *something else* during this last portion of his second life. He needed a bigger space than I could have provided here."

"Where?" said Seckry. "Tell me where she is. Kayne could be doing anything to her right now."

"Seckry," Sanfarrow said softly. "You are going to have to forget Eiya. In less than an hour, she will no longer be with us."

"What are you talking about?" Seckry screamed. "I know you switched the results, I know that it was actually my name that came out of that test."

Sanfarrow smiled wryly.

"Vance. Of course. I guessed he would work it out at some point, but withholding the results from him would have been even more suspicious."

"What is Kayne going to do to her?" demanded Seckry.

"Kayne is simply taking her with him."

"Taking her where?"

"To what he believes is the eternal afterlife," said

Sanfarrow. "He's had somewhat of a religious conversion over the last few months."

"He's . . . going to kill her?" said Seckry.

"Yes. We've discussed it in great detail, and the thought of Elenya spending a second lifetime with you is repulsive to him. He has spent most of his time in this undead state being antagonised by the idea that his wife is out there, being courted by some boy named Seckry Sevenstars. The ultimate reward for having to endure that torture is taking her with him into the afterlife, so they can spend eternity together forever."

"This is ridiculous!" Seckry yelled. "You can't let this happen!"

"It's the only way!" Sanfarrow yelled back. "The only way I can repay him for saving my life, and the only way I can redeem myself for fleeing Endrin and leaving him to Darklight."

"Look," said Seckry, forcing himself to stay as calm as possible. "I understand how crushing it would be for him to have to accept that his wife never did return from the dead, but you cannot kill Eiya just to give him some final ray of happiness before he dies. You have to tell him the truth."

"Don't tell me what I can and cannot do," roared Sanfarrow, spittle spraying from his bearded mouth. "Have you ever owed somebody your life and then left them to die when they needed you most? No! You have no idea of the torment."

"You need to tell me where she is," Seckry said. He couldn't waste any more time arguing. "You need to tell me where she is, now!"

"Fine," said Sanfarrow, slowly. "She's in Warehouse Twenty-Two. I found a pair of keys to the place in Darklight's old stuff. Kayne's been living there. It doesn't really matter that I've told you. You're not going to be able to save her."

"Why?" demanded Seckry.

"Because you're going to die before she does," said Sanfarrow. "Yes, both you and this Gedin forsaken monorail renovation project will die together, tonight. It was doomed from the start. The government were right in thinking it was a cursed project. It's time to end everything. I'll make it look like you broke in and hijacked the test vehicle." Sanfarrow opened a drawer underneath his desk and pulled out a pistol.

Seckry fumbled for Vance's stun gun, but as soon as it was out of his pocket, Sanfarrow shot it out of his hand.

"I never wanted things to come to this, Seckry, I honestly didn't. But I know you will never be able to live without Eiya. It is best to save you from that misery, and end it before it begins."

Sanfarrow strode towards him, the pistol aimed directly at his forehead. Seckry had no options.

"Goodbye, Seckry Sevenstars," Sanfarrow said, and slammed the butt of his gun into Seckry's temple.

Chapter Forty-Two

History Repeats

Seckry was aware that he was moving. Moving fast.

He opened his eyes, his head pounding. As his vision slowly sharpened, he saw the interior of a monorail driver's compartment, and Sanfarrow's words echoed through his mind.

It's time to end everything. I'll make it look like you broke in and hijacked the test vehicle.

Seckry tried to move, but he was taped securely to the driver's seat. He stared out of the front window at the whizzing city in horror. He knew the track still wasn't finished.

He wriggled violently until he was able to squeeze one arm out of the tape, and reached for the control panel. He pulled a few different levers, but they came apart in his hands. Sanfarrow had to have dismantled them to render them useless. This monorail was heading towards its death and there was nothing Seckry could do to stop it. The only option he had was to flee.

Seckry bit into the tape closest to chest, tearing it apart. It felt like his teeth were being ripped out of his jaw, but the pain was being numbed by pure adrenalin and fear.

When he was free, he kicked the rusty door beside him with all his force and it swung open violently, slamming into the side of the carriage from the speed, nearly coming off its hinges.

Seckry poked his head out and saw several metal ruts leading onto the roof of the carriage.

He reached out and began to climb, gripping the ruts so

tight that he thought his fingers were going to start bleeding. As he climbed, he turned his head to the wind. Through the hair that was whipping his face, he could see, in the distance, the scaffolding that signalled the end of the track. He had just minutes before the whole thing plummeted off the edge of it.

He yanked himself up onto the roof and scrambled, nearly slipping in his haste. The only thing he could do was run across the carriages, just to give him a few more moments. He had no idea what he would do then, but it was the only thing he could think of to bide his time. The only option he had once he reached the end was to jump, in the faintest hope that he would be able to catch a part of the track and hang on for his life. He knew he had almost zero chance of catching anything, and if he did catch something, he would probably be electrocuted by it.

But it was his only chance.

He sprinted as fast as he could, diving over the gaps between the carriages. But his pace slowed as he realised the carriages beneath him were tilting. The entire thing, the train and its track, were crumbling. The weight of the moving vehicle had been too much for the unfinished structure.

There was nothing Seckry could do. He was about to plunge to his death. The first carriage had already hurtled over the edge and was exploding into a fiery furnace.

This is it, Seckry thought. *This is where I end.*

As he stood, helpless, he saw the Mechaner's cliff approaching. And as the weight beneath him began to fall, he saw a car screech to a halt at the edge of the cliff, spraying rocks and dust.

It was Vance's car.

Suddenly, Vance burst out of the driver's seat and threw himself over the cliff edge, his suit jacket flying off his back.

There was a deafening screech of metal and Seckry's world turned upside down as the carriage below him dropped completely. Freefalling and tumbling into the flames, all Seckry could see was Vance hurtling towards him, his arm outstretched, a stream of red and orange vapour pouring from it.

Was it the *teleportation device?*

As the scorching heat of the explosions beneath engulfed them both, Vance slammed into Seckry, and pressed the teleporter to his chest.

There was a blinding flash of light and every muscle in Seckry's body seized up. Then came a loud bang, and Seckry hit the laminated floor of Vance's classroom.

Office papers billowed upwards as Vance hit his own desk, cracking the wood, and bits of molten metal panged around them along with a couple of bent screws and bolts.

"The force of gravity comes through too," Vance groaned.

Seckry couldn't say anything, partly because he was winded from the impact, and partly because he was in utter shock at what had just happened.

Eventually, he stammered, "The . . . teleporter . . . it . . . it worked."

"I did a bit of work on it this evening before the banquet. I thought I'd have time to test it before actually using it though."

"You didn't test it?" said Seckry. "How . . . how did you know it was going to work?"

"I didn't," said Vance.

Seckry had no time to contemplate this.

"Eiya," he said desperately. "Kayne wants to kill her. He's got her in Warehouse Twenty-Two. I have to save her."

"My car's sitting on the Overhang," said Vance. "But I think Mr Pegglewim's still here, working late. I'll get his car keys."

As Vance ran to speak to the geography teacher, Seckry looked through the classroom window. The city was in carnage. Black smoke was pluming into the air from the wreckage, and he could hear the sirens of ambulances and fire engines in the distance.

Seckry tore his gaze away and ran down the stairs, ready to meet Vance in the staff car park, but felt a buzzing in his pocket.

It was Tenk.

"Man, I've got an awesome new weapon for Bash-" he started, as Seckry picked up, but Seckry cut him off.

"Tenk, Eiya's in serious danger. I have to go."

"What? What are you talking about? Where?" said Tenk.

"Warehouse Twenty-Two," said Seckry, and hung up, diving into the passenger's seat of Mr Pegglewim's car as Vance unlocked it. With a screech, they sped out of the Estergate grounds.

As they swerved to a stop outside the warehouse, they saw that Sanfarrow had already made his way there, and was stationed outside with his pistol. They saw as well that the warehouse itself was barricaded all around by several rows of red lasers.

Seckry and Vance jumped out, and Sanfarrow's face became one of horror and confusion.

"You . . . but . . . you were . . . you should be *dead* in that wreckage, for Gedin's sake!"

"We're going in," said Vance.

But Sanfarrow raised his gun up at him.

"There is no way in," he said manically. "You walk through those beams, you get sliced in six."

Seckry could see that the beams were being projected by thin pillars that had been stationed at each corner of the building. He wasn't sure, but it looked like there was a small keypad on each of them.

"You can try if you want," Sanfarrow said, noticing Seckry's line of sight. "But there's no way you'll guess the keycode. There's only one person who knows that code, and that's me."

"That's where you're wrong," came a female voice.

Sanfarrow turned.

His wife, the current CEO of Endrin, Jenniver Layne, stepped out from behind the far corner in her white lab coat, pointing her own pistol directly at her husband's head.

"Jen . . . Jenniver," Sanfarrow stammered. "How did you? I kept all this a secret from you . . . I had it all under control."

"Do you really think I wouldn't work out that something

was up?" Jenniver said angrily, striding towards him. "I bugged your office yesterday after being suspicious for too long, and I heard everything you said to Seckry."

As she came nearer, Seckry could see that she was trying to keep her face as composed as possible, but was struggling to hold back tears.

"You bugged my office?" Sanfarrow said. "My own wife?"

"I had every good reason to. How could you do this, Ropart? How *could* you?"

"I had to," Sanfarrow pleaded.

"I thought you were different from him," said Jenniver. "But you're just like Darklight."

"No!" Sanfarrow spat. "I'm nothing like Darklight!"

"You're right," said Jenniver. "You're even worse than him. Darklight was a cold-hearted sociopath. We all knew that. But you . . . you *have* a heart . . . you *care* . . . and the fact that you can do this to Eiya and Seckry with that caring soul makes you worse."

She suddenly grabbed her husband and ripped the pistol out of his hand, throwing it to Vance. Then she pressed her own gun to Sanfarrow's temple and dragged him to the nearest laser pillar.

As she began tapping numbers into the keypad, Sanfarrow tried to break free.

"No!" he screamed. "If you truly loved me, you'd understand that I have to do this for Kevan! You know I have to pay him back for saving my life!"

"Ropart, I'll shoot, I swear to Gedin, I'll do it!" Jenniver screamed back, her eyes no longer able to contain the liquid that was filling up inside of them.

With a final press, the lasers surrounding the warehouse powered down with a sigh and vanished.

Seckry wasted no time in running towards the giant roller shutter door and clasping the bottom of it. Vance did the same a little further down, and with a heave, they flung it upwards.

Chapter Forty-Three

The Nightmare Begins

Seckry barged in and caught his breath as he saw what had become of Kevan Kayne. Sanfarrow had told him that Kayne's body had become too big for the Chronoway Crossing office, but nothing could have prepared him for this.

Kayne barely resembled a human being anymore. The only thing left of his original form was his head and his naked torso, embedded into the back wall of the warehouse, with lines of organic tubes pumping blood into the rest of his mass, which had filled the warehouse like an overgrown creeper.

There were eyeballs popping out of unidentifiable limbs, and fingers and ears and other features growing out of other bulging bits, all of it alive and moving, but diseased-looking and decayed.

Then Seckry saw Eiya, and he screamed her name.

She was trapped in one of the birdcages that Darklight had left behind, hanging close to Kayne's chest, and gripping the bars in fear, her eyes pouring tears. There was also something attached to her head, but Seckry had no idea what it was. It looked like a rusty, old torture device, but had a wire coming out of it, travelling all the way down to a cluster of computers in the far left corner of the warehouse.

"Seck!" Eiya pleaded. "Please, help . . ."

"What is the meaning of this?" Kayne demanded, and even his voice sounded inhuman now. "Ropart, you said you would guard this place!"

"This is over!" said Jenniver, pointing her pistol at Kayne's head. "Eiya's not going anywhere with you."

Seckry was looking for a way to lower the chain that was holding the cage, but before he had time, two of Kayne's flesh tentacles shot out of the nearest wall and clasped around his wrists, dragging him backwards.

Vance fired a few shots from Sanfarrow's gun into the flesh, causing them to shudder, but they reacted by squeezing Seckry's wrists even tighter, making him yell out in pain. As he was slammed into the wall beside the entrance, the tentacles shoved his hands into the clasps lined along it, and clicked them shut, locking him in.

"No!" Seckry screamed, trying to yank himself free.

Jenniver began firing too, straight at Kayne's head, which burst with green pus. But a string of what seemed like muscle tissue latched onto her and sucked her into a pulsating mass close to the entrance, squeezing the gun out of her hands and making her gasp for air, allowing her husband to break free.

Tentacles were slithering close to Vance too, trying to catch his feet, but he was firing in rapid succession, severing the tips before they could reach him. The distraction, however, was enough for Sanfarrow to kick Vance to the floor, snatching his gun back. Vance tried to get up, but was pinned down by hundreds of quick, eel like threads.

Sanfarrow turned the gun on Seckry, walking slowly towards him.

"You should have died on that monorail!" he seethed. "How am I going to explain your death now? I'll be locked away!"

He held the gun to Seckry's head, his grip tight, but his arm shaking.

There was nothing Seckry could do. As much as he was trying to rip his hands through the clasps, they wouldn't budge. He looked up at Eiya, his eyes staring into hers.

"Get away from him, you evil monster!" she screamed at Sanfarrow.

"I'm not a monster!" Sanfarrow roared, turning around. "Does nobody understand this? I'm doing this for Kevan!"

There was the sudden sound of several battle cries, and Tenk, Tippian, Loca and Kimmy all burst into the warehouse, diving on Sanfarrow's back and toppling him to the ground.

"We got him!" shouted Tenk, and then went silent as he looked around at the hideous warehouse that was intertwined with Kayne's mutated form.

"Stop ruining my final moments!" bellowed Kayne, his face now dripping with green slime from Jenniver's bullets.

The group were snatched away from Sanfarrow individually by slimy tentacles that were as thick as tree trunks, wrapping around their waists and propelling them through the air before smashing them into opposing walls of the structure, making the whole thing shake.

It had knocked all of them unconscious except for Tenk, who was groaning in agony.

"These are my final moments in this world with my wife," Kayne growled. "And you *dare* to take them away from me?"

"Eiya's not your wife!" Seckry yelled. "It's all a lie. Everything Sanfarrow has told you is a lie! He switched the names on the results."

"Shut your mouth, you revolting boy," Kayne said.

"What is that thing on Eiya's head?" Seckry demanded. "What does it do?"

"That is a simple headpiece," said Sanfarrow, getting back to his feet, "designed to pierce the temple with a thin pole. I have hooked it up to Kayne's life monitor, so that when his consciousness disappears, the latch will trigger and it will pierce Eiya's brain. It will be a quick and painless end to her life in this world."

"And then we will enter His Kingdom together," said Kayne.

"No!" Seckry screamed. "I won't let this happen!"

"Seckry!" Eiya pleaded, unable to say much else through her tears. "Please . . ."

Seckry yanked and yanked his wrists, so much so that he could feel blood dripping into his hands. But the clasps were too tight.

"She's not your wife!" Seckry screamed again. "You're not listening to me! Sanfarrow switched the names. She's Eiya, and she was created from me!"

Kayne roared in anger and frustration, before wrapping a huge tentacle around Sanfarrow's waist.

"Why does he keep saying that, Ropart?"

"The . . . the boy's deluded!" Sanfarrow whimpered. "Of course he is! He just wants Elenya all to himself."

But Kayne yanked Sanfarrow towards his torso, the bearded man scratching the floor of the warehouse like a rat trying to scuttle away.

"K-Kevan . . ." Sanfarrow said desperately "He's lying. The boy's deluded. Of course he is."

Kayne slowly lifted Sanfarrow into the air until he was face to face with the man.

"Ropart," Kayne said calmly, squeezing Sanfarrow tight. "Look me in the eyes and tell me that the name on those results was Elenya Kayne. And bear in mind that I can tell when my closest friend is lying to my face. I've known you long enough."

Sanfarrow stuttered a few times and began lying, but Seckry could see Kayne's face becoming angrier and angrier.

"Look . . . Kevan . . ." Sanfarrow said weakly. "You were never meant to find out. I mean . . . I was just trying to give you what you wanted . . . I was giving you your dying wish! I was just doing what any true friend would have done. Kevan . . . Kevan, what are you doing?"

But Kayne said nothing. He just stared into Sanfarrow's eyes as he squeezed and squeezed and wrapped his thick, snake-like, bloated tendons tighter until Sanfarrow's mouth started spilling blood.

When he had squeezed all the life out of Sanfarrow, he dropped his dead body to the floor in a crumpled, disfigured heap.

"That's it!" shouted Seckry. "You know the truth now. Disconnect Eiya from that thing! You can go in peace on your own!"

"Shut your mouth," Kayne said with disgust. He smashed through Sanfarrow's equipment until he found the computer screen calculating his remaining lifespan.

"Five minutes," he said, before taking a deep, violent

intake of breath. "She's still coming with me."

"No!" Seckry screamed.

"I killed Ropart because he lied to me," said Kayne. "Not because of the worthless test results. It explains nothing. What about the memory she keeps having of our wedding day?"

"I don't know," Seckry said honestly. "But I don't care. I don't even care if the machine was wrong and she *was* your wife in her previous life. She's Eiya now and she wants nothing to do with you. Can't you see that? Listen to her. *Listen* to her!"

Eiya was screaming crying, trying to break open the cage door.

"No!" Kayne roared. "She would have remembered long ago if it wasn't for you corrupting her. You've poisoned her mind, you sick, little boy."

"Seckry!" Eiya screamed between tears. "Seckry, please!"

"Stop. Saying. That. Boy's. *Name!*" shouted Kayne, and slashed the cage with a tentacle, making it rock back and forth.

Kayne looked to his left.

"Four minutes," he said, changing his tone. "The time is almost here, my beautiful girl. Gedin will give you back your memory when we are both safe in His Kingdom. This was always His plan for us. Both of us died, and both of us should have embraced Gedin's arms when He opened them to us. We resisted Him, and we came back to this planet unnaturally. It is time for us to go. It is time for us to embrace His welcoming arms together."

Seckry thrashed about like a tormented animal, screaming through clenched teeth over Kayne's religious rant. He didn't care if the bones in his wrists snapped. He just needed to break free and save Eiya somehow. Broken bones and ripped skin were painless in comparison to losing Eiya.

But even with his wrists dripping with blood, he still couldn't get his hands through. He was trapped, and he needed another way to save Eiya.

He needed his powers.

If only he could create something, just something to wedge a solid barrier between the thin pole and Eiya's temple, so that when it sprung, it wouldn't touch her. Just something small, something tiny. That was all that was needed to prevent her from dying.

He closed his eyes and had never concentrated so hard on something before in his life. The two halves of the creogen symbol appeared in his mind, as sharp and as real as ever, but the more he concentrated on them, the more they started shaking and repelling each other, trembling from Seckry's aggressive force.

He turned his gaze downwards, so that he could focus more, but the harder he tried, the more the two halves repelled each other until they were noticeably drifting apart.

He let out a cry of anguish. This was it. It was just like in his recurring nightmare. Eiya was about to die in front of him, and there was nothing he could do about it.

"Two minutes," said Kayne.

As the creogen symbol halves dispersed from his mind, Seckry's vision came back and he realised that Adelbert's electronic diary was lying on the ground of the warehouse in front of him, its screen still displaying the hacked entry. It had to have dropped out of his pocket as he had been flailing around.

Seckry could do nothing but stare at it, his energy completely depleted and his wrists soaking with blood. Without realising it, his eyes were reading the words. The words he had been about to read back in the flat:

I will never forgive Rikard for what he has done to all of us. I will never forgive him for destroying our plans just to prove his theory of nurture beating nature.

He did the unthinkable. He switched the elements before their lives even began.

My child has been infused with creogen, and his, with exorophon.

Chapter Forty-Four

The Trinity Awakens

The two segments of the exorophon demon symbol suddenly materialised in Seckry's vision and slammed together uncontrollably. All sound then became distant, and everything seemed to go into slow motion.

Seckry could sense his body flooding with something. Something powerful. It felt like all the anger and fear and determination he had inside of him was surging into his hands.

He suddenly felt the clasps around his wrists cracking and snapping and folding in on themselves before bursting into sharp shards. Seckry was aware that metal splinters were piercing his skin, but he could feel no pain. As he ripped his arms free, he saw jet black liquid pouring down the bulging veins of his forearms.

He wasted no time. He focused on the device attached to Eiya's head and it burst into fragments, before taking half of the cage with it.

Eiya fell out, crashing to the floor, but picked herself up, trying to scramble to safety.

Kayne's tentacles immediately reached for her, coming from all directions, but Seckry used all of his mental force to tear each throng into bits of ragged flesh before they could touch her.

"Stay. *Away*. From. Her," Seckry roared.

Two tentacles soared towards Seckry, but he caught them and held them tight in his fists, his veins almost bursting out of his skin.

"Elenya's coming with me!" Kayne fumed, green ooze

dribbling from his manic eyes.

"Her . . . name . . . is *Eiya*," Seckry said. "And she's going *nowhere*."

With a gargantuan cry, he sent all of the power within him to his fists.

The skin on the tentacles began splitting, ripping giant seams towards Kayne's body. The power surged outwards to all of the other strands too, bursting the muscle tissue that had rooted into the building, and freeing Vance and everyone else. As Seckry continued to scream, sending all of his power through his hands, the steel beams that were holding the warehouse together began to buckle and collapse, and the aluminium roof started disintegrating. Sanfarrow's computing equipment was also exploding into shards of glass and plastic that then popped, while the power cords snapped, forming billows of fire that plumed before sucking into themselves and vanishing.

As the last remaining section of wall crushed itself into nothing, and only Kayne's torso and head were left, Seckry sent a final pulse of power, ripping what remained of the undead scientist into pieces that contracted and swallowed themselves in mid-air.

When the only things left were the people around him, standing or lying amidst the rubble in the open night air, Seckry fell to his knees.

Chapter Forty-Five

The Trophy

Seckry had very little memory of what happened after that. The only thing he could recall was Eiya running towards him, screaming his name, and Vance holding her back, shouting, "No! Don't touch him!"

The rest of the night was a blur, as if all of his consciousness and energy had poured out of him to destroy Kayne.

"Eiya," Seckry said, and realised he was lying in his bed back at the flat. "Eiya . . . what time is it?"

Eiya's face looked pained through his blurred vision.

"It's midday," she replied.

"Midday?" Seckry said, surprised. He jolted up and blinked until he could see clearly. His mum and Leena were in the room too, sat on Eiya's bed.

"Eiya's told us everything that happened, love," said his mum, wiping tears from her eyes. "I'm just glad you're both alive, okay?"

"I told them about your powers and everything," said Eiya. "I had to tell them."

Seckry looked at his bedsheets.

"I'm . . . exorophon," he said. "Me and my dad . . . We're not even infused with creogen. We're infused with *exorophon*."

"Vance was the first one out of the rest of us to work it out, I think," said Eiya. "None of us really knew what was happening when you were destroying everything, until he explained it to us afterwards."

"I . . . destroyed everything. The entire warehouse."

Eiya smiled.

"I think Cartell will be pleased," she said. "He'll be able to build his new clinic now."

"We'll leave you two alone for a bit," said his mum, and led Leena out of the room.

All Seckry wanted to do was to hold Eiya and never let her go, but he still couldn't, in case she dissipated.

"Vance wants to talk to you about this not being able to touch each other thing," she said. "He wants you to meet him at Estergate whenever you're ready. Just send him a text to arrange it."

Seckry's face lit up. Would Vance be able to help them? But thinking of Vance just reminded him of the monorail and how he had nearly died.

"Eiya . . . I . . . if it wasn't for Vance, I would have died, and you would have died too. He saved us both. I . . . would have failed you again."

"Seck, what are you talking about?" said Eiya. "You've never failed me. Seck . . . *you* saved my life last night. You're my hero."

Seckry spent the following couple of days recovering, and being incredibly cautious in case he accidentally destroyed anything else using his powers inadvertently. He had been anxious about Tenk, Tippian, Loca, and Kimmy, too, but thankfully, they were all fine, and back to their usual selves. They met up as soon as Seckry was ready to leave the flat, and talked about everything that had happened, and were mainly all in awe of Seckry's newly discovered power of destruction.

The city was recovering too.

The collapse of the monorail had killed four people in total, and had injured forty seven. The government had said it was somewhat of a miracle that the casualty count wasn't higher.

Jenniver Layne had given the Patrol her audio recording of Sanfarrow's plotting, and had sorted out all of the legal issues that might have incriminated Seckry and the others, but

Seckry hadn't seen or heard from her. He guessed she needed a lot of time alone. He couldn't imagine what she would be going through at the moment; finding out what her husband had been doing, and then watching Kayne kill him.

When Seckry was ready, he arranged to meet Vance at Estergate, and was greeted by a smile as he entered the classroom.

"Rikard switched the elements," he said. "None of us saw that coming, did we?"

"No," Seckry said. "No, we didn't."

"It makes perfect sense, though," Vance continued. "Rikard said that he believed nurture and upbringing was what defined a person, not their DNA. I guess he wanted to prove to Adelbert that he could raise a decent human being, even with an element inside that should have made the child evil by default."

"So this means . . . that Lux is actually the one infused with creogen," said Seckry.

"Another thing that makes sense now," said Vance. "I'm a bit rusty on my Ancient Klax, but I found out recently that Lux is actually the Klaxion word for 'light' and 'goodness' and 'creation.' Lux may have given himself that name to signify his creogenic power. The information also changes one very important thing. If he did lose his arm as a child, once the creogen awoke inside him, he would have been able to regrow that arm. It broadens the possibilities of who he could be incredibly. All we know now is that his original name began with an 'F.'"

"I still can't get my head around the fact that I've got exorophon inside me," said Seckry. "And . . . I was actually able to use it."

"It explains why you had so much trouble trying to push creogen segments together," said Vance. "No wonder they kept repelling each other. Which leads us on to the main reason I wanted to meet with you, Seckry. To discuss Eiya's transparency whenever you touch her."

Seckry nodded, hoping that Vance would have some kind

of solution.

"Have you worked it out yet?" Vance asked, but didn't wait for an answer. "It's the exorophon doing it. Zovak seemed like the obvious culprit, because it started happening shortly after the Andersun Wellworth award ceremony, but what was just days before the ceremony? The date your powers awakened. It seems that Eiya's unique composition is so fragile, the exorophon is affecting her even without you pushing those segments together."

Seckry hadn't even contemplated it; he felt like he hadn't even had time to think straight since everything that had happened. But what Vance was saying made perfect sense.

Then it hit him. There was no getting rid of the exorophon. It would have been better if Zovak had poisoned him. At least then they could have made an antidote.

"I can never touch her again," Seckry said, his eyes welling up.

"Seckry," said Vance, putting a hand on his shoulder. "I haven't been idle these last few days. You know how much I love a scientific challenge."

He pulled something out of his pocket, something that Seckry hadn't seen for a long time. It was one of Darklight's Pro-Tek Chips.

"Don't worry," said Vance, smiling. "It's not scanning for helitonium anymore. I've been modifying the technology inside. Instead of gathering data, this should now suppress any exorophon within a ten metre radius of it. Which should effectively stop it from affecting Eiya. You won't be able to use your powers whilst wearing it, but that may be a good thing. You wouldn't want to accidentally think of those segments and start destroying things around you. I would recommend leaving it on at all times unless you are in a dire situation in which you think your powers are needed."

"This is incredible," said Seckry.

"Well, it's not completely finished," said Vance. "It'll take me a couple of days to make sure the components are stable, but I will let you know when it's ready to collect."

Seckry felt overwhelmed with emotion. Soon, he would

finally be able to touch Eiya again, and it was Vance that had made it possible.

"Sir . . ." he said, a lump forming in his throat. "I just . . . don't know how to thank you . . . I mean, you jumped off the Mechaner's Cliff to save me. You could have died if that teleporter hadn't worked."

"Well," Vance chuckled. "I tend to have good faith in my own scientific skills. I was ninety-nine per cent sure it was going to work."

"I need to repay you," Seckry said, feeling utterly indebted.

"Seckry," said Vance, seriously. "You really don't need to." He paused for a moment, then said, "Actually . . . there is *one* thing you might be able to do. Do you think you could persuade your mum to forgive me for putting you in danger when I took you to Draindug?"

Seckry laughed.

"My mum? I'm sure she's already forgiven you by now."

A guilty smile appeared on Vance's chiselled jaw.

"Does that mean there's a chance I will get an ellonberry pie this year, after all?"

Seckry woke the following day feeling invigorated. Not only would he be able to touch Eiya again in a matter of mere days, it was also just a matter of days before the date he would be meeting his father. He also felt a huge relief at knowing that he could now activate his powers, despite being a power he was expecting to have the opposite of, and felt relief at the fact that he hadn't been going mad trying to push those segments together.

There was only one thing that didn't make sense to Seckry. If Eiya truly was created from him, as was revealed in the DNA test, then why did she keep having that vision of the word 'echo', a vision that Kayne was convinced was from his own wedding day?

Seckry decided to try to forget it. The results had proven that Eiya had nothing to do with Kayne or Elenya, and that was all that mattered to him.

When they got up, Seckry and Eiya planned to spend the

day playing video games in their pyjamas, but Tenk rang and asked them both to come over to his flat, along with Loca and the others.

"I still haven't told my nan about Richelle," Tenk admitted over the phone. "But granddad's coming out of hospital and she's going back to live with him, and I have to tell her before she leaves. I have to man up and just say it. But I need the moral support."

When everyone met up in Kerik Square that afternoon, Loca still couldn't believe Tenk hadn't revealed all.

"She must have cottoned on," she said. "I mean, your nan hasn't seen the girl for nine months. I think she may have an inkling."

"Yeah, you're probably right," said Tenk. "She's probably just been too ashamed to actually let herself believe it."

When they all filed into the flat, Tenk's nan was sat watching some kind of antique auction show.

"Whatever you lot have come here to do, you'd better do it in silence," she said, her eyes not moving from the screen.

"Nan, there's something I want to tell you," said Tenk, but his nan cut him off.

"Tenk, whatever it is, it can wait. I want to see if this vase is really Ancient Klax or not."

Tenk took a deep breath, then did something Seckry was not expecting. He stood in front of the television and pressed the power button, zapping it off.

Tenk's nan stood up slowly and glared at her grandson.

"Nan," Tenk said, puffing out his chest. "I'm . . . I'm not with Richelle, and I haven't been for months. I'm single and I'm proud of it."

Tenk's nan blinked a few times before narrowing her eyes on him. "How dare you be so rude to your grandmother? And what are you talking about? You don't have a girlfriend after all?"

"No, I do not," said Tenk.

"I don't get it. What are you trying to tell me? That you're gay?"

"No . . . nan, that's not it . . . but there would be nothing wrong with it if I was."

"Then what is it?" she demanded.

"Look, nan, I shouldn't have to be ashamed of being single. I'm sixteen, I'm a teenager, I've got the rest of my life to find someone. I can be single if I want, and I'm not going to let you intimidate me anymore."

Tenk's nan looked horrified, and threw an offended look at her daughter, but all she got was a blank response.

"I'm not gonna defend you, mum," she said. "Tenk's absolutely right. You treated me exactly the same way when I was growing up, and now you're doing it to your grandkids. I'm glad Tenk's got the courage to say something, because I never had."

Tenk's nan huffed and said, "Loada bleedin' nonsense, the lot of you. There's something wrong with you if you can't get a girlf-"

"Nan, I don't want to hear it anymore," Tenk interrupted defiantly. "Like I said, I'm single and I'm proud of it."

"Yeah . . . me too," said Tippian suddenly, nudging up next to Tenk and puffing out his small chest.

"Yeah, me too!" shouted Loca and threw her hat on the floor for emphasis. "*I'm not really*," she whispered quickly to Kimmy. "*Just got caught up in the moment!*" She blew him an apologetic kiss.

Tenk's nan grabbed her coat (even though the weather outside was pretty hot), and said, "Come on, daughter, we're going shopping. I need a new brooch to cheer me up after this."

When they left, Tenk's dad shook his son's hand.

"You're a brave lad, son," he said dramatically. "Much braver than I."

Shortly afterwards, Tenk's dad left to go pick up some champagne to celebrate his mother-in-law's departure, and Seckry and the rest of them popped out to grab some chips from the local chippy, with Longo tagging along.

But as they returned to Tenk's flat to eat them, Longo

threw his arms out, saying, "He's done something to the front door!"

"Who?" said Tenk. "Raymus?"

"Of course Raymus! Who else is in there?"

Seckry squinted to see, and could just about make out that the front door was slightly ajar, with something balancing on top of it.

"Round the back," said Tenk. "We can sneak in through my bedroom window and jump him."

"Always avoid Tenk's place," said Loca. "Why do I never listen to myself."

As they snuck around the back of the flats and crept silently into Tenk's room one-by-one using his rope ladder, they could see Raymus through the open door to the living area, hiding behind one of the kitchen units, giggling to himself uncontrollably and shaking his head from the sheer ingenuity of his prank.

They could also see from where they were that it was a mop bucket sitting atop the front door, leaning precariously and dripping with a sticky looking mixture that Seckry guessed was probably flour and water. Seckry also noticed that there were a few white feathers scattered around Tenk's bedroom, and one of his pillows was now just an empty sack, explaining what was probably sitting atop the gloop.

"*He thinks he's a Gedin-damned pirate,*" Tenk whispered. "*Well the joke's on him now. Let's get him, guys!*"

"I'm quite happy leaving you to beat your brother up," said Loca.

But before Tenk could rush out, there was the sound of keys jangling.

Raymus slapped his leg and stood up excitedly, waiting for the door to open, and Seckry and the others could only watch, mouths open, as Raymus screamed, "Take that, you little suckers!" and the slime dropped onto Mrs Binko and Tenk's nan before blasting them with a plume of feathers.

Tenk's nan reacted by squawking and flapping about like a chicken being taken for slaughter, and Mrs Binko just glared at Raymus, shaking the slop from her hands.

"It was . . . it was Tenk . . . it was Longo!" Raymus cried.
"Don't even *try* it," Mrs Binko hissed.

After his prank, Raymus was sentenced to a summer of slavery from his younger brothers, whilst being banned from seeing his own friends or going anywhere on his own. Despite arguing that he was currently twenty-two years old and was a fully grown man, their mum stuck firm to the decision that if he was adolescent enough to cover his mother and grandmother in feathers, then he was adolescent enough to be grounded.

Seckry imagined he'd be let off the hook when the situation calmed down, but the thought of Raymus having to do anything Tenk told him to did bring him a little bit of enjoyment, since he still remembered vividly the day Raymus had squirted fire extinguisher into his face.

That evening, they ended up at Tippian's house because he wanted to show them a new project he was working on; some kind of hover shoes. But as they walked through the front door, his mum handed him an official looking letter.

"It's from the Science Committee," he said, tearing it open, and began reading, excitedly. "Dear Mr Furst, in light of the recent revelations about the winning invention, our judging panel have decided that your invention, the Voicemaster, should now be rightly crowned as the true winner. However, since the trophy was engraved with Zovak McVorak's name and we do not have the budget to make another one, you will not be receiving one. This does not affect the fact that you are officially now the winning inventor, and your invention can be commissioned."

By the end of the letter, his voice had become slow and quiet.

"I'm not getting a trophy," he said, and Seckry could hear the disappointment in his tone.

When Tippian excused himself and went to the bathroom, Kimmy said, "This is terrible. I wish there was something we could do for him."

"You know . . ." said Tenk. "There is *something* we could do for him."

Two days later, they returned to Tippian's house with Tenk holding something proudly in his arms. Tippian's mum let them in and stared bemusedly at them as she told them Tippian was up in his bedroom.

"Guys?" said Tippian, as they entered his room. "What are you doing here?"

"Tippian Furst," said Tenk. "We are proud to present you with . . ." he paused for dramatic effect, but left it a little bit too long for comfort. " . . . The Tenk's Mum Young Inventor of the Year Award!"

"The *what?*" Tippian spat.

Seckry and the rest of them had spent the last two days building a trophy out of a plastic cup and some other bits and bobs that they'd managed to get their hands on.

"We couldn't afford any Andersun Wellworth utainium," said Loca.

"Why's it the Tenk's Mum award?" said Tippian.

"Oh yeah," said Tenk. "She provided the glue that holds it all together, making her our official sponsor. You can think of her as the poor man's Andersun Wellworth."

"The glue?"

"When I say glue, I mean her porridge. Same thing really."

Tippian sniffed the thing and raised his eyebrows.

"Wow," he said. "Brings back some memories. It hurts my jaw just smelling it."

"We couldn't let you just get robbed of the trophy when you put all of that effort and hard work in," said Loca. "We know it's not the same as the real thing, but if you look at it from a distance it kind of looks like the real thing . . . kind of . . . well . . . not really. Dear Gedin, Tenk, you could have at least tried to get the handles symmetrical."

"Guys, I . . . don't know what to say," Tippian mumbled, then started to laugh. "Thanks . . . I guess."

When they were leaving later that evening, Tenk said,

"Where do you think he's gonna put it on his pyramid? On the bottom row? Or maybe just on the carpet next to it?"

"Let's not beat around the bush," said Loca. "I wouldn't be surprised if it goes straight in the bin."

They headed for the closest monorail station, but halfway there, Seckry realised his phone was no longer in his pocket.

"I must have dropped it," he said. "I'll be back in a minute."

He jogged back to Tippian's and found it lying on the driveway. He had to have dropped it when he had text his mum to say they were heading back.

As he picked it up, he glanced up at Tippian's bedroom window, and in the warm lamplight, he saw Tippian's silhouette place the award they had made for him at the very top of his pyramid, in the empty space he had reserved for something very special.

Chapter Forty-Six

Maybe, Just Maybe

When Seckry and Eiya got back to the flat, they were feeling hyper from all the pop they had drunk at Tippian's, and Seckry could barely contain himself because the day of meeting his father was tomorrow. He was also excited because Vance had given him the modified Pro-Tek Chip earlier that day. Seckry had put it on and activated it straight away, but Vance had advised him to wait at least one day before trying to touch Eiya, so that it could suppress all of the exorophon first.

"I'm never going to be able to relax tonight," he said. "There's just no way it's gonna happen."

"Me neither," said Eiya. "I'm just . . . buzzing with energy. I feel claustrophobic in here, and it's really hot. Oh, Seck! Let's go up to the roof."

Seckry thought it was a great idea. Even with the window open, the humid summer air was stifling, and there was usually a nice breeze up on the roof.

"I can't believe we still haven't managed to get Mr Mulk to activate that telescope after all this time, though," said Eiya, as they climbed the grating. "It's been months since we found it."

Seckry stopped as they reached the top floor, his mind going into overdrive, and suddenly feeling angry at Mr Mulk again. Eiya was right. The miserable old man had got ruder and ruder towards them every time they asked him politely to press the button in his flat, and Seckry thought it was time to take action.

"How about we press that thing ourselves?" he suggested.

"What?" Eiya said, shocked. "Seck, are you serious?"

"Yeah, I'm fed up of him," said Seckry. "And I'm too curious to forget about it."

A fire suddenly lit up in Eiya's eyes.

"Yeah, you're right. Someone made that beautiful telescope and carved those coordinates into the wall so that someone could look through it and see something specific. We can't let that telescope rust away without anyone ever seeing what it's pointing at."

"We'll need to knock on his door and then lure him out somehow, then sneak into the flat and press it, and run back out before he catches us."

"What can we lure him out with?" said Eiya. She fumbled around in her pockets and pulled out a fluffy, pink keyring.

They looked at each other.

"It'll do," said Seckry, and Eiya placed it at the opposite end of the corridor.

"Hopefully he'll come out and see it, and go to see what it is," she said.

Seckry nodded and they rapped a couple of times on his door, before hiding around the closest corner.

As planned, they heard Mr Mulk cursing before opening the door. Then they heard him walking towards the keyring, and they made a dash for it.

Eiya ran straight to the button and pressed it, but Seckry stopped dead in his tracks, staring at Mr Mulk's living room desk.

On it were several different, beautiful, clockwork telescopes, some half made, and some finished.

"Let's go!" Eiya whispered, but stopped as soon as she saw the desk too.

"Eiya . . ." said Seckry. "I think . . . I think Mr Mulk built the telescope *himself*."

"Yes, I built that telescope myself!" came Mr Mulk's voice sharply behind them.

They turned around sheepishly, to see Mr Mulk glaring at them, his face bright red with fury.

"And it's none of your Gedin-damned business!" He took

a few wheezy breaths. "Since you've hounded me for the past year and have now broken into my flat, I have two options," he said. "I can either call the Patrol . . . or I can leave the bleedin' thing on and put this to rest for once and for all."

He threw the keyring back at Eiya.

"Follow me up to the roof," he said sharply.

Seckry and Eiya could do nothing but obey, astounded.

Once they had climbed up the ladder, following Mr Mulk slowly, he led them to the telescope, which was glowing with the reflection of the bright night's moon.

"Go ahead," he said as they approached, the resentment and temper now missing from his tone of voice. "You've been trying to get the thing working all this time, here it is. Go on, take a look. You've waited long enough." What was present in Mr Mulk's tone now was a sheer exhaustion.

Eiya carefully placed her eye on the eyepiece and removed it a few moments later with a slightly confused frown on her face, letting Seckry take a look.

Seckry pressed his eye against it.

Through the lens, he could now see that it was pointing at a narrow gap between two dark buildings, and through that gap was a segment of Gallica's Wall. A very particular segment.

Graffitied on that segment of wall was the ornate writing that read:

I love you, Itraya Rosebloom.

"I knew her for just a year," Mr Mulk said softly. "Itty, she was called, for short. She used to work at Softspoon's bakery before it closed down. I'd be in there every other day for a slice of her delicious teraflower tart. But it wasn't the food I kept going in for. I just wanted to see her. Eventually I plucked up the courage to ask her out."

Seckry removed his eye and saw that Mr Mulk was now leaning on the railings, gazing out at the moonlit cityscape.

"She said yes," he continued. "Believe it or not, I actually think she felt the same way about me. I had my moments, but

I wasn't always this cranky old croon. We went out to dinner a few times, but I was just so embarrassed around her. My mouth would go dry, I'd start stammering, I'd be sweating, you name it. I loved her. But I couldn't say it. So I came up with this elaborate plan to build a telescope on the roof and paint the words 'I love you' onto Gallica's wall. Who knows what was going through my mind at the time? I guess I thought it was romantic, and it solved the problem of me plucking up the courage to actually say it out loud to her."

He stopped for a moment, lost in his memories.

"When I finished the writing and set up the telescope, I got my best suit dry-cleaned and ready to wear that evening, and she went to visit her family in the north partition on the newly built monorail that ran from Chronoway Crossing to Mechaner's Village. But that was the day the carriage came off the tracks."

Mr Mulk smoothed his hand gently over the brushed metal of the telescope.

"She never got to see the message at the other end," he said.

"Mr Mulk," said Seckry. "We . . . had no idea . . . we're so sorry."

Mr Mulk smiled weakly.

"You know, one of the things I miss the most about her is that she smelled of that delicious teraflower tart even when she wasn't working. I guess when you're making the thing every day, the smell probably sinks into your skin. It was divine. I'd always be able to tell if she'd visited the flat while I was out, because she would leave a trail of that sugary scent wherever she went. It's funny how it's the small things like that that you remember and miss the most."

Mr Mulk stayed with them for a while on the rooftop, watching the blinking lights of the city in silence. But there was a moment in which he very quietly, and very slowly, inhaled a deep breath, and Seckry was sure the old man could smell the very same aroma of teraflower that he and Eiya had been enjoying for months.

Seckry wasn't one to usually believe in spirits or ghosts,

and was almost certain that the smell was still coming from Softspoon's Bakery. But in the back of his mind, there was the faintest thought that maybe, just maybe, Itraya Rosebloom did finally get to see the message at the end of that telescope.

Chapter Forty-Seven

Back to Draindug

Seckry and Eiya stayed on the rooftop once Mr Mulk had left them, still surprised that it had actually been him who had made the telescope after they had been mad at him for so long.

After staring out at the starry sky and the smoggy buildings for a while, Eiya said, "How long do you have to wait for that Pro-Tek Chip to work, Seck?"

"Vance said to wait a day for it to work properly," Seckry replied.

Eiya pulled her phone out of her pocket and looked at the screen.

"It's gone midnight," she said. "It's . . . technically tomorrow." She slowly put her phone back into her pocket and reached out her hand. "Just touch the tips of my fingers."

Seckry hesitated. He had been so used to having to prevent any contact with Eiya over the last few months that even touching her fingertips seemed wrong and sinful, but as he reached out and made contact, his whole body relaxed.

"It's working," Eiya said, half laughing, half whimpering, her large, brown eyes wet. She let her fingers slip between Seckry's, so that they were intertwined with his, and then pulled him gently to her until the tips of their noses were almost touching.

Seckry felt euphoric. He placed his other hand on the back of her neck, under her hair, feeling her moist, summer skin beneath his palm, and it was as though years' worth of longing was flooding out of him.

Seckry ran his hand gently around her neck until he was

touching her smooth cheeks, and brushed the hair away from her eyes, savouring every moment of the sensation, bringing his face even closer to hers. As their noses met, all he wanted to do was connect her soft, sweet lips to his, but there was something he wanted to tell her first.

"Eiya," he said softly. "I've been too embarrassed to say it, but I should have said it a year ago. I don't want to end up like Mr Mulk, having never said these words. Eiya, I am in love with you. I am head over heels in love with you. I love you Eiya Tacana."

Eiya's beautiful chestnut eyes stared into his own, wobbling with happy tears.

"I love you too, Seckry Sevenstars," she said, and placed her lips upon his.

Seckry slept peacefully that night, but woke up with his mind swimming with thoughts of his father. He got showered and dressed in a complete daze, unable to think of anything other than the fact that he would be meeting him. Today.

Even the car journey back to Draindug with Vance and Eiya was a blur, because he was completely lost in his own world, wondering what his father would look like now, and what he would say to him. There were so many questions. Had his dad been watching them from afar? Did he know about Eiya? What had he been doing all these years whilst in hiding?

When Vance pulled up outside The Axe and Cleaver Inn, Seckry stepped out, feeling as though he was walking on water.

They were ushered upstairs once again, to Grolt's macabre looking workshop, but found the man with a distressed frown on his round face.

"Pawl," Seckry said desperately. "Is he here?"

Grolt shook his head and stared out of the window, shrugging his shoulders.

Seckry's heart sank and his stomach churned. He didn't know if he could take it if his father didn't turn up. He didn't know if he'd be able to keep his emotions under control.

"We'll wait here, if that's okay with you," said Vance, and Grolt nodded.

They waited that day for around seven hours. The owner of the inn offered them food at one point, which Vance and Eiya gladly accepted, but Seckry couldn't eat anything, sick with worry and anger and confusion. His dad had specifically told him to come back on this date to meet him. And he was nowhere to be seen.

Eventually, they had to leave.

When they arrived back at the flat, Seckry went straight to his bedroom and curled up into a ball on his bed. After a while, Eiya sat beside him gently.

"We'll figure this thing out, okay, Seck? We'll figure it out together. There must be a reason he wasn't there."

But Seckry didn't know what to think. All that kept going through his mind was what Leena had said to him months ago. That if their dad had really loved them, he wouldn't have run when the xinary turned red. He would have stayed and protected them.

They sat on his bed for a couple of hours, both lost in their own thoughts, and eventually, Eiya fell asleep beside him, her face buried into his hip.

Seckry got up slowly to get changed into his pyjamas, laying Eiya's head carefully onto his quilt, and wondering if he would even recognise his father now. He had no photographs of him. All he had were his mum's very rare descriptions.

As he opened his wardrobe, he noticed something sitting at the bottom of it; something he had forgotten about. It was the memory helmet Vance had given him, the one that had been designed to help Eiya recover her lost memories when they thought she had amnesia. Seckry had imagined he'd have no use for it, and had shoved it into storage, but he was now having second thoughts. Would it be able to help him remember his father? Would it be able to reach that far back into his past?

It was worth a try.

Seckry knew he was probably going to get even more upset if he started remembering his father vividly, but he couldn't help himself. He just wanted to remember his face, his voice, and his mannerisms.

It took him a few moments to figure out how to switch the helmet on, but when he did, he sat down on Eiya's bed and placed the heavy thing on his head.

"Scanning for memories," said an electronic voice, and Seckry heard the thing begin to whir. He had no idea how it was going to work. Would he be able to choose from a list of memories to recall?

But before he had a chance to contemplate it, the voice said, "An artificially suppressed memory has been found. Attempting to reconstruct."

An artificially suppressed memory?

Seckry had no time to feel confused, as the memory helmet clamped to his head tightly, sending a searing pain through it.

He gripped the machine and tried to yank it off, but it wouldn't budge. It was locked onto his skull until the process had finished.

Seckry's phone began buzzing. He took it out of his pocket, but as soon as he pressed the 'answer' button, the pain in his head became so severe that his hands seized up and he dropped the phone to the carpet.

"Seckry," said Vance's voice, tinny through the broken reception. "I've just been analysing some of the documents you brought back from Site Origin, especially the one that revealed the letter F underneath the name Lux. It was so eroded that the human eye couldn't pick it up, but the computer detected another extremely faint line at the bottom of the letter. Seckry, it's not an F . . . It's an *E*. Seckry, are you there? Seckry?"

"Memory reconstructed," said the machine, and Seckry's eyes rolled into the back of his head.

Chapter Forty-Eight

The Missing Memory

Seckry arrived at the guildhouse feeling relief that he was away from the creepy Kevan Kayne, but there was something about the atmosphere that made Seckry feel like he was being watched.

He hesitated as he reached for the bloodlion doorknocker, because he was once again struck by how lifelike it was. Its eyes were piercing, and the snarling teeth that clenched the metal ring looked ready to bite his hand off. Seckry told himself that his imagination was getting the better of him, and closed his fist around it. But as he did so, a large, firm hand covered his mouth tightly, and another strong arm clasped around him, pinning him to the spot.

Seckry was about to scream, when a deep voice whispered, "*Seckry, don't make a sound.*"

If it had been any other voice, Seckry would have bitten down on the hand and fled. But . . . this was a voice that Seckry knew.

"Come with me. We need to get away from this place," the voice said, and Seckry was led firmly away, still gagged and unable to see the man behind him. He was pushed firmly but gently forward until they came through a clearing and emerged into what must have been the Mechaner's Overhang.

"I'm not going to hurt you," the voice said. "Do you know who I am?"

After a moment, Seckry nodded silently.

Seckry stood there for a while, the hand still clasped over his mouth, but releasing its pressure gently.

"The view is beautiful, isn't it," the voice said slowly. "It almost looks like the cityscape is spelling something out."

From where they stood, the giant letter E protruding out of the Endrin headquarters was positioned directly to the left of the chococorp factory, whose first three letters were visible before being obstructed by another building, forming a rugged 'Echo' written across the skyline.

The hand let go, releasing Seckry so that he could turn around. But he was frozen to the spot. All he could do was just stare at the word 'echo' written across that skyline, unable to believe what was happening and completely overwhelmed with emotion.

Behind him was the man he had thought about every day of his life for the past ten years. The man he had been waiting to see once again since the day he disappeared.

Holding back tears, Seckry very slowly turned on the spot, until he was looking into his father's eyes.

"Dad?" he said in barely more than a whisper.

Pawl reached out and gripped his son in a tight embrace.

Seckry buried his head into his father's long, fair hair, and hot tears began flooding from his eyes.

"Gedin, son," said Pawl. "I've missed you. I've missed you so much. I've missed you all."

When Seckry was ready, he stepped back and looked at his father properly. He had aged from the image he had always had of the man in his memory; there were lines under his eyes that hadn't been there before, and his shoulder-length, golden hair was now flecked with grey. But the most noticeable thing was that he was covered in scars.

"Did Lux do this to you?" said Seckry.

"In a way, yes," said Pawl. "But more accurately, it was Grolt."

"What?" said Seckry. "In that torture chamber?"

"Torture chamber?" Pawl laughed lightly. "Gedin, it *did* look like it at times. But Seck, Grolt is who the people of Draindug consider their doctor. Most of them can't afford health insurance so they pay Grolt cash instead. He does what he can with the tools he has. It's completely against the law, and the Patrol have tried stopping him a few times, but the

Patrol are too scared to keep coming back to Draindug. They'll sweep something under the rug if they don't want to deal with it. I went to Grolt for surgery. I went to him to ask him to cut me open and remove every single tracking device that my captors had planted inside me."

"Captors?" said Seckry.

"Yes, captors. You . . . you remember the night I was captured, right?"

"What?" said Seckry. "I thought you were in hiding. I thought you ran away the night the xinary went red so that Lux wouldn't know we existed. To protect us."

Pawl's eyes searched his momentarily.

"Ran away?" he said, his own eyes filling up. "Seck . . . I didn't run away. I would never have left you. I know you were probably too young to remember, but doesn't your mum remember what happened?"

"We woke up and you were gone," said Seckry. "We had no idea what had happened for years, until we came to Skyfall and me and my teacher, Vance, started uncovering things."

"I should have known," Pawl said, agonised. "They wiped your memory. They must have wiped all three of you."

"What?" said Seckry, unable to believe what he was hearing. "So . . . you didn't leave in the middle of the night to protect us from Lux? To stop him finding out about our existence?"

"No Seckry. When that xinary turned red I got ready to fight. I was ready to face my brother. I thought the xinary turning red meant that Lux had escaped from the labs there and then, but it was a trick. He had escaped a long time before that. He was already standing outside the house. And he wasn't alone. He had brought an army of followers. I was no match against them, and they took me. I lived as a captor for eight years, until I escaped last year. The first thing I did was find out where you, your mum and your sister were living, then I found out about Grolt, and got him to rid me of Lux's tracking devices."

"Did . . . Grolt get rid of them all for you?" Seckry asked.

"It's very hard to tell," said Pawl. "Which is why I've

stayed away from you until now."

"Why . . . why have you chosen now to reveal yourself?" Seckry asked.

"Because I need to give you instructions, Seckry," said Pawl, his kind eyes growing dark. "I need you to prevent Cartell Quinn from healing the patient he has been given. Because the patient he's attempting to heal is -"

Pawl was cut off by the screech of a car as it sped into the Overhang, coming dangerously close to them.

An old man jumped out; the old man that had brought Eryk to Cartell.

"Wilbus," Pawl said with horror.

"Mr Ringold," said Wilbus, striding forwards. "Did you really think you'd be able to remove all of our tracking chips? We've known where you've been the whole time. We were just waiting for the right chance to snatch you again. That time has come."

"No!" Pawl roared, and dived on the old man, toppling him to the ground.

"Seckry!" Pawl shouted. "Run!"

But Seckry couldn't. He couldn't just run away after everything his father had just revealed to him.

Before Seckry could make a split decision, there was a zapping noise and Pawl was blasted off Wilbus, flying through the air and landing with a heavy crash on the edge of the cliff, almost sliding off it.

"Dad!" Seckry screamed, running to his father, who was lying unconscious.

"Seckry," said Wilbus, getting back to his feet. "It's no use resisting this. Your father is coming with us."

"He's not going anywhere!" Seckry yelled, but before he could say any more, the rock beneath him and his father shifted, and a giant crack tore itself across the ground.

The impact of his father hitting it had to have been too much. The Overhang was collapsing.

Seckry grabbed his father and heaved, pulling his heavy body backwards as fast as he could.

Within seconds, the Overhang broke into giant segments

and crumbled down the side of the cliff, dragging bits of grass with it. Then, with a humongous crack, the tree that sheltered the Overhang was dragged with it, its roots popping out of the rock, sending dust and stone splinters everywhere. With an awful clang, it smacked into Sanfarrow's half-finished monorail track, sending the whole construction bending and breaking into a mess of scaffolding, pummelling to the ground.

It was carnage. But Seckry had to think about the moment. He used the distraction to dive on Wilbus, knocking his stun weapon out of his hand, a cylindrical baton of some sort that was fizzing with blue energy.

"You're not taking my dad anywhere!" he shouted.

But Wilbus was surprisingly strong for an old man, and toppled Seckry over before getting up and grabbing his weapon once again.

Seckry got to his feet but could already see that Wilbus was coming for him, the baton poised. Seckry searched around him for something. Anything.

The only thing he could see were several shards of sharp rock that had materialised from the collapse. Seckry quickly clasped one in his hand and swung it as the old man bore down upon him. Wilbus shielded with his fist, and the shard opened a deep gash across his knuckles, making him drop the baton once again.

Wilbus immediately snatched the shard out of Seckry's hand, kicked him to the ground, and drove the sharp end straight down into Seckry's open, right palm.

Seckry yelled out in pain.

"Do you have any idea what you and your father are?" Wilbus said manically. He pulled a thick syringe out of his pocket that was filled with bright green liquid, strode over to Pawl, and plunged it into his chest.

"No!" Seckry screamed. "What is that?" He raced towards them and shoved Wilbus off before ripping the syringe out of his father's chest and throwing it to the ground, where it cracked and began leaking.

But Seckry seized up and fell backwards as he was zapped

in the back by Wilbus's baton.

"Don't worry," Wilbus said breathlessly. "That solution will keep your father alive while we prevent him from ruining our plans. Yes, we don't want to kill him just yet. He's far too valuable for that."

Seckry could only watch, immobilised, as Wilbus opened his car boot and dragged a large ottoman out of it. As he opened the lid, an icy vapour escaped into the air, and the entire thing emanated an eerie, neon blue glow.

"We'll awaken him when we need him," said Wilbus, and dragged Pawl's heavy, limp body into the container before slamming the lid shut and locking it.

Seckry was trying to scream, trying to yell for help, but even his mouth was paralysed. All that was coming out of it was foaming spittle.

Once Wilbus had shoved the ottoman back into his boot, with Seckry's dad inside, he picked Seckry up and began dragging him back to the guildhouse.

By the time they got there, Seckry was just about regaining some feeling and movement in his limbs and his face.

"Aren't you . . . going to . . . kill me?" he said, just about forcing his lips to move.

"No, no, Seckry," said Wilbus. "We have an incredibly important healing process to embark upon. The last thing we want is the Patrol on our backs about a missing teenager. No one will come looking for Pawl. He's been missing for several years. But there'd be uproar if *you* went missing." He leaned in close to Seckry's ear and whispered, "*Don't worry, your impure blood will be spilled in due course. He has very specific plans for you.*"

Seckry tried to free himself, but had nowhere near enough control or movement in his limbs to do so.

Wilbus looked at his watch.

"Twenty minutes wipe," he said. "That should do it."

He pushed Seckry's face up against Cartell's door, and pressed something cold and metal against Seckry's right temple.

"You won't remember a thing," he said. "Your father will still be a mystery to you. Some vague figure that disappeared a long, long time ago."

There was a blinding flash of blue light and Seckry's consciousness slipped away.

Epilogue

The Angel of Light Rises

Cartell smiled for the first time in weeks. Everything was falling into place. Finally, he had been granted permission to build his new clinic on the Warehouse Twenty-Two plot, and his work on Eryk Valenkar had come to completion. All that was left to do was to administer the final modified helitonium into Eryk's brain that would recover the parts that had been damaged, allowing him to move again and talk again.

He sat alongside Wilbus, watching Eryk through a glass screen in an adjacent room, so that they weren't exposed to the helitonium. Joining them were Trixa, the girl Eryk had waited so long to see again, and Flynt, the one-armed man Seckry had sent his way.

As Cartell looked through the glass at his first patient, he felt overcome with emotion. The man's strange condition had been incurable until now, and he, Cartell, had found a way to reverse all the damage it had done.

Cartell placed his hand on Wilbus's shoulder.

"This is the beginning of a new era, Mr Valenkar," he said. "A new era of science and medical discovery."

"A new era indeed," Wilbus said slowly.

"We did it. We actually did it. Your son will be healed completely in a matter of minutes."

"Shall I begin the process?" said the nurse in Eryk's room.

"Go ahead," said Cartell, and she pressed a few buttons on the machine hooked up to Eryk, before leaving and joining Cartell and the others.

"This must be an incredible moment for you," Cartell said to Wilbus, but he noticed that the old man had a strange expression on his face.

"Mr Quinn," Wilbus said darkly. "I have a confession to make. Eryk . . . is not my son."

Cartell laughed briefly.

"Excuse me?" he said.

"Oh, Mr Quinn," said Wilbus. "You have absolutely no idea what you have just begun, have you?"

Cartell swallowed. "Mr Valenkar . . . what are you talking about?"

The old man got up and pressed himself against the glass, his eyes peering at Eryk in admiration.

"What's he talking about?" said Flynt.

Cartell looked to Trixa for an explanation, the woman who was supposed to have been Eryk's former lover, but she too had an odd expression on her face, and joined Wilbus close to the glass.

"I apologise that I had to lie to you to get you to help him," said Wilbus, "but it was for the greater good. You have healed the one who will will change this world forever, and along with him, his powers that will allow him to do it."

"His . . . powers?" said Cartell.

"Yes," said Wilbus. "His powers of purity. His powers of greatness, of goodness." He suddenly turned to Trixa. "The greatness and goodness that you chose not to believe in," he said with disgust.

"But . . ." said Trixa, her face fearful. "I was wrong. I should never have questioned him. I am here to plead for forgiveness. To worship him."

Wilbus chuckled darkly.

"We thought that Seckry would find you and send you here if he talked about you enough. And sure enough, here you are."

"I had a lot of time to think," said Trixa. "I was foolish to oppose his plans. I am with him now. I have come to my senses. I love him."

Wilbus laughed again, but there was no humour in it.

"You think he brought you here to forgive you?"

"This is madness!" said Cartell, who had heard enough.

He turned to the nurse. "Can we stop the procedure? I have no idea what's going on."

"The procedure has already completed," said the nurse, her voice trembling.

On the other side of the glass, Eryk was slowly awakening, cracking his joints and moving his limbs for the first time in years. As he locked his eyes on the group, Cartell could see that his pupils and irises were disappearing, leaving just eerie, pure white spheres for eyeballs. His veins also began to protrude out of his skin, and were filling with white liquid.

Cartell couldn't believe what he was seeing. He could only watch in horror and confusion as Eryk began levitating out of his chair, the tubes and wires that were connected to his body snapping and popping off him.

Wilbus's eyes were wild and wide.

"Rise, Angel of Light. A new age is about to begin."

Trixa was still pressed against the glass.

"I was foolish to ever doubt you," she said desperately. "Please, forgive me. Please. I am with you. I am your loyal follower."

Eryk, still floating in mid-air, extended an arm in Trixa's direction, which Cartell, at first, thought was a sign of reciprocated affection. But a spear of glass suddenly burst out of the pane in front of Trixa's mouth, piercing straight through it and out of the back of her head.

As Trixa gargled blood and went limp, Flynt shouted, "It's you!" with fascination flashing in his wide open eyes. "It's not Seckry I should have been worshipping, it's you. You are the one who can create from nothing. You are the one that can heal me."

Eryk then lowered himself and smoothed his hands over his precious ottoman that was sitting at the bottom of his surgery chair, looking at it with a strange expression that Cartell couldn't fathom, before raising his head, his eyes focusing directly on Cartell's.

"Who . . . in Gedin's name . . . *are* you?" Cartell said.

Without Eryk even moving his body, fresh blood began appearing on the pane of glass that separated them, materialising out of nothing and smearing itself into letters that read:

I AM LUX

Seckry's adventures continue in…

Seckry Sevenstars and the Fate of the Fractured
The Seckry Sequence Book Three

If you enjoyed Seckry Sevenstars and the Trinity Awakening, Joseph would love you to share your thoughts in an Amazon review!

Also, if you want to be the FIRST to know about Joseph's new books, and get some exclusive free content, you can join his mailing list by visiting:
www.josephevansbooks.com

Other places you can connect with Joseph Evans:
TikTok: **@josephevansauthor**
Instagram: **@josephcevans**
Facebook: **/theseckrysequence**